CHALLENGES
OF THE
HEART

CHALLENGES OF THE HEART

Louis Tabor

ReadersMagnet, LLC

CHAPTER 1

New York City was a fun place to live. I always seemed to be getting in trouble whether it was stealing a loaf of bread for supper or cheating when playing marbles for pennies. However, I had to say I enjoyed every minute of it. Mom would always lecture me about staying out of trouble but she had her hands filled with my younger brother and sister. Our Dad was killed over in Germany during World War ll. That had been six years ago but it seemed much longer than that. My sister Nellie never saw her Dad since she was born while he was overseas. Nellie was now six years old with the brightness red hair and very smart for her age. Tommy was now eight years old and he loved playing sports especially baseball. As for me I was twelve now but at times I felt like I was eighteen years old mainly because I had to take care of my brother and sister while Mom worked to pay our rent and keep food on the table. I really didn't have a hobby but I just love to sing. My friends would call me Rory the Canary of the Bronx.

We lived in a little two-bedroom apartment on the second floor in the Bronx. Our Mom worked in the garment district running a sewing machine. Her hours were long and the working conditions were terrible. I guessed that why they called the place the sweat house. I guess Mom was about thirty-five years old now but she was very pretty with her long auburn hair and blue eyes. She only weighed about 110 pounds which was about what I weighed. All Mom and Dad's ancestors came from Scotland so nobody messed with the hard nose Ann McClure. Mom said that all of our relatives came to the United States on a boat from Scotland and most of them went out west but our Dad wanted to stay here because he was a news reporter and New York is where the news is. Mom took it very hard when Dad got shot but she knew she had three kids to raise and she was counting on me to help her.

Although I was only twelve years old, I would hustle around the neighborhood looking for jobs to help Mom out with some extra money. The one place I could always get some work was the fish market scaling fish. The owner, Mr. Anthony would always want me to sing because it would draw customers to his stand. I didn't mind because sometimes the customers would throw me a couple nickels. My only problem was that I only knew three songs and one of them was from Saint Patrick's Catholic Church where I went to school. The nuns at the school told me I had a great voice and even made me join the boys' choir. Sister Reynolds would always say to me, "Rory, "God has given you a special gift and you need to use it for his glory." I kind a thought she was right but a lot of the guys would make fun of me and call me sissy. One day I asked Mr. Anthony about my singing and he said, "God gave you a gift and the other boys sound like frogs. They are just jealous of you and stupid." Lucky for me my best friend Sonny was the tough kid in our neighborhood so nobody would mess with me or they would have to answer to Sonny.

I always felt sorry for Mom because all she did was work and she never had any fun. I sometimes wished she would find another man or at least go out on a couple dates. Men would ask her out all the time and she would politely turn them down. I think she was still in love with my Dad and she needed to let him go and find a new life for herself. Mom's life was basically the same day after day and there seemed to be no way of changing her. Mom was a firm believer in God and always said he would take care of us and provide what we need. She was a very proud woman and when we walked in church on Sundays everyone knew it. At the age of twelve she really didn't expect much from me except to keep the apartment clean and watch my brother and sister. One day Mr. Anthony give me the music for three songs and said that once I learned them, I could sing at his fish stand on Saturday and he would pay me one dollar. Since my buddy Sonny was Italian, he knew the songs from his family singing them so he helped me learn the tune. When I stated singing at Mr. Anthony's fish stand more people came to buy fish from him. Every Saturday the people would just be waiting for me to come and sing and Mr. Anthony's business was growing so he raised my pay to two dollars. Sonny kept telling me I could be a famous singer like Frank Sinatra and make tons of money. I was just happy to give Mom the two dollars for groceries each week.

One afternoon while sitting on our building's front steps watching the kids get soaked by the fire hydrant water a man in a brown suit carrying a briefcase walked up to me. "Excuse me, do you know if a Mrs. Ann McClure lives here?"

"Yes sir, that is my Mom. I'm her oldest son."

"Is she home?"

"No sir, she is at work over in the garment district, why?"

"I need to talk to her about something very important. What time will she be home?"

"Usually about six o'clock."

"Here is my business card. Tell her I will be back to see her this evening."

As he walked away, I started reading his business card. It said, Mr. William Jones Attorney at Law. I couldn't figure out what an attorney needed to see Mom about. Maybe it had something to do with my Dad's military benefits or something like that. When Mom got home that evening, I told her about Mr. Jones and gave her his business card. She said it was nothing to worry about he was just probably trying to sell something.

That evening about seven o'clock there was a knock on our apartment door. Mom slowly walked to the door and looked out the peep-hole to see who it was.

"Rory, is this the man you were talking to today?"

Looked out, "Yes Mom, that is Mr. Jones."

Then Mom opened the door. "Yes, can I help you?"

"Are you Mrs. Ann McClure?"

"Yes I am."

"May I come in so we can talk? I have some very important news to tell you."

"All right, come in, we can talk at the dining room table. Now, what do you want to talk about Mr. Jones?"

"I am the legal representative for your husband's uncle, Weston McClure. A few months ago, Mr. McClure passed away and he left his entire estate to you and your children."

"Oh my God, what's this mean?"

"Well, for one thing you are now very wealthy. However, Mr. McClure did have one condition in his will."

"And what might that be Mr. Jones?"

"You and your children have to live on the McClure Ranch and keep it operating."

"A ranch, I know nothing about running a ranch. Where in the world is it?"

"It's in Wyoming. Way out west. Let me explain the entire will to you Mrs. McClure. Your husband's uncle left you and your children everything he owned which in monetary value comes to about $1.7 million dollars."

"Oh my God, I am dreaming."

"The biggest part of the value is the McClure Ranch which stands on 170,700 acres and has a beautiful modern house for your kids and you. The ranch is a cattle ranch and is presently managed by Sam Wesley. All you have to do is sign the papers and live on the ranch."

"Mr. Jones I could kiss you but give me those papers to sign first."

"You take a week to pack up your things and handle any business you need to and I will get four train tickets for Saturday morning for your trip to Cheyenne, Wyoming. Once you get there, which will take several days, someone will pick you up at the train station. Also, Mrs. McClure here is two hundred dollars for spending on your trip. Don't flash it around because you don't know who is watching."

"Thank you so much Mr. Jones. This will give us a new life and my children a good future."

"You are welcome Mrs. McClure. I will drop your tickets off in a couple days. Good evening."

All night Mom tossed and turned and she was up and down. I finally got up to talk with her. "Mom, what do we have to lose. We have nothing here and you are killing yourself working those long hours. Dad would want us to do this"

"I think you are right Rory but it is scary moving when you don't know what you are walking into."

"Mom, it can't be any worst then what we have here."

"You are right, so Wyoming here we come!"

Mr. Jones made all the arrangements for us to travel out to Wyoming. On July 18, 1950 we left our apartment for good to head out west. Mom sold everything we had in the apartment so she had a little bit of money for the trip. When we got to Grand Central Station Mr. Jones was waiting for us and he give Mom $100 for expenses we might have. When we got on the train the conductor showed us to what he called a State Cabin and Mom had to tip him fifty-cents. The cabin was really nice it had four like roll up beds and big soft seats where you could look out the window and a small bathroom. Mom, commented, "I bet this cost a pretty penny for four tickets. See how rich kids live."

As we pulled out of Grand Central Station, we all waved good-bye to New York. The train ride would take several days according to Mr. Jones and we would have to change trains in Chicago. It was an enjoyable ride for us because we had never been out of New York City. I couldn't believe all the beautiful trees, mountains, and rivers we saw. It puzzled me why everybody lived in the city when there was so much open land outside of it. When it came time to go to the dining car, we had no idea what to expect. As we walked in the car a waitress came over to us and showed us to special seating area and she gave us a menu and told us to order whatever we wanted and that it had all been taken care of by Mr. Jones. Of course, she had her hand out for Mom to tip her. After hearing that we were eating free we filled our bellies until we were about to explode. It was really hard sleeping on the train with all the noise from the train wheels on the tracks.

Several days later the conductor called out "Cheyenne" which was our stop. When we got off of the train everything looked so different from New York City. It looked like everyone was moving at a real slow pace and they all seemed polite and not in a hurry. Almost all of the men had on cowboy boots and hats. The thing I said to Mom was, "I have to get me one of those cowboy hats."

Mom just laughed as she was looking around for the person who was suppose to be picking us up here at the station. Finally, a young dark skin, black haired man came up to her, "Are you Mrs. McClure?"

"Yes, I am, and these are my children."

"I was sent by Mr. Wesley the McClure Ranch boss man to pick you up and take you to the ranch which is just outside of Sheridan. My name is Dinja. I will get your suit cases and you can follow me to the car."

When we got to the car it was an old beat-up jeep woody station wagon. All I kept thinking was let's get moving because it was so hot you could fry an egg on the street. As we headed for the highway, I kept looking at Dinja and finally said, "Are you an Indian?"

"Rory, stop asking questions and let Dinja drive."

"It's okay Mrs. McClure, yes I am a Shoshone and we are American Indians. Mr. Wesley has many Shoshone brothers working for him. We are good with the cattle and horses."

"How big is the ranch, Dinja?"

"Rory, stop it now!"

"It is many thousand acres and cattle everywhere. You will like it."

I wasn't sure if I would like it but I had to admit it was different.

We saw a big sign hanging over the entrance that said McClure Ranch. As we turned in and rode down the dusty road, we could see a huge white house with other buildings around it. As Dinja pulled up in front of the house he said, "Here you are at your new home."

As we got out of the car an older Indian man and woman came down the steps to meet us. "Hello, Mrs. McClure, I am Samoka and this is my wife Nija. We take care of the house and cooking for you and your family."

"Nice to meet you Samoka and Nija."

"Come we will show you the house and then Boss Wesley will be here."

The interior of the house was huge. It started with a large foyer that flowed into a western style living room with a stone fire place. Between the living room and dining room was a Grand Piano. The dining room had a huge table that must seat about twenty people and the kitchen was modern with all the latest appliances. This house was a woman's dream. "What is back here?"

"The downstairs bathroom and Boss Wesley's bedroom and the doors to the back patio. "Mr. Wesley lives here?

"When Boss McClure got very sick Boss Wesley moved into the house to take care of him until he died. I will show you the patio and then we will go upstairs."

The view on the patio was breath taking and the patio was fantastic with a barbeque made out of stone. Next, we went upstairs where there were four bedrooms each with their own bathroom. The master bedroom was still filled with Mr. McClure's things and Samoka said, "This is your room. You are now Boss McClure."

Mom had the three of us pick our bedrooms and said she would sleep with Nellie for a while. We didn't ask any questions we were so happy. I think my bedroom was bigger than are entire apartment back in New York.

As we were settling in our rooms, we heard the front door open and apparently it was Mr. Wesley because Samoka and Nija kept calling him boss. When we came down stairs, he was standing in the living room waiting for us to come down. Sam Wesley was about six feet tall, looked very muscular and was about my Mom's age. He looked like a cowboy right out of the comic books with his cowboy boots, jeans with a huge belt buckle, a western shirt, and a black cowboy hat. I wanted an outfit just like his. When he saw us, he immediately said, "Welcome Mrs. McClure it is nice to meet you. Your husband's uncle spoke very highly of you."

"It is a pleasure to meet you Mr. Wesley and I look forward to learning all about the ranch from you."

"Please, just call me Pitch. That is what everybody calls me."

"Okay, Pitch, I am Ann. These are my children Rory, Tommy, and Nellie. I assume you already know my husband was killed in World War ll."

"Yes, his uncle told me all about him. He sounded like a great guy. I will get my things out of here this evening."

"Please stay Pitch, it will make me and the kids feel a little safer until we get to know this place better."

"That will be okay for a while. I have to go now we are in the middle of branding."

"You are having dinner with us tonight, aren't you?"

"If you would like me to. I am sure you have tons of questions. I'll see you at six."

After Nija fixed us some lunch I went outside to check things out. I walked around the back of the house and there were four buildings. The first two I looked in were stables for the horses. The next one must have been their equipment barn because it had a tractor, tools, and feed. The last one, when I opened the door there was a young boy about my age. "Oh, I'm sorry for interrupting you."

"I'm just cleaning up. My name is Reno. I take care of the bunk house for the wranglers until I get old enough to ride with them. Samoka and Nija are my grandparents. We all live up in the village."

"I'm Rory, just got in from New York City."

"You must be the new owner?"

"Well, my Mom is. I was just checking out the place."

"This is where the wranglers who aren't married live. Boss McClure gave the married ones a piece of land on the south side where they have built houses for their families. It is like a small village but no t-pees just houses. I'll take you there some day to meet my friends. I better get back to work. Nice meeting you Rory." When I went back in the house, I could tell Mom didn't know what to do with herself since she was always working and never had any free time back in the city. She asked Samoka and Nija if she could help with anything but they told her no. For some reason she decided to go upstairs and went in Mr. McClure's bedroom to look around. He had guns and swords hanging everywhere but she did find a picture of him hugging my Dad when he was a boy. She guessed at one time they were very close. For some reason at that point she decided this room was now her room and called down to Samoka to bring her some boxes. She started taking things off the walls and packed then in boxes to be stored. It was obvious that Mom was going to be the new Boss McClure.

When it was dinner time Pitch knotted on the door and Mom answered it. "Pitch, you live here, you don't have to knock. Come on in, dinner is smelling really good." We all took our chairs for dinner and surprisingly Pitch remembered our names. Then of course, Mom said grace and we passed the food plates around. Then Mom politely said, "Pitch, I want you to tell me everything I need to know about this place."

"I don't know where to start."

"How about, how much land do I own?"

"Okay, you own 130,700 acres. Your husband's great, great, grandfather came out here after World War 1 and brought the land

and settled here when there was nothing. He became very good friends with the Shoshones and they built this ranch together. The last time I checked you had approximately $245,000 in the Sheridan State Bank which is handled by your accountant John Riggins who is located in Sheridan. Let's see, you have about 9,000 head of cattle, about 40 horses and 32 employees working for you. The majority of them are Shoshone. They are very good wranglers and are very trustworthy. You have an account at Sears in Sheridan where you can buy anything you want. They have everything and John Riggins pays the bill each month. As for groceries, you tell Samoka what you want and he does the shopping. We have a Shoshone village to the south which Boss McClure gave to the Shoshone for their families. It is all houses, not t-pees and that is where the married wranglers live. I will take you there one day. Your children will go to school in Sheridan. Dinja will drive them there and pick them up after school. Oh yea, we also have three cars and three trucks. Do you drive?"

"No!"

"Well, you will have to learn quickly so you can get around. Also, we have a horse for each of you so you all need to learn how to ride. It is the easiest way to get around the ranch. Samoka and Nija take care of the house, laundry, and cooking. Dinja will be your driver until you learn how to drive. I think that is about it for now. Do you have any questions?"

"It is obvious that we need some western clothes."

"Dinja will take you to Sears tomorrow and you can buy all the clothes you need. He will also show you around the town and take you to meet John Riggins. Anything else before I call it a night?"

"I am re-doing the master bedroom so I will need paint, curtains, new furniture and some other things."

"You just pick out what you want at Sears and they will deliver it."

That night all I could think about was how I would look in my cowboy boots and hat. Plus, I was getting my own horse. I had to come up with a good name like Thunder. But then I thought the horse would already have a name, that's okay. I also kept wondering if they had any kids around here and what they did for fun. All I see is work, work, and more work. But since I was the owner's son, I should just be giving orders. If my friends from the city could see me now.

Everybody was up bright and early. I guessed they didn't realize it was summer and everyone slept in. When I came down the stairs breakfast was on the table.

"What time is it Samoka?"

"A little after eight o'clock and your breakfast is getting cold."

I was surprised that Mom, Nellie, and Tommy were already finished with breakfast and were outside ready to go to Sheridan. I had some, eggs, bacon and toast which was like heaven compared to my usual Cheerios back in the city each morning. When I went outside Mom was talking to Pitch and Nellie yelled, "Come on Rory, let's get going. I want to see the town and my new school." We all jumped in the car and Dinja headed down the dusty road to the highway. The ride took about twenty minutes or so. Dinja told us we were going to see Mr. Riggins first because the stores were not open yet. Mr. Riggins secretary was waiting for us and took us right into his office. My first thought was it is Santa Claus and then Nellie yelled out, "Santa Claus" and Mr. Riggins just started laughing. Mom started to apology but Mr. Riggins told her it was all right. Mr. Riggins explained everything to Mom that Pitch had already told her. However, he did tell her to watch over her land carefully because many free-loader miners were moving on to rancher's land and drilling for uranium without permission. Next, we rode around town and saw the school we would be going to in the fall.

The town had several churches and one big Catholic church called Saint Joseph's which made Mom very happy. Then we pulled up to the Sears store and we all got excited. I couldn't remember the last time I got to buy new clothes. We must have shopped for three hours in the clothing departments. I got two pair of cowboy boots, five pair of wrangler jeans, five shirts, a hat, big belt buckle, underwear, socks, and a suit for church. Tommy, Nellie, and Mom all got about the same thing as me, only the girls got dresses for church. When the bill came it was almost two thousand dollars and Dinja told the clerk to put it on the McClure account and that this is Mrs. McClure for the future reference. Then we all wanted to go home and get our new clothes on but not Mom. She went and picked out paint for her bedroom, then curtains and bed things, and then a complete bedroom set. Sear promised they would deliver it tomorrow but Mom took the paint and brushes with her. We were finally done, so we thought. Mom told Dinja to take her back to Mr. Riggins office. We had no idea what for. When we got to his office, she told us to stay in the car. When she came out, she had a hand full of money. "I needed some pocket money. Now we can go have lunch Dinja."

When we got back to the ranch, we all quickly went to our rooms to change into our new western clothes. I had to admit I did look like a cowboy but knew nothing about what it means to be a cowboy. When Mom came down stairs, I couldn't believe how good she looked. The western clothes showed off her good figure and she was very attractive after having three kids. I wondered what Pitch thought of her since he was not married. Then I heard her calling Samoka and he came running. "Yes, Boss McClure!"

"I want all of this furniture except for the desk to be moved out of here so this bedroom is ready to be painted tomorrow."

"Yes, Boss! What do I do with the furniture?"

"Give it to somebody in the Shoshone village who needs it. Just get it out because I have new furniture coming tomorrow and I will need a crew to paint tomorrow."

"I will take care of it right now Boss Lady. By the way, you look very nice."

"Well, thank you Samoka."

At dinner that evening Pitch commented on our new western clothes look. Mom told him what she was doing with the master bedroom and he seemed okay with it. While we were eating, I said, "Mr. Pitch can I asked you a personal question?" "Rory, Pitch does not have to answer your questions."

"That's okay what is it Rory?"

"How did you get the name Pitch?"

"Well, let's see where to start. My Christian name is Samuel or Sam but when I was growing up, I was the pitcher on all of our baseball teams so all my friends just started calling me Pitch and it just stuck. I pitched in the Major Baseball League for the Brooklyn Dodgers for three years until I blew my elbow out in 1946. Then I decided to come back home to Wyoming to be a cowboy. I was lucky when I met your uncle and he took me on and I eventually became his ranch manager. We became very close friends and he treated me like I was his son. I moved in the house at his request and took care of him until he died. Now you know the whole story of Pitch."

All at once Tommy spoke out, "You pitched for the Brooklyn Dodgers, Mr. Pitch?" "Forgive him Pitch, he is baseball crazy and the Dodger's are his favorite game."

"Yea, Tommy, I pitched for the Dodgers. You are too young to remember but one day I will show you all the things I have from playing in the big league."

"That's great, can we do it now?"

"Tommy, Mr. Pitch said some day. So, stop buggy him or he won't show you."

"We will do it as soon your family is settled in Tommy, I promise."

"What do you like better, being a cowboy or professional baseball pitcher."

"Rory, now you are starting up."

"It's okay Ann, I loved playing baseball but my first love is being a cowboy."

"How come you are not married?"

"That's it, all you kids go get washed up for bed. Right now!"

After the kids took off up the steps, "I'm so sorry Pitch but you know kids."

"It's okay. Thanks for dinner. I'll be turning in also, and the answer is I haven't found the right woman yet. Good night!"

The next morning things were really jumping. Samoka had a four-man crew already painting in the master bedroom and the

Sear's truck showed up with Mom's furniture and stuff. Mom started giving orders left and right. I knew it was time for us kids to get out of her way. We decided to go out to the barn and look at some of the horses. Nellie and even Tommy were a little scared because the horses were so big. Once they began feeding them a few carrots they were okay and liked petting them. There was this one beautiful rusty red horse at the end of the stable. Just then Reno came walking in, "That is one beautiful horse. Her name is Galant. She was the Big Boss's horse so I guess she will be your Mom's horse now. Boss Pitch takes her out every now and then to let her run a little. I guess your Mom will learn how to ride?"

"Mr. Pitch said that we all would have to learn to ride and we will have our own horse. I can't wait so I can go watch the wranglers."

At that point Nellie asked Reno, "Does the village have any little girls there?"

"Sure, there are plenty of them all around your age."

"Do they have doll babies?"

"Of course, only they are Indian dolls not white dolls."

"That's okay, I would like an Indian doll."

We all started laughing, but Nellie.

After we had lunch I went over and sat at the grand piano. I played around with the keys for a while to see how they all sounded different. When I got an idea of how they went I tried to pick out the song Yankee Doodle Dandy. After working on it for about an hour I finally got it down where it sounded pretty good. I would mess up a little here and there but each time I played it the song got better. I finally got it down when Samoka came over to the piano. "So, you have learned to play the piano. It sounds very good."

"Oh no, this is just the first time I have tried to play a piano. We had one at our school back in the city but I never tried to play it."

"Your uncle Boss McClure played the piano usually after he had a few drinks. He told me he played by ear. I didn't know what that meant because I always saw him using his hands. Maybe that is what you were doing?"

"I guess you are right. Maybe I get it from my Dad's side of the family."

"There are all different kinds of music papers in the bench you are sitting on just pick up the top of it. Perhaps you can learn to read the music or they probably have a piano teacher in Sheridan who could give you lessons."

I got up off the bench and opened the top and there was all kinds of music sheets. As Samoka walked away I started going through the music. I was all excited and decided to look for a western cowboy song. Then I saw it, Home on the Range. I pulled it out of the pile and started picking at the keys. I was getting no where mainly because I didn't know how the song went. I kept trying over and over again and finally got some of the beginning. Then Nija came in from the kitchen. "No, no Mr. Rory that is all wrong. Your uncle played that song many times. It going like this and she started to sing it, Home, home on the range where the deer, and the antelope range." She went through the entire song.

"Nija, start singing again while I figure out the notes."

That didn't work very well so I started singing the song with her over and over again until I got the tune in my head correctly.

After a good half an hour I finally had it and Nija went back to the kitchen singing. I worked on finding the right notes on the piano and after about two hours I finally had it down. It was time for a break so I went outside to see what Tommy and Nellie were up to. They were over by the coral watching the wranglers break in new horses. I was hoping one of them was for me.

As we watched the horses throw the men to the ground, we would laugh but they would just climb back on the horse and ride them until they were broken in for regular riding. All of a sudden up behind us was Mr. Pitch. "See any of them you kind a like for your horse?"

"They all look mighty big for me Mr. Pitch," was Nellies comment.

"Don't worry Nellie we have a nice little pony for you named Princess. "Can I see her, can I see her?"

So, we all went with Mr. Pitch to the barn to see Princess. When we got to her stall, I thought Nellie would go nuts just jumping up and down. Then Mr. Pitch opened the stall gate and picked Nellie up and sat her on Princess. "How does she look boys?"

"Like a real cowgirl," was my remark.

"Now Nellie every day you need to come out here and use the ladder here to climb up on Princess and you two talk to each other and you feed her carrots."

"Horses can't talk, Mr. Pitch!"

"Oh, you will be surprised. All right, let's go wash up for dinner."

We had a wonderful dinner and the entire evening Nellie wouldn't shut up about Princess. When we were done eating, I said, "Everyone stay here."

I went over to the piano and started playing and singing Home on the Range. Mom and Mr. Pitch were totally shocked. When I was done playing it a couple times, they all applauded. "Rory, where did you learn to play the piano?"

"I didn't Mom. Nija sang the tune to me over and over again so I could find the right notes to play. It's the only song I can play."

Then Mr. Pitch spoke out, "Playing the piano was great but I was really impressed by Rory's singing. He could be another Gene Antry."

Nellie says, "Who is that?" Then Tommy and I said the same thing.

"He is a real famous western singer and he makes a lot of movies."

"Rory just loves music, he sang in the boy's church choir and in the fish market. In the fish market? Well, you could look into getting him piano lessons in Sheridan since you have this nice grand piano here."

"Can I Mom, can I?"

"We will see Rory. It would be nice to have music in the house."

While Tommy, Nellie and I were playing around with the piano Mr. Pitch said to Mom, "Come on, take a walk with me I want to show you something."

"Okay, where are you taking me?"

"You will see!"

They went out into the barn and Pitch walked her to Galant's stall. "Oh, what a beautiful horse. Its hair is almost the color of mine. Is this your horse Pitch?"

"No Ann, it is your horse."

"You are kidding me, right?"

"No, her name is Galant and she is waiting for you to learn how to ride her. Actually, I think she is tired of me exercising her and can't wait for you to take over."

"When can I start learning to ride?"

"First things first, you have to learn to drive so you can go anywhere you want, any time you want."

"Okay, when do I start learning to drive?"

"Well, are you all done with your bedroom?"

"Yes, for now."

"I will have Dinja start teaching you tomorrow morning."

"That's great. Good night Galant."

As they walked back in the house, they both were laughing about something. "Okay, time to wash up for bed. Come on, get upstairs. I'll be right up."

As I laid in in my bed that night, I thought this was a great day. It was almost like we were a real family with a Dad.

CHAPTER 2

Morning comes early on the ranch so Mom was out on the front steps waiting for Dinja to come with the car. When he pulled up it was not the old woody jeep station wagon but a beautiful red Cadillac with steer horns on the front of it. Quickly Mom said, Dinja where is the old smaller car?"

"Well, Boss Lady, this is your car and it is an automatic shift and not a stick shift so it is much easier to drive."

Mom jumped in the car and Dinja started telling her how everything in the car worked. After she got most of it, they switched positions and Mom got behind the steering wheel. She put the car in gear and slowly jerked down the dusty road. The three of us stood there and said a little prayer so Mom wouldn't crack upthe Cadillac.

The next morning Ninja took Mom to Sheridan to get her learner's permit. After she had her legal permit, he let her drive home from Sheridan. When they got home, Mom told Dinja to leave the car out front and to give her the keys. Of course, he had a big question mark on his face but she was the boss lady so he did what she said. Mom would go inside do a few things and about an hour later come out jump in the car and drive down the road then turn around and come back to the house. She would do this all day long and everybody, including us, thought she was going crazy. At least once a day she would have Dinja take her out on the highway and around Sheridan. I could tell her confidence was building and she felt good behind the steering wheel. After three days of this she had Dinja set up two barrels for her to practice parking. Mom would practice, practice and practice some more. Mr. Pitch would watch her trying to put the big Cadillac between the barrels. "Now, that is one determined woman!"

Mr. Pitch told Mom that he would not be at dinner this evening because he was going to town with the boys to let off some stream. I guessed that meant they were going drinking. Dinner that night was boring. I think we all missed Pitch. Nija could see the sad looks on our faces. "Boss Pitch doesn't drink much. He just goes with the wranglers so they don't get into trouble or have too much to drink so they can't work tomorrow."

"Thank you Nija, but Mr. Pitch is a grown man and he can do whatever he wants in his spare time."

"Yes, Boss Lady, I understand, sorry."

"Does Dinja work on Saturday?"

Then Samoka jumped in, Yes Boss everybody works on Saturday and they all have off on Sunday so they can go to church. Only Nija works to do the cooking for the big house."

"Tell Dinja I want him out front with the car on Monday morning at nine o'clock. I am going to take my driving test."

"Yes Boss, I will tell him tonight."

At dinner I started playing around with the piano while Tommy, Nellie, and Mom played Go Fish at the table. I was working on how to play the three songs I sang at the fish market. I finally got Camp town Races down and started singing it. When I was done the three of them applauded. "Rory as soon as I get my license, we are going to town to look for a piano teacher for you."

"That would be great Mom since we have this big piano,"

"All right kids its time to wash up for bed. I will be up shortly."

I guessed Mom was waiting to see if Pitch was coming home then I heard her come upstairs. I tried to stay awake to see when Mr. Pitch came in but I fell fast asleep.

When I came down stairs, I asked Nija where my Mom was and said, "Out front driving that big red car up and down the road."

"Where is Mr. Pitch?"

"I don't know he is the Boss, not me. Come over here and eat your breakfast."

After I finished eating, I went outside to find Tommy and Nellie. They both were in the stable and Nellie was sitting up on Princess. Tommy and I decided to look at other horses in the barn figuring these must be the extra ones since the wranglers were all out working. One was white with black spots all over it. I think I heard them calling it an Appaloosa or something like that when they were breaking the horse in the other day. Tommy really liked him. When I looked in the next stable there was a horse that just looked like Roy Roger's Trigger. I think a Palomino. What kind of cowboy am I, don't even know the type of horses? We settled on these two horses but knew Mr. Pitch would have the last say about that.

Mom finally got done practicing with the car. Just as she pulled up in front of the house a big truck with the name RJ's Catering pulled up beside her. As soon as Mom got out of her car Samoka came running out of the house waving to the truck driver to go around the back. "Samoka what is going on here?"

"Boss Pitch is having a barbeque for all the wranglers this afternoon so you can meet them."

"That is a great idea. What time does it start?"

"At three o'clock to give the wranglers time to clean up before we eat."

"Do you need any help?"

"No, Boss Lady, I will take care of everything. We have had these before with Boss McClure."

Mom waved okay and went into the house. It was only minutes later when Pitch came running in the house. "Ann, I'm sorry, I forgot to tell you about the barbeque."

"That's okay Pitch, it is a great idea. The men should know who the new boss is and to meet my children. Are their families coming from the village?"

"No Ann, it is just the men who work for you. I'm going to put my horse up and then I'll be back to clean up myself."

"Okay, I'll see you later."

When I walked out back, I could smell all the good food cooking. They had everything steaks, ribs, hamburgers, and even a few hot dogs. When Mom came out, she looked beautiful with a red cowgirl shirt and her hair hanging down. As she walked out on the patio things got very quiet and the wranglers just looked at her. Then Mom spoke out, "I would like to welcome all of you to our little get together. I am Ann McClure the new owner and these are my children Rory, Tommy. And Nellie," as she tapped us on our heads. "I look forward to learning all about the ranch from Boss Pitch and getting to know you all better. Enjoy yourselves and have fun."

Samoka had a table reserved for us and Mr. Pitch and another man I did not know. After we all got our food and sat down Mr. Pitch said, "This Kinno he is the ranch foreman and third in command after you and me. He has been with the McClure ranch over ten years and his family lives in the village. Rory, I think you met his son Reno?"

"Yes sir, we are becoming good friends."

Then Kinno said, "It is nice to meet the McClure family and if you need anything just ask me."

Tommy quickly wanted to change the subject, "Mr. Pitch, Rory and I saw two horses in the stable we would like to have for our own."

"Let me guess, one is an Appaloosa and the other a Palomino."

"You are right, can we have them?"

"Yes, Kinno had the boys break them in a couple days ago and also you get to name them because right now they do not have any names."

Tommy and I took off for the stable and spent the whole afternoon sitting on boxes thinking up names for our horses. Tommy final settle on Domino and I liked the name Dancer. When we came back to the barbeque most of the men had already left for their homes. We told Mr. Pitch and Mom the names we picked out and they liked them. "Mr. Pitch, when can we start learning to ride them?"

"As soon as your Mom gets her driver's license so I can teach all four of you at the same time."

"Don't worry kids I will get my license on Monday and we can start learning Monday afternoon. If that's okay with Pitch?"

"You seem very confident!"

Just before we were about to call it a night Mr. Pitch said, "Ann, Sheridan has three churches a Baptist, Methodist, and Catholic. I am going to Saint Joseph's the Catholic church but if you want to go to one of the others, I will have Dinja take you and the kids."

"Oh no, Saint Joseph's is fine we are Catholics. What time will we be leaving?"

"Around eight thirty so we can make nine o'clock mass."

"We will be ready to go and thank you for all you have done for us. I really appreciate it."

"No problem. Good night."

Sunday morning, we all loaded up in the Cadillac with Mom driving and Mr. Pitch in the front. We all had our Sunday best on and even Mr. Pitch had a western suit on with one of those sting ties. Mom did a good job parking the car and when we walked in the church everybody kept staring at us. I could tell Mr. Pitch wanted to sit in the back seat but Mom kept walking up to the front to the fifth row. All through the church service the priest kept looking at us and smiling. When I looked around, I saw many of the wranglers and their families and the Reno waved to me. I guess the Shoshone could be Catholics just like us. After church. it was a nightmare trying to get out when everybody was coming over to meet Mom. It took us forever to get out the front door of the church where the priest was shaking hands. "You must be Mrs. McClure, I am Father Daniel, welcome to Saint Joseph's church. Are your children going to go to school here?"

"I guess they will. I haven't had much time to think about it."

"Well, September is almost here. You should go see Sister Mary at the convent"

"Yes Father, I will do that this coming week. Have a nice day Father, it was nice meeting you!"

We all quickly got in the car and Mom drove away. As we passed by this parked car. This old bald fat man waved to Mr. Pitch and he waved back.

"Who was that Pitch?"

"That is Mr. Todd Gallon the city's mayor and the biggest crook in the town. Believe me, never trust one word he says and don't believe it for a single minute." "Mom, Mom, look over there, the sign says music lessons by Mrs. Louise Lambert."

"Write that phone number down Rory we can call her this afternoon>"

I had to admit Mom was a pretty good driver. When we arrived at the ranch, we all couldn't wait to get out of our Sunday clothes and to check our horses.

As we were getting out of the car Kinno came over to Mr. Pitch and pulled him over to the side. Mom was watching them carefully, it looked like something big was up. Mom and I could hear Pitch giving out orders to Kinno. When they got finished talking Pitch came over to Mom. "Ann, one of Kinno's relatives saw free-loaders on your property up north and he said it looked like they were planning to drill for uranium. So, I am taking three men with me and we are going to stop the drilling even before they start. Kinno will be in charge while I'm gone."

"Why can't Kinno go and you stay here?"

"There are a couple reasons, one is Kinno runs our ranch wranglers and takes care of the cattle and second if there is any shooting, we need to have white-man there and not all Shoshone Indians. I should only be gone a few days and Kinno and Samoka will take care of everything around here."

"You honestly believe there will be shooting?"

"There are people who want to get rich quick and will do anything including

shooting people."

"Why don't you get the Sheriff involved?"

"Dinjo is already on his way to town to inform the Sheriff of the situation but every man or woman has the right to protect their land. I have to get going, we need all the daylight so we can get there faster."

"Pitch, you and the men be careful and don't do anything risky."

"We will, now I have to really go, Ann."

I think at that point Mom felt like hugging him.

After Pitch and the three men rode away with their pistols and rifles, we went back in the house to get out of the heat. I could tell Mom was thinking hard and that she was worried. "Mom, how about if we call the music teacher to find out what the story is on piano lessons."

"That sounds like a good idea. What was her name?"

"Mrs. Louise Lambert, here is her phone number."

It was like Mom and this Mrs. Lambert were old friends. They talked on the phone for almost an hour. Finally, Mom hung up the phone, "So, what did she have to say Mom?"

"Louise is from New York so we had a lot to talk about. She went to the Peabody Conservatory and studied piano so she must be really good."

"Okay, Mom, what about the lessons?"

"All right Mr. Patience, she will give you lessons on Monday and Thursday. The good part she is coming out to the ranch for your lessons because she heard Mr. McClure had this beautiful grand piano and she only has an upright piano. She will be here at six-thirty after dinner. I think I have made a female friend. I could use a friend with all these men around here."

"That's is great, Mom. Do I start tomorrow?

"Yes, Louise said she would be here after their dinner to get started with you. Oh, she did ask if my other children want to take lessons?"

Tommy and Nellie were shaking their head no at a hundred miles per hour.

After dinner that evening, the four of us went down to the stable to be with our horses. We all took turns climbing up on our horse in their stable even Mom. "Mommy, you have to talk to Galant so she knows your voice and feed her carrots so she likes you. Mr. Pitch told me that."

So, we all started following Nellie's advice. After an hour or so we went back inside and had some ice cream.

"Mom, are you worried about Mr. Pitch?"

"Yes, Rory and also the other men. Any time I see guns that means trouble."

"Do you think there will be any shooting?"

"Mr. Pitch is a reasonable man. I think he will just try to get the free-loaders off of our property. Enough of that now, quiz me on my driving test questions"

Mom was up early and I knew she was looking for Pitch's return. Finally, Dinja pulled around the front in the red Cadillac all cleaned up. "Wish me luck kids"

"We will say a prayer for you Mom."

Mom, took off down the road to Sheridan's Department of Motor Vehicles which was located on the back-bottom floor of Sears. The place was almost empty so she got to take the written test immediately. She aced the written and then this older lady with what looked a bird's nest on her head came over to us and said, "Mrs. McClure?"

"Yes, I am McClure."

"I am your driving tester for today. My name is Mrs. Clark."

"Nice to meet you Mrs. Clark. These are my children."

"Oh, what a nice-looking family. Where is your husband? Most women bring their husband because they are the one who have taught them now to drive."

No, my husband was killed in the war."

"Sorry to hear that. Now, if you show me to your car we can get started."

When we walked out the back of Sears she said, "What car is your car?"

"That red Cadillac over there."

"Oh my God, what a beautiful car. I've never ridden in a Cadillac before."

Mrs. Clark told Mom where to drive and where to turn while talking about the Cadillac the whole time. After about a half hour driving all over town Mrs. Clark had Mom pullback around behind Sears and pull up to the curb. This is just nice here Mrs. McClure, you have passed the test and after I sign it you can take it inside to get your license."

For a minute Mom thought about asking her about the parking test but did not bring it up. Mom went inside and they stamped her permit PASSED. Mom, thanked Mrs. Clark and told her she hoped to see her around town. Then all of us went out the door screaming and jumping up and down for Mom. When Mom came driving up the dusty road to the house, she was waving her license out of her car window. Everybody started cheering for her even Samoka and Nija. When Mom got out of the car, we all hugged her over and over again. Then she said to Dinja, "Go put this car away and get out the old woody jeep. Now you have to teach me how to drive a standard shift."

"I'll be right back Boss Lady."

Mom drove up and down the road at least twenty times learning to shift gears properly and we could actually see her getting better. She finally called it quits and told us to clean up for dinner because we had Mrs. Louise coming for my piano lesson.

After we, ate, I sat patiently on the front steps waiting for my instructor. Then finally, I saw an old car coming up the driveway and it was Mrs. Lambert. I called back to Mom to let her know Mrs. Lambert was here and she came right out. Mrs. Louise Lambert was a very tall woman I would guess about six feet tall and on the skinny side. She had blonde hair tied all up in a knot on her head and wore really small framed glasses that sat down on her nose. She was about Mom's age or maybe a little older with tons of make-up on her face. Mom invited her in the house and then they did all the women's chit-chat. Finally, she walked over to the grand piano. "I have heard about this beautiful instrument and it is in fantastic looking condition. It probably needs a tune- up. I understand that Mr. McClure used to have the nuns come out and do the tuning."

"These are my children Rory, Tommy, and Nellie. Rory is the one with the music talent in the family. The other two are not interested right now."

"Well okay, let Rory and me get started."

I was ready to start banging away on the keys. What do you know about reading music Rory?"

"I can play a few songs."

"Let me hear one of them."

"Okay, how about Home on the Range."

"That will be fine, go ahead."

I started playing and about half way through Mrs. Louise stopped me. "So, you are playing and singing by ear?"

"Everybody has been saying that for years to me but I have no idea what it means."

"How did you learn this song?"

"Nija, sang the song and I learned to sing it from her and once I knew it good then I picked it out on the piano keys."

"That is what playing by ear means. You know how the song sounds and your brain relays that to your hands. It is a gift that most people don't have. However, to be really good you have to learn how to read music so you can just pick up a sheet of music and play it even if you don't know the tune. Reading music is where we are going to start with you. First, you need to learn and understand the music scale. It goes like this, Doe, Ra, Me. Fa, So. La, T, Doe. Now, you try it. No, listen to me again."

Finally, I got it right and she played the notes on the piano. Now, you sing with me. You have a beautiful voice Rory."

"Thank you, what is next?"

"Now, I will explain what all these notes mean on the music sheet, little by little. As we go on you will learn the difference and meanings."

Mrs. Lambert and I went on for about an hour and a half and the only thing I got to play was the music scale. For practice until our next lesson on Thursday she wanted me to be able to play the music scale with my eyes closed. Needless to say, when she left, I was very disappointed. Then Mom told me if I wanted to be good, I would have to do it the right way and practice what she is teaching me and not what I wanted to do. I knew she was right and I wanted to be good.

"All right kids, it is time for bed."

Sam, Pitch, Wesley and his men reached the uranium drilling crew's location just before dark on Monday night. He had one of his men go scout ahead of them to see how many were there. When he heard four owls' hoots, he knew there were four men. They tied their horses about a hundred yards away from where the drillers camp was and walked quietly closer to take a look at what they were up against. The four of them together came up with a plan. They would wait until the drillers were asleep and then sneak up to them, knock them out, tie their hands and feet and secure their weapons.

After waiting about an hour, they could hear the men snoring so they put their plan into action. Each one of the drillers had a pistol, rifle and two of them had knives in the boots. The wranglers collected all the weapons and put them in their wagon where the uranium drill, shovels and tools were. Since the drillers were out cold, Pitch told the men to fix something to eat and coffee. After they ate the Shoshone 's went over and kicked the men in the sides to wake them up. When they finally came to Boss Pitch said, "Good evening boys, did you have a nice nap?"

There apparent leader spoke out, "What the hell is going on here" and he reached for his pistol with his hands tied. "No boys, I should be asking you what you are doing on McClure Ranch property? There are No Trespassing signs posted all over the place. Even a blind squirrel could see them."

"We just got our direction messed up a little. We'll pack up our equipment and be off your land in minutes."

"Okay, I'll play your game being lost. Show me your drilling permit from the state of Wyoming."

Then their leader said, "We accidentally forgot it."

"Or maybe, you didn't want to drill where the state would let you. You just decided to go trespassing and drill where you wanted to. My Indian friends here just can't wait to scalp trespassers." Boss Pitch said something to his men in Shoshone and they grabbed their knives and pointed them at the drillers. The Shoshones took the men and stood them next to a big tree trunk and wrapped rope them about six times and made it tight so all they could do was stand. Next the got an old shirt from the wagon, tore it into pieces and tied the pieces around the driller's mouths. "Now, I want you men to be very quiet so we can get some sleep. Now, if you decide to make noise trying to get away, we will take your shoes and socks off so the red ants can have a feast on your toes and feet I hope you don't give the ants a chance to go up your pants. So, be very quiet gentlemen."

They were all shaking their heads okay!

Pitch and his men got a good seven hours of sleep before the sun came up. They had their breakfast of beef jerky and coffee and then took off the driller's mouth covers.

"Are you going to let us go or just going to kill us?"

"Oh no, we want you to tell all your trespassing friends to stay off the McClure Ranch property because the next ones found on this property will be scalped."

Pitch's men pulled out their knives again and made like they were scalping. "Not yet boys, just a little longer." Then all the wranglers started laughing.

Pitch told one of his men to hook up the horse to the wagon and tie all the others to the back of the wagon and head for the ranch and the rest of them will catch up with him. "Where are you going with our equipment wagon and our horse?"

"I'm glad you asked. We are taking them to the Sheriff's office in Sheridan. You can go claim them at his office. However, I must tell you he will probably charge you with trespassing and give you boys a fine and ten days in jail. Oh yea, if you don't claim them in thirty days the Sheriff will auction your things off and the money will go to Saint Joseph's. You boys get all of that?

The drillers were really pissed off because drilling equipment was very expensive.

As the wagon pulled away Boss Pitch told his men to untie one of the drillers.

"Okay, young man take off all of your clothes and boots."

"What!"

"You heard me or would you like these two Shoshone brothers to help you?

The boy started taking all his clothes off. When he was done, they tied him back up and did the same with the other two free-loaders. Once they had all the drillers tied back to the tree the Shoshone's started throwing their clothes and boots way up in a tree. Then they took the four of them over to a huge thorn bush and told the drillers to jump in it and lay on their backs. At gun point, they did it and were screaming very loud. You could see the thorns cutting into their skin. "Well, free-loaders it is time for us to go. I hope this is a good reminder to stay off McClure land. This is your only warning. If we catch you here again, we will put a bullet in your head and bury you where you fall. If you think you can come back with more, I have many more at the ranch plus the entire Shoshone nation backing me up. So, men be smart and go on some other rancher's property. Let's go men and catch up with the wagon."

As Pitch and his men rode off, they could hear the drillers yelling and screaming as they tried to get out of the thorn bushes.

During the night I could here Mom going down stairs and I even thought I heard her knock-on Mr. Pitch's door to see if he was back yet. In the morning Samoka told us Mr. Pitch was not back. Mom decided to go drive the woody jeep around without Dinja and I think she got the gear shifting down. She decided to go to Saint Joseph's to register us for school. However, Dinja begged her to take the Cadillac and not the woody jeep because

Boss Pitch would kill him. Mom understood what Dinja was saying and didn't want to put him in trouble with Pitch so she went flying down the highway in the Cadillac for the first time by herself. When she met with Sister Mary, they both decided I was in the sixth grade, Tommy in the fourth grade and Nellie in the second grade. Sister Mary told her tuition was three hundred dollars a year for each child but most of the parents don't pay it because most of the children are Shoshones or Arapahos and they don't have that kind of money so they pay what they can. Mom told her she would have Mr. Riggins give her a check tomorrow for a thousand dollars. "Mrs. McClure it is only nine-hundred dollars."

"That's okay Sister, I'll just give a little extra to help out because I have many Shoshone who work for me."

"Are you pregnant, Mrs. McClure?"

"No, where did you get that idea?"

"Aren't you and Mr. Pitch married?"

"No, he just manages the ranch for me. My husband was killed in the war when Nellie was born."

"I'm sorry Mrs. McClure. Please forgive me. I am new here and I thought Mr. Pitch was your husband. You look like such a nice family in church."

"That's fine Sister Mary. I'll see you when school starts."

When Mom came out of the convent, she was talking to herself and laughing at the same time. "Where in the hell did she get this pregnant idea. Do I look pregnant?"

Mom got home as fast as she could to see if Pitch got back yet. When Samoka told her no, you could tell she was very disappointed and worried. The more she thought about it the more she worried. The trouble was Mom had to much time to think. "You kids want to be cowboys and cowgirl but you do nothing on this ranch that you can call work. When Mr. Pitch gets back, I am telling him to give you all some jobs around here."

We all just looked at her like she was nuts. "Don't worry Tommy and Nellie, Mom will forget all that working bull when Mr. Pitch is back."

"I'm not sure Rory. We had to do things when we lived back in our little apartment."

"Stop worrying Tommy, she will forget because she has all kind of people to boss around.

"I just hope you are right. All I want to do is ride Domino."

About four o'clock Wednesday afternoon Pitch and his men came back to the ranch and they had a wagon and a bunch of extra horses. Mom came running out, "Pitch is everything all right?"

"Yes, Ann everything is fine. I will tell you all about it at dinner."

Then Pitch rode over to the stable to take care of business. "Kinno, you and Dinja take the wagon, equipment and horses into the Sheriff and tell him it is from the trespassers and no guns were fired. Tell him I will come in tomorrow morning to tell him all that happened."

After taking care of his horse, Pitch went in the back door to his bathroom to clean up for dinner.

When we all sat down for dinner it was not food on our minds but Mr. Pitch's adventure up north. However, what was on Mr. Pitch's mind was some good home cooked food. Now, ladies and gentlemen I am not talking about the uranium free-loaders until I enjoy this wonderful meal prepared by Nija. So, everybody started eating as fast as we could including Mom. Mr. Pitch just shook his head and started laughing out loud. "I can see I better start talking before the four of you choke on your food."

"We can wait Pitch I know you must be hungry and tired of beef jerky."

"It's okay Ann. I'm going to have to tell what happened sooner or later."

Pitch told us everything about the meeting up with the four men and they were getting ready to drill for uranium before he and the wrangles stopped them. He said that he took their wagon, equipment, and horses and right now Kinno and Dinja were taking it all to the Sheriff. Pitch said he warned the men not to come back on our property. That was all he had to say about the entire situation. However, I knew there was a lot more he wasn't telling us but I figured I could find out from the wranglers because they liked to tell stories in the bunk house. Then Mom said, "Did anybody get shot?"

"No, Ann there was no shooting at all and hopefully they will take my warning to heart. So, what has been going on around here?"

"Show him Mom!"

Pitch looked at Mom, "Show me what?"

Then Mom pulled her driving license out of her pocket and waved it at him. "Oh my God, they let anybody have driving licenses these days"

Everybody broke out laughing including Mom. "Mr. Pitch, we have something else, Rory had his first piano lesson from Mrs. Louise. Then Nellie said, "He learned Do,You, Me, We Them."

"That's not right Nellie."

"How are the lessons going Rory?"

"I have only had one lesson and I am bored to death."

"I see, well after I see the Sheriff tomorrow morning and check out the ranch how about it if we start your riding lessons?"

Then little Nellie spoke out, "While you were gone Mr. Pitch I was in charge and had them all sit on their horses and talk to their horse and feed them carrots. I told them that was your orders."

"Outstanding Nellie, I'll remember to always put you in charge. Let's say we will start the riding lessons about two o'clock because you have a lot to learn about horses. Is that okay with you, Ann?"

"That is fine Pitch. Rory has his next piano lesson after dinner tomorrow."

Then the three of us kids went over to mess around with the piano and Pitch and Mom went out to sit in the patio so Pitch could smoke his cigar. "I went and registered the kids for school today at Saint Joseph's."

"So, they are all set. When does school start?"

"It starts right after Labor Day. You want to hear something funny?"

"Sure, I could use a good laugh."

"When I was registering the kids with Sister Mary, she asked me if I was pregnant."

"What, are you kidding me?"

"She thought you and I were married."

"Would that be so bad?"

Ann just smiled. "I better go get the kids up to bed. It is really nice to have you back home and no it wouldn't be bad."

Ann, got up and hurried in the house before Pitch could say a word.

Bright and early the next morning Pitch went to Sheridan to talk to Sheriff Dan Douglas. He explained everything that happened including the clothes and thorn bush parts. Sheriff Douglas got a big laugh out the whole story. "Maybe they learned their lesson Pitch?"

"I doubt it Dan, I think they will be back at it again. Maybe not the McClure Ranch but in your territory. Well, I have to be on my way. Let me know if anything comes up or if you need my help. See you later, Dan."

When I came down stairs in the morning, I was all excited because I would have my first riding lesson and my second piano lesson. Also, I could smell Nija's wonderful pancakes or as they say out here flapjacks. After I ate, I went down to the chicken coop because Mom usually collected the chicken's eggs in the morning. Nellie yelled at me as I walked over to them, "Rory it is riding day and Princess is just waiting for me."

"Hey Mom, where is Mr. Pitch?"

"He had to go see Sheriff Douglas and then he had to go check the new fence the wranglers put up on the west side. He said he would be back by lunch. While you are here go and get a bag of feed for the chickens. We already collected their eggs." I did what Mom asked me too and then went into the bunk house to see if Reno was working in there. I yelled in the door and Reno answered, "Is that my City Slicker friend from New York?"

"I won't be one of them much longer. Today is my first horse riding lesson. You want me to help you out in here?"

"That would be great. Then I can finish early and go watch you fall on your butt. How about washing the dishes and cleaning the table off while I finish up in the bathroom?"

"Okay, I think a City Slicker can handle that."

While we were working, I asked Reno if any of the wranglers that went north with Mr. Pitch told him anything more about what really happened? "I heard them talking at dinner last evening about what Mr. Pitch said and what the true story was. He didn't tell your Mom the good parts."

"Tell me, tell me, what did Mr. Pitch do. I knew that he was not telling the total story."

"What I heard was that Boss Pitch made the four men take off their clothes and the wranglers threw their clothes high up in a tree. Then Boss Pitch made the four of them lay down in a huge thorn bush."

"That must have really hurt!"

"The one wrangler said as they were riding away they could hear the guys yelling and screaming when the tried to get out of the bushes."

"I bet they won't forget about that for a while."

"Now, you have to promise not to tell anybody because you will get me in trouble. What is said in the bunk house is supposed to stay in the bunk house because that is the Shoshone code. Can I trust you?"

"Sure, I won't tell anybody, but it is really funny.?

Before I knew it I heard Nija ringing the bell for lunch and just as I ran out the bunk house door Mr. Pitch came riding in on his horse Thunder. "Come on Rory let's wash up for lunch.

The others must be inside already. I got a lot of work to do this afternoon so move out young man."

"I thought we were going to have our riding lesson this afternoon?"

"Believe me that will be a lot of hard work teaching you easterners." We just laughed and walked in the house after we washed up.

"Oh, you are back, Pitch."

"Yes Ann, it didn't take long with the Sheriff and the boys did a great job on the west fence. What's for lunch. I'm really hungry?"

"Good old hot dogs and potatoes chips. What did Sheriff Douglas have to say about the free-loaders on our property?"

"Dan told me there are these type of surface miners popping up all over the county. He said they use Geiger counters to locate the uranium and then start drilling or blasting. The problem is, they are doing it on other people's property and they have no right to be there."

"Do they make a lot of money doing this?"

"They can fill a wagon or truck with uranium ore and sell it for about ten thousand dollars in about a week's time. Then they look for another area. In 1948 the Atomic Energy Commission (AEC) started over seeing the purchase of uranium. The AEC announced that it would purchase uranium from private companies. This opened the door for the uranium boom. The race was on to locate uranium and submit it to the government for purchase with no questions asked. The news soon reached those interested in making a quick killing off of uranium. With the ability to make some quick big money it brought out miners, prospectors, rock hounds, and weekend dabblers to our territory. So, now Sheriff Douglas is fighting these small uranium crews everywhere. The problem has grown all over the west. These hot dogs are good!"

With lunch almost done Nellie said, "Are we ready now?"

"Are we ready now? What are you talking about Nellie? I got work to do!"

"But you promised we would ride the horses this afternoon?"

"I'm only kidding. Come on let's all go to the horse stable."

CHAPTER 3

"**B**efore we get started the four of you have to promise to listen and do everything, I tell you. This is very important and will prevent problems down the road. Let me hear it."

"We promise, Pitch!"

"It is very good that the four of you have been getting to know your horses and them you. Horses, even though they weigh about 1000 pounds, all but Princess, are really big sissies. They spook easy, so you want to avoid fast movements around them and don't make loud noises. Always have a calm, "It's okay" attitude around them."

"Now let's pull each horse out of their stable and let them stand in the middle of the barn so I can explain things to you. As you can see Kinno put all the equipment used in horse riding on your horse already. He did it mainly because the saddles are very heavy. All the equipment together is called Tack. What is it called Nellie?"

"Tack, Mr. Pitch."

"Now, the first part of the tack is the saddle. To keep the saddle on tight you have the Girth. This is a strap that goes around the horse's belly to hold the saddle on. Next is the Bridle, which goes over the horse's face. This is called the Bit which goes in the horse's mouth and connects to the Bridle like this."

"Pitch, does that hurt their mouths?"

"No Ann, they get used to it. Next, are the Reins, the leather straps which allow you to guide the horse. Okay, Rory tell me what the Tack consist of?"

"There is the saddle, girth, bridle, bit and reins."

"Very good."

"Now the four of you are going to mount your horse. You always mount your horse from the left side. Place your left foot in the stirrup, pull yourself up by the horn knob on the saddle, then swing your right leg over to the other side. Very good job! Now we will walk the horses slowly out to the corral and Kinno will be there if you need help. Just walk them nice and easy. Now, take the reins in your right hand and pull them to your right hip bone. Good, see how the horse turns that way? Now try it with the other side. When you want the horse to stop you pull straight back on the reins and say Woah. Once the horse stops you release the pressure on the reins. Are you with me Nellie?"

"Yes, Mr. Pitch, I got it."

"Now, I want all of you to slowly walk your horses around the corral, nice and easy. That is really good, go around again. Now, turn your horse to the left. Very good, keep walking them. Now turn to the right. Okay, pull back on both reins and make the horse stop. Everybody is doing great. Now, one at a time and Kinno will be running beside you I want you to get your horse to trot. Now maintaining your balance is important. You go first

Ann. Just give a little easy kick in the sides of Galant and she will start trotting around the corral."

Then the kids did the same thing. "That was really good. Now do the same thing without Kinno running beside you. Okay, keep practicing. Turn them in different directions to get used to turning and stopping."

Pitch just sat on the corral rail and watched us go around and round for about a half an hour. Okay, let's see if you can get off the horse. Great job! Kinno will take the horses back to the stable. That's enough for today. You all did very good and I want you to think about all you learned today when you are laying in your bed tonight. We will practice this for a few days and then I will show you what to do with your horse after you are done riding for the day. Maybe by the weekend we all can go for a ride out on the ranch."

"Okay, kids let's get cleaned up for dinner because Mrs. Louise is coming this evening."

My piano lesson went fine and Mrs. Louise started showing me where the notes are on the piano and the difference between whole notes and half notes. Things like that which was interesting to me. The only problem I had was that I was picking it up faster then she wanted to show me which meant I was getting bored very easy. Our riding lessons were going great and I was anxious to go riding out on the ranch. I was excited when the weekend got here but Mr. Pitch decided we were not ready yet so that was very disappointing for me. Kinno took over showing us, all but Mom, how to take care of our horses after they got all lathered up from exercising in the corral. However, that part of riding I didn't like because it was very hard work. I tried to saddle Dancer by myself but Kinno kept telling me it was no good and the girth was not tight enough and the saddle would fall off once Dancer started running. I guess I needed more muscles like the wranglers have. The only good part about the weekend was in church Reno told me the Shoshone village was having a Labor Day celebration and we all were invited. I had been wanting to go to the village since I got here. Mom said we would go with Mr. Pitch in the Cadillac. Reno said there would be all kinds of different games to play and plenty of food to eat.

After church on Sunday Kinno was waiting for me on the church front steps. When he waved me over to him, I didn't know what to expect. I initially thought I did something wrong with Dancer. "Rory, come over here. You and your family are coming to the village tomorrow for our Labor Day celebration, right?"

"Yes, we all are going in the Cadillac with Mr. Pitch. I can't wait to meet all the kids."

"I want you to do me a favor."

"I had a big question mark on my face. "What can I do for you Kinno?"

"I hear you singing all the time and you are really good. The Shoshone villagers would appreciate it if you would sing God Bless America tomorrow?"

"Are you sure? Most of the people that will be there are Shoshone."

"Rory, we are also Americans. Just like you are Scottish and American."

"Kinno, it would be my honor. Just let me know when you want me to sing."

"There will be no music for you to follow, Rory."

"That's okay I think I can handle it if I practice some tonight."

We shook hands and went our separate ways.

When I got in the car Mom immediately said, "What was that about with Kinno?"

"He asked me to sing God Bless America at the village celebration tomorrow."

"What did you tell him?"

"That I would do it."

"Pitch, isn't that a little strange with all the Shoshone people there?"

"Ann, they do it every year. Last year they had this young woman sing it and she was absolutely terrible. I think they do it because they have adopted the American way of life and appreciate all that America has provided for them. And don't forget they are American Indians."

"Rory, you better really practice today and make us proud of you tomorrow."

After dinner I practiced and practiced. Tommy and Nellie said it sounded really good. After about an hour I stopped completely because I didn't like it. I wanted to run it by Mom and Mr. Pitch but they were nowhere in sight. "Tommy where did Mom and Mr. Pitch go?"

"Mom said they were going for a walk down by the pond and will be right back."

I decided the only choice I had was to call Mrs. Louise and talk to her about it. I told her I was having problems with the way it started off. Her idea was to sing the second verse first and then the first and the second again. When I tried that arrangement, it sounded much better so I decided to do it that way. As I practiced it started sounding good.

Pitch, this country out here is so beautiful. Are you from Wyoming?"

"Yes, I grew up right outside of Cheyenne. We lived on a cattle ranch where my father was the foreman. I was a three-sport athlete in high school and had a college scholarship to play baseball before I went into the army. I spent most of my time in France while I was in the service. When I got discharged, I tried out for a minor league professional baseball team and within a year I was playing for the Brooklyn Dodgers. Two years later I hurt my arm bad and after two surgeries my baseball career was over. I moved back to Wyoming and hooked up with Mr. McClure. That is about all there is."

"Did you have any women in your life?"

"Oh yea, my Mom and my sister. My whole family has passed away. They are buried in Cheyenne."

"That's not what I mean!"

"Oh, you mean romantically?"

"Yes, smart ass!"

"I had a girl friend in New York and when I got hurt bad, she dumped me like a hot potato for another guy with money. However, it didn't matter because it really was not serious anyway."

"Okay, Ann now you know all about me, what about you?"

"Let's see, my grandparents came to New York from Edinburgh, Scotland and they had a small carpenter shop in Brooklyn. I met my husband in high school and we got married when we both were eighteen years old. He was a newspaper reporter and wanted to report on the war over seas. We already had Rory and Tommy and I was pregnant with Nellie when he left. He was only in Germany for about six months before he was killed."

"I'm sorry, Ann."

"It's okay now Pitch. I had three kids to raise so I got a job in the garment district running a sewing machine. I had to work ten-hour days and really had no time for myself. Then God blessed me with this wonderful gift, the McClure Ranch. This is the happiest I have been in seven years. I actually feel like a new woman out here."

"It sounds like you have had a hard life. However, the thing I do know about you is that you are one determined woman. What happened to the rest of your family when you stayed in New York?"

"They all left for the gold rush in Colorado. My Dad and my uncle found gold and were mining it. My uncle sent two workers to town for supplies and equipment. When they returned, they had a gang and wiped my entire family out over the gold. It was hard to believe that happened but men go crazy over gold. At least that was what the sheriff said. I didn't know much about our Uncle McClure. Only that my husband used to visit him when he was a boy. There is a picture of them together in his bedroom or I mean my bedroom now."

"Do you like it here now?"

"Absolutely, sometimes I am afraid I am going to wake up and be back in New York working in the sweat shop again. I really do appreciate all you have done for me and the kids. I think you are part of God's blessing on me. I really need to get back to put the kids to bed for school tomorrow. I'll race you."

When we pulled into Shoshone village I was really impressed. There were about twenty houses that made up three different dirt streets. There were about ten cars and two pick-up trucks parked by the houses. They had a large stable and corral and at the end of one street was the Shoshone Village Community Center. That is where the celebration and the cook out were being held. As we pulled up to the center Chief Warki came over to welcome us with his son Kinno. They had the barbeque pit going and were roasting a pig. They had many picnic tables set up with all kinds of food on them. Then Reno came running over and told Tommy, Nellie and me to come with him. We went over where all the kids were playing games and he introduced them to us. Not that we could remember all of their Indian names. A few of the kids had regular English names with another name added to it. Like Reno's cousin Johnny Hawk and Reno's little sister was Sara Song. Sara was about Nellie's age and she had a bunch of little girl friends so Nellie went off to play with them. Tommy and I went with Reno to check out some of the games they were playing. They had horse shoes, volley ball, shooting arrows at a target and some game with a ball and sticks with a net at the end of the stick. Reno told me the game was called Lacrosse. I always wanted to shoot a bow and arrow so the three of us went over to that area. Reno showed Tommy and me how to hold the bow and pull the sting back to shot the arrow. We were probably about thirty-yards away from the target that had a red circle in the middle. When I shot my first arrow it got about half way there. My next arrow got a little bit further and my third arrow hit the bottom of the target. Reno immediately said, "Not good Rory! This is a short distance target so I would have to say you really stunk." We all started laughing hard. Then it was Tommy's turn. His first arrow hit the bottom on the target with power. His next arrow went right into the red circle of the target. Reno yelled, "Tommy, you must have Indian blood in you. We will now give you an Indian name and call you Warrior Tommy." Tommy really liked his new name and told me to call him Warrior Tommy from now on. Reno, Tommy and the other village kids were having a ball laughing at me shooting arrows. "Hey, Tommy is the athlete in our family he loves any kind of sports. I am the music guy in the family."

But they continued laughing because I was really, really, bad.

The whole family was having a great day and we made so many new friends. Reno told us that most of the kids here go to Saint Joseph's school so we all will get to know each other better. The roast pork was done so everybody settled down at the tables to eat. When Nellie came to the table, she had an indian doll baby in her arms.

"Nellie, where did you get that baby doll," was Mom's question?

"Sara Song gave it to me and said I could keep it."

"Are you sure, Nellie?"

"Yes Mom, here is Sara Song just asked her."

"It's okay Mrs. McClure I have plenty and Nellie needs an indian doll baby to keep her safe. "Then okay, Sara Song, you will have to come to the house and play with Nellie."

Both Nellie and Sara Song started jumping up and down in joy. "All right girls, sit down and eat now."

I could say one thing for the Shoshone, they could really eat and eat some more. When everybody had their bellies filled Kinno walked up to a microphone they had hooked up from the community center. He made a few announcements and thanked us for coming and thanked Mom for providing the pig. Then

Kinno said, "To give thanks to our nation we love, Rory McClure will be singing God Bless America for us. Kinno yelled out, Rory come on up here."

I slowly walked to the microphone on the top step of the community center. Everyone was sitting very quiet and then I started. "God Bless America, land that I love. Stand beside her and guide her. Through the night with a light from above. From the mountains to the parries. To the oceans white with foam. God Bless America, my home sweet home."

Once I finished the three verses, I didn't know what to expect. Then everybody stood up and started applauding really loud. In fact, I started turning red in the face from all the cheering and yelling. Mr. Pitch came up to me with Mom, "Rory that was absolutely breath taking. You can really sing beautiful, son."

All of my new friends came up and patted me on the back. Then Reno said, "You can't shoot arrows very good but you really have a great voice brother. Your new indian name is Rory Voice." We all laughed.

The Labor Day celebration at the Shoshone village is one I will never forget. I knew after singing that song with no music my life would be all about music and singing. It was finally time to go home but I knew I would see all my new friends at school tomorrow. On the ride home I kept wondering if they would call me Rory Voice or just Rory in school. In the back seat I could hear Mr. Pitch talking to Mom about my singing. I couldn't hear all they were saying but I did hear Mom say, "I have to find a way for him to use his God given talent."

If I knew Mr. Pitch he would check around with his friends and try to come up with an answer for Mom. As soon as we got in the house Mom said, "Okay kids, up stairs and a bath for all of you. First day of school tomorrow."

We all thanked Mom and Mr. Pitch for the great day we had at the village.

The next morning, we were all loaded in the woody jeep heading to Saint Joseph's school at eight-fifteen in the morning. When Mom dropped us off, we saw many of the Shoshone kids we had met yesterday and that was a good feeling not to be a stranger. Of course, the three of us went to different class rooms but we would see each other at lunch time. My teacher was Sister Martin and to be honest I thought she was half Indian or Mexican by the color of her skin. Sister Martin was about thirty years old, just a little younger than Mom. We had the usual school subjects, English, Math, and History so I figure it was just like the schools back in New York.

When Mom got the mail that afternoon there was an invitation from Mayor Gallon to a black tie at his home to promote Frank Barrett for governor of Wyoming on next Saturday evening. The invitation was addressed to Mrs. Ann McClure and Mr. Samuel Wesley. Mom took the invitation and quickly went out side to find Pitch. When she saw him over by the corral, she walked over to him. "Pitch take a look at this."

Pitch read the invitation, "I know Frank Barrett from my days back in Cheyenne. He would make a great governor. Do you want to go? It might do you good to have a night out without the kids."

"I don't have anything to wear and you would have to wear a tuxedo."

"Well, let me see, you can drive and you know where the stores are. As for me, I have a tuxedo in my closet. So, what is the verdict, Ann?"

"Let's do it!"

"Okay, call the mayor's office and give them our RSVP. Now, can I go back to work?"

"Yes, please do. Oh, do you know how to dance?"

"Get out of here Boss Lady!"

As Pitch was watching the new cattle being branded in the cattle corral, Ann came out of the house, jumped in the woody jeep and flew down the dusty road.

"Hey, Boss Pitch, Boss Lady in a big hurry?"

"Yea, Kinno, it's shopping time."

Ann spent the entire day in town shopping. She even stopped for a nice relaxing lunch. While she was sitting in the restaurant by the window, she saw the mayor across the street with four tough looking men in dirty torn up clothes. She watched them talking and it looked like they were arguing about something. Finally, the four men got in an old beat up truck and took off out of town. After she ate lunch Ann decided to shop a little more and then she could just pick up the kids from school. While she was looking in a jewelry store, she saw a beautiful gold Rolex watch. As the store owner took it out of the showcase and handed it to her to look over, she really wanted to buy it for Pitch. The store owner told her it cost $15,000. Ann thought about just buying it but she wasn't sure how Pitch would react so she decided not to buy it.

The kids came flying out of the school doors and when they jumped into the jeep there were tons of bags in the back. "Mom, what did you do, buy the stores all out?"

"Oh, be quiet Rory, it's only a few things. The mayor has invited Pitch and me to a black tie at his house so we can meet Frank Barrett who is running for governor."

"You and Mr. Pitch going out on a date?"

"No, we are just going together."

"That sounds like a date to me."

"We were invited separately, not together. How about we get some ice cream, it is only two-thirty?"

"That's its Mom, change the subject but ice cream sounds good."

When we pulled up to the house Mr. Pitch yelled, "Where have you cow hands been the horses all are getting hot waiting for you.?"

The kids started jumping up and down. "Get in the house and change your clothes."

Ann, picked up all her shopping bags out of the jeep. "You need some help there? It looks like you brought the stores out. I'll be right out, it won't take me long to change."

When we all came back out, we were all ready to ride in our jeans and boots.

"All right, let's mount up properly. Kinno, open the corral gate. We will be back in about an hour."

"Mr. Pitch, are we going to ride the range?"

"Yea Rory, we will see what you all remember. Just walk the horses out slowly and do what I tell you."

The five of us headed out the gate and Mr. Pitch said, "Okay, let's trot them a little while."

We rode up the top of a hill and looked down in the valley and there were thousands of cattle. "Oh my God, are all of those our cattle?"

"Yes Ann, that is some of them. We have a lot more over on the south side of the ranch."

"What do we do with all of them?"

"We sell them at round-up for the best market price. Let's ride down the hill slowly. Now, remember the horses spook very easy so ride slowly around the cattle."

Mr. Pitch showed us another beautiful pond and the cattle were there drinking. We went around the herd and back towards the ranch where the ground was pretty flat. "Okay team, here is your challenge for the day. We are going to run the horses back to the ranch. When you see me stopping, you stop! Understand me?"

"Yes sir!"

"All right let's go."

The five horses took off running and I was loving every minute of it. We ran the horses for about ten minutes and then Mr. Pitch pulled up and so did we.

"Now, let's get off our horses and walk them in from here. That way they can cool down some before we get to the corral."

"Mom, how did you like that ride?"

"I loved it Rory. I think we are getting the hang of this cowboy stuff."

"Oh, come on Ann, we all know you always wanted to be a cowgirl."

"Me to Mommy!"

"You really looked good running Princess, Nellie."

"All right, do you all remember what we do when we get to the ranch?"

"Mr. Pitch, I know."

"All right Nellie, tell me."

"We give the horses a good drink, take them to the stable and take off their tack, then brush them down and give them some hay to eat."

"You got it all right, Nellie."

When I had my next piano lesson, Mrs. Louise told me I was the talk of the town. She said everybody had heard about the wonderful voice I had. Mrs. Louise asked me if I would sing the song for her but I politely made up an excuse about my throat. I was getting pretty good at reading sheet music and Mrs. Louise agreed that we should pick up the learning pace. I really liked Mrs. Louise but she was interested in making me a great pianist and I only wanted to learn to play the piano to help with my singing. To me this was a big problem. I tried talking to Mom about the situation but she would always say, "Mrs. Louise knows best for you Rory."

One day when I was helping Reno in the bunk house, I told him what was going on. "Rory, why don't you talk man to man with Boss Pitch about your problem. You know he followed his dream to be a professional baseball pitcher so he will understand about what is in your heart."

"That is good advice Reno. I didn't know you were so smart."

We both laughed when I said that. I laid in bed that night and was really puzzled. I got up out of my bed and went down stairs and knocked on Mr. Pitch's bedroom door. After I knocked the second time he came to the door. "Rory, is something wrong? Is everybody okay?"

"Mr. Pitch can I talk to you a few minutes about something troubling me? I could really use some help."

"Sure, Rory, come on in and we can sit on the bed. What is going on with you?"

"I have a big problem and thought you might be able to help me out."

"Tell me what your problem is."

"You know Mrs. Louise is giving me piano lessons and she is good at it. Only, she wants me to be a great pianist and I only want to learn to play the piano to help my singing. I also want to learn to play the guitar. What I want in my heart is to be a great singer, not a pianist. When I talked to Mom about it, she says Mrs. Louise knows best. But, Mr. Pitch, she doesn't know what's best for me."

"I got the picture Rory. I had a similar situation when I was growing up. I'll tell you what. Let me sleep on it tonight and I will get with you tomorrow and together we will find the right solution. Is that okay?"

"Yes, thank you Mr. Pitch."

Then Mr. Pitch hugged me and said, "It'll be all right."

When I got back in my bed, I felt much better. I thought, "That must be how it feels when you have a Dad to talk to."

When we got home from school I came running in the house as usual and Samoka was waving to me to come over in the kitchen. "What is it Samoka?"

"Boss Pitch says for you to get your jeans and boots on and meet him behind the bunk house. Keep it quiet and let everybody think you are going to help Reno in the bunk house but you go behind the bunk house and Boss Pitch will be waiting for you. Now, you hurry up. Don't keep Boss waiting!"

I quickly changed my clothes and walked slowly towards the bunk house. When I got to the front door I quickly turned and ran around behind the bunk house. Mr. Pitch was standing there holding the reins of Thunder and Dancer. "Come on Rory, we will take a ride out to the Shoshone burial grounds up north. As we trotted along, we talked about my problem. "Well, today while you were at school, I made a few phone calls and came up with a plan. Do you want to hear it?"

"Yes sir, Mr. Pitch!"

"I talked to Bob Steward who owns the Steward Music Shop in Sheridan and to Sister Martin while you were having lunch. Between the three of us we think we can solve your problem."

"Okay, okay, tell me what the plan is?"

"First of all, I will be taking you to Bob's shop so you can pick out some music and get a good guitar. Sister Martin will call Bob and tell him what kind of guitar you will need. Sister Martin is part Arapaho Indian and learned to play the guitar in college before she became a nun. Sister thinks you can learn to play the guitar by yourself with an instruction book we will buy at Bob's shop. Then Sister Martin will be available on Saturdays to help you with problem areas. You will continue to take piano lessons from Mrs. Louise but Sister says focus on reading the music more than playing the piano. Now here is the whole ball game. On Thanksgiving Day, the Sheridan City Council has a talent contest and you are going to win it and get your picture in all the newspapers, right? You have to know two songs really good for the contest. And the thing to remember when you are picking your songs is the judges are all adults so pick songs they can relate to and absolutely no kid songs. You want modern day songs they play on the radio. Are you okay with this plan, Rory?"

"I really like it but what about Mom?"

"I will take care of her but it will take some time. You good?"

"Yes sir! I'm getting excited now."

"We will go to the music shop on Saturday so start thinking about the songs you want to sing. Look at that hill right over there. It is the Shoshone burial grounds for their relatives. It is considered sacred ground by the Shoshone and you cannot even go riding through the area. Your Uncle McClure gave them that piece of land and it is the only land not owned by your Mom. We better get back your Mom will be looking for you."

When we got back to the ranch Mr. Pitch told me to go in the house and he would take care of Dancer for me. When I went in the house, I closed the front door quietly and went straight up stairs to my bedroom. I got a new notebook out of my desk and started writing down all the things that Mr. Pitch said were in our plan. I called the book Rory's Journey and from now on I was going write everything down about my singing in it. Just as I was finishing, I heard, "Rory, where are you? Rory, where are you?"

"I'm up here Mother dearest. I have a lot of homework."

"Okay, I just missed my good-looking son. I'll call you when dinner is ready."

When Saturday rolled around Mr. Pitch and I headed to town in one of the ranch trucks. He had told Mom we were going to get some feed and he wanted to show me where the feed store was and what to buy. Mom, thought that was a great idea and it was actually the truth, at least part of it. We pulled in a parking space right in front of Steward's Music Shop. They had all kinds of guitars and violins hanging in their front window. When we walked in Mr. Steward greeted us. "How have you been Pitch? It is good to see you."

"Bob, this is Ann McClure's oldest son, Rory. He is the music genius I was telling you about."

"Yes, I heard about him and his God Bless America performance at the village. Nice to meet you Rory."

"Nice to meet you Mr. Steward," and we shook hands like real men do.

"All right, let's get started. I talked to Sister Martin, God she is a wonderful person, and she wants you to have this special Gibson guitar. And believe me I would never question what she says about guitars because that nun was the best guitar player in Wyoming before she became a nun."

Mr. Steward handed the guitar to me. "It is really big. I thought it would be smaller."

"Sister Martin wanted you to have a professional guitar. She said absolutely no kid guitar which are smaller."

Mr. Pitch and I just smiled at him. Then Mr. Pitch said, you will learn to handle it and you will be fine, Rory."

"Okay, let's move on. Sister Martin wants you to have this instruction book on how to play a guitar by Hank Williams. Rory, in learning to play the guitar the key part is learning the cords. Once you get that down it is a piece of cake."

I just listened to Mr. Steward and nodded my head yes.

"Okay, now you need to go over to that music rack and pick out the songs you want to learn. Get about two or three now and you can come back later and get more when you are ready."

"Rory, get three sheets of music. Remember, songs adults would like to hear."

"Okay, Mr. Pitch, I have a few in mind."

As I walked over to the music rack, I could hear Mr. Steward's cash register ringing up the items I was getting. It must have been a lot but Mr. Pitch just paid for it. Then I saw Mr. Pitch filling out some form and I had no idea what that was all about. After I went through most of the music sheets, I finally settled on three songs I liked and walked back up to the counter. Here are the songs I picked."

Mr. Steward said, "Let me see what you have, Ramblin Rose, There's No Tomorrow, and Some Enchanted Evening. They are great selections Rory. However, I don't know about Some Enchanted Evening by Ezio Pinza on a guitar."

"Oh, no sir, I picked that one to be played on the piano."

"You play the piano?"

"Yes sir, I play by ear and Mrs. Louise Lambert has been giving me piano lessons."

"That is fabulous, Rory."

"Okay Bob, we got everything and we need to get moving. Good seeing you again."

"You to Pitch. Oh, wait a minute. Rory you have to sign this form."

I looked at the form and it was the entry form for the Thanksgiving Day talent contest. As I was signing it, I looked at the line for parent signature and it said, Ann McClure. Apparently, Mr. Pitch had signed Mom's name for me to participate.

We jumped back in the truck and Mr. Pitch headed down the street. "Where are we going now, Mr. Pitch?"

"To Henry's Feed Store so I can show you where it is and how much feed to buy. To be honest you will never have to do this because Nija takes care of it all the time. We will buy a couple bags because we told your Mom that was what we were going to do."

"What do you mean we?"

"That's its Rory be a little smart ass."

We both started laughing.

It didn't take long in the feed store but at least I could say that I have been there.

"Where are we going now, Boss Pitch?"

"Just hold your pants on cowboy."

As we were riding, I said to Mr. Pitch, "What are we going to tell Mom when she sees the guitar?"

"I told you to hold your pants on! I hope you don't think I'm dumb or crazy. I haven't forgotten about your Mom."

A few minutes later we pulled up in front of Saint Joseph's convent. "What are we doing here?"

"Just grab your music stuff and follow me."

Mr. Pitch rang the convent door bell and Sister Martin opened the door. "Good morning Sister Martin."

"Good morning Pitch and Rory. Let's go into the sitting room so we will not be bothered. I see you got everything I told Mr. Steward. That is a beautiful Gibson guitar. I really think you will like it Rory."

"Sister play us a little tune."

"Okay, Pitch, just so Rory can hear the quality of it. Let me tune it a little. I'll play a song you know, Rory."

Sister Martin started playing God Bless America on the guitar. Both Mr. Pitch and I started smiling and laughing. "I didn't know you could play that song on a guitar."

"Rory, you can play any song on a guitar. But you really have to be the master of the instrument and it takes years of practice. When I played professionally before I became a nun, I used to practice a minimum of eight hours a day when I wasn't performing."

"Okay, Sister here is the game plan. You are going to be Rory's guitar instructor and we will come to see you on Saturday for help and advice."

"Okay, so far Pitch."

"We are going to leave all the music stuff here with you today. You can tune the guitar up and mark up the instruction book for Rory. Then on Monday Rory will bring the music stuff home when his Mom picks him up after school."

"Okay, so far again."

"We will tell Rory's Mom that you offered to give him guitar lessons because of his music abilities."

"What about the guitar showing up?"

Ann will think the school lent it to him and we will just leave her think that."

"It isn't the absolute truth Pitch"

"I know Sister but we are not lying either."

"I guess I can go along with that but if Ann asks me, I will have to tell her it is Rory's guitar."

"That is fine Sister but I guarantee you she will not ask you."

"Okay, so Monday Rory, I will give you a few instructions and mark the instruction book up to denote key things. Now, you two cowboys get out of here so I can play with this wonderful guitar."

"Thank you, Sister Martin."

Mr. Pitch and I were out of the door in record time. "Mr. Pitch that is a great plan and Mom will never know."

"Don't count her short, Rory. She will eventually figure it out. Your Mom is a very smart woman."

Everything went as planned on Monday and I came running out of school with the guitar in one hand. When Mom asked about the guitar, I told her Sister Martin was going to give me lessons and that was the end of it until we got home. When I got out of the jeep Mom took a closer look at the guitar. "Rory, that looks like a brand-new guitar?"

"Sister Martin really takes excellent care of them. I had to promise that I would also."

"Are you still going to take piano lessons?"

"Yes, Mom, it is good to know how to play several instruments."

I couldn't wait to get to my bedroom to start working on what Sister Martin wanted me to do. I told Tommy and Nellie not to touch the guitar because if they broke it Mom would have to pay for it and it was very expensive.

It didn't take me long to learn a bunch of cords. I think it had a lot to do with my ability to play by ear. After dinner I went out on the patio step and was just messing around. Since I knew how Home on the Range went, I decided to give it a try. After a couple times I had it down pretty good. Then Mom yelled out to me, "Rory, that sounds really good. You are picking it up fast on the guitar."

Now all I had to do was learn the new songs and win the talent contest.

CHAPTER 4

The evening of the mayor's black-tie affair was only four hours away and Mom was all excited and running around like a jack rabbit. Although the cocktail hour didn't start until six o'clock an hour before dinner Mom could have been ready at three o'clock. She kept asking me where is Pitch? I told her about a thousand times he was out on the ranch working. "What is he doing out there, Rory?"

"They are moving a herd of cattle to a different grazing location. He will be back in plenty of time Mom."

Finally, about four o'clock I heard a bunch of horses coming in out front. I looked out and it was Mr. Pitch and four wranglers. "Mom, Mr. Pitch is back."

"Go asked him what time we are leaving?"

I walked into the stable where Mr. Pitch was putting Thunder back in his stall. "I know Rory, what time are we leaving, right?"

I started laughing. "You got the big question crazy lady wants to know."

"Tell your Mom about ten minutes to six. We don't want to be the first ones there." "I'll tell her but if you here yelling it is not at me."

"I can handle it. Just tell her."

About twenty minutes to six Mom came walking down the steps. She had on a red backless gown with some shiny gold things in the gown, red high heels, and gold earrings and gold necklace. "Mom, you look so beautiful. I didn't know you were that skinny."

"It's just the gown, Rory."

"I want a dress like that Mommy."

"When you are a little older, Nellie."

Then Mr. Pitch came out of his bedroom in his tuxedo. "Mr. Pitch, you look like one of those models in the magazines."

"Not, what I was hoping for, Rory."

"You really do look handsome Pitch."

"I hope so because I don't want to embarrass this lovely lady I am going with."

Then walking through the front door came Nija in a black suit. "Your chauffer is here. Are you ready to go?"

Then Samoka said, "Let me take some pictures first."

When Mr. Pitch put his arm around Mom her eyes made her look like she was in shock. I guess a man hasn't put an arm around her since my Dad did many years ago. Nija opened the door for them and they got in the back of the Cadillac together.

Mom rolled her window down. "You kids behavior yourselves or you will hear from me tomorrow."

Then I responded, "Okay, Mom, have a nice date."

She looked at me and waved her fist. We all started laughing as Nija pulled away.

About quarter after six Nija pulled up in front of the mayor's house. As Pitch and Ann walked in the cocktail area all the men were eyeing Ann up and down. Pitch looked at her, "Looks like you have a lot of new fans!"

Just then Mayor Todd Gallon came over with his wife Margaret to welcome us. After the usual greetings Mrs. Gallon who was a short, fat, ugly woman started throwing draggers at Ann. "I thought you were a lot older with three children, did you have one before you were married, it must be nice to get out of that dirty city you lived in? I guess you are not very good at ranching?"

Then Pitch came to the rescue, "Come on Ann I want you to meet my old friend from Cheyenne Frank Barrett and his wife." As they walked away, "Thank you Pitch. I just wanted to punch that old bitch's eyes out."

Pitch couldn't help but laugh because Ann was really steaming.

Frank Barrett and Pitch had been friends for many years. Frank knew Pitch when he was still pitching for the Brooklyn Dodgers. When Pitch introduced Ann to him, he said, "I must say Mrs. McClure you look radiant this evening and I think all the other women are envious of you."

"Thank you, but there are many beautiful women all over this place."

Pitch and Frank talked about old times a little and Mrs. Barrett asked Ann all about her children. Then the dinner bell rang for everyone to take their assigned seats with their names on a reserved for signs. After looking around a little their seats were near the front. They started to read the names of who was sitting at their table. The first name was Mr. & Mrs. Robert Steward, next was Sheriff Douglas and his wife, then came Mr. & Mrs. Lambert and the final placement sign said Mr. & Mrs. McClure. Pitch looked at it and just smiled. However, Ann was very upset and kept apologizing to Pitch for the screw up. "Ann, it is okay. You are not the one who messed up. I kind of like the Mr. & Mrs. Part. When he said that Ann didn't open her mouth.

All of the couples at the dinner table were really nice. They all laughed, told jokes and made fun of the way different people were dressed. Ann and Sharon Steward were really getting along and that worried Pitch because he brought Rory's guitar in her husband's store. The dinner was fabulous and the Sheriff made it very clear that the city of Sheridan was paying for all of this and not the mayor. As dinner ended. Mayor Gallon got up and made a little speech and while he was talking Sharon Steward leaned over to Ann and said, "You know his wife?"

"Not, really, I just met her this evening."

"Well, she is a real ass hole!"

Ann almost burst out laughing and had to hold her hand over her mouth to prevent it. "That is funny Sharon. I called her an old bitch after I met her."

They both had to hold their laughter back. Then Pitch said, "What in the world is going on with you two?"

They just smiled at him. When the mayor was finished, Frank Barrett got up and asked everyone for their support and vote for him to be the next governor. When he finished everybody stood up and applauded.

It was almost nine o'clock when the band started playing. They were pretty good but as usual most people sat and listened to a couple songs before they got out on the dance floor. Pitch could see Ann singing along with the music and she was tapping her feet and hands. Then the band played a slow song, Forever and Ever by Perry Como and Pitch said, "Come on Ann let's dance."

It immediately hit Ann this was waltz type music to dance. She just looked at him and he just took her hand and walked her out to the middle of the dance floor. When they took their posture for the slow dance Pitch's hand was placed right in the middle of Ann's bare back. She looked petrified and cold chills went down her spine. "Are you okay?"

"Yes, just dance!"

Throughout the evening they danced about six times and Ann complimented Pitch on how well he could dance. "Thank you, don't forget young lady I lived in New York for several years and to have fun you had to know how to dance."

About quarter after ten Pitch said, "It is time for us to be leaving Mrs. McClure. I told Nija to pick us up between ten and ten-thirty so he will be waiting outside. Are you ready to leave?"

"Oh, yes, this has been a delightful night and one that I needed."

After everyone said good-bye to each other Sharon Steward said, "Ann, let's have lunch one day next week? I'll call you."

"Sounds great Sharon, any day is fine with me."

When they, walked out the front door the Cadillac was sitting there waiting. As Nija pulled away Ann said, "Nija take the long way home Boss Pitch and I need to talk a little."

The alarm went off in Pitch's head and knew this could mean nothing but trouble. Nija rode around the town at a slow speed. "So, Pitch, how much did Rory's guitar cost you?"

Pitch knew he was trapped and the truth was the only way out. "Listen to me carefully Ann, Rory wants to be a singer, not a pianist. He came to my bedroom in the middle of the night to talk about it. He said he tried to talk to you about it but you kept telling him Mrs. Louise knows best. Of course, that is correct if you want to be a pianist. I can't help it but I really love your kids and I would do anything for them. Sometimes boys need a man to talk to for advice. Nellie has you and I see you and her talking all the time about women things. You heard Rory sing at the village and you said he sung in the fish market back in New York. The kid has a great talent and all he wants is to follow his dream. I did what I had to do to make him smile again. I'm sorry if I offended you."

"You didn't offend me. I want to thank you because sometimes I don't pay enough attention to the boys and I know they need a man every now and then to talk to and get advice from. Everything you did for Rory is wonderful and I know the two of you did not lie to me. I want to support his dream and not get in his way."

"Well, when he sings in the talent contest on Thanksgiving Day you better be there to cheer him on. By the way, I signed your name on the entrance form because it needed parental permission."

"All of us will be there to cheer him on. Pitch, please promise me when my boys come to you with something, tell me about it so I can help you."

"I promise Ann, no more secrets."

As Nija finally headed to the ranch Ann talked about the great time she had and thought that Sharon and her could become close friends. Then she said, Pitch, I want to pay you for the guitar. Sharon said it cost $700 because it was a special Gibson. I don't feel right with you spending your hard-earned money."

"We need to get something straight between us. You know I had a five year contract with the Brooklyn Dodgers."

"Yes, I know that. Tommy keeps reminding me."

"You do know that professional baseball players make a lot of money?"

"I guess so."

"Well it is true, and the money I got for playing baseball I invested very wisely. So, to be honest with you, the truth is, I am a millionaire."

"What, you are a millionaire? Then why do you work on the ranch?"

"Because it is what I love. It is that simple."

"Oh, my God, I was out dancing with a millionaire tonight. Who knows this?"

"Just my investment firm and you."

"I still don't feel right about you paying for the guitar."

"Here is what you can do, Sister Martin is working with Rory on his songs for the contest. If Rory wins the contest you give

Sister Martin the $700 for her music program at Saint Joseph's. Deal"

"You have a deal!"

Nija finally arrived at the house and we thanked him for being our chauffer. "Oh, no, I thank you for the overtime pay and for my delicious dinner."

Both of us laughed out loud. We walked in the house around eleven-thirty and it was pure silence. Standing on the bottom step of the stairs to her bedroom, "Pitch, thank you for a great evening and for just being you."

She bent down to kiss him on his cheek and instead he quickly turned and their lips met for the first time. He kissed her softly and then softly again and then passionate and much longer as she responded. Then she took a step back while breathing heavy and looked Pitch in his eyes. Good night Pitch and she ran up the steps.

The next morning the kids wanted to know all about the black-tie affair. "Come

on Mommy, tell us all about it before we go to church."

"Okay, Nellie, Mr. Pitch and I had a great time and we danced a lot. I made a lot of new friends and I think Sharon Steward and I will be good buddies."

"Who was that Mom?"

"You know Rory, Bob Stewards wife Sharon. They own Stewards Music Shop in Sheridan. I'm sure you been there! The dinner was really good and Mr. Pitch met up with one of his old friends Frank Barrett who is running for governor."

"Mommy, I bet you were the most beautiful lady there?"

"Come to think of it Nellie you are absolutely right. I was a knock-out and all the men couldn't stop looking at me in my red gown."

"How about Mr. Pitch?"

"Oh, he was the most handsome man there."

"So, it was a great date Mom?"

"Yes Rory, it was a great date!"

"Mommy, did Mr. Pitch kiss you?"

"Now, Nellie, you know girls never kiss and tell."

All of us started laughing out loud. "All right let's get dressed for church."

"Is Mr. Pitch going, Mom?"

"I think so Rory. Why do you need to talk to him?"

Before we knew it Mr. Pitch pulled up out front in the Cadillac and blew the horn. We all ran out and jumped in the car and he took off down the dusty road. Nellie had no patience, "Mr. Pitch, how was the thing last night? You know where you and Mom went."

You could tell Mr. Pitch was thinking. Nellie, it was absolutely wonderful and we had fun and met many nice people."

"What was the best part, the food?"

"No, the most fantastic part was the end of the night and I couldn't get it out of my head all night long. That is it no more questions unless your Mom wants to answer them. Understood!"

"Yes sir. Mom already told us all about it."

When we got in church Nellie wanted to go sit with Sara Song. Mom finally told her it was okay but to come back over here after church. Seeing this little white girl sitting between all the dark skin Shoshones really looked funny. However, I guess God made all of us so what difference did it make. When church was over Mom stayed behind a little and I could not understand what was going on. Then I saw Sister Martin coming out and Mom went over to her. "Sister Martin, I want to thank you for all you are doing for Rory. Sister, I know Mr. Pitch bought the guitar for Rory so you don't have to worry about keeping their secret anymore."

"Thank God, I have been praying about that situation."

"However, Rory does not know yet that I know. I am stringing him along for a while to see what he will do."

It was killing me because Mom had her back towards me and I couldn't see what she was saying and Sister Martin was just shaking her head. I really needed to talk to Mr. Pitch but I couldn't catch him alone. When we all got in the car Mom started talking about Sister Martin. "Pitch, did you know Sister Martin was a professional guitar player before she became a nun. Supposedly, she was the best in the whole state of Wyoming."

"Okay, okay Mom, Mr. Pitch bought the guitar for me. It is my guitar and not one I got from Sister Martin"

"I know Rory and we will be cheering you on to win the contest."

Tommy looked at Mom. "What contest? A rodeo?"

"No Tommy a talent contest on Thanksgiving Day where Rory will be singing."

"Oh, I thought it was something exciting. Singing not for me!"

As time rolled by, I was really practicing hard and many hours for the contest. Mr. Pitch found out there were twenty contestants and only four were kids and I was the youngest one. That meant I was going up against sixteen adults. This made me very nervous. To top things off Reno told me one of the contestants was a beautiful twenty-two-year-old lady who sang in the Country Western Night Club in Sheridan and all the men loved her. When I put all of this together the chances of a twelve-year-old boy from New York winning this contest were about zero to me. My confidence was going down the toilet and fast. My best friend Reno knew what was going on in my head and did everything to help me turn it around. "Look Rory, there are twenty contestants and then they will break it down to three finalists. If you make it to the finals that is great for a twelve-year-old kid. You will definitely make it to the newspaper which will give you exposure that's what you want."

Everything he said made good sense but everyone was counting on me winning, not just making the final three. I was really worried. I kept wondering if Mr. Pitch and Mom knew the deck was stacked against me. One night after dinner when they both were sitting out on the patio, I decide to go talk to them. "Can I talk to the both of you for several minutes?"

"Sure Rory, what's on your mind?"

I explained to them all the circumstances of the contest and the odds of a twelve-year-old boy winning it"

I think Mr. Pitch already knew all of this but it was obvious that Mom didn't because she looked very surprised. "Rory. Is your dream to become a great singer and have a professional career?"

"Yes Mr. Pitch. But to be honest I am not very mature and I'm so scared I could piss in my pants right here!"

"Okay, that is fair but please hold it in for now. I want you to think about one thing with all of these facts going on in your head. If all these people in the contest were really that good then why are they still in little old Sheridan? Perhaps they only think they are good. When you are twenty-years old where do you think you will be?"

"I would think Nashville or California."

"Rory, trust in yourself and the talent God has given to you. Do you honestly think he is going to let you waste it.?"

"No, I don't think so."

"Why do you think he put you here with a grand piano in your living room and a world-famous guitarist player at your school and a Mother who would give her right arm for you. God does things for a purpose and that is why he put you out here in Wyoming. Now, he wants you to give back to him by doing the best you can and practice hard so there is no doubt that you will be giving the very best performance you have in you. Excuse my language but to hell with the competition. You are the one they have to beat."

"You are absolutely right Mr. Pitch. It is up to me, not up to them. I will show this entire town who is the best singer."

I walked over and hugged Mr. Pitch and then Mom. "Thank you both for your support and for believing in me. I have to go practice now."

When I walked away Mom almost had tears in her eyes. "You okay, Ann?"

Yes, I am fine but I have to go in the house right now."

She got up and bent down and kissed Mr. Pitch passionately, firm and long on his lips. "Thank you so much for being Rory's Dad tonight." Then she walked up the patio steps back into the house leaving Pitch sitting by himself. He looked up in the beautiful sky with stars shinning bright and said. "Dear Lord I love that woman so much it hurts but I don't know whether to tell her or not. I really need your help, Big Boss."

I was really practicing hard with Sister Martin and she even came out to the house a couple times. Then a couple of lucky things happened that I could not believe. The young woman night club singer took off for Nashville. Next, the Sheridan Prairie Newspaper had an article in it about this brilliant young, up and coming music genius Rory McClure. The article was written by Louise Lambert a graduate of Peabody Conservatory. She made me sound like the greatest thing since sliced bread and that Sheridan should be proud of me. I really started getting my confidences back and I was determined to win.

Late Saturday afternoon Mr. Pitch got a phone call from Sheriff Douglas. "What is on your mind, Dan? It is almost beer time."

"I can taste them now but I felt I needed to talk to you about what happened today. This morning I had the auction for all the equipment and horses you took from the free-loaders on the McClure property. Guess who bought them at the auction?"

"I have no idea, Dan."

"Our wonderful Mayor Gallon and he paid $2,000 for everything."

"What in the world does he want with all that equipment, he is not a miner.?"

"That was my thought and where did he get the $2,000? He doesn't have any money that is why he wanted to be mayor. Shit, I don't think their little dress shop makes enough for the two of them to live off of these days. Most of the women go to Sears for their clothes. I would bet you one thing, if the city did a professional audit he would be in big trouble."

"How in the hell did he get elected mayor in the first place?"

"I think you were just arriving at the McClure ranch when all of this happened. We had an election for mayor and nobody but Gallon wanted the position so he automatically got the job for eight years. His term is up this year."

"Okay, Dan I will keep an eye on the property and let you know if anything comes up. Talk to you later. Go have your beer."

That night at dinner Pitch told Mom all about his conversation with the Sheriff. When he told her, who bought the stuff at the auction Mom hesitated for several minutes. "I remember now! I forgot to tell you about the mayor and these men because I was so excited about my new gown. When I was shopping, I stopped for a late lunch and was sitting at the restaurant's front window when across the street I saw Mayor Gallon talking with four tough looking men. They seem to be arguing back and forth about something. The one guy must have been their leader because he did most of the talking. After about fifteen minutes they got in an old truck and took off. I meant to tell you when I got home but forgot with all the excitement."

"Ann, do you remember what they looked like?"

"Of course, their clothes were all dirty and had holes all in them. The one doing all the talking was about six feet tall, looked to be about 25 or 26 years old, kind a on the skinny side and his hair hanging out the back of his hat was dirty blonde or like brown and blonde mixed. Let me see, he had on brown pants, a dark green shirt and a black hat. That is all I can remember."

"You are doing great. What about the other men?"

"I couldn't see much of them because the mayor was blocking my view. Wait a minute, one of the guys was really young. I couldn't see his face good because he didn't have a hat on. I think he must have been about seventeen or eighteen years old. Oh yea, one of the other two men was really short. About as tall as Rory. Sorry, that is about it Pitch. Does that help?"

"That was great Ann. I am pretty sure they are the same men who were on your property."

"What in the world is the mayor doing with them?"

"Sheriff Douglas believes the mayor used the town's money to buy back their equipment and horses at the auction this morning. I'll be giving him a phone call or we will go see him in the morning because he is downing beers right now."

After dinner was over, Mom kept looking at Mr. Pitch and I could not figure out what was going on. Then Mr. Pitch said, "All right Tommy you are coming with me."

"Where are we going?"

"Just follow me no questions or I'll have to shoot you."

We all laughed as Tommy followed Mr. Pitch back to his bedroom. Mr. Pitch pulled a big box from under his bed and opened it up on the bed. It was everything from his baseball days. Tommy really got excited and asked Mr. Pitch tons of questions. Then Mr. Pitch went to his closet, "Tommy, I have something for you. It is a little big but you can probably use it to sleep in at night. Mr. Pitch pulled out his jersey from the Brooklyn Dodgers.

Tommy started jumping up and down all over the bedroom like a crazy kid. "Settle down cowboy."

The jersey was white with Dodgers written across the front in blue letters. The back had the number 33 in the middle and Wesley written across the top of the back. "Come on partner, let's try it on you."

It swallowed Tommy whole but he was really happy. Then they started talking about baseball and Tommy told Mr. Pitch his favorite position was shortstop. Tommy asked him why more kids around here don't play baseball? Mr. Pitch told him several years ago he tried to organize some little league teams but he couldn't get enough players for two teams so he gave up the idea. "Tommy, I just guess baseball isn't very big in Sheridan County like it is on the east coast with the Yankees, Orioles, Senators and all the other teams."

They had been in Pitch's room for about an hour and Tommy wanted to go show off his jersey to the others. When he walked in the living room, we jumped all over him and kept feeling the jersey. You could see how proud Tommy was. Finally, Mom told us it was time to get to bed. Tommy, immediately said, "I'm sleeping in my jersey."

"Okay, now get upstairs all of you."

After the kids went upstairs Ann went and got a glass of whiskey and a cigar, "Come on Pitch, let's go sit on the patio because you deserve a relaxing break."

"Well, that is mighty nice of you cowgirl."

They sat on the patio while Pitch smoked his cigar. "That was really nice what you did for Tommy."

"Well, he has been so good about all the attention Rory has been getting, I just wanted to pick up his spirit a little."

"I think you did more then that. I just think he really misses sports. That was all he did back in New York. He was always playing something and just as happy as he could be."

"I got an idea how we may be able to help him out."

"Let me know if you need my help."

"I surely will this time. I promise!"

They talked about everything but what was really on their minds.

Ann stood up, "I guess it is time to go in it is getting a little chilly."

Pitch then stood up and looked her in her eyes and kissed her tenderly. Ann responded and put her arms around him with another soft kiss. Then Pitch put his hands on her butt cheeks and pulled her tightly to him while kissing her very, very, passionately. Ann finally broke the kiss off and just looked into his eyes and said, "Thank you for everything, Pitch. You are a wonderful person."

Then she heard Nellie crying, I have to go. "You need my help?"

"No, she has bad dreams every now and then. Good night, Pitch."

As she walked away Pitch couldn't take his eyes off Ann's butt. He really wanted to make love to her bad but he was afraid of being too aggressive with her. He thought about telling Ann he was in love with her but then he thought maybe she was just happy the way her life was. He knew her entire focus was on her children and apparently, she didn't date anyone back in New York. Pitch decided that if anyone was going to say they were in love it would have to be her first. However, it will be very difficult trying to keep his hands off her. She is a very special woman.

Everybody was happy to see Saturday roll around and Pitch told the kids they would go for a horse ride in the early evening. A little after ten o'clock Pitch came in the house calling Ann. "Yes, Pitch, what do you want?"

His brain immediately felt like saying, you. "I need you to go to town with me to talk to Sheriff Douglas about the men you saw with the mayor."

"Okay, let me go change my shirt and we can go."

When they got to the Sheriff's office, Ann told him what she had told Pitch. "Pitch, what is your take on all of this?"

"I have an opinion but I'm not sure it is the correct answer. I think Mayor Gallon know he is not going to be re-elected and is trying to build a little nest egg for him and his wife when he is out of office. By quick drilling uranium and selling it he can make some big bucks before he is out of office. I think part of the mayor's responsibility with the crew was to keep the authority off their back. However, my visit to their camp site was a surprise and the mayor didn't hold his end of the deal up. I believe that is what Ann saw them arguing about."

"I think you hit the nail on the head Pitch."

"Dan, put some feelers out to see if you can find out where these boys are staying. If we know that you, me, and a few of my wranglers can pay them a visit."

"Okay, Pitch, I'll let you know how I make out."

Ann and Pitch drove down Main Street a little way and he parked the truck. "Now where are we going?"

"Do you have your money with you, rich lady?"

"I have some but I have my check book if I need more, why?"

"We are going in Fred's Sporting Goods to buy you a gun so you can shoot me because I am in so much pain,"

"What? What in the world are you talking about?"

"I am only kidding you. Come on and bring that fat check book."

They walked in Fred's and of course Pitch was good friends with him. "Good to see you Pitch."

"Fred, this is my boss Mrs. McClure, she needs a pistol."

"What are you talking about Pitch? Nice to meet you Fred."

"Do you have all the things I told you to order?"

"Yes, right here in the back."

They all walked to the back of the store. "Here is what you ordered Pitch; two lacrosse stick, a midfielder and attackman stick, a dozen lacrosse balls, a lacrosse goal, a ball feeder, and a instruction and rules book. Did I get everything?"

"What about the lacrosse helmet and shoulder and arm pads?"

"They are on back order and will be here next week."

"Okay, we will take all of this and add the bill up for Mommy big bucks here. Don't forget to add the cost of the helmet and pads."

"Okay, let's go up to the counter."

When they all got to the counter, Pitch began seriously thinking about a pistol for Ann. "Fred, let me see that thirty caliber Colt pistol over there."

Fred handed the pistol to Pitch. It's not to heavy. Ann, take this in your hand. Is it too heavy for you to hold?"

"No, not really. Is this supposed to be for me?"

"Yes, I think you need to have a gun in your bedroom for emergencies."

"I don't know with the kids around all the time."

"You don't put the bullets in the gun unless you need to use it. Ann, you live on a ranch out by itself. Everybody on the ranch has a gun even Dinja."

"Our cook and house keeper have a gun?"

"Yes! We will take it Fred and three boxes of bullets."

"Well that be it?"

"Yes Fred, what is the total?"

"That comes to $842 with sales tax and Pitch's discount."

"All right lady big bucks pay the man."

"Can I write you a check?"

"Absolutely, Mrs. McClure and thank you for your business."

When they got back in the truck Ann had this mean look on her face. "Pitch, I am not crazy about having this gun around the house with the kids coming and going."

"Ann, listen to me, this is only for you and the kid's protection. Please, I know what I am talking about. Here is what you do. You put the Colt in safe place where the kids are not allowed. You know like your pantie's drawer. The bullets you hide on the top shelve of your clothes closet so you are the only one who knows where the bullets are. That is a safe arrangement with kids in the house. While the kids are at school, I will show you how to load and fire the gun. We will practice way in the back until you get good with the pistol. You know the old saying, Better Safe than Sorry."

"Okay Pitch you have convinced me this is not a bad idea. Please don't tell the kids about me having a pistol."

"I promise, this just between the two of us. Are we okay?"

"We are good to go."

"Do you still love me?"

Ann just looked at him and didn't say a word. "I'm just kidding, lighten up."

However, Pitch was testing the water to see what would be her response and he was not pleased with the result. In fact, it made him very depressed so he decided to go in town to one of the wrangler's birthday party and have a few beers to cool off.

This was the first time Pitch had disappointed the family because he was gone and there was no evening horse ride. The kids were really upset and Nellie said, "Mommy, what did you do to Mr. Pitch?"

Then the boys jumped in to help Nellie, "Yea, Mom, this is not like Mr. Pitch to not keep his promise to us. Why did you make him mad at all of us?"

Ann was really puzzled and also had left Tommy's lacrosse stuff in Pitch's truck so she couldn't cheer him up as planned. Of course, she knew nothing about lacrosse and Pitch needed to be there to explain the game. "Samoka, do you know where Boss Pitch went?"

"Kinno said something about a birthday and they were going to town to have some beers."

"One more question Samoka, does Dinja have a pistol?"

"To be honest Boss Lady yes she does."

After dinner Ann went out and sat on the patio by herself. It was really different without Pitch there to talk with and smell his cigar. She wondered what he was doing at this time and thought about things that would make him just run off for some beers with his men. It wasn't the lacrosse equipment because she paid for it and listened to him about buying the pistol. Then it hit her, he asked me if I still loved him and I didn't say a word. That can't be it, I let him kiss me all the time and he grabbed my ass and I just let him. He must know how I feel. Although, he did get very quiet after he said he was just kidding. Perhaps, I should have told him that I loved him. I really want to tell him but I am afraid to love. I have my children to look out for. He must understand that? Oh, he probably just forgot about the evening ride and just needed to go out with the boys. That's it!

Ann put the kids to bed and went in her bedroom and just laid across her bed with her eyes open. Then she started thinking about Pitch's kisses and how his hands felt on her back and butt. She was wishing that he was laying right next to her and she could fall to sleep in his arms. She began thinking she really messed up and what if he is in some other woman's arms right now. Ann would doze off for a little while and wake up picturing Pitch. About eleven o'clock she heard him come in the house. He was very quiet but at least she knew he was home. Ann finally fall to sleep and woke up at about two o'clock calling Pitch's name.

She looked around her room and said, "Dear Lord, please help me. I am so troubled." About an hour later she woke up again and for some reason got out of bed put her robe on and slippers on and went down stairs. Oh God what am I doing? The next thing she knew she was walking down the hallway to where Pitch's bedroom was. She stopped at his door and thought for several minutes. Then she knocked on his bedroom door. Then she knocked again and started to walk away when Pitch opened the door. "Ann, are you all right?"

He was standing there only in his boxer shorts and she could she all his muscles. "Ann, what is going on?"

She hesitated for a few seconds, "Pitch, I just wanted to tell you that I love you very much and I am scared to death and I need time. That is it!"

She started to walk away and Pitch took her hand and pulled her to him and kissed her over and over again. "I love you very much Ann and you can have all the time you need."

He kissed her again very, very passionately. "You don't taste like beer?"

"I drank Coke and thought of you the entire night."

They kissed four or five times more. Then Pitch said, "Go back to bed Ann, church is very early tomorrow morning."

"I do love you, Pitch."

Sunday morning Nellie did not let Mr. Pitch off the hook for braking his promise. He told her he was sorry but he had forgot it was one of the wrangler's birthday and he had to go to his party. "That's okay then, I love birthdays myself."We will all go for a family ride this afternoon and Rory can show us where the Shoshone burial grounds are."

"How does he know?"

"One of the Indian spirits called Rory Voice in the night and showed him."

Tommy looked at him, "That's bull Mr. Pitch."

"Oh yea, the spirits told me they left something in my truck for Warrior Tommy."

"What is it? Let's go look now."

"The spirit said we will have to wait until after church."

On the way to church we kept making fun of Mr. Pitch and his Indian spirits "Oh, Tommy the great spirit wants to wear your Dodger jersey." Even Nellie joined in, "Mommy, the great Indian spirit wants you to cut all your hair off." We all were laughing at that one and even Mom had to laugh with us. Church was as usual only this Sunday Sara Song came over and sat with us. Nellie and her had become best friends like Reno and me. As we were leaving church Mom was talking to Sister Martin and I thought she was checking up on how I was doing. When we all got back in the car Mom said, "Guess what I found out?"

Immediately I said, That I am doing great."

"No, you are wrong."

"Everybody give up?"

Then Mr. Pitch asked, "Do I get a guess?"

"Sure, big boy! Let's see how smart you are."

"You found out who the judges are for the talent contest."

"Yes, how did you know that?"

"The great Indian spirit told me."

We were laughing so hard at Mr. Pitch I thought I was going to pee myself. When we all settled, "Well, tell us Mom."

"Okay, there are six judges and the good news is three of them know and like Rory. The judges are; Sister Martin, Mrs. Louise Lambert, Mr. Bob Steward, Mayor Gallon, Dick Boone and Fred Jackson. "Who in the world are Dick Boone and Fred Jackson, Mom?"

"I have no idea Rory. Maybe Pitch knows who they are?"

"I do! The great spirit just told me."

"Come on Mr. Pitch be serious."

"Dick Boone owns the largest ranch in Sheridan county and he is part owner on the Sheridan Trust Bank where your Mom has all her money. Fred Jackson is the Sheridan City Controller and everybody knows he does whatever the mayor says. That means Rory has at least three votes probably for him, two votes against him, and Dick Boone is probably on the fence. All this means is Rory has to win the audience with his performance and he will win,"

Nellie and Tommy started cheering, "Rory, Rory, Rory!"

When we got home, we all immediately wanted to look in Mr. Pitch's truck right then and there. Mom quickly put a stop to that, "All of you go right upstairs and change out of your Sunday clothes. Right now!"

We all went running in the house as Mr. Pitch quickly went to his truck. He got the Colt pistol and the bullets out of the truck and wrapped them in his coat and handed it to Ann and told her to take them up to her bedroom. Mom quickly ran up the steps to her bedroom and came back out and threw Pitch's coat down to him. Ann yelled at the kids from her room, "All of you wait for Mr. Pitch in the living room. Do not go out to his truck. I will be right down."

With everyone assembled in the living room. "Here is what we are doing. I am staying in here to help Nija and Samoka make lunch for us the rest of you go with Mr. Pitch to his truck and bring in the stuff the spirits left."

"Oh Mom!"

"Go, go, get out of here."

We all ran to the truck even Mr. Pitch. He opened the back up and sure there was a bunch of stuff. Nellie looked at it, "What is it?"

Immediately Tommy shouted, "It is lacrosse equipment. You know Rory the game the Shoshones play up in the village."

"You are right Tommy. Only their sticks are handmade and not manufactured."

We all picked up some of the equipment and Nellie lead us into the house carrying the two lacrosse sticks. We laid everything on the living room floor and Mr. Pitch started to explain what everything was. "Mr. Pitch, how is the game played?"

"I'm really not sure Rory but we have a book of instructions and rules. Maybe if Tommy, you and me read it we can figure it out."

"I'll try to help but I have a lot of practicing to do for the contest."

"Just do what you can."

Then Mom told us to come and eat lunch and we can figure it out later. As we were going to sit down for lunch, I saw Mr.

Pitch lightly put his arm around Mom's wrist and she just smiled. I really didn't know the meaning of this but it made me smile.

Lunch was really good especially the apple pie. Tommy and Mr. Pitch were looking at the lacrosse instructions and trying to figure the game out. "There are ten men ot the team it says here, Tommy. I felt so sorry for Mr. Pitch because he was not much help to Tommy. This was out of his league, he was a baseball player. While Nija and Samoka were cleaning up after lunch they were watching and listening to what was going on in the living room. Out of nowhere Samoka said, Boss can I talk to you and Boss Lady out on the patio?"

They looked at each other and said, "Sure Samoka."

Both Mom and Mr. Pitch knew it was rare for Samoka to interrupt family things so they knew it must be important. Once they got out on the patio Samoka said, "I have something to say that I hope may help you with Tommy if you have time to listen to me, Bosses."

"Sure Samoka, tell us what is on your mind?"

"Here is the whole story I need to tell you first. The Shoshones have played lacrosse for many years and start playing at the age of 5 or 6 years old. Dinja played at the village and then he played at Sheridan High School where he was an all-star. The University of North Carolina gave him a college scholarship to play lacrosse for them because he was so good."

"What happened Samoka?"

"Boss Pitch, Dinja worked during the summer on the ranch as a wrangler. One day a wild steer put its horn in Dinja's thigh. They almost had to cut off his leg. You see him walk with a limp now that is from the steer. He never got to go play college lacrosse. I am telling you this because Dinja is the person to teach Tommy how to play lacrosse. He still loves the game and helps all the village kids. If you give him a chance, I promise you Tommy will be a great player one day. That is all I have to say."

Ann walked over to Samoka and kissed him on the cheek, "Thank you for sharing that with us."

"Samoka, take the truck and go to the village and bring back Dinja with you."

"Yes sir, Boss Pitch. I will be back in about twenty-minutes."

After Samoka departure Pitch looked at Ann, "Praise the Lord Ann, he has answered my prayers because I don't know shit about lacrosse, baseball is my game."

They hugged each other. "Pitch, should we pay him?"

"If we offer to pay him, he would not like it and probably wouldn't take the money. What we can do is put an extra twenty-dollars in his pay check each week. If he ask me, I'll tell him I don't handle the money that he needs to go talk to Boss Lady. When he comes to you, just tell him that he got a pay praise."

"You think that would work?"

"He won't argue with you but he will eventually figure it out for himself."

Pray that this works, Pitch."

When Samoka returned with Dinja Pitch said, "Dinja, Boss Lady and I want you to do us a favor. Her son Tommy wants to learn to play lacrosse. She bought him all the equipment but he needs a good teacher so we are asking you to be his teacher and coach."

Dinja looked at them, "You know Bosses I have a bad leg and cannot run?"

"We are asking you to coach, not run! Let Tommy do the running. He is a good athlete and with your help he can be a great player as you once were."

"What will Tommy think of this Boss?"

"He wants to learn so bad and he knows I don't know shit about lacrosse. You are the only hope he has. You will have all the freedom you need to do what you need to do. And Tommy will listen to you."

"Are you sure Boss and Boss McClure?"

"Please Dinja do this for us and for Tommy."

"Okay, I will be Tommy's lacrosse coach."

All four of us walked in the living room from the patio then Ann said, "Tommy come here."

"Yes Mom, what do you want?"

"I want you to meet your new lacrosse coach, Dinja."

"Really, he coaches the village team."

"He can help you become a great lacrosse player and you can go to Sheridan High School and break all of his scoring records."

Tommy went right over to Dinja and hugged him. "When do we start coach?"

"Tomorrow right after you get home from school."

After Dinja showed Tommy a few things like how to keep the ball in the net by cradling the stick, Mr. Pitch looked at his watch and it was almost three o'clock. "Dinja that is enough for today. You take the truck back to the village and bring it back in the morning,"

Dinja thanked his bosses and went out the door.

"Okay, McClure it is time to saddle up our horses so we are back in time for dinner. Out to the stable they all went and they all walked the horses out of the barn and they all climbed in their saddles. "All right Rory lead us the great spirit burial grounds of the Shoshone. The five of them, as they rode out on the range looked like a family going for a Sunday afternoon ride. Tommy and Nellie kept asking me if I really knew where the big spirit ground was or were, we just riding around like a bunch of dummies. I told them the great spirit only talks to Rory Voice. We were having some much funny kidding around that we rode ahead of Mom and Mr. Pitch. I kept looking back at them to make sure we didn't get to far ahead and I saw Mr. Pitch reach over and kiss Mom. Something was cooking between those two and they were not talking.

CHAPTER 5

Dinja coaching Tommy was working out great and he could cradle a lacrosse ball in his stick about a week later. Dinja would take Tommy to the village games and explain what was happening and why players did certain things. Tommy loved hanging with him and paid attention to every word Dinja said. When Dinja would get his pay check with the extra twenty-dollars in it all he said to Ann was, "Thank you Boss Lady." Ann just smiled back at him.

Thanksgiving Day was just a week away and Rory was practicing every chance he got. The funny thing was he also practiced on the piano not just the guitar. Ann got a letter in the mail telling her all about the contest and rules. There were now only fourteen contestants, there are six judges and it said who they were, the initial elimination round would start at nine o'clock. The three finalists would come back at seven o'clock in the evening to compete, and it would take a majority vote to win. If there is somehow a tie, the performances will continue until there is a winner. The winner will receive a $1,000 in cash, a trophy, and interviews with several newspapers. The city auditorium will be open to the public free of charge. After the winner is announced the city will have a small fireworks display. Ann showed the letter to Rory and Pitch. Then the three of them argued about what Rory should wear for the competition. Ann decided that the solution was for her to take Rory shopping.

Sharon Steward called Ann about having lunch together. During lunch Sharon told her about the Sheridan Women's Association and she begged Ann to join. There are thirty-two women in the association and Sharon told her all of them are very nice except for a few like the mayor's wife. Sharon told her that being from New York she would be really shocked at the women. Most of them are good ole girls which to her meant they just do what their husbands tell them and don't think for themselves. Sharon was the president of the association and she let it be known that she was not a good ole girl. From what Ann could tell the women did a lot of wonderful things for the children of Sheridan and for the Shoshone and Arapahoe Indian families. Before their lunch was over Ann joined the association and Sharon was really excited but Ann couldn't figure out what the big deal was.

When Mom got back from lunch in the jeep, she saw Pitch down by the coral with about four of his men. It looked like they were breaking in horses. She looked down to where Pitch was several times and when he saw her, he waved. All of a sudden, her feet started walking down to the coral and when she got to where Pitch was, he said, "Yes, Ann, do you need something?"

"As a matter of fact, I do. A kiss!"

Pitch was totally shocked and wasn't sure he heard her right. "What was that Ann, it is pretty loud here with the horses and all?"

101

"I said, I need a kiss!"

At that point Pitch did not hesitate and bent down and kissed her tenderly but very long on the lips. When they parted Ann said, "Thank you Boss Pitch. I'll see you at dinner this evening."

Then she turned and walked back up to the house. Pitch was still somewhat in shock because his men were watching all of this and it was Ann's first outward display that she cared about Pitch romantically. The men were just standing there looking at him and he had a big grin glued to his face.

That evening after dinner Tommy saw Mom pat Mr. Pitch on the butt and say to him, "Not bad big boy," and he smiled. A little later Nellie saw Mr. Pitch whisper something in Mom's ear and she smiled back at him. The kids had no idea what was going on between Pitch and Ann. Then Rory said, "Nellie, Tommy, let's go to the stables and check on our horses." When they got there Rory said, "Are the two of you seeing what I am seeing?"

Nellie said, "I think so, what are you talking about?"

"He is talking about Mom and Mr. Pitch being together."

"Tommy is right. Reno told me some of the wranglers were talking about Mom kissing Mr. Pitch."

"Does that mean Mr. Pitch is going to be my Daddy?"

"No Nellie, but something is going on and it is about time we know about it."

They all went back up to the house and Rory took the lead. "Mom can we talk to you and Mr. Pitch?"

"Sure Honey, we are right here. What is on your mind?"

"What is going on between you and Mr. Pitch?"

They both just looked at each other for a second. Mr. Pitch started off, "Well, kids your Mom has agreed to be my girlfriend. We both really care about each other and you kids. Is that okay?"

"Are you getting married?"

Ann quickly handled that question. Nellie, we don't know for sure right now but we might down the road a little later."

"In fact, I am taking your Mom out on a date tomorrow night, so it is good you know."

Ann just looked at Pitch because this date thing was surprise news to her.

"Are you kids okay with that?"

We all started singing, Mom is going on a date, Mom is going on a date.

After a little while the kids all went their own way. Nellie had her doll baby, Rory had his guitar and Tommy his lacrosse stick. When the timing was right Ann said, "So, I'm going on a date with you and you didn't even ask me?"

"Ann, will you please go on a date with me?"

"Where are we going?"

"Sorry, that is a surprise only the spirits know."

"You and your dam spirits. Okay, then what time do we have to leave here?"

"About eight o'clock will be just fine."

"Isn't that a little late? Should we eat dinner at six?"

"Maybe a little something, like a salad or soup. Not too much."

"How do I dress for this date?"

"Your cowgirl clothes would be super."

"The more questions I asked, the more I'm not sure about this date."

"Just trust me Ann."

"Okay, I will but remember I have a gun."

The entire day Friday Ann kept thinking about their date and tried to figure out what Pitch was up too this time. When dinner time rolled around both of them just had a salad which upset Nija because she thought it was her cooking. "I guess I'll go get dressed for my date."

All the kids thought that was funny and laughed as she walked from the table. "Oh Ann, I forgot to tell you to wear your cowgirl hat."

"My hat, I only wear that when I go riding."

"Please, pretty please with sugar on it."

"I can't believe I'm going out with this nut!"

When she came back down stairs she looked like a model with her slim figure and tight jeans.

"Do I pass your inspection Pitch?"

"Absolutely, and the hat makes the outfit."

"Oh, give me a break about the hat. Are we ready to go?"

"Yes, Boss Lady your chariot awaits you."

When she walked out front Pitch's pick-up truck was setting there. "Where is the Cadillac?"

Sorry, my lady, it is a Ford tonight.

They jumped in the truck and headed toward Sheridan and Ann still had this big question mark on her face. They came down Main Street and then Pitch made a left turn on to this narrow street. Right in front on them with its neon lights on was the Coyote Western Night Club. Pitch pulled the truck in a parking space. "Come on Ann, now I will show you some real dancing, not that black-tie junk." As they walked in the Coyote everybody started saying hi to Pitch. The Coyote had a real long bar with stools, small tables and chairs all over the place, a big dance floor and a stage where the band was setting up to start playing at nine. The entire place was decorated with western stuff including a buffalo's head hanging on one of the walls. They took a table near the dance floor and Pitch stood up. "Everybody this is Ann McClure my future bride so all you other ladies stay away from me."

"Pitch, will you sit down, you are making an ass out of yourself. They are going to kick us out of here."

Next the waitress came to their table. "Hi Sophie, this is Ann."

"I heard!"

"We will have twenty barbeque buffalo wings and two Pioneer beers and keep them coming."

About ten minutes to nine the leader of the band, Wes Holder, came over to talk to Pitch. "How have you been Pitch? I haven't seen you in a while."

"Don't get down town on the weekends much anymore. Wes, this is Ann McClure the only love ever in my life."

"Nice to meet you Ann. You are one lucky lady to catch this guy. It's time to tune up. Hope you both have a good time."

"You must have spent a lot of time in this place?"

"To be honest, which I promised you, I own this place. Stony Mason runs it for me. He will be in about ten o'clock so he can close up tonight."

"You are full of surprises."

At nine o'clock the Wes Holder Bandit Band started playing I'm So Lonesome I Could Cry recorded by Hank Williams. Unlike the black-tie affair, here everybody jumped right out on the dance floor. "Come on Ann, it is time to do some two stepping."

Ann and Pitch laughed and carried on the entire night. They were having fun just like her kids do every day. They even did a few crazy western line dances which Ann was totally lost, but she kept going on. They had really worked up a sweat and must have kissed a hundred times. At one o'clock Pitch said, it is time to go Ann. Stony will be closing at two. They danced their way to the truck and sang songs all the way back to the ranch. Pitch kept kissing her right up to the front door. Before they went in the house Pitch looked Ann in the eyes, "You know I want to make love to you?"

"I know and I want to give myself to you, my whole self. Please be patient with me Pitch it has been a very long time. I'm not sure I know how to act with a man."

"Ann, all you have to do is be yourself."

When they walked in the house, they looked around just in case one of the kids were up. They kissed very passionately and she told Pitch she really loved him with her whole heart. "Ann, I would marry you tomorrow if you would let me."

"It's shower time lover boy, we are starting to smell bad. Ann ran up the steps and threw him a kiss from upstairs.

Ann woke up Saturday morning hearing somebody yelling, "Shoot, shoot, shoot to the corner." When she looked at the clock it was almost ten o'clock. She had not slept that late in years. Ann just laid there thinking about the fun they had last night and all the fun they had at the Coyote Club. She had a big smile on her face when Nellie came running in her room. "Hey, sleepy head, time to get up. Did you have a good time on your date Mommy?"

"Yes, I did Honey. Mr. Pitch and I went dancing. Who is that yelling outside?"

"That is Dinja teaching Tommy how to play that game."

"Oh, you mean lacrosse. Where is Rory?"

"Mr. Pitch took him in to practice with Sister Martin. I think they left before nine o'clock this morning. Mommy, can Sara Song come down and play with me today?"

"Go tell Samoka to call her Mom and ask her. Tell Samoka to tell her he will come get her and to ask her if Sara Song can stay overnight. We will bring her to church with us tomorrow."

Nellie went flying down the steps. Ann thought for several minutes. This is like a real family, all but one thing.

Thanksgiving Day was finally here and I think everybody was nervous for Rory. I think Sister Martin must have told him a secret on how to handle his nerves from her days as a professional guitarist. For clothes, Ann went with the western look but no jeans, dress pants. The family including Pitch arrived at the auditorium at eight-thirty.to give Rory time to warm up and the contestants had to draw numbers to see who went when. They were not expecting many people to the early morning elimination round. It was mostly family members and a few other people. They had a baby grand piano on the stage for anybody who needed it for their performance or accompaniment. The judges told the contestants that now there was only twelve competing, two others dropped out. Rory drew the number five which was almost in the middle of the performances. Pitch said, "It is better to be near the end because that are the performances the judges remember the most."

The contest was ready to start and the mayor lead the people there in The Pledge of Allegiance to the Flag. The first contestant was a man about forty years old who played western violin music and missed a lot of notes. Then there was a tap dancer who must have been sixty years old. The next performer was a real surprise. It was a very skinny little young woman who sang Mule Train. Nobody could believe this deep voice coming out of that small body. However, she did a good job and was not too bad. Finally, it was Rory's turn to perform "Ramblin' Rose." He sat on a stool with his guitar, "Ramblin' Rose, rambling rose. Why you ramble, no one knows. Wild and wind-blown, that's how you've grown. Who can cling to a ramblin' rose." He sang it so beautiful and with feeling that it almost made you cry. The judges were all looking a each other and writing things down. Even with a very small audience Rory got a lot of applause when he finished. Next, performing was a guitar player and then a drummer. Everybody in the place wanted the drummer to stop. Listening to a drum solo at ten o'clock in the morning is not what people want to do. The next contestant was a young girl around seventeen or eighteen years old. She was a pianist and played "Far Away Places" very beautifully. The judges started writing again. We all thought this was the person Rory had to beat. The last two contestants sang off key and you could tell their nerves had them all tongue tied. After all the performances were over the judges thanked the performers. Then they went off stage to deliberate and promised to be back in fifteen minutes.

When the judges returned, Mayor Gallon stood in front of the microphone with a piece of paper. "Ladies and gentlemen, we have decided who are three finalists are. The first finalist is Mary Thomas a singer." Everyone applauded, this was the little skinny woman who sang Mule Train. "Our second finalist is Rory McClure singer and guitar player." The applause from the people there was very loud. "The last finalist is Victoria Schwartz pianist." The people there also applauded for her. Then the mayor said, "Our finals are at seven o'clock tonight. The finalist needs to be here at six-thirty. Now, go home and have a nice Thanksgiving Day dinner with your family. See you tonight."

When Rory got in the car, we all patted him on the back and congratulated him for making the finals. On the way home Rory was laughing because Nellie and Tommy were trying to sing Ramblin Rose. When we got home, everybody was waiting to see how Rory made out. Nija told us Thanksgiving Day dinner would be at two. Samoka went over to talk to Mr. Pitch. "Boss, can I go to the village to tell my people Rory made it to the finals and they should come to help support him this evening."

Absolutely Samoka and I'll go tell the other boys in the bunk house."

Our Thanksgiving Day dinner was fabulous and we all thanked Nija. She was all smiles. From about four o'clock until we left for the finals you could feel the tension in the house. When we arrived around six-thirty the auditorium was filling up and there were plenty of Shoshones from the village. The judges had the finalist draw again to see the order of their performance. Rory drew number two. The mayor did his little speech again and then the finals started. First up was the woman with the deep voice who sang Mule Train in the elimination round. She sang the same song again. Mr. Boone asked her if she knew any other songs? "I know some, but not very good."

They thanked her and now it was Rory's turn. He came out real slow with his guitar and took a seat on the stool and started to play and sing. "There's no tomorrow when love is new. Now is forever when love is true. So kiss me and hold me tight. There's no tomorrow. There's just tonight. When he finished the entire auditorium, which was about six-hundred people gave him a standing ovation. Now, it was Victoria Schwartz's turn and she played Far Away Places. She was really good. About half of the people stood up for her but no Shoshones. The mayor then told the audience they needed a few minutes to deliberate. You could see them talking back and forth and doing a little arguing. It took about fifteen minutes until the mayor came to the microphone. "Ladies and Gentlemen, we have a tie between Rory McClure and Victoria Schwartz. We will give the two finalist ten minutes and we will have the tie breaker performances."

Ann looked at Pitch, "What happen with the vote?"

"I bet Louise Lambert flipped her vote to the Victoria girl. I heard that Louise has been teaching her for a long time and she is a pianist."

"You could be right."

The ten minutes was up and they drew to see who went first and it was Victoria. She played Far Away Places again. She was really good and Rory had his work cut out for him. He came walking out on the stage carrying his guitar. However, this time he put the guitar up against the stool and walked over to the piano. Rory started playing and singing. "Some enchanted evening you may see a stranger. You may see a stranger across a crowded room. And somehow you know, you know even then. That somewhere you'll see her again and again." When he finished the place went nuts. Finally, the mayor had to settle the audience down. The mayor went and deliberated with the other judges. Mr. Pitch looked at Ann, "Rory really has some guts. That was a risky move."

"No Pitch, he has confidence in himself."

This time it didn't take the judge long. Mayor Gallon came to the microphone. "The winner of the Sheridan Thanksgiving Day Talent Contest, by unanimous vote is Rory McClure."

Every one stood and applauded and Victoria even hugged Rory. Ann was just full of pride. Pitch just sat back down in his chair. "Pitch, is something wrong with you?"

"No Ann, I am just totally amazed by your son. That boy can really sing and play. I think he needs to make records in Nashville that's how good he is."

"Pitch, he is only twelve years old and not even in high school."

"I know Ann but talent like Rory does not come along to often."

Mayor Gallon presented the trophy to Rory and the $1,000 prize money. There were two newspaper reporters there and they interviewed and took pictures with Rory for about an hour. Pitch knew the reporter from the Sheridan Prairie newspaper so when he was done with Rory, Pitch went over to talk to him. "Sid Walter, how are things going with you and Sophie?"

"Well, Pitch, since you gave her a job at the Coyote, we have been saving money and talking about getting married and buying a house. Sophie told me you were in love and announced it to the world the other night. I hope that I just didn't get her in trouble?"

"Sid, how can she get in trouble for telling the truth? My girlfriend is Rory's mother."

"The ranch owner Ann McClure?"

"You got it buddy, she is right over there with her other two kids. I wanted to talk to you about Rory. He showed some great guts today by switching from guitar to piano, didn't he?"

"That boy can be a county western singing super star."

"That is why I need your help. I want Rory to get exposure all across the country. So, I have a deal for you and Sophie."

"Go ahead, I'm listening. What do you have on your mind?"

"You write the best article you have ever written in your life about Rory and put it on the Associated Press (AP) line so the world can pick it up and print it in their papers and you call all your newspaper reporter friends and ask them to do you a favor and run the article in their newspaper."

"What's in this for me?"

"Here is what I will do to help you and Sophie get married and buy a house. I will give Sophie a $50 a week raise in her Coyote paycheck and put her on the big tipper's tables. She will probably pick-up a couple hundred dollars in tips over the weekend from those tables. If I calculated correctly that is about a $1,000 extra a month. More than enough for a mortgage payment without the extra work"

"That is a great deal, Pitch."

"Well, your article better be great! Sid, are you in or out?"

"I'm in all the way."

"When you write this article write as if Rory was your son and run it on Sunday. The only thing at risk here is you better hope Sophie really loves you because all the money will be coming to her."

"Is it okay to tell her what is going on?"

"You better and remind her I can also turn the money flow off."

When Pitch got finished talking to Sid, he went out front to watch the fireworks with the kids and Ann. "You were talking to that reporter a long time."

"Just trying to make sure Rory gets some good press."

"Pitch, I still am wondering what happened with the tie vote. I talked with Louise and she said it was Dick Boone who voted with the mayor and Fred Jackson to make it a tie."

"Let me tell you what Sid said the mayor told him about the tie vote."

"I can't wait to hear this!"

"On the tie vote Louise voted with Jackson and Mayor Gallon to make it a tie. Dick Boone voted for Rory every time which I expected."

"Why did you think that?"

"Ann, ranchers stick together and Rory comes from a ranch."

"So, the bottom line is that Louise straight out lied to my face. What a bitch!"

"Yea, go punch her eyes out."

"You know sometimes you act goofy. I think I should fire her ass."

"Talk to Rory about it first and if he doesn't need her fire away."

Nellie came running over to Ann and Pitch, "What are we going to do now Mommy? We have off school tomorrow so we can stay up."

Of course, she turned and looked at Pitch. "Why are you looking at me?"

"Because you're the man with all the ideas and answers. I thought about going for ice cream but all the places are closed for the holiday."

"I know where we can get some ice cream."

"Where, the places are closed?"

"The Coyote Club!"

"I can't take the kids in a club where everyone is drinking."

"Ann, it is closed."

"Oh, I wasn't sure."

"We will have some ice cream, play the jukebox, and just celebrate Rory's day."

"Let's do it."

It was about nine o'clock when they pulled up in front of the Coyote Club with the neon light shining bright. The kids were all excited, "Are we going in the Coyote," was Tommy's question. "No, stupid, it is closed," was Rory's response. Then Nellie had enough, "Mr. Pitch what is going on here?"

"I asked the great Indian spirit to let us have fun tonight and celebrate Rory's victory battle. Come on let's go!"

Ann just looked at him. "Here we go again with the crazy spirit stuff."

The kids jumped out of the car as Pitch and Ann just followed them slowly up to the door. Pitch put his big hands over the door locks and put in the key so the kids couldn't see the key. After he unlocked the door, he did the same little cover-up trick with the security pad while he put in his pass code. Then he stood back a little from the door, "Great spirit I command you to open the door." He went to the door and pushed it open and he walked into the Coyote. The kids were going crazy and laughing their heads off. Pitch turned on all the lights and the kids just walked around looking at everything. Ann looked at him, "You are just too much," but thought you have to love him. He went over to the jukebox and turned it on automatic play so you didn't have to put nickels in it. "Rory come over here and select the songs you want to hear. Just push the number and it will play that song."

"I got it Mr. Pitch I will play some good tunes."

"Who wants an ice cream sundae?" He went back to the kitchen and while he was gone Ann showed the kids all the western decorations hanging all over the place. Tommy just stood in front of the huge buffalo head, his eyes were glued to it. "You okay, Tommy?"

"I never thought they were that big, Mom."

Ann had to hide her face from laughing. Ann started dancing with Nellie on the dance floor and told her this is where Mr. Pitch and her danced on their date. A few minutes later Mr. Pitch came walking out of the kitchen carrying a tray with five sundaes on it. They had three scoops of vanilla ice cream, chocolate syrup, and a cherry on top. They all sat at a table and began eating away. When they were finished, Mr. Pitch said, "Come on, your Mom can show you all how to do a Texas line dance. They had a ball laughing, falling, and just making up steps. It was fun for the whole family. Finally, Mr. Pitch said, "Sorry it is time to go it is ten-thirty." He turned off the jukebox and as they walked out the door Ann said, "What about the mess me made. We could clean it up."

"It's okay Ann, just leave it." Then she remembered he owned the place. The ride back to the ranch was nothing but fun on top of fun. When the kids got out of the car, they all thanked Mr. Pitch for a great and funny night. Nellie said to him, Mr. Pitch this was almost like Christmas."

When they got in the house Ann immediately said, "Okay, everybody upstairs and right in to the shower because you all stink."

All four on them ran up the steps and since each of them had their own bathroom and shower they were quick. They put on their pajamas and Tommy his Dodger jersey and jumped into bed. Now go to sleep immediately because the spirit asked so." The kids all laughed. "Good night Mom!"

Ann went to her room and showered quickly while her mind was racing. She sat on the edge of her bed and all she could think of was how great Pitch was with the kids. It seemed Pitch was always doing something for one of her children just like he was their father and he was what made them a true family. She looked at herself in her mirror, "Ann, tonight is the night! It is time to show Pitch your love for him has no restrictions." She got up from the bed and went to her clothes drawer and looked at different nightwear. Finally, she pulled out a silk, violet teddy. She put it on and thought, I have never had this on before but it does show off my good parts. Quickly, she went to her closet and pulled out a beautiful silk white three-quarter length robe. Ann decided to for-go the bedroom slippers and to go bare feet. She took one last look in the mirror and fixed her hair and make-up. Then she took a deep breath and walked the steps with her heart beating very hard. She was really nervous and somewhat hesitated.

When she reached the bottom of the steps the place was dark all but for a little night light. She walked in her bare feet down the hallway to where Pitch's bedroom was. She hesitated right before she got to his door. Talking to herself again, "Ann, this is good you love him and he loves you."

With all the courage in her she knocked lightly on Pitch's door. That was all it took and he was at the door in just the pants of his pajamas, no top. He just stared at her for a few seconds, "Ann you are just so beautiful and very sexy. You make my heart skip a beat when I look in your eyes. He gently took her hand and moved her close to him and first kissed her on her forehead, then her cheeks, neck, and then her lips. As he kissed her again, she looked him in his eyes, "Pitch, I want us to make love together to tonight. I am still a little afraid because I haven't been with a man in over six years."

Pitch, picked her up in his arms and carried her over to his bed. He sat on the bed with Ann sitting on his lap, "You have nothing to be afraid of because I love you so much and want only what you want."

He laid Ann down on his bed and laid down beside her and held her in his arms tight. He kissed her very gently several times and casually untightened the robe from around her wrist. As she helped him get her robe off, he saw the sexy teddy she had on for him. "Let me see this so I can carry this picture around in my mind all day when you're not with me."

Pitch kissed her very passionately over and over again. Ann wasted no time in helping get his pajama pants off as he worked on getting her teddy off. When she was completely naked, he just looked at her body. "You are just so beautiful my Darling Ann. God has truly blessed me by bringing you into my life."

Ann put her hands on his face and kissed him and kissed him. They made passionate love all throughout the night and Ann fell asleep in Pitch's arms. Something she had dreamed about many times.

Ann woke up and looked at the clock and it was seven-ten in the morning. She hadn't planned on spending the entire night in his room. She decided to let Pitch sleep and put on her robe and tip-toed out of his bedroom down the hallway. When she got to the living room, she heard some noise and looked in the kitchen and there was Nija getting ready to make breakfast. Ann just give a short hi wave with her hand as Nija stood there smiling from ear to ear. When she got to the steps, she took off running upstairs.

Since the kids were off from school Pitch took Rory and Tommy out on the range so they could see what the wranglers did. When they got to where the herd was Pitch told them to get down off their horses. He pulled something out of his saddle bags and the boys were not sure what he was doing. "I have a present for you boys."

He handed both of them a pair of chaps. "When you are around long horn cattle you need to have chaps on to protect yourself."

The three of them put on their chaps and got back on their horses. "Okay, now we can ride down to the herd and see what Kinno is doing today."

As they approached Kinno yelled, "Hey, boys look we got help coming. It's good to see that you cowboys have chaps on because some of these steers are mean and remember the cattle spook easy just like the horses."

Mr. Pitch asked Kinno what they were doing today? "This herd has gotten very large in size since the babies have grown up so we are splitting the herd and taking half of them over to the west valley."

"Kinno, is that going to be very hard to do?"

"Rory, let me explain it the easiest way I know. When you had to leave your friends in New York city did you want to go?"

Tommy didn't give Rory a chance to respond, "I told Mom she could leave without me. I was not leaving my baseball team and all my buddies."

"Well, that's how the cattle feel and they will fight us to stay here with the other part of the herd, some of them will really get mean and that is why we wear chaps. They will try and fight you with their horns but the chaps will just make their horns slide off to the side."

Tommy asked, "Is that what happened to Coach Dinja?"

"Coach Dinja, yea Tommy. Dinja didn't have chaps on and a spooked steer got his leg with a horn and now he walks with a limp. One last word before you start helping the wranglers. The two of you do what Boss Pitch and I tell you at all times or you will get hurt and Boss Lady will shoot the both of us."

Mr. Pitch kept us on the outside of the herd and showed us how to use our lasso to get the steers to go the way we wanted them to move. We did see the wranglers fighting off a couple of the bad boy steers. The wranglers got the herd split and we started traveling west. A couple of wranglers stayed behind to keep the other half from following us. We were out on the range about four hours or more. When we got back Mom and Nellie were sitting on the front step and walked down to the stables. "Ann, Nellie, I want you to meet two real cowboys."

Tommy couldn't wait to tell them all we did. Then Mr. Pitch yelled, "Take care of your horses and put your chaps in you saddle bags for the next time you need them."

He looked at Ann, "How is the Boss Lady feeling today?"

"Like a spring chicken!"

Pitch couldn't stop laughing at Mom. Then she yelled, "All right you wranglers go get cleaned up for dinner and I mean showers for all of you. I don't want my house smelling like steers. Move out!"

Saturday evening, we had a little barbeque out by the patio and Sara Song's family, Reno and his family, Dinja, Nija and Samoka were invited. Ann had somebody from Sheridan come to do the cooking and grilling. Ann felt good about getting to know her kid's friends' families. Many times Pitch stood with his arm around Ann's waist. Then Sara Song asked, "Are you two getting married like my Mom and Dad? Pitch did not know what to say so he dumped the question in Ann's lap. "I think we may one day Sara Song but nothing is for sure until you make it happen."

Quickly, Sara Song's parents pulled her to them so she couldn't ask any more questions. The entire evening was a lot of fun and the McClure's were making new friends all over the county.

Pitch couldn't wait to get his hands on the Sunday newspaper to see the article Sid wrote about Rory. He had sent Samoka to town to get the paper and told him to read the article and if it was good to buy ten copies. Pitch waited, but not patiently, and then saw Samoka coming up the road in the truck. As Samoka pulled up Pitch opened the truck door and took a copy off of the pile in the front seat. He sat down on the front step and didn't have to look far because Rory's picture was on the front page. The

Sheridan Parrie's Newspaper headline read, "McClure Brilliant Look Out Nashville. The article talked about how mature and cool Rory was for being only twelve years old. It emphasized his great ability to play the guitar and piano. However, the highlight of his performances was his voice. The article compared him to many great country western singers like Hank Williams. It said he was a young cowboy from the Bronx looking for a start in the music profession business. Sid Walter's ended the article by saying a voice like Rory's doesn't come along that often and record companies and agents should be lining up at his parent's door. Pitch felt Sid did a great job and the article was picked up by the Associated Press which meant all other newspapers could pull it off the line and use it in their newspaper. Samoka gave Boss Pitch all the other newspapers he bought and Pitch walked in like a newspaper boy selling papers. "Newspapers, Sunday newspapers, read all about it, Rory McClure is brilliant and walks away with a unanimous vote for the Sheridan City Thanksgiving Day talent contest."

Everybody came running and took a newspaper from him even Nija. They all sat down and started reading the article. Pitch explained what the AP stood for. Mr. Pitch do you think they will get this article in the Bronx?"

"I'm not sure Rory but a little later I can call my New York friends to find out." Ann told Rory he needed to start a scrap book for all the paper articles he will have in the future. She also instructed him to open a bank account to put all of his future winning. Rory sounded back, "But, Mom I want to give the money I won to Sister Martin for her school music program."

"Rory you put your money in the bank and I will take care of Sister Martin for you."

"Yea, that's right, your Mom has a little bet to pay up."

"Okay, Pitch, I'll go see Sister Martin tomorrow. Rory are you still planning to take lessons from her going forward?"

"Absolutely Mom!

"What about Louise Lambert?"

"I think I can play what I need to and can continue to learn on my own."

"It will be my pleasure to give her the bad news. Rory looked at her and saw the mean look from when she lived in the hard city.

When Ann went to visit Sister Martin, she decided to go by herself, no kids. They went for a walk in the parish garden and sat down on a bench there. "Sister, Rory wants to continue his lessons with you. He has learned so much from you. Mrs. McClure."

"Ann, please."

Ann, you know Rory does not want to be a professional guitar player like I was. He wants to be a singer. To be honest he has come a tremendous way in such a short time. I think his ability to play by ear has really helped his progress. Ann, Rory is not only a very good singer he is very intelligent. Here is what we can do. Tell Rory I said for him to continue to learn on his own and if hits a problem area he can come see me on Saturdays."

"I think that will work Sister because he will know you are still his coach. Sister Martin, I know you are not going to want this but here is $700 for your music program."

"Ann, I don't want any part of Rory's money he won!"

"It is not Rory's money. He put his $1,000 in what he calls his performance bank account."

"Good for him. Then what is this?"

"This is from Pitch and me so you can continue helping other children like you did for Rory."

"Are your sure Ann? This is a lot of money."

"I am sure Sister."

"With this I can buy a couple guitars and a violin. Nothing like the Gibson Rory has."

"Sister Martin, it is almost noon on this beautiful Saturday afternoon can you go to lunch with me? I really want to pick your brain about some things."

"That sounds great Ann. Let me go tell Sister Mary I am going to lunch with you."

Ann took them to the restaurant where she saw the mayor and the men, only because she liked it so much. After some chit-chat they ordered lunch. "Sister, I am worried that we may be pushing Rory to fast into a music career. You saw the article in the newspaper last Sunday which will probably give him exposure to the music world and people will come knocking on our door. I know you were a professional guitarist at a young age and thought you had some advice for me."

"I worry about that with Rory too, Ann. To be honest when I decided to become a nun the Lord was calling me to serve him and at the time, I was twenty years old and completely burnt out. I had so much pressure on me. People wanted me to be in two places at the same time. Of course, you know I am part Indian and my parents were poor and I had three brother and two sisters. My family needed the money and by me performing they now have a nice life in Laramie. Since my mother was an Indian and my father a white cow hand everybody assumed that they were dumb and tried to take advantage of them. Our pastor at our local church convinced them to hire an agent for me. When you have an agent all they care about is the money and their percentage comes right off the top. The more performances the more money for them. I could go on and on Ann but there is no need to tell you all I went though."

"It sounds like you were not happy even though you loved playing the guitar?"

"You are right, Ann. My life ended up being my guitar and God and finally I made the right decision, God."

"What do you suggest I do for Rory?"

Rory is just going to be thirteen years old but he is a talent all the record companies and agents will come after very shortly. My suggestion is that you be his agent and Pitch can help you. Do not hire an agent for Rory at his age. Together, you and Pitch decide where and when he sings. You have to remember he will have to travel a lot so the two of you can pick and chose where he goes. It is important that you let him be a kid and get his education. When he gets out of high school then you can get him an agent and he can take care of himself. By then you will know which are the good agents who will care about your son."

"Sister Martin, you have been so helpful."

"Ann, if you need help just pray to the Dear Lord."

After dropping Sister Martin off on the way out of town Ann had a lot to think about and really wanted to talk to Pitch. She knew Pitch would protect Rory like he was his son. Before she left the town, she decided to go talk to Louise Lambert at her teaching shop. As she walked in the place Louise yelled to her from a piano, "Ann, I am almost finished with this lesson. I'll be about five minutes longer."

Ann thought about telling her the spirits told her to fire Louise but laughed and changed her mind. When Louise was done, "What can I do for you, Ann?"

"Louise, I came here to tell you I am cancelling Rory's lessons with you."

"Oh, no, Ann, didn't you hear how good he played in the contest?"

"Yes, I did Louise and I know he learned that song all on his own with no help from you."

"But Ann, he can be a great pianist."

"Rory wants to be a great singer and not a great pianist. Besides, I heard you voted against Rory in the contest?"

"That's not true, it was Dick Boone."

"I don't think so Louise, even the mayor said it was you because Victoria Schwartz has been a student of yours for many years. When I asked you about the vote at the auditorium you lied to my face and I don't like liars. Consider this your cancellation notice and Rory will not be coming here anymore."

Ann turned and walked out the door.

It wasn't until after dinner that Ann got to talk with Pitch about what Sister Martin had said. He agreed with everything Sister Martin told her and all the reasons she gave. They agreed that they would be Rory's agent until he graduated from high school and made sure he still had the opportunity to just be a kid. Ann looked at Pitch, "So, we have a partnership? I'm the brains and you are the muscle."

Pitch started laughing and Ann joined him.

CHAPTER 6

P itch's friend in New York told him the article on Rory was in the entertainment section of the New York Times with the article title, Bronx Boy Next Star. Pitch thought if the Times picked up the story to run it, stands to reason this many other newspapers would also.

Ann had received many letters in the mail from agents wanting to represent Rory. With Christmas not far away Ann and Pitch thought this would be a good time to get people to hear and see Rory perform. Pitch thought they should get Rory all the exposure they could in the state of Wyoming and branch out from there. They both talked to Rory and told him he needed to learn some Christmas songs, maybe four or five.

Ann continued to get letters from agents and tons of phone calls. It got so bad she got sick of picking up the phone. Then she came up with a plan. Ann told Samoka to answer the phone in Shoshone to totally confuse the agents. He was having a ball with this because he could understand them but they couldn't understand him. Ann also received postcards at different times from RCA, MGM, and Capital record companies telling her to have Rory's agent call them. It became very obvious that Rory's name and talent was out there in the music industry. One day she got a letter from the University of Wyoming. Ann just put it on the side thinking it was just an advertisement for the college.

That evening after dinner Pitch was sitting on the sofa and saw the letter from the University of Wyoming laying on the end table beside the lamp. He picked it up, "Ann what is this letter here?"

"I think it is just some type of advertisement for the college. Open it up and see what it is."

Pitch opened the letter and it was from the universities Director of Music, Terry Bowden. As Pitch read on the director was asking them if Rory would like to sing the National Anthem at the University of Wyoming Cowboys football game against the University of Missouri on Saturday December 14th at the Jonah Field War Memorial Stadium in Laramie, Wyoming. If they were interested to call his office for more details. Pitch read the letter over and over again.

"Ann, do you know what this is?"

"No, that's why I asked you to read it. What is it?"

"This is an invitation for Rory to sing the National Anthem at a University of Wyoming football game."

"Is that good?"

"Ann, there will be tens of thousand people at the game. The exposure Rory would get from this is unbelievable."

"Okay, let's do it then."

"The director wants you to call his office if you want Rory to do it. By the way the game is in Laramie."

"What do you think?"

"What do I think? I thought you were the brain of this outfit? My opinion is we should jump on this immediately. You need to call the music director Terry Bowden the first thing in the morning."

"I know nothing about Wyoming or football. You call him, you are Rory's co-agent so you can speak for him. Plus, you will know what he is talking about. I won't have a clue."

"That will cost you!"

"What will it cost me?"

"A visit to me by the sexy spirit tonight."

"Oh, now I'm a spirit?"

"Only in my heart Ann."

"You know what? We better check with Rory to see if he wants to do this. Singing in front of thousands of people can get to your nerves. Ann went over to the upstairs steps. "Rory, come down here a minute."

"Okay, Mom, I'll be right there."

When the other kids heard Mom wanted to talk to Rory, they followed him right down the steps. "What is up Mom?"

"Mr. Pitch needs to talk to you about something important so listen carefully."

"Rory, the Director of Music Terry Bowden at the University of Wyoming wants to know if you would sing the National Anthem before one of their football games." Before Pitch could finish Tommy yelled, "Football game, when we going, who is playing, I don't care, when is it?"

"Mr. Pitch it sounds like a great opportunity for me. What do you think Mom?"

"You know there will be thousands of people there and all kind of stuff going on with the band, cheer leaders, flag girls, and the players."

"Where will I be singing?"

In Laramie at the War Memorial Stadium."

"I would like to do it. This will challenge me for the future."

"Okay, Mr. Pitch will call the director tomorrow morning and see what he has to say."

That night as Pitch and Ann cuddled in his bed Ann worried about Rory alone singing to a big crowd. "Ann, Rory won't be alone. The entire family and I will be with him."

"What are you saying Pitch?"

"If Rory gets this opportunity, we all are going to Laramie with him. We will have a road trip in the Cadillac."

"Can we do that with the kids?"

"Absolutely, we will get adjoining rooms in a hotel and you sleep with Nellie and I will sleep with the boys. We can go to the football game and can show them all the things in the city of Laramie."

"Now you got me all excited. Can we tell the kids?

"Let me talk to Terry Bowden in the morning and find out all the details and if everything is a go then you can tell Tommy and Nellie about the road trip."

"That is why I love you so much. Come here Mr. Wesley!"

Pitch waited until ten o'clock to call the office of Terry Bowden. He got Mr. Bowden's secretary. "Mr. Wesley you need to talk to Don Reese the stadium events manager. Just hold on and I will transfer you."

Don Reese answered the phone and Pitch explained who he was. Mr. Reese said he had read the article in the Laramie newspaper and thought it would be great if Rory could sing the National Anthem for a home game. Pitch told Mr. Reese that Rory would love to sing for the Cowboys audience. Then Don Reese went into details and said Rory would have to be at the stadium Friday December 13th to rehearse for game day. They will have to check the acoustics with his voice sound.

"You know he will be singing acappella?"

"What is that Don? I'm not a music guy, just a cowboy?"

"It is when he sings without music being played. There is no accompaniment."

"I'll have to tell him that."

"Also, tell him to learn the National Anthem by heart if he doesn't already know it. How many people will you have so I can reserve seats up front for you?"

"Counting Rory that would be five."

"You can stay at the Hilton Hotel. They give the university big discounts. I guess you will need two rooms?"

"Yes Don, adjoining rooms because we have kids."

"I will take care of that but you call the Hilton tomorrow to confirm your reservations. I think that covers everything."

"One more thing Don. How should Rory dress for this?"

"Where does Rory live?"

"His mother owns the McClure ranch."

"Then by all means tell him to dress like a real cowboy."

"Thanks for all your help Don."

"Same here Pitch. Can't wait to meet the family.?

After Pitch hung up, he went to find Ann. She was out working in her vegetable garden. When she saw him coming, she said, "There is my lover boy!"

Pitch had to laugh and he told her everything that Don Reese said.

"We better tell Rory he has to sing acappella and that he needs to memorize the National Anthem."

"That is your job co-agent. I have to go check on the boys and the herd."

It didn't take Ann long to find Rory. He was over in the bunk house helping out Reno. She told him the news and he causally said, "Okay Mom, I got it. Don't worry I will be ready."

Ann was nervous about all of this and here was Rory cool as a cucumber. Ann went back to work in her garden but couldn't stop thinking of all the things Pitch had done for her kids. "I really need to marry that guy and soon."

That night after Ann told Nellie and Tommy, they all were going to Laramie for the weekend so they better be good or she would leave them with Nija. Mr. Pitch asked Tommy how his lacrosse practice was going? "Coach Dinja says he is going to let me play in the 10 to 12 year old village lacrosse league very soon. I am going to play the attackman position and score lots of goals."

That is great Tommy. We all will have to come see you play was Ann's response. Then Nellie said, "Yea, we can watch Warrior Tommy the attackman."

We all laughed and Tommy looked at us seriously, "I am Warrior Tommy."

Then Mr. Pitch jumped in, "We know you are Warrior Tommy and the other team better watch out or you will take their scalp."

With that all the kids went to do their own thing while Pitch just studied every movement Ann made. "What is on your mind cowboy?'

"Would you like to take a walk down the hallway?"

"Get out of here. Are you nuts it is only seven-thirty?"

"Love has no time Ann."

The week of the football game was here and every day you could hear Rory practicing. Ann bought him a record player and the National Anthem record so he could hear how the music went. One evening Dick Boone called Pitch and told him he found areas on his ranch where somebody had been drilling and blasting for uranium. "It was right near the Boone/McClure property line. When I called Sheriff Douglas, he said you ran some men off of Ann's property not long ago." "I will take a ride out there tomorrow to see if I can find the men or a lead. Dan is trying to find out where these guys are living so we can pay them a visit. Ann saw them one day talking with Mayor Gallon."

"It figures, he is a big crook and we need to get his ass out of office this coming year."

"If I find anything Dick, I will give you a call. Talk to you later."

On Wednesday evening Rory went for a final rehearsal at Saint Joseph's school with Sister Martin. She had invited all the nuns, priest, and staff to come to the school assembly hall to hear Rory. He had no idea what he was walking into and that was the way Sister Martin wanted it. She wanted to see if this had any impact on his singing. When Sister Martin and Rory walked in the assembly hall with all the people there his eyes lite up. "This is a nice surprise Sister. I hope they enjoy my performance."

Sister Martin took a seat with the others and Rory started singing the National Anthem acappella. When Rory was done it was dead silence. He just looked at them, "I'm done!"

They all stood up and applauded loudly. They told Sister Martin he was ready. Sister Mary said, "Rory, you have a great voice and will do great in Laramie. We all will be praying for you."

When Pitch came to pick Rory up, "How did you like your little surprise?"

"I enjoyed it."

Pitch was always amazed how calm and cool Rory was. "You got guts kid. I would be shitting in my boots if I had to sing in front of all those people."

At ten o'clock on Thursday morning they were loading up the Cadillac. The drive to Laramie was about three-hundred miles and it would take five to six hours to get there. When Pitch yelled, "Let's load up," the kids were in the car before he finished the sentence. The scenery along highway I-25 south was beautiful and the kids didn't miss a thing to point out. Luckily, Pitch had been to Laramie many times before so he kind of knew his way around when they got into the city. When he pulled up to the Hilton Hotel doors, the baggage boys took all their luggage on a carrier and Ann and Pitch went to the desk to check-in. The kids were just looking at everything in the lounge about the old west. They took the elevator up to the third floor and opened the doors to their two rooms. One room had a king size bed which Ann immediately informed them this was Nellie and her room. The other room had two double size beds. Tommy looked at them, "Where are you going to sleep Pitch?"

"Right in this bed here and that one is for you and Rory."

"Wait a minute here, they get that huge bed and I have to sleep with Rory?"

"Tommy, it will be just like it was back in the Bronx."

They all started unpacking. Ann started reading all about the hotel from a brochure on the night stand. "Oh my God, they have an in-door swimming pool on the top floor."

"How can we go swimming Mommy without our bathing suits?"

"Nellie, if you are good, we can go to the store in the lounge and I am sure they have bathing suits for sale."

The kids started cheering.

They decided to take a walk around the city and look for a place to eat dinner. Pitch told them to make sure they stayed together because there were many people in town for the football game. Tommy spotted a restaurant called the Old Wagon Wheel and suggested they eat there. The kids loved it because they got cheeseburgers, French fries and a milk shake. It took then a good two hours to get finished eating and then they headed back to the hotel. Pitch said, "Let's go check out the hotel store for swimming suits. They found one for each of the kids but Nellie didn't like the color of the one for her. You could tell Ann was getting tired from the long day, "Nellie, it is that suit or no swimming pool for you."

"Okay, I will take it."

They decided before they went to bed that Mr. Pitch would take Rory to the stadium in the morning because there was no need for all of them to go. Tommy had a fit because he wanted to see the inside of the football stadium. Finally, Pitch gave in and said he could go with them if he went right to sleep. When Ann kissed Pitch good night, he looked at her, "Cotton pajamas! I prefer your teddy."

"Be quiet, go to bed."

Pitch and the boys were at the stadium on time in the morning. Inside the stadium it was like a three-ring circus with people practicing everything. Don Reese came over to them and they did the usual introductions. The stadium crew did a sound check. Then Mr. Reese give Rory some instructions. "Rory, we are going to run through this about three times and check things like acoustics and vibration factors. Is that okay with you?"

"Yes sir, Mr. Reese."

"Are you ready, go!"

Rory sang the National Anthem all the way through and while he was singing the entire three-ring circus paused to listen. Don Reese, just looked at Rory and was shaking his head saying, "Amazing, Amazing, where did this kid come from? He turned to the sound crew and they give a thumbs up. You are done Rory."

"Mr. Reese, I thought you wanted me to sing it three times?"

"Rory, it doesn't get any better then you just did and the sound crew got everything they needed from one take. Pitch, here are the family's tickets for tomorrow and sideline passes for you and

Rory. Now, go enjoy a day in our city." He turned and went off to other jobs for the game.

When they got back to the hotel rooms the girls left a note stating they went to breakfast at the hotel restaurant. When the boys arrived at the restaurant Ann immediately wanted to know how Rory did but Nellie wanted to know what they were going to do today? Ann wasn't sure what to say. "We all can take a walk around the city to see what kind of stores they have."

Tommy just stared at her, "Mom, no shopping, no shopping!"

"Would all of you like to know what Rory's co-agent would do on a nice day like today?"

After they all said yes, Pitch went into his play for the today. "First, we will go to the Laramie Historic Railroad Depot, there are really old trains, you can get on some of them and look like you are driving the trains. Your Mom can take pictures of you as the engineer. After we are finished there, we will go to the Laramie Plain Museum. This is an old mansion built in 1892, the old wooden floors make noise and we will probably run into a ghost or two. Lastly, if we have time, we will go to Spruce Mountain Lookout Tower. We will go high above the forest up where the birds fly and this time of year, we probably can see the mountains covered with snow. Does that sound good instead of shopping?"

"Great Mr. Pitch let's go now. Also, can we go swimming when we get back."

"Nellie, I will make sure you get to swim after our tour."

"See kids, that is why I let him hang around with us."

They all just laughed at both Pitch and Ann.

They all had an enjoyable day in Laramie and when it was bedtime the kids were dead on their feet. Ann put them all to bed and told them that she and Pitch were going down to the cocktail lounge to have a drink and so Pitch can smoke a cigar after a day as their tour guide. She instructed Rory not to open the doors for anybody. She had her key to get back in when they returned.

Pitch and Ann sat at a small table in the cocktail lounge where there was a total of seven people. "Pitch, you showed the kids a great time today and okay me too. Are you sure you want the responsibility of raising three kids twenty-four hours a day, seven days a week?"

"No, Ann!"

She looked at him confused. "I want the responsibility of raising four kids! "She almost fell out of her chair. "Are you saying you want to have a baby with me or am I misunderstanding what you just said?"

"Ann, to be honest, all I want right now is you on a permanent basis. It is getting very hard to just fit our love in just when you can. I want it all the time."

"That is the best I can do right now Pitch. I am sorry I cannot guarantee you that I will be there when you want me. All I can tell you is that I do love you and want to be with you."

All the way back to the rooms they kissed and talked about their love for each other.

Game day was here and Rory looked good in his new western clothes and hat. Since they had to get to the stadium early Pitch thought parking would be no problem. When he pulled into the parking lot people were tailgating every where and drinking at ten o'clock in the morning. They finally found a parking space far from the entrance gate and had to walk about five blocks. The kids were just watching all the fans cooking, drinking, and acting crazy in Cowboy jerseys. Once they got into the stadium

Pitch took Ann, Tommy, and Nellie to their seats and then him and Rory went on to the sideline. Don Reese came over to them, "Rory, you look good, only leave the hat with Pitch, you do have to take it off. I got some others things to take care of. I will be back in a little while."

The players just finished their final warm ups and headed back into the locker room. The University of Wyoming marching band then came on the field and performed a few songs with their fantasy marching maneuvers. Don Reese came back over while the band was still playing and walked Rory and Pitch up the sideline to the fifty-yard line. "Okay, Rory, here is what is going to happen. The announcer will introduce both teams and they will come running out of the tunnel to their proper sideline. Pitch, you make sure the players don't knock Rory down when the Cowboy's come to this sideline. Straight out in front of you in the center of the field will be your microphone. After the players are at that sideline you slowly walk out to the microphone. Once you are there the announcer will make an announcement to the fans and when he is done that is your sign to start singing. Before, you start singing take a deep breath and wait for the silence. Is everything clear?"

"Yes, sir Mr. Reese, I got it."

The announcer came on, "Ladies and gentlemen, at this time would you please stand and remove your hats for our National Anthem being sung by Rory McClure."

Everybody stood up and the stadium got dead silent. Rory took a deep breath and started to sing. "Oh, say, can you see, by the dawn's early light. What so proudly we hailed at the twilight's last gleaming? Whose broad stripes and bright stars, thro' the perilous fight. O'er the ramparts we watched, were so gallantly streaming? And the rockets red glare, the bombs bursting in air."

Rory continued through all four verses. The stadium was so quiet you could hear a pin drop. When he finished the stadium of sixty-thousand fans went crazy with applause for Rory. As the captains of both teams were coming out to the center for the coin toss, they stopped Rory and shook his hand. Once off the field Rory walked off to where Pitch was and Pitch gave him one big bear hug and told him his performance was great. As the game was getting under way, they walked to their seats with Ann, Tommy, and Nellie. Ann was crying her eyes out and the others were hugging their brother any place they could. As the game went on Don Reese came over to the family and told Ann that any time Rory wants to sing here, he can. At half time Terry Bowden the Director of Music at the university came over and praised Rory's performance. He told Rory that he hoped to see him at the university as a college music student when he was old enough. The only thing that went wrong all day was that the University of Wyoming Cowboys lost 36-17. Before leaving the stadium, Ann had to buy the kids a souvenir. Of course, Tommy got a kid's Cowboy football jersey. As they walked from the stadium to their parking space, they could hear people saying, "There is the young boy who sang the National Anthem."

By the time they got back to the hotel through all the traffic they all were drained and had no energy left. When Pitch asked them where they wanted to go for dinner they almost cried and Ann put her head under her pillow. Pitch could understand because he was tired and knew he had a long drive ahead of him tomorrow.

"I got a plan, there is a good restaurant about twenty-five blocks from here that we can walk to in about forty-five minutes."

They all looked at him like he was absolutely nuts and then threw their pillows at him. Ann looked at him, "Do we have to go, we are worn out from all the walking today?"

"I have a better restaurant and you will love it better then any one in this entire town."

"Okay, what is it called and how far away is it?'

Pitch looked at her and then the kids, "Room Service!"

They all jumped for joy and they all picked out what they wanted from the menu in the room. Then Pitch said here is the plan, "Ann you call our order in and it will take the kitchen about an hour to get the food here. While you do that, I will take the kids for a swim."

His plan worked great and even gave Ann time to take a shower. They just got back to the room from the pool when the food arrived at their room. They had French fries, buffalo wings, ribs, hot dogs, hamburgers, soda to drink and a chef salad for Ann. After their showers and with their bellies filled everybody but Pitch was asleep by nine-thirty. Pitch made sure the doors were all locked and laid down on his bed and started wondering about the future and how much he loved this family. Finally, he said to himself, "That's it Christmas day I am proposing to Ann and she will have to commit to me or reject me."

They left Laramie at nine o'clock Sunday morning. The kids slept about half of the way and they only heard a sound from them when it was lunch time. They pulled in at the ranch about four in the afternoon and the kids were ready to go play while Ann and Pitch were drained. The news of Rory's performance was all over Sheridan and Sid Walter had written an article about Rory performing at the football game. Ann started getting calls for Rory to sing at local Christmas events. Ann told him he needed to learn four or five Christmas songs which should not be too hard because he knew most of them back in New York. The Sheridan's Women's Association was having a Christmas party and they hired Rory to sing two carols for $200. Ann was having a hard time keeping track of where he was singing. Between the places Rory needed to be to sing, decorating the house for Christmas, shopping for presents, and the kids, Ann had her hands full. Rory quickly learned all the words and music to White Christmas, Silent Night, Rudolph the Red Nose Reindeer and Frosty the Snowman. With all of this going on Ann had not spent much time at night with Pitch, Tommy, and Nellie. When she finished her day, she had no energy left for a night walk down the hallway. She kept apologizing to Pitch and he would always say he understood and not for her to worry. However, Ann always made sure she kissed Pitch and hugged him every day. Late one night while they were talking about what he should get the kids for Christmas, out of nowhere, he grabbed her and kissed all over her body and it was passionate kisses. Then he looked in her eyes and said, "Ann, if you don't come to my bedroom soon, I am coming upstairs to your bedroom."

Ann calmly reached for his hand and they walked down the hallway together. It was a night filled with excitement, love and passion and Ann said to him, "I wish this could be every night. I love you so much."

Pitch had to go to town to take care of some business at his Coyote Night Club. Since he was in town already, he decided to do his Christmas shopping since the big day was just around the corner. He first went to Sears mainly because they had everything. In the toy department he got a nice baby carriage for Nellie to take her babies for a walk. Next, he went to the sports department and got Tommy a pair of cleats for lacrosse and luckily, he had checked Tommy's size at home. Then he went to the women's department and bought Ann some perfume, a beautiful red teddy, that he would give to her in private, and a going to church dress that would show off her figure. He didn't know what to give to Samoka and Nija because he had no idea what they needed so he bought a $500 gift card for them. When he was done at Sears, he walked down Main Street to the western store and bought Ann a pair of chaps. Next, he went to Stewards Music shop and bought Rory a two-sided harmonica that came in a green leather case. A little further down the block he spotted the sign for Geyer's Jewelry Store and decided to go look at rings. George Geyer had been good friends with old Mr. McClure for many years and George had gotten to know Pitch through him. George was happy to see Pitch and gave him a big hug. "What can I do for you Pitch?"

"I need to look at engagement rings."

"They are over here in the front show case. Is this for you? So, you have someone special in your life now?"

"I hope it is. These look very nice George but to be honest I have not lived in New York city for a while they look cheap."

"Well, Pitch I don't have many requests for expensive engagement rings because most of the people in Sheridan who are getting engaged are young and don't have a lot of money to spend on a ring."

"I understand George but I was looking for something that would knock her eye balls out."

"You stay here I have a beautiful ring in the back that I want to show you."

It did not take George long and he came back with a ring laying on a black velvet cloth. "Take a look at this beauty Pitch. I keep it in the back because it is very expensive."

Pitch looked the ring over closely. "Now, this is a ring George!"

The diamonds equal a ten karat. It has twenty small diamonds surrounding the big center eye catcher."

"George do you know or have a good guess at Ann McClure's ring size."

"From seeing her in church and shaking hands my expert eyes would say that her size is about a five. But that doesn't really matter because after you give it to her and if it does not fit, she can bring it in and I will size it for her. Do you want to know the cost of the ring before we go any further?"

"Sure, lay it on me."

"It cost $5,000 but I will give you a 10% discount so the cost to you is $4,500. If that is too much maybe we should look at ordering one?"

"That will take too long and I want to give it to her on Christmas. George, I am taking the ring. Put it in a fancy box for me and I will write you a check."

"She will love this ring."

"I just hope she takes it!"

As Christmas got closer on Saturday around one in the afternoon Sister Martin came driving down the McClure dusty entrance road. When she got out of the church's old station wagon Ann could not believe her eyes. Sister Martin had on jeans, a red cowboy girl shirt and cowboy boots with her long black hair hanging down over her shoulders. She was gorgeous looking with her copper skin color and her slim figure. Ann welcomed her and said, "This is a pleasant unexpected visit and by the way you look fabulous. We just finished lunch. How about some tea and a piece of Nija's apple pie?"

"That sounds wonderful Ann."

As they sat at the kitchen table Sister Martin told Ann why she came to the ranch. "Father Daniels sent me out here on a mission. Saint Joseph's would love to have Rory sing Silent Night at the Christmas Midnight Mass. I will be his accompaniment if he would let me use his Gibson guitar."

"You can play Silent Night on a guitar?"

"Ann, I can play anything on a guitar, even Beethoven. If he is willing to sing Father Daniels says we can put a sign out in front of the church to let people know he is singing and Father will announce it at mass on Sunday. We would love to fill the church for the midnight service. Usually, we only have about thirty people attending it."

"I really like the idea. We will have to see what Rory thinks? Samoka, please find Rory and tell him we need to talk with him, thank you."

"Ann, between you and me if Rory agrees to do this, I would like to record it on tape and send it to a friend of mine in the recording business. Would that be okay?"

"Sure, what could it hurt."

Just then Rory walked in and greeted Sister Martin and they told him about what Father Daniels wanted. Rory had no problem with doing it and said, "I can't wait to hear you play this on my guitar."

"Thank you, Rory, you will be helping the church out if this increases attendance."

Rory went back outside and when he saw Pitch, he went over to him. "Mr. Pitch, you need to go in the house right now and see Sister Martin. You will not believe your own eyes."

"What is it Rory?"

"Go see for yourself."

Pitch went straight into the house because he had no idea what Rory was talking about. When he saw Sister Martin, "Now, I see what Rory was talking about. You are a knock-out Sister Martin."

Ann yelled, "Pitch!"

"Well she is!"

"Thank you Pitch."

"Rory is going to sing at the Christmas Midnight Mass."

"That is great, I will tell everybody I know to make sure they come."

"Here is the other surprise, Sister Martin is going to accompaniment him on his guitar."

"There will be standing room only at the mass."

"Guess, what the song is? Silent Night! Can you believe Sister is going to play it on the guitar?"

"Yes, I believe it because I have heard her play Rory's guitar."

"Okay, you two that is enough! We haven't performed yet. Since the kids are out of school for the holidays, I think we should practice Monday, Tuesday and Wednesday and then we will be ready for the midnight service on Wednesday night. What time is good for you Ann?"

"How about three o'clock because we eat dinner at six?"

"How about two-thirty since I eat dinner at five?"

"That will work so that is our plan. You know Sister if you want, I can bring Rory to the convent to practice?'

"Ann if you don't mind, I would like to come out here in the fresh air and it reminds me of where I grew up. You know my Dad was a cowboy."

"Then it is settled here at two-thirty. You know Sister, you can have dinner with us"

"Maybe Tuesday evening but I have to check with Sister Mary first."

"Okay, whatever you want to do."

"I have to run now. I will see you in church tomorrow. Father Daniels will be so happy now that Rory is singing."

As Sister Martin drove down the dusty road, Pitch looked at Ann, "I am going to make sure that church is filled for the midnight mass."

Sunday morning, they all went to church and there was a big sign about Rory singing at midnight mass where everybody could see it. When Father Daniels did the church announcements during mass, he told the congregation that they don't want to miss Rory's singing. In the afternoon they went for their Sunday family horse ride to the north edge. Ann and the kids were becoming really good horse riders and Pitch was very proud of them. When they got to the ridge something looked funny to Pitch in a distance. "Let's take a ride over there, I need to look at the area a little closer."

When they got to the location Pitch was talking about, he saw an area that had been blasted. "It looks like the uranium diggers have been at it again. I'm not sure it is the same guys but this is getting out of hand. I will have to call Sheriff Douglas on Monday."

"Please Pitch, no trouble during the Christmas holidays."

"I agree with that Ann. It will have to wait."

Rory and Sister Martin practiced really hard and sounded wonderful. It was almost unbelievable hearing the guitar with Rory's singing of Silent Night. Sister told Ann that she had permission to have dinner at the ranch on Tuesday. Monday afternoon Rory and Nellie were watching Tommy practicing lacrosse. He was looking really good and in a couple months he would get his chance to play for a team in the village league. Nellie just happened to look down the ranch entrance road and somebody was walking towards the house. She pointed the person out to Rory and Tommy and they all walked over to see what the person wanted. It was a young boy and he looked terrible. His clothes were all raggedy and dirty and he had an old WWII knapsack on his back. As they greeted him, Rory figured he had to be about fifteen or sixteen tears old, was skinny to the bone, and looked like he was ready to fall on his face from exhaustion. "Can I help you? I am Rory McClure the ranch owner's son and this is my brother Tommy and my sister Nellie."

"It is nice to meet you all. I am Anthony Donovan from Virginia,"

"You are a long way from home."

"To be honest, I really don't have a home any more. Do you mind if I sit on the steps, I am really tired from the walk from your town?"

"You walked from Sheridan? Yes, Anthony, sit on the steps."

"You can just call me Tony."

"Okay, Tony, what are you doing out here?"

"I am looking for work and a nice lady in town, if I remember correctly her name was Mrs. Steward, told me I might find work out here."

Nellie go in the house and get Mom. Tell her about Tony showing up here."

Ann came out of the house immediately and as Tony stood up, he almost fell over."

"Please, sit down young man. I am Ann McClure the ranch owner. How can I help you?"

"Mrs. McClure, I need a job. I am all out of money and need money to support myself."

"Mom, Sharon Steward told him he might get a job out here."

"Yes, she was a very nice lady."

"Tony, when was the last time you had something to eat?"

"I think about three days ago Mrs. McClure."

"Where is your family?"

"They were all killed in a train accident outside of Richmond, Virginia so I have fended for myself."

"How old are you Tony?"

"I am fifteen years old Mrs. McClure, almost sixteen."

Ann had tons of questions she wanted to asked him but now was not the right time. Ann was thinking hard what to do for this poor soul. "The ranch manager who does all the hiring is out with the herd so you have to wait until he comes back to the ranch. However, in the meanwhile, Rory is going to take you to the bunk house to wait for the ranch boss. Tommy, you go tell Nija to prepared a plate of food for Tony and you bring it to the bunk house. Rory, you tell Reno to come see me immediately."

They all went their separate ways and Reno came to see Ann in about ten minutes. "Yes, Boss Lady, what do you need?"

"Reno, you see that young boy with Rory? I want you to get him some clothes from the bunk house closet, show him where the shower is and a bed where he can lay down. You stay with him because Rory has to practice. Make sure he eats before anything. Nija is preparing a plate of food for him and Tommy will bring it to you."

"I got it Boss Lady. But there is one problem. The clothes in the closet are for the wranglers and they will not fit that skinny boy very good."

"Find the smallest size you can and roll them up. Take your knife and put extra holes in a belt. Do the best you can Reno and throw his clothes away outside the bunk house because they smell."

"I will take care of it Boss Lady."

Ann was all upset by the situation this young boy was in and wanted to help him. She knew what it felt like to all of a sudden be on your own and have nobody to look out for you. Ann faced that shock when her husband was killed in the war. She had no idea what kind of job the ranch had for him, if any at all. It was obvious that he had no wrangler experience and probably never been on a horse. Maybe Pitch could come up with something but Tony really needed to be in high school and not working for a living. She decided to walk over to the bunk house to see how things were going. When she walked in, "Boss Lady, he is over there sleeping in the bed."

"Thank you, Reno."

"He ate all the food Nija sent over and he had a shower and I found the smallest clothes I could for him but they are still big on him."

"You did a good job, Reno. Now, we will just let him sleep."

When Ann looked at Tony in the bunk bed, he was skinny to the bone. He probably didn't even weigh a hundred pounds. She went back over to the house but could not get Tony off of her mind.

When Pitch returned to the ranch Reno told him the Boss Lady needed to see him immediately. Of course, he thought something was wrong so he hustled over to the house. Ann greeted him with a little kiss and told him all about the boy. Pitch had no idea what to do and said, "Ann, why in the world did Sharon send him out to the ranch. She knows all we have is wrangler type jobs and you said the kid was an easterner."

Pitch told her to let him think on it a while and talk to the boy when he wakes up. "I'll tell Kinno to keep an eye on him until we figure this out."

"Thanks, you are my darling, lover boy."

"You only talk like that when you want something!"

"So, do you, so do you!"

Pitch had to laugh.

When Sister Martin arrived to practice Ann told her all about the boy.

"Ann, I have no idea what to do but that young boy belongs in school."

While Rory and Sister Martin were practicing Tommy came in to see his Mom. Mom, can Tony have dinner with us this evening? He has nobody and he is out in the middle of nowhere."

"I guess that would be all right. I'll tell Nija we are having one more for dinner."

When Tommy left, he went over to the bunk house to see if Tony was up yet. He asked Kinno if he had any jobs that the new boy could do? "Tommy, to be honest, I don't think so but it is really up to Boss Pitch. If I were you, I would talk to him and see what he has to say."

Finally, Tony woke up and saw Tommy just sitting there looking at him. "Hi, buddy your name is Tommy, right?"

"It is really Warrior Tommy but you can just call me Tommy."

"Has the boss man come back yet so I can talk to him?"

"Mr. Pitch knows you are here and when he wants to talk to you, he will find you."

"Oh, he must be a mean boss?"

"No, just the opposite. He is a great man and cares about everybody. You will meet him this evening because Mom said you can have dinner with us."

"Is she a good cook?"

"Yes, but she is the boss lady and does not cook any more. Nija does all the cooking and she is a super cook."

"Tommy, why does that Indian over there keep watching me?"

"That is Kinno, he is the boss over all the wranglers and he is watching you because Mr. Pitch told him to keep an eye on you."

"I don't want to seem stupid but what is a wrangler?"

"They take care of the herd and work the ranch on horseback. Why did you come to Wyoming?"

"Is that where I am?"

"You don't even know where you are?"

"I jumped a lot of trains and just went where they were going as long as it was west."

"I would show you my horse Domino but I don't think Kinno will let you leave the bunk house. It's been nice talking to you Tony but I have to go practice lacrosse."

"You play lacrosse?"

"You know about lacrosse?"

"Yes, it is a big sport in Virginia and my older brother played it in high school."

"Where is your older brother?"

"He got killed in the war."

"When Mr. Pitch lets you walk around free you should come see me practice."

When dinner time came Mr. Pitch sent Rory out to get the new boy. When Tony walked in the house, he was looking all around the place. "This is really one beautiful house Mrs. McClure. How long have you lived here?"

"I think going on seven months but it seems like a lot longer. The ranch belonged to the family's uncle and when he died, he left it to me."

Mr. Pitch kept eyeing Tony up and down, while Tony kept looking at the great food on the table. He started to reach for a hot roll when Pitch informed him that Grace is said before they eat. When dinner was almost over Mr. Pitch started his cross-examination. "Why did you leave Virginia and come out west?"

"I thought I could come out here and find gold and be rich."

"Son, the gold rush was over many, many years ago. How old are you?"

"I will be sixteen on January 15th."

"Where is your family?"

"I don't have a family any more. My parents were killed in a train accident and my older brother was killed in the war. I have no relatives in the United States but I might have some in Ireland."

"Did you go to school in Virginia?"

"Yes sir, I was a freshman in high school and a straight A student. In fact sir, I loved school, especially math."

"Do you have any skills or anything you are good at doing?"

"Only math sir, but I am a real hard worker and a very faster learner."

Ann was sitting across from Pitch, almost in tears listening to his story. Pitch could tell Ann wanted him to help this young boy. "I'll tell you what Tony. Here is what we are going to do for now. You stay in the bunk house with the wranglers. Do you know what a wrangler is?"

"Yes sir, Tommy explained what they do."

"They have breakfast at seven o'clock in the morning and then leave for work. When they leave, you go help Rory and Tommy feed the chickens, pigs, horses and clean out the stables. You can have lunch with the kids and dinner with us until I figure this out. Do you follow me?"

"Yes, sir, and thank you very much."

"Tony, listen very carefully, do not cross me or do anything to hurt this family."

"I will only do what you say and I thank God for all your family has done for me."

"All right we are clear. Now, go to the bunk house and catch up on your sleep."

After the kids went upstairs Ann thanked Pitch and promised to reward him.

The next morning with three of them working together the boys were all done with their work by ten o'clock. Ann came out with Nellie to see how they were doing. Tony, kept pulling his pants up to keep them from falling off and he had the sleeves of his shirt rolled up because they were so long. He also had his own tennis shoes on and were falling apart. She said to herself, "That's it I can't take this any longer. Boys, go wash up, the five on us are going to town."

Ann drove straight to Sears parking lot. "Here is the plan, Nellie, Tommy and Rory here is a hundred dollars each for your Christmas shopping. Remember, you buy nothing for yourself! Rory you keep Nellie with you and Tony and I with catch up with you later. "Tony you are coming with me."

Ann went straight to the boy's department and started picking out clothes for Tony. He did whatever she said including trying things on and coming out of the dressing room to show her what the clothes looked like on him. When she was finished, she bought him two pairs of jeans, dress pants, two casual shirts, a dress shirt, cowboy boots, a hat, underwear, socks, and a belt with a big buckle. Tony couldn't believe she was buying all of this for him. "Why are you doing this Mrs. McClure?"

"Because if you are going to live on my ranch, I want you to look like a rancher." They walked around Sears and found the kids and they had just finished their shopping. "Rory quickly said, "Mom can we go to lunch?"

Ann looked at her watch and said, "Okay, but I have to find a phone to call Nija so she doesn't make lunch for us. They had a lot of fun at lunch and Tony fit right in with the other kids. They got home a little after two just in time for Rory's practice with Sister Martin.

Sister Martin stayed for dinner that evening and when Ann told her Tony's story her heart was broken for him. "Ann, God will bless you for taking this young boy in your home." Pitch stopped her right there, "Sister, we haven't taken him in as of now."

"I know you will do the right thing Pitch because you are a good man."

CHAPTER 7

C hristmas eve was finally here and the kids were excited about getting presents. Tony looked good in his new clothes that fit him but you could tell he was still a lost soul with no idea what was ahead of him. At dinner Pitch looked at him.

"What religion are you Tony?'

"My family went to a Presbyterian Church in Virginia so I guess that is what I am."

"Well, tonight you just became a Catholic."

"That is okay with me Mr. Pitch because God doesn't care what religion you are."

Ann's eyes watered up again. Pitch knew this boy had gotten to her heart and he really didn't know what to do with Tony going forward.

About eleven o'clock that night they all got in the Cadillac including Tony and made it to Saint Joseph's by twenty minutes after eleven. There were people everywhere and we were lucky that Sister Martin had reserved the front row for the McClure family. We quickly took our seats and the church filled up. Pitch turned to Ann, "I told you it would be standing room only."

The mass started and the organist played some beautiful Christmas music but everyone was waiting for Rory. According to the church bulletin Rory was scheduled to sing during the offertory part of the Mass. The bulletin also said that he was singing Silent Night/O Holy Night. We had no idea what that meant because we thought he was just singing Silent Night. During the announcements part Father Daniel mention Rory singing accompanied by Sister Martin on guitar. The offertory part finally got here and Father said a few things about giving to God and then Sister walked out in her nun habit carrying the Gibson guitar and sat on a stool as Rory followed her out to the microphone. Sister Martin played a beautiful introduction and the ushers dimmed the church lights. Rory started singing, "O holy night the stars are brightly shinning. It is the night of the dear Savior's birth." As they continued, they switched songs. "Silent night, holy night all is calm, all is bright, round yon Virgin mother and child. Holy infant so tender and mild sleep in heavenly peace. Long lay the world in sin and error pining. Till he appeared and the soul felt its worth." They kept going back and forth between the two songs. Their mixture of the songs was perfect and it gave everyone cold chills. It almost made you feel like you were there looking at Jesus in the manger. Ann was crying her eyes out and Tommy and Nellie were hugging each other. As they finished Rory said to the congregation, "Please join Sister Martin and me for one stanza of Silent Night." The entire church started singing with Rory. It was loud and very beautiful. When the song was finished the congregation stood up and applauded in appreciation. Father Daniel came over and hugged both Sister Martin and Rory. As Father finished the mass Pitch looked at Ann, "Are you okay?"

"Yes, I am just so proud to be Rory's mother."

As they were leaving the church Pitch shook hands with Father Daniel, "I bet your collection is the most this church has seen in a long time."

"Yes, I believe you are right and we thank you for your efforts to fill the church."

Pitch just smiled and walked to the car. As they waited for Rory, Tony said, "Who thought Rory to sing like that?"

Nellie looked at him, "Of course, God did!"

As Pitch was driving home from church the kids asked Ann if they could open presents when they got home because it was really Christmas since it was one-thirty in the morning. Ann firmly told them absolutely not and do not come down stairs until nine o'clock. The kids argued with her but it did no good. When they got to the house Tommy said, "Mom, since it is late can Tony sleep with me? My bed has plenty room for the two of us. Besides, he might wake up the wranglers if he has to go to the bunk house."

Nellie looked at him like he was crazy, "What wranglers Tommy, they were all in church."

Everybody had to laugh. "I think that will be fine Tommy. What is he going to do for pajamas?'

"Mom, he can sleep in my Dodger jersey since it is so big and long."

"That will work, just as long as the two of you go right to sleep."

After the kids went upstairs to bed, Pitch said to Ann, Let's get a drink and go sit on the patio and look at the stars. It's not too cold tonight and we can just stay out a little while."

"Okay Pitch, that might help relax me."

They went out and sat on the patio steps and Pitch held her in his arms and they kissed a few times. Then Ann said, "This has been one great day. Don't you think so?"

"Yes, I do and I hope it is going to get even better."

Then Pitch got down on his one knee and pulled out the ring box and opened it. "Ann McClure will you do me the honor of marrying me?"

With no hesitation Ann jumped him and they rolled together on the patio floor. "Yes, yes, a thousand yeses. I love you so much."

Pitch then put the ring on her finger. "Pitch, it is so beautiful. It must have cost you a lot of money?"

"Nothing but the best for my girl. Are you getting cold?"

No, in fact I am really hot! Really, really hot!"

"Would you like to go for a walk down the hallway with me?"

"I thought you would never ask!"

At seven o'clock in the morning Ann made it back to her bedroom. There was no Nija to see her come from the hallway because she had told Nija that breakfast would be at ten o'clock on Christmas morning. This gave Nija and Samoka time in the morning to spend with their family. It was nine o'clock on the dot when the kids came running down the steps with Ann behind them. Tony lagged behind and he washed up and got dressed and slowly walked down the steps to the front door to leave. Pitch was all dressed sitting in the kitchen drinking coffee when he saw Tommy at the front door. "Where do you think you are going? Get your skinny butt over here."

Tony pointed at himself, "Me?"

"Yes, you Mr. Donovan."

Tony quickly came over and took a seat to watch the kids open presents. Rory started putting presents from under the tree in front of each person. To Tony's surprise he had five presents sitting in front of him. "All of these presents are for me?"

"They have your name on them so they belong to you."

All of a sudden Nellie spotted Ann's ring and ran over to her. "Mommy, where did you get that beautiful diamond ring?"

"Last night Mr. Pitch asked me to marry him and this is the engagement ring he gave me."

The living room went nuts with all the kids jumping on Mom. They were hugging and kissing her all over."

"I take it with all this joy you are happy I said yes to Pitch's proposal?"

Rory responded for all of them, "Absolutely we are happy we couldn't believe it took this long. We know you both are in love."

Then all of them started asking questions like when are you getting married, are you going to have a big wedding, and if they could be in the wedding? Then Nellie turned to Mr. Pitch, "Can I call you Daddy now?"

Pitch almost had tears in his eyes. "Not yet Nellie but very soon."

She ran over and hugged Pitch and so did Tommy and Rory. Nija and Samoka were standing in the kitchen all smiles when they heard the good news. After all the emotion, it was time to get serious and open presents. Rory had each one take a turn opening one present and he would go from one person to the next. It was Tony's turn, "This is from Mr. Pitch." He quickly opened it and it was a work jacket for around the ranch. The next time it was his turn, "This is from Mrs. McClure." When he opened it everybody started laughing because it was a work jacket like Mr. Pitch give him. "Tony, we will take it back and get you a dress jacket for church and other times."

"Thank you, Mrs. McClure."

After all the presents were opened it was obvious everybody loved what they got. When Rory opened up his harmonica from Mr. Pitch, he could not put it down. He played with it a little and started playing Santa Claus is Coming to Town. Both Pitch and Ann walked over to Nija and Samoka and each handed them an envelope. When they opened them there were two gift certificates from Sears for $500 each. Ann and Pitch thanked them for all they do for the family. Nija was really tickled, "Now, I can get my new living room set from Sears."

"Maybe after I get my new hunting rifle," was Samoka's response to her. Pitch and Ann just laughed and wondered if they would be like that when they got old.

After breakfast the kids went to play with their new toys and games while Ann and Pitch still sat at the kitchen table drinking coffee. "Pitch what are we going to do about Tony?"

"I don't know Ann. The boy has really had a hard time and if he leaves here and keeps jumping trains some drifter is going to beat the shit out of him and take everything he has and more likely leave him to die. What do you want to do?"

"I really would like to keep him with us and make him part of the family."

"I knew that. Do you remember when I told you I wanted four kids?"

"Oh yea, I remember because I could not see me pregnant at my age."

"Well, I think the Dear Lord has sent us our fourth kid."

"That is why I love you so much."

"No, it's because you always get your way."

"Yea, but I do reward you!"

They both started laughing and the kids looked over to see what was so funny.

"Later, you and I need to sit down and figure out what we need to do."

About a half hour later Tony said, "I guess I should go to the bunk house? Thank you all for my presents, I only wish I had something for you."

"You stay right where you are Tony you are spending the entire day with us"

Pitch went out on the patio to smoke one of the cigars Rory bought for him. His mind was working over-time on the Tony situation. He thought many different things and finally came up with one he liked. "Ann, can you come out here, I need to talk to you in private?"

Ann came right out and they discussed Pitch's solution. He could tell Ann was tickled with it. "Ann called Tommy to come out on the patio. "Tommy we are trying to help Tony out and we were wondering if you would mind if Tony stayed with you in your room? Once your Mom and I are married he can have my room for his?"

"That is great with me. I love having a buddy at night. Is he going to be part of the family?"

"We are working on it but not yet. Don't say anything to the others when you go inside."

Ann and Pitch talked some more and finally went back inside.

When they came in, they sat in the living room where the kids were. "All right everybody listen up and Tony you come over here by Ann and me. Tony, this is what Ann and I have decided to do concerning you. First, you will move out of the bunk house into Tommy's room and he is happy to have a buddy. You will do everything with the family. I will take you one day to register you for high school. The school bus for Sheridan High School will pick you up in front of our entrance. You will continue to help Rory and Tommy with their jobs. On Saturday Dinja will drive you to a business I own and you will work for Stoney Mason until noon. Tony, you need to get your education. That is it for now. Are you okay with this plan?"

Tony started crying and Ann when over and hugged him. "You people are so good to me. I don't know what to say."

The kids yelled, "Say yes!"

"Yes, and many thanks."

Rory and Tommy helped Tony move his clothes and other things from the bunk house to Tommy's room. "You know Ann, I could just move in with you and Tony could have my room now."

"It is like this Pitch. This ring does not buy you that privilege it is the other little gold one that does the trick."

"Well, we better get on those wedding plans immediately!"

Sister Martin played the tape of Rory and her performance over and over. She wanted to send it to her friend David Sarnoff who was now the president of RCA records. Sister was not sure he would even remember her from her professional days. She made another copy of the tape and decided to send the tape to David figuring she had nothing to lose. However, she decided that she would sign the little note with the tape Sister Martin/ Sylvia Reynolds. She knew he was aware that she became a nun but didn't want to take any chances. Sister packed the tape up with the note and took it to the post office. She knew the odds of him actually getting the tape were very slim and if he did get it she was not sure what he would do. All she could do now was pray.

Pitch took Tony in to meet Stoney Mason at the Coyote Night Club. Stoney knew they were coming because Pitch called him and told him what was up. When Stoney met Tony, he asked him what he could do? "Whatever you need to do Mr. Stoney."

"Pitch says you are good with numbers?"

"Yes, sir, I love math."

"Here is what we are going to do. You work with the girls to help them clean this place up from the night before and the last hour you work with me in the office. I will start teaching you how the books are kept and how to run this business. I will only keep doing this if you have the skills for accounting. Are you agreeable?"

"Yes, sir, that sounds good to me."

"For the four hours you work here I will pay you $10."

At that point Pitch said, "It looks like we are set. He will start next Saturday Stoney."

Pitch's next job was to get Tony in Sheridan High School. He knew that registering Tony would be a tricky situation because he had no previous school records and no birth certificate. Luckily, he knew the principal of the school Don Lark really good from playing poker with him many years. Pitch made a call to Don and told him the issues Dan told Pitch not to worry he would talk to the registration clerk Mrs. Arnold and she would get Tony registered. The next morning Pitch took Tony over to Sheridan High School to get him registered. When they arrived, they were greeted by Mrs. Arnold even though school was closed for the holidays. She knew Tony's situation and told him to sit down at a desk and take the test she handed to him. The test took about a half hour and then Mrs. Arnold evaluated Tony's answers. She informed Pitch the test was designed to tell what grade a student should be in by their knowledge. "Mr. Pitch the test shows by Tony's answers that he should be in the ninth grade or possibly the tenth. So, I will register him for the Fall semester in the ninth grade."

When they filled out all the paperwork, Pitch used the McClure ranch as his address and Ann McClure as his guardian. Mrs. Arnold took the paperwork, "You are all set, Tony. The classes start back up on January 5th at nine o'clock. You will be in Mrs. Melany homeroom on the second floor. She will know you are a new student and will assign one of her students to show you around until you get used to the school."

Pitch thanked her and they were out the door headed back to the ranch. During the ride Pitch looked at Tony, "You better do really good and make Mrs. McClure proud of you."

"Don't worry Mr. Pitch, I will."

The Sheridan Women's Association was having a New Year's Eve Party and Ann was the head of the decoration committee.

This was just a suit and tie for the men and Sunday dress affair, no black-tie. Sharon Steward the president of the association was working with Ann on the decorations. When Sharon saw Ann's ring, she could not believe the size of it. Of Course, she wanted to know how Pitch proposed so Ann had to tell her. She laughed when Ann told her she actually jumped him. While they were putting up the decorations Sharon causally said, "How is that boy Tony Donovan doing Ann?"

"Why did you send him out to the ranch?"

"Because I knew you had a warm heart and would give the boy the help he really needed."

As they decorated every now and then one of the ladies would come over and chit-chat with Ann for a while. It was lady after lady and Ann thought it was a little out of the normal but didn't say a word. When the hall was decorated completely it looked great and Sharon announced that Ann was responsible for the planning and design. All of the women applauded.

"Sharon it wasn't just me!"

"You were in charge of the committee."

Ann had this funny feeling something was going on but she couldn't figure it out. Then she thought it was probably just my imagination.

New Year's Eve was here and Pitch told Dinja just to bring the Cadillac around front and he would drive them. When Ann came down stairs, she had on a pretty navy-blue dress with navy high heels and the way the dress fit around her body made her looked sexy. When Pitch saw her, he wanted to skip the party and go right down the hallway now. When they arrived, the place was packed already but Sharon had reserved a place for them at her table. The affair had an open-bar so Pitch went to get Ann and him a drink. The band started playing dancing music and Ann was ready to kick-up her heels. Throughout the evening women with their husbands or boyfriend kept coming over to talk to Ann. Pitch looked at her, "You are very popular tonight!"

"Pitch, some of these women I don't even know but they seem to know me?"

"It is probably because you are the most beautiful women here."

"Sure, Pitch, sure!"

As it got closer to midnight Sharon as president of the association got up and made a few announcements about the charity the money from the event was going to and then she said, "We all need to thank Ann McClure for the beautiful decorations." The entire hall of people stood up and applauded for Ann. When Pitch turned and looked at Ann, she had a big question mark on her face. "You must be their hero Ann?"

"Oh, give me a break Pitch. Something is going on and I don't know what it is."

The clock was getting close to midnight. The countdown started 3, 2, 1, Happy New Years. Everyone was kissing and hugging and they all wished for a great 1951. By the time they got home it was two o'clock in the morning and they both were bushed so they both agreed no hallway tonight and went straight to bed.

They all went to church on Sunday and when it came time to go for their afternoon horse ride, they didn't know what to do about Tony. "Pitch we can't leave him behind!"

"What do you want me to do?"

Pitch thought about it while he had a cup of black coffee. He got up and made a phone call to somebody. Pitch went outside for something and about twenty minutes later he came back in the house. "All right cowboys and girls let's go saddle up the horses. Rory and Reno had made a pulley lift that hung from the top of the rafters and centered in the middle of the exit. With the pulley Rory could bring his horse to the middle and put the saddle on the lift and then pull it up on to the horse's back. Pitch thought this was fabulous because Rory could saddle and unsaddle a horse without the help of an adult. "Come on Tommy and Nellie I will help you saddle your horses. "Mom, what about Tony?"

Mr. Pitch jumped in, "Don't worry about Tony he goes with me." The kids and Ann went out to saddle their horses. "It's time to go Tony, wait a minute. Go upstairs and get your hat."

"Yes, Mr. Pitch."

Tony came running down the steps and the two of them went straight to the stables. Pitch told Rory to get Thunder out with his horse and Pitch brought out Pale Face which was Kinno's horse. The kids and Ann looked at Pitch like he was crazy. "Tommy, show Tony how to get up on his horse the right way and a quick lesson on what the reins do."

They all mounted their horses. "Tony will ride with me."

"Pitch are you sure about this? He has never been on a horse in his life, let alone to go for a ride."

"Rory you lead and Tommy and Nellie you stay with Rory. We are going to the east side of the ranch Rory."

"I got it, Mr. Pitch."

"Make sure you stay ahead of us I don't want to spook Pale Face."

They all started to trot their horses to the open range when Mr. Pitch said something in Shoshone and Kinno's horse started trotting. Ann kept looking at Tony up on Pale Face. Then Mr. Pitch said something else in Shoshone and Pale Face slowed down to a walk. Pitch looked at Tony, "How are you doing cowboy?"

"Really good sir, I love this and can't wait to ride like the other kids."

"Don't worry, they were like you when they started, it just takes time."

Ann looked at Pitch, "Let me see if I have this figured out right. You asked Kinno if Tony could ride his horse Pale Face. Because the horse only listens and responds to Shoshone commands. You speak Shoshone so you are the only one that controls Pale Face."

"I knew I was marrying a genius!"

"Well, thank you Love."

As they were riding Pitch was looking for any signs of uranium mining. Rory yelled, "Over here Mr. Pitch. It looks like they have been blasting again."

When Pitch looked at the area, Rory you are right."

Pitch knew he had to stop this because now it was getting bad. "Ann, remind me to call Sheriff Douglas tomorrow."

They came back to the ranch after about a three-hour ride. They immediately took care of their horses and when they were walking up to the house Tony was walking a little bowl-legged. Pitch pointed it out to Ann and she smiled. "Tony, After you shower for dinner, I have some salve you can put on the inside of your thighs to help the pain. Once you really learn how to ride you will not have that problem."

"Thank you, Mrs. McClure because it does not feel very good right now."

It was Monday and school was back in session. Pitch told Tony he would take him to school because he had to go see Sheriff Douglas anyway. Pitch could tell as they rode in the truck that Tony was really nervous. "Tony, you will be all right don't worry about it. Just think of all the things you did and have been through. None of these high school kids have experienced what you have in life. Your skin is tough."

"You are right Mr. Pitch, thank you, this is a piece of cake!"

Pitch dropped Tony at the school's front door. He yelled at Tony as he walked away from the truck, "Second floor, Mrs. Melaney's homeroom class. If you can't find it ask somebody."

Tony waved to him as he walked in the front door.

Tony found Mrs. Melaney's classroom without any problem. When he walked in she was standing in front of the class. Mrs. Melaney saw him, "You must be Anthony Donovan, come up here. I am Mrs. Melaney your homeroom and math teacher. Mrs. Melaney was about thirty years old, very tall, with blonde hair, and by the way she talked you could tell she was from the east coast. She told him to take a seat in the front. When the bell rang, the class said the Pledge of Allegiance to the flag and a student read a verse from the Bible. She introduced Tony to the class and told them to help him get around and that he was from the McClure ranch. Then she called this young Indian girl to the front of the class. "Anthony, this is Maomi Warki she will take you to all your classes and help you out for a little while."

"You can just call me Tony. Nice to meet you Momi."

"It is Maomi and it is nice to meet you Tony."

The bell rang again and it was the signal to go to your first class of the day. Maomi was very nice and also very pretty. You could tell she was very proud of being an Indian because some of her clothes were Indian attire. As they walked to each of the classes, they questioned each other about their background. Maomi couldn't believe all that Tony had been though for such a young boy. She told him she was Shoshone and that many of her relatives work on the McClure ranch. The entire day went by fast. Maomi introduced him to many students. At the end of the day as they were walking out of the building Tony looked at her, "Do you have a boyfriend?"

Maomi just smiled at him and went on her way. Dinja was blowing the horn for Tony and when Tony saw him, he jumped in the truck and Dinja took off for the ranch.

That evening at dinner everybody wanted to know about Tony's first day in high school. He told them everybody was nice and he liked Mrs. Melaney who was his homeroom and math teacher. He told them he had no problem with his classes and he projected he would get all A's.

"Oh yea, there is this nice girl who is taking me to all my classes until I get to know the school better. She is an Indian and her name is Maomi Warki."

Pitch looked at Ann with a surprised facial expression. "Is something wrong?"

"Do you know who Maomi Warki is?"

"No, I have a hard time with the different Indian names."

"She is Chief Warki's youngest daughter."

"You mean the Chief of the Shoshone tribe?"

"Absolutely, I think she is about sixteen. You better not mess around with her Tony or the chief will have you scalped."

Tony looked at Pitch with concern. Tony he is only kidding you. The Indians don't do scalping anymore."

"Thank you, Mrs. McClure, I was worried for a while because I really like her."

Nellie, could not miss this opportunity, "Tony's got a girlfriend!"

Since Pitch missed the Sheriff yesterday, he went back today knowing he was in his office. Pitch told Sheriff Douglas about the two blasted areas on Ann's ranch.

"Pitch, this is getting out of control and I need to put an end to this. "You are right Dan but we have to catch them at it."

"We had no luck in finding where these free-loaders live but one of my deputies did find out something interesting. Curly took a shot in the dark and went to the surveyor's office to see if anybody was looking at properties. He found out that the only person was our own Mayor Gallon."

"I told you he is connected with this some way."

"What do you think our next move should be Pitch?"

"I think our best chance of finding these guys is to follow the mayor. Why don't you put a stake-out on the mayor? That's if you have enough deputies to do it. It may take a week or so but I believe the mayor is going to meet with them to tell them where to blast next."

"I like that idea and my deputies need something to do anyway. I will call you if they come up with anything."

"Okay, I'll see you later Dan."

Ann went to her next Sheridan Women's Association meeting. Once again, all the women were patting her on the back and chit-chatting with her. When Sharon Steward called the meeting to order she went over general business and then said, "This is an important time for Sheridan. It is our responsibility to do what is right for our city. In two months, our territory will be electing a new mayor and we need to get Mayor Gallon out of office. To do this we need a good, smart, dedicated, and strong candidate. As president of this association I would like to recommend to you that we back, support, and nominate Ann McClure as our candidate."

The place went crazy with all the women standing up, applauding and chanting Ann. Ann, Ann, Ann for mayor!"

Ann's face turned bright red and her mouth was wide open as she just sat there in her chair. She had no idea what to do as they kept chanting. "Ann, come on up here"

Sharon kept calling her and Ann was shaking her head no, no. Finally, several ladies grabbed Ann by her arms and walked her up to the front where Sharon was. Sharon and the entire association actually forced her to speak. "I am honored that you all want me to run for mayor. I really don't know what to say at this time mainly because this surprised me. I wish I could tell you yes but I have to talk this over with my family and fiancé'."

"Come on Ann with Pitch's support behind you, you can't lose," was the comment from someone in the group. "I will talk this over with them and give you my answer in a couple days."

They all started cheering again and began yelling "Ann for Mayor."

After the patting on the back by association members they settled down and Ann went to talk to Sharon.

"Sharon why did you put me in this position?"

"For a number of reasons. First, you can win, second your kids are all in school and you have the time to do a great job. You are very tough and will straighten this town out for the good and won't take shit from anybody."

"I don't know anything about being a mayor?"

"You will learn as you go along and you will have a staff that will do most of the work for you. Ann, the bottom line is, do you want all your children to grow up in a city under Mayor Gallon for another eight years."

"No, but can't somebody else run against him?"

"Ann, the last election nobody ran against him and he got the office by default. We want you to ran because you will do what is right for the city. Pitch is totally loyal to you and he will support every move you make."

"If I am reading between the lines you all figure it is Pitch and me running for mayor and you wouldn't want me to run if I didn't have Pitch?"

"See, I told you that you are one smart cookie."

"Why don't you run?"

"I have two small children who are not in school yet, plus I need to help Bob with our store. I keep the books and pay the bills. Without me, I think the store would go under."

"I understand now, but there is nobody else in this town who could run?"

"Most people fear Mayor Gallon and all the crooks he has working for him. We believe Pitch as your husband will not let anybody mess with you."

"All I can say right now is that I am surprised, confused, and not sure what to do. I definitely will have to talk to Pitch and the kids. What they decide is what I will do, one way or the other."

"That is fair enough Ann."

As Ann drove back to the ranch her head was spinning. When she got in the house, Nija asked her if she was all right. "I think I will go lay down for a little while, Nija. I am just tired from that long association meeting."

Ann laid on her bed but kept thinking how she should handle this mayor situation with the kids and Pitch. The conclusion she came to was that she needed to talk to Pitch first see what he thought she should do. The kids would go along with whatever Pitch and she wanted to do. She could not turn her brain off to even get a little nap. She needed to decide how to approach Pitch. She knew if she really wanted to do this, he would back her because he loves me so much. However, she didn't want his approval that way. She wanted his approval because he thought she could do a good job and would help the city. Once she decided on that she fell asleep for a short nap.

When dinner time came Ann did not say a word about running for mayor. The kids talked about school and Pitch about getting part of the herd ready to go to the meat dealer auction that was coming up. Ann was very silent as they ate and Nija was keeping an eye on her. Pitch also noticed her silence, "Are you okay Ann?"

"I am fine. When you are done eating can I talk to you out on the patio?"

"Absolutely, just give me a couple minutes."

When they went outside, "Pitch, I have something very serious to talk to you about and please don't get mad at me."

"Our wedding plans!"

"No, but we do need to start working on them. I am almost afraid to talk to you about this."

"Ann, I love you and whatever you have to say will not change that so shoot."

"The women's association I am in want me to run for mayor against Gallon."

"Hallelujah! This is great news. Are you going to do it?"

"I have not committed yet. I wanted to talk to you first."

"I think it is a fabulous idea. We need to get Gallon out of office and you can do it."

"You have no protest or argument against me doing this?"

"Do you really want to do this?"

"The more I think about it the more I do."

"Ann, what you went through in New York with your husband being killed and having to raise three kids by yourself has made you a very strong, determined, tough woman. For my comparison only, Lady you have a big set of balls!"

Ann had to laugh at his comparison. Pitch hugged her and said, "Let's do it! Remember, you told me I was your muscle so just let anybody shit with you."

"God, I love you so much Pitch."

"Let's go tell the kids I know they will be jumping all over the place."

The next morning Ann called Sharon and told her the good news. Sharon was tickled to death with Ann's decision. "Okay, Ann, now we have to get your campaign committee together and develop our winning plan. Then we need to announce that you are running for mayor. I will head up the committee and recruit the members we want on it. I have one suggestion that will really help us. Pitch is real good buddies with Sid Walter of our newspaper. Tell Pitch to get him to write an article about you and why you should be our next mayor. That will shock the shit out of Mayor Gallon "

"I'll see if Pitch will do it."

Sid's article came out in the Sunday newspaper and the headlines read, "Ann McClure the Future of Sheridan." It said Ann was a strong business woman, a family woman, and a good Christian. Sharon was excited about the article and had her committee put up posters all over town. Everywhere you looked you saw Ann's pretty face. Sharon had arranged for Ann to talk at various organizations and businesses. Pitch had Stoney put posters all over the Coyote and announced that if Ann won the election it would be free beer all night. It was obvious that Mayor Gallon knew he was in trouble and he tried a dirty campaign against Ann. Pitch felt like punching Gallon's eyes out. Pitch also knew that Gallon would try something with the voting machines to make him win. When he talked to Sheriff Douglas about this Dan said he would do two things. Since this would be the first time the voters would be using the voting machines, he would check with the manufacturer to see if there were ways to cheat. The second thing was that his deputies would monitor the voting on election day. It looked like everything was under control.

Pitch reminded Ann that January 15th was Tony's sixteenth birthday. Ann decided to have a party for him and went to the high school to talk to Mrs. Melaney. She explained that she wanted to have a birthday party for Tony's but he had very few friends and thought she could get his classmates to come.

Mrs. Melaney said she would tell the kids to come to the party and give a list of the student's names so she could send them an invitation to the party. Ann hired a party company to take care of everything. When Tony's birthday came on Friday nobody at the house said a word to him, not even a Happy Birthday. They all made like they didn't know it was his birthday. When Tony came home from working at the Coyote in the morning on Saturday, Ann immediately told him to go clean up because they had to go somewhere. Since Tony would never question Ann he ran upstairs and was back in ten minutes. Ann told him she wanted to show him something on the patio and when he walked out everybody yelled, "Surprise and Happy Birthday."

Tony thanked all his new friends for coming and went over and hugged Ann. The entire afternoon the kids ate and played games and Tony opened presents. It was a great party and when the kids left, they thanked Tony for inviting them. After they all were gone Pitch walked over to Tony, "Hey cowboy, Ann and I have two more presents for you."

"Pitch, the party was enough. I had never had a birthday party in my life until today."

The family all stood around Tony. Pitch handed Tony a little card of some type. "What is this, Mr. Pitch?"

"It is an insurance card to allow you to drive in the state of Wyoming. I will take you to the Department of Motor Vehicles to get your learner's permit and Ann will teach you how to drive."

Tony was so excited he was hugging everybody. "We are not finished, we have one more present." Then Pitch whistled and Kinno came from around the corner leading a horse. "Tony, here is your own horse. His name is Outlaw."

Tony started crying and Ann had to hold him up from falling. "Come over here and say hello to Outlaw."

Tony went over and started kissing the horse's face. Tony told the family this day was the greatest day in his life,

Sister Martin kept checking the mail every day hoping to hear from David Sarnoff. A couple more weeks passed by without any response and she was upset. Sister decided to call RCA headquarters to see if she could reach David. She got the corporate operator and told her she needed to talk to David Sarnoff. The operator explained to her that she had strict instructions on forwarding calls to the president's office. Sister Martin said, "Please don't hang-up I am a nun and was a good friend of David's and I need to talk to him badly."

"Sister, I feel sorry for you but I could get in trouble. Wait a minute, I will forward you to his secretary Mrs. Royal she is not the president. Here goes Sister I hope she answers the phone."

"Hello, this is Mrs. Royal, Mr. Sanoff's secretary, can I help you?"

"This is Sister Martin, please don't hang-up. I am an old friend of David's. Before I became a nun, name was Sylvia Reynolds."

Before Sister Martin could finish the secretary cut back in, "Sylvia this is Jane Orr.

You remember me?"

"Yes Jane!"

"Royal is my married name. It has been a long time back when David was just the general manager."

"Jane, I sent David a tape of a boy singer and haven't heard back from him."

"He has been over in Europe opening a new operation for RCA. After that he is going on vacation with his family. I don't expect him back for a month, perhaps a little shorter. I'll tell you what Sylvia, oh I'm sorry Sister Martin. The mail room has been holding some of David's mail. I will contact them to see if there is a package from you. If they find it I will personally put it on his desk with a note from me. What is your phone number in case he wants to call you?"

"God bless you Jane. I really appreciate all your help."

Sister Martin, I know this boy must be really good for you to call David."

"He is Jane, thank you again."

After the call Sister Martin felt much better and she knew the wheels were turning now. She only hoped that Jane locates the tape and that David listens to it. She decided to pray more.

CHAPTER 8

Ann's campaign for mayor was going strong and surprisingly she had very little work to do herself, the committee did most of it. Ann did go to various organizations and businesses to give short speeches. Most of the time she would use the same speech because she thought it was great. Her committee developed a slogan for her campaign, "Honestly Starts with the Mayor's Office." Since she had time on her hands in between speeches she decided to start planning for the wedding. She picked the date of July 18th and would run it by Pitch but didn't think he would have a problem. Next, she called Father Daniel to make sure that Saturday July 18th at one o'clock was good on his calendar. Once the church was taken care of, she called the catering company. They were fine with the date but they wanted her to come in and pick out the menu. She talked to Nija to see if the village ladies who had a little flower business wanted to provide the flowers for the wedding. As for chauffer she decided that since Tony had got his license, he could be their driver in the Cadillac. Now, came the hard part, who would be in the wedding? Of course, Nellie would be her flower girl and Tommy could be the ring bearer. From that point her and Pitch needed three people each to fill out the wedding party. She thought it would not be hard for Pitch because Rory would be one of his ushers. However, it would be a different story for her. She went over what she should do while laying in his arms in bed. He kissed her over and over. "See, this is why you would make a good mayor, you get things done."

It was getting close to the election and Mayor Gallon knew he was going to lose and be out of office. Late one night he left his house. Curly who was steaking out the mayor's house thought this might be the break they were looking for. He followed the mayor out of town and through the north valley. It was hard for Curly to see because he didn't have his headlights on because he thought they would alert the mayor that somebody was following him. Curly saw an old miners cabin sitting on the ridge and the lights were on inside. The mayor parked his car in front and went inside. Curly had what he needed so he turned around and went back to town. Since it was only eight o'clock, he called Sheriff Douglas at home and told him the mayor and was at the miner's cabin. The sheriff told him not to tell anybody and he would see him in the morning to hear all the details. When Curly came in the next day at noon because he had worked late, he told the sheriff everything. They took a ride out to the cabin and the old truck that was in front of the cabin last night was gone. With caution Curly and Dan walked up to the cabin with their guns drawn. Dan called out to the cabin, "This is Sheriff Douglas, come out with your hands up."

After calling several times they slowly approached the door of the cabin. When they finally went in there was nobody there but the stove was still hot. After looking around for any clues that might tell them where the free-loaders went they decided to leave. As they were riding back to town Curly said, "I bet the mayor told them of a new place to blast last night."

"I think you are right."

"Are you going to tell Pitch about the cabin?"

"I don't think so Curly, at least not yet. The election is a week away and he needs to keep his focus on helping Ann so we can get this ass hole mayor out of office."

"I got another idea Sheriff, "I can go back and talk to the surveyor office manager to see if he noticed the mayor paying special attention to any particular area. If I get lucky again maybe we can run them down before they start blasting."

As the election drew near Ann was getting nervous so Pitch decided to take her for a canoe ride on the lake. This was another new experience for Ann but she loved the peace and quiet. She told Pitch more about the wedding plans and they both needed to determine the other three people for him and her. Ann said, "To be honest I don't have three close friends. You know the buddy type."

"I got an idea let's just make it two people each, nothing says it has to be three. My suggestion would be that Nija be your maid of honor because she has been like a big sister to you and Sharon as your bride's maid. I will have Kinno as my best man and Rory as my usher. What do you think?"

"I like it, let's do that and we will be done."

"We are done!"

After the canoe ride, they went to see how things were going. Sharon quickly cornered them, "We may have a problem. The ranches around here carry a lot of votes and we are not sure how they are voting."

Pitch responded, "That is all taken care of Sharon. Dick Boone and I had a meeting with the owners and they all want Gallon out of office. My take is Ann will get the majority of the votes from the ranches."

"Now I know why Ann loves you so much!"

"Sharon, one more thing. Ann has a question for you."

Ann looked at Pitch like he was crazy. "The wedding, remember?"

Then it hit Ann, "Sharon would you please be a bride's maid in our wedding?"

"I thought you would neve asked. Absolutely Mayor and they hugged.

When they got home, Pitch looked at Ann. "Okay, I will go talk to Nija and you go talk to Kinno when he gets in from the herd."

Ann went into the house and Nija was mopping the kitchen floor. Nija was about forty years old but still very beautiful with her long black Indian hair. "Nija, come over here and sit down with me."

That put a big question in Nija's mind and she thought she was in trouble. "Yes, Mrs. McClure, what can I do for you?"

"Just relax this is something good, you are not in trouble. Since I came to the McClure ranch you have been like an older sister to me. You take care of my family, give me advice and you keep secrets between us. I honestly love you and consider you and Samoka part of my family. So, what I am going to ask you is out of love for you. I want you to be my maid of honor in my wedding party?"

Nija just looked at Ann in shock and a few tears fell from her eyes. "Mrs. McClure, I am not sure what to say."

"By the way Nija I want you an Samoka to start calling me Ann. I actually hate being called Mrs. McClure or Boss Lady."

"I am not sure about being a maid of honor. I would be the only Shoshone in your wedding party."

"That is not true, Kinno is going to be Pitch's best man, Rory is his usher, Nellie is my flower girl, Tommy is the ring bearer, Tony is going to our chauffer and the only person you don't know is Sharon Steward who will be a bride's maid. Plus, you don't have to do anything on the wedding day but look pretty and enjoy yourself. So, will you do this for me?"

"Yes Mrs. McClure, I mean Ann."

They hugged and Ann kissed her on the cheek.

Pitch asked Kinno and Rory to be in the wedding and both said yes. Rory was tickled that he got to have an adult role. Ann took care of Nellie and Tommy so the wedding party was all set.

It was the Saturday before the election on Tuesday and it was Tommy's first lacrosse game in the village lacrosse league. His teams name was Tomahawks. Pitch had been funding the league for years and the only person that knew this was Chief Warki because had to to give the money to Dinja for equipment and uniforms. Nobody questioned the Chief as to where the money came from. There were about one hundred people at the game, most of them Shoshone. Tommy looked funny out on the field because he was white and all the other players were Shoshone. When the game started Tommy's team got the face-off and they passed it to Tommy behind the goal. Tommy quickly made a move and ran around the left side and shot at the right corner of the goal for a score. The whole family cheered and Ann hugged Pitch. "Ann, Tommy is really good. Dinja did a great jog training him. The game ended with Tommy's team winning 12-7 and Tommy had five goals. After the game Pitch took everybody, the whole team, for hot dogs and milk shakes. He must have had ten kids in his Cadillac. Ann thanked Dinja for the great job he did with helping Tommy. "He has a long way to go Mrs. McClure but Tommy has the desire to be great. I am sure he will break all my scoring records when he gets to Sheridan High School."

Election day was here and people came out early to vote. Sheriff Douglas had positioned two of his deputies by the voting machines to make sure everything was legal. When Ann and Pitch came to vote the Sheridan Prairie Newspaper took pictures of them at the voting machine. When Mayor Gallon and his wife came to vote all the people in line to vote started booing him. Since the voting was open until seven o'clock Ann had a long wait to see if she had won. About five o'clock with most of the votes in and Ann far ahead Mayor Gallon conceded to Ann. When her campaign team heard the news, the place went nuts with everybody yelling and screaming "We won, we won, we won!"

Pitch looked at Ann, "Can I have the first kiss from Mayor McClure?'

Ann jumped him with her legs around his waist. "I can't believe I did it Pitch! Who would have thought eight months ago in New York that I would be the mayor of a city with over 12,000 people living in it."

"I am really proud of you and know you will be good for this city."

Not to forget his promise, Pitch called Stoney and told him free beer until closing.

"Boss, tell Ann congratulations from me and Sophie. We voted for her. "Pitch wanted to take Ann for a great quiet dinner at a nice restaurant but the four kids put on their Mayor McClure tee-shirts and insisted on going to Dairy Queen. By the time they got home Ann was totally exhausted but really wanted Pitch badly. After she showered, she came back down stairs and went to Pitch's room. He was just finishing up in his bathroom and said, "Ann, go lay on the bed I will be in shortly." When Pitch walked over to the bed Ann was sound asleep. He moved her over a little and jumped in beside her and fell asleep with Ann in his arms. He quietly said, "Dam, I love this woman!"

Since there was a transition period of fifteen days before Ann actually took office, she had to deal with Mayor Gallon and his staff. Knowing Mayor Gallon was basically a crook Ann went to see John Riggins her financial advisor. His advice to her was to have his firm do an audit of the city's books to see if everything was done properly. Ann, under regulation A51 you have the right to an audit before taking office."

"Thank you for letting me know that and when can your firm start the audit?"

"We can start tomorrow because things a little are slow around here. Plus, you want to know the results before Gallon leaves office. Ann, you need to understand that we can not have the mayors staff getting in our way.""I will take care of that as soon as I leave your office today."

Ann wasted no time, she had two stops to make and the first one was the most important. She went straight to the office of the City's Financial Controller, Fred Johnson. Lucky for Ann,

Fred was in his office but the mayor was out of his office. This made the timing ideal for the conversation she needed to have with Fred Johnson. Ann greeted him cordially, and he said, "Can I help you Mayor elect McClure," which implied she was not his boss yet. "As a matter of fact, you can. Fred, I know you are a good family man and a good Christian. I am willing to bet that you want to keep your job going forward?"

"Yes, I do Mayor McClure," which was a sudden change of attitude. "If I don't keep this job, I will have to pack my family up and move to where I can get a job."

"Here is my thought Fred. I think you are an honest man and you just did whatever Mayor Gallon wanted you to do so you could keep your job."

"I am honest and what you say is correct Mayor McClure."

"I am having John Riggins firm do an audit of the city's books starting tomorrow. I want you to fully cooperate with the auditors and if you do that for me, I will think about letting you keep your present job. Do we have a deal?"

Fred Johnson hesitated for several seconds. "Yes, Mayor McClure, we have a deal as long as you remember I took orders from Mayor Gallon and anything the auditors find is on him and not me."

"Fred, do not cross me!"

Ann left the city building and went straight to Sheriff Douglas' office. Dan congratulated her on her victory and asked her what he could do for her? "Dan, I need your help. I am having an audit done on the city's books starting tomorrow. I would like you to assign a deputy to oversee the audit because I will almost guarantee you that the mayor is going to try and interfere. According to the city regulations as in coming mayor I have the right to do an audit. See, it says it right here in regulation A51. John Riggins showed me the regulation or I would have never known about it."

Dan read the regulation. "Ann, you got it, one deputy at the city's office in the morning to oversee the audit. I will give him instructions and a copy of the regulation in case he tries to interfere."

"Dan, I know this is terrible to think but I wouldn't put it pass Mayor Gallon to burn down the building to cover his trail."

"That is something to think about. Once you start your audit and the mayor becomes aware of it, I will have a deputy steak-out the building just in case."

"Thank you, Dan. no wonder Pitch says you're a great guy."

The sheriff just smiled at her. When Ann got home and told Pitch what she did he was amazed. "I think the city is in good hands now.

Sister Martin waited patiently to hear from David Sarnoff. About a week after she called, Sister got a phone call from Jane Royal. "Sister Martin, the mail room found your package to David. You have to forgive me but I listened to the tape. That young boy can really sing. How old did you say he was?"

"Rory is twelve years old almost thirteen."

"How did you discover him?"

"His mother owns a ranch her in Sheridan, in fact she just got elected mayor."

"Is that you playing the guitar?"

"Yes Jane, that is me."

"I see you still got the magic fingers girl."

"Well, I am still retired and a Catholic nun. This is all about Rory McClure and his future in the music world."

"Don't worry Sister David will make that boy a singing star. Let me asked you one more question before I let you go. Who did the arrangement of those two songs together? It actually made me cry and makes me want to get closer to God."

"I did the arrangement Jane with the help of God's hands."

Fred Johnson did not tell Mayor Gallon about the up coming audit when the mayor returned to his office. Bright and early the next morning the auditors and the deputy showed up at the city office building. When Mayor Gallon saw them, he said, "What the hell is going on here?"

Right away the deputy stepped in, Mayor Gallon, according to regulation A51 of the city code, the incoming mayor has the right to perform an audit of the city books before taking office. Mayor elect Ann McClure has decided to exercise that right. I would greatly appreciate it if you would stay out of the way of the auditors. Thank you for your cooperation."

Mayor Gallon was totally pissed and immediately said, "Fred, I hope you have done everything by the book and nothing is wrong."

The mayor went into his office and was slamming things down left and right in his office and finally he decided to leave. The auditors worked until six o'clock and had a lot more to cover. The deputy reported everything that happened that day back to Sheriff Douglas. Dan sat in his big desk chair thinking things over. He figured if the mayor was that pissed off, he might try something stupid. Dan called Curly into his office, "Curly I want you to steak-out the city office building from dark to dust. Take another deputy with you."

"Dan, I can handle this by myself."

"No, do what I said because there might be trouble and I feel better if you had a back-up. Also, if there is trouble it helps to have two deputies telling the same story. Be careful, I think something big might happen."

Ann had a meeting with Sharon to talk about Ann's staff. Ann told her all about the deal she cut with Fred Johnson. "Ann, most of the people who work on Gallon's staff are good honest people who have been misled. It probably got to the point where they did what Gallon said or it cost them their jobs. Here is what I think you should do. Keep all the staff members because they have experience and they know what needs to be done. Tell them they still have their jobs on a trial basis. Then you keep an eye on them and if you need to make changes fire the ones that you can't trust."

"I told you Sharon, that you should have been the mayor."

About three o'clock in the morning Curly saw a man looking at the city building with something in his hand. Curly immediately woke up the other deputy and pointed out the man to him. "What the hell is he up to Curly at three o'clock in the morning?"

Curly was figuring out what they could do to prevent the guy from running away. "I got it, here is what we will do. Since we have a plain car, you drive up along side on him and I will jump out and put my gun in his back. Then you get out of the car and help me with him."

"I think that will work Curly but be careful you don't know if he has a gun."

They put their plan into action and in seconds Curly had his gun in the guys back. "Put whatever you have in your hand on the ground slowly."

The man started to talk. "Don't say one word until I tell you to talk. Put your hands behind your back nice and slowly."

Curly handcuffed him and when he searched him, he found a pistol. "Sit down on the sidewalk. What are you doing here at this time of night?"

"Curly there is gas in the can!"

"You plan on setting this building on fire?"

"What are you talking about? My truck ran out of gas."

"Where is your truck?"

"Down by the Coyote Club."

They put the guy in their car and drove down to the Coyote Club.

"Where is your truck?"

"It is gone, somebody must have stolen it."

"Sure, they did. It looks like jail for you partner unless you got something you want to tell us."

"What are you charging me with? Walking down the street with a can of gas?"

"No, for starters possession of a concealed weapon. Don't say another word or I'll knock your ass out."

When Sheriff Douglas came to the office in the morning, "Well, well, what do we have in our lovely jail?"

Curly stayed with the prisoner all night and told the sheriff the entire story. "You can't hold me here! Let me out of here!"

"Oh yes I can my dear young man. How old are you about twenty? Let's see by the time you get out of the state prison you should be about thirty or thirty-five."

"That's bull shit. You don't have charges to put me in prison."

"Let me see, possession of a concealed weapon, resisting arrest, and striking an officer."

"I didn't do all of that!"

"That is what the report says. You know I am tired of hearing you talk so keep your mouth completely closed or I will handcuff you and put tape over your mouth. No warning, one more word that's what will happen. While you sit in our beautiful jail you might want to think about telling us the truth because ten years in prison is a long time."

The auditors started back at it in the morning and Fred Johnson was a great help to them. They were finding misappropriation of funds left and right. One of the auditors questioned, "I see the city bought a commercial truck for $15,397.13, where is the truck?"

Johnson replied, "It is over at the mayor's business shop and their business name is written on it. The mayor signed off on the purchase."

"What about this $21,950.23 for an addition construction?"

"It was for an addition to the mayor's house so he could work at home."

The list of missed used city funds went on and on. The auditors decided to go check with their boss Jon Riggins. They told him just this year they found a total of $172,911.79 of misappropriated funds and most of it was for his own personal purpose. They asked John if he wanted them to go back into other years? He told them to hold up until he talked to Mayor

McClure about the situation. With all this evidence it looked like Mayor Gallon would be going to jail for a long time.

Sheriff Douglas decided to give Pitch a call to see if he could identify the young man in his jail as one of the men blasting on Ann's property. "If Pitch can identify him, he might start talking and tell him where the others are drilling.

When Riggins told Ann about the misappropriation of city funds, she really did not know what to do next. "Ann your City General Attorney, what's his name?'

"You mean Tom Berry? But isn't he a Gallon guy?"

"I think so but that is your only course of action. He needs to develop the charges against Gallon and then issue an arrest warrant so the sheriff can lock him up."

Ann went to see Tom Berry in his office. She showed him all the facts from the audit and told him he needed to file charges against Mayor Gallon and issue an arrest warrant. Berry said, "Let me study this information over night because it is dinner time now and I'll meet you first thing in the morning to discuss the situation. If I feel the charges are justified, I will do the paperwork and Sheriff Douglas can go lock the mayor up."

"Why can't we just do the paperwork and the sheriff is waiting for you to give him the word."

"Ann, you can't rush these things and you have to be right so let me study the information tonight and we will handle the arrest in the morning."

Ann saw Berry was not going to move off of his position so she backed off and told him she would see him in the morning at eight o'clock. When she got home, she told Pitch about Berry's position and that she really didn't like him or his attitude. "You are right, I always saw Berry as a little sneaky guy that you don't turn your back on." As Ann laid in Pitch's arms that night, she wondered how much money Gallon had taken from the city funds over his eight years in office. "Ann, stop thinking about it. We are going to lock his ass up."

"How do you know what I am think?"

"We are one now, Love."

Ann was up early and had breakfast with Pitch. She wished that he could go with her to meet Tom Berry but Pitch was splitting the herd for the up coming cattle auction. After breakfast Ann went straight to the city building and Tom Berry was not there yet. Finally, a little after nine o'clock he came strolling in his office. Ann jumped right on him, "I told you we were meeting eight o'clock this morning. You see what time it is?"

I am sorry, I had a problem at home I needed to handle."

"Well. Did you study the facts and see what a crook Gallon is?"

"Yes, but perhaps he has some reasoning behind what he did."

"You know Berry I am getting tired of your bull shit. Fill the dam papers out and issue the arrest warrant or pack your shit up and get the hell out of here."

"Okay, I will get right on them."

"How long is this going to take?"

"No more than a couple hours."

"I will be back in one hour and if them dam papers and the arrest warrant aren't waiting for me consider yourself fired."

Ann got up and walked out the door. She had to go see Sister Martin so she headed to the convent.

When she arrived, she had to wait for the school's morning recess. Sister Martin told Ann about David Sarnoff of RCA Records. Ann thought what she did was wonderful. She told Sister Martin that Rory was tired of singing for organizations and businesses and singing the same type music. Rory kept telling her that he wanted something more challenging and to sing modern country western songs. Ann asked Sister Martin if she knew of anything that could help Rory out? Sister knew from her professional days that many singers didn't make it because there was no challenge and then they lost interest. She told Ann she would call her friend Jane Royal to see if David had returned from his trip. "Ann, I also have a few contacts in Laramie where Rory could go and sing over the weekend."

"You can check them out Sister and if you find something, we can talk about it. Right now, I am involved in taking over as mayor and Pitch is getting the herd ready for auction. So, we aren't really available to take him to Laramie for the weekend."

"Let me see what I come up with and then we can figure out the logistics."

"That sounds good Sister. I got to run, I am trying to put a big crook behind bars."

After leaving Sister Martin, Ann went straight to Tom Berry's office and the paperwork for the charges was sitting there with the arrest warrant. "It is all completed properly and I will have someone take it over to Sheriff Douglas."

"I well take it over myself. Thank you for your cooperation. I do have one more thing to say to you. If we are going to work together you better change your attitude or you will be looking for a job."

Ann turned around and walked out the door. When she arrived at the sheriff's office, Dan here is all the charges paperwork and the arrest warrant. Have your men go get the son of a bitch?"

"Boys, go get Mayor Gallon and lock his fat ass up. Ann do you want to wait here until they bring him in.? I have a fresh pot of coffee."

"Thanks Dan but I need to get back to the ranch to see how Pitch is doing."

"Tell Pitch I need to see him. You are going to be one tough mayor Ann and you can count on me to back you up,"

The deputies went straight to Mayor Gallon's office and he was not there. Since it was noon they went to the restaurant where he ate lunch. no luck. Curly said, "Let's go check his business shop." They went to his tailoring and sewing shop and it was closed. "Boy's. it is time to go to his house," was Curly's direction. When they got to his house both his car and the shop truck were gone. They knocked on the front door, "Sheriff's Department."

After knocking several times and the front door was locked, "Okay, men let's try the other doors around the house."

Curly tried to look in a window but the shades were pulled down. The side doors were also locked. Curly went around where the swimming pool and the patio were and tried the glass sliding door and it was unlocked. He called in several times with no answer and all the deputies went in with guns drawn. They quickly realized that the place was empty all but for an old sofa and chairs. One of the deputies checked upstairs, empty. It was apparent that the Gallon family had packed up and left town with all on their belongings. They looked around for any clues that might tell them where the Gallon's went. Curly then said, "Let's go check their shop to see what we can find there."

Since the shop property was rented, they got the owner to open the door with his key. The deputies searched the shop good and did not find a clue as to where the Gallon's went. "Okay boys, that is a wrap. Let's go report to the sheriff."

When Curly and the other deputies came walking through the department's door empty handed, "Curly, where the hell is Gallon?"

"Sheriff, he and his family and all of their belongs are gone. He skipped town probably late last night."

"Are you shitting me?"

"No sir, we searched everywhere including their shop. It is almost like someone tipped him off."

"You found no clue where they were going?"

"Nothing sheriff, absolutely nothing."

The sheriff immediately had his office clerk put an alert out on the National Crime Information (NCI) network with their description and what Gallon was wanted for. "Sheriff, I figure they must have had a rented moving truck and towed the car behind it and his wife drove the commercial truck. I would think that he changed license plates, painted over the sign on the truck and didn't tell the moving truck company where they were really going. Gallon is no dummy so he probably really covered his tracks good."

"I think you are right Curly. Put that information on the NCI network also. Now, I have to tell Ann McClure about the situation."

Ann had Samoka saddle her horse and headed out to the herd to see what Pitch was doing with the herd. She wanted to know and understand everything about the cattle business. Pitch greeted her with a little kiss and asked her if everything worked out with Berry? "The sheriff is serving the arrest warrant and is going to lock his fat ass up."

"Good job Ann!"

Pitch explained what he was doing with the herd and told her once they had all the cattle, they wanted to sell together they would drive them to the train station where the meat buyer's auction takes place. "I think we will get top dollar for your herd and fatten up your bank account."

As they rode back to the ranch together, they were laughing and carrying on like two young kids in love.

When they got to the house, Nija came out on the front steps, "Ann, Sheriff Douglas has been calling you every fifteen minutes and said it is important that you call him back immediately."

Pitch told her he would take care of her horse and for her to go call Dan. When she called Sheriff Douglas, he told her the entire situation with all the details. "I can't believe Gallon got away."

"Ann, we think somebody tipped him off and as we speak the deputies are checking around town to see if anybody knows where they went. I also put the arrest warrant on the NCI network hoping someone would spot them and make the arrest."

"I guess you have done all you can?"

"One more thing Ann, we think Berry is the one who tipped off Gallon."

"You might be right, since he dragged out the entire process to arrest Gallon. I will have to keep an eye on him."

"If I were you, I would get him off of your staff very quick."

Ann thanked Sheriff Douglas for all the good work his department did. "We will get him Dan somebody will spot them very shortly."

"I hope so Ann. Oh, by the way tell Pitch I need him to come to my office when

he can."

"I will tell him."

At dinner that evening Ann told Pitch all the details of Gallon's escape. She also told him that the sheriff thought Berry told Gallon they were coming to arrest him so he had time to get away. Later that evening Ann handed Pitch a glass of whiskey and a cigar, "Let's go out on the patio I need to talk with you about something concerning Rory."

Once they got settled on the patio, Ann told him about Sister Martin and what she was trying to do for Rory. Pitch puffed on his cigar and Ann could tell his mind was working big time. "I have a solution but you may not like it."

"At this point I am worried about Rory and will listen to anything."

"Okay, but let me finish before you start yelling at me. Rory wants to sing modern country western music and use his talent. I own a country western night club where they play current music every weekend. No talking, you promised. I could get Wes Holder to let Rory sing with his Bandit band on Saturday nights when there is a big crowd. Rory could sing three or four songs from eight o'clock to nine o'clock. You and I would take him there and bring him back home after nine o'clock."

"I like the idea but I am worried about the drinking and bar atmosphere."

"From eight to nine o'clock nobody is drunk yet. They are just warming up and the place is really enjoyable."

"I never thought about that. This might work and he wouldn't have to travel to Laramie on the weekend.

"The places in Laramie are going to be just like the Coyote club."

"Let's give it a try and see if it works."

"Hold your pants on mama, I have to talk with Wes Holder to see if he is willing to go along with this plan. It is by no means a done deal."

"I understand, you talk to Wes and then we can tell Rory if Wes agrees. Oh, I forgot to tell you earlier that Dan wants you to come in and see him."

"What does he want?'

"I have no idea, he just said it was important."

"I'll go see him tomorrow and then go talk to Wes Holder."

The next morning, Pitch went to see Sheriff Douglas. Dan walked him into the jail part of the department. Do you recognize this young man Pitch?"

"Absolutely, Sheriff, he is one of the guys who were blasting on Ann's property. Hey, young man, do you remember me? You probably still have some thorns in your ass."

The young boy turned his face away from Pitch and the sheriff. "Let me see now, adding these charges to the other ones his sentence probably will be thirty years in prison."

"That is a long time for a pretty young boy to be in a prison."

"Yes, Pitch, I will bet he will be somebody's girlfriend in there."

"You two stop all that bull shit!"

"We are not bull shitting you son. By the way we got your big boss, the mayor, and an arrest warrant is out for his ass. He will be joining you in prison."

"What kind of deal are you offering me if I talk?"

"Because you are such a young man and can change your ways, here is what my one and only one-time offer is to you. You tell us where your crew is blasting next and we catch them all, I will let you go free but you must leave the state of Wyoming."

"Are you serious about your offer or just lying?"

"Going once, going twice."

"I'll take your offer."

"Son, let me make myself very clear. If what you are going to tell me is bull shit, I will make sure the municipal judge gives you thirty years in prison. Okay, now tell us what we want to know."

"The crew moved out of the cabin because the mayor told them to move. They have a camp site about three miles north of the cabin in the woods on Boone's side of the property. On Monday they are going to started blasting and drilling on the north ridge of the McClure property. The mayor told them from the survey report there should be tons of uranium there."

"Why are they waiting until Monday?"

"Because they know the McClure family goes horseback riding on Sunday and they are afraid they might get spotted. On Monday the McClure wranglers will be on the other side of the property working with the herd. That is all that I know but if you go there Monday you should catch them blasting or drilling."

"Well, thank you, young man, if what you say is true and we catch them you will be out of jail in no time. Pitch, how about it if we meet at nine o'clock on Monday and go get them. That will give them time to get started and we can catch them in the act."

"Sounds good Dan, I'll see you then."

From the sheriff's office Pitch went straight to the Coyote Night Club where Wes Holder and his band would be practicing for today. "Wes, I have request to make of you and your Bandit band. I hope you can help me out."

"What do you have on your mind Pitch?"

"You know Rory McClure?"

"Of course, the great kid singer. Sure, everybody in Sheridan knows about him."

"Well, he needs a challenge and I thought singing with your band would do the trick."

"I would love to have him sing with us but you know we play until two in the morning."

"Here is my plan. You let Rory sing three or four songs from eight to nine. Ann and I will come with him and after his last song we will leave and take him home before the club gets to crazy."

"I really like that and if we advertise that he is singing we will pack the club. When do you want him to start?"

"Now about next Saturday?"

"That will work. Here are our four songs we are going to play next week. He will have to learn them and come to practice next Wednesday at seven o'clock and Saturday at one o'clock so we can iron out any problems. Tell him to learn it like it is on the music sheets."

"Thank you, Wes. The kid is going to love this."

Pitch wasted not time in getting home to tell Ann that Wes was good with their plan. They called Rory in the house and Pitch said, "Here is something for you," and handed Rory the sheets of music. Rory looked at the sheets of music and said, "What am I supposed to do with these?"

Ann could not hold back any longer, "Learn them because you will be singing them next Saturday night at the Coyote club."

Rory looked at Ann with a big question mark on his face. "What are you talking about Mom?"

Then Pitch cleared things up, "Rory you are going to sing with Wes Holder and his Bandit band."

Pitch explained what the deal was and that he needed to learn these songs so he could practice with the band. Rory started hugging them both, "Thank you God for answering my prayers. I am going upstairs and start practicing right now."

Rory ran up stairs to his guitar. "You owe me big time Mayor McClure."

"I will pay my debt tonight Boss Pitch!"

Before Pitch knew it, Monday was here and the Sheriff, his deputies and Pitch were headed out to find the free-loaders. As they approached the area where the boy said they would be they heard blasting. "Our timing is right Dan. Let's be very careful because they are carrying guns."

When they got to the location the six of them spread out and the Sheriff called out, "The Sheriff's Department put your hands up in the air."

The free-loaders turned around and pulled out their guns and started shooting like crazy. Dan's first shot hit one of them and he went to the ground. The other two were like mad men and just kept shooting. Dan looked over and Pitch was laying on the ground and Curly came over to where Pitch was and blasted the guy with his two-barrel shotgun. The last one standing dropped his weapon and got down on his knees. Curly ran over to Pitch on the ground. "Sheriff, Pitch has been hit and he is bleeding badly."

"Where is he hit?"

"It looks like the shoulder but I can't really tell. It could be his chest."

They did everything they could to stop the bleeding. "Curly, help me get him on his horse. I got to get him to the hospital immediately or he will die. One of the deputies can go with me to help keep him on his horse. We can put him between us. You and the other deputies take care of the situation here. Come on let's go. I hope he can make it!"

CHAPTER 9

They could not ride very fast but the good thing was that Pitch was semi-conscious. When they got to the edge of town Sheriff Douglas flagged down a car and told the driver he needed his help. They carefully put Pitch in the car and Dan told the deputy to take the horses. "Sir, I want you to drive this dam car like you are in a race. Now, get us to the hospital, blow your horn so these ass holes get out of your way. Keep blowing!"

When they arrived the emergency room entrance of Sheridan Memorial Hospital the nurses and a doctor came running out to assist Dan. "We got him sir, you can stop holding. We will take care of him from this point on sheriff."

Dan had Pitch's blood all over him and he was really shaken up. Dan was having a hard time breathing. One the nurses saw him gasping for air and she called for assistance. They took him in the hospital and checked his vials and determined it was the stress he under so they give him something to calm him down. After about a half an hour Dan was breathing normal and felt much better. He was really worried that Pitch was in big trouble and wanted to know what was going on with him. Dan got up out of bed and walked to the nurse's station. "Where is Pitch Wesley?"

"Sir, you should still be in bed until the doctor checks you again."

"Will you please answer my question, right now!"

"Sheriff, Mr. Wesley is in surgery. The bulleting cut through an artery."

"How long will he be there?"

"I have no idea sheriff."

"Give me that dam phone!"

"Calm down sir or your breathing will get difficult again"

"Hand that phone over here."

"Sir, that phone is for hospital use only."

Dan went around the nurse's station and picked up the phone. "How do I get an outside number. I need to call the mayor. That is her husband."

"You dial nine first then the phone number. Here let me help you. What is the phone number?"

"I don't know the dam phone number off the top of my head."

"Calm down, I will call information get you connected to the McClure ranch."

Nija answered the phone at the ranch. "Here you go sheriff a lady named Nija is on line."

Nija, this is Sheriff Douglas, where is Ann?"

"She is out in the barn with the chickens."

"Go out and tell her Pitch has been shot and he is at Sheridan Memorial Hospital. Tell her he is in surgery right now and she needs to get here fast."

"I'm on my way Sheriff," as she hung up the phone. Nija came sprinting out of the house and Samoka was yelling at her. "What is the matter?'

"Get the car and bring it out front, now!"

Nija came yelling into the barn, "Ann, Ann!"

"Nija what is the problem?"

"Mr. Pitch has been shot and is at Sheridan Memorial Hospital. Sheriff Douglas says you need to get there fast. Boss Pitch is in surgery."

"Oh my God, oh my God!"

"Samoka is bringing the car around to take you to the hospital. I will take care of the kids. Here is Samoka, go, go!"

Ann jumped in the car and Samoka flew down the dusty road. It only took fifteen minutes to get Ann to the hospital. She ran in the emergency room knocking people out of her way. "I am Mayor McClure, where is Pitch Wesley?"

"Calm down Mayor McClure."

"Did you hear what I said. Dam it, answer me."

Then a nurse came running to where Ann was with Sheriff Douglas right behind her. "Ann, Ann! "Dan where is Pitch? I want to see him right now."

"Ann, you can't, he is in surgery and it will be a while before you can see him. "The nurse said, the doctor who is doing the surgery will come to talk with you after the surgery is finished. Let's go sit in the waiting room so they know where to find you."

"Dan, what happened?"

"Sit down and I will tell you everything.

"Dan went through all the events that happened and told her what he knew about Pitch's injury. "I am so sorry Ann. I probably should not have let him go with us in the first place. "

"Dan, don't get stupid on me. Pitch wouldn't let you go without him so put that out of your mind."

They waited for three hours and finally the surgeon came to talk to them. "Mayor McClure, I am Doctor Alexander and here is an update on Mr. Wesley's condition. He got shot in the shoulder and the bullet cut an artery which caused him to bleed so much. The surgery went fine. I removed the bullet and fixed the artery and a couple other things. He is in recovery right now so we can keep a close eye on him. He will be in recovery for about two hours and then they will put him in the Intensive Care Unit (ICU). Once they have him settled in his room and sedated you can go see him. He will be under heavy pain medication and will be in and out of consciousness. Please don't be alarmed by all the tubes and wires that he is hooked up to. These are monitoring his heart, blood pressure and some other things. The good news is he could recover over time but that may take a while. Do you have any questions?"

"Dr. Alexander, is he in danger of dying?"

"To be honest with you, right now he has a 60% of full recover but that baring no complications down the road. We will stay in contact with you and let you know how he is coming along and when you can see him."

"Thank you, Doctor Alexander."

It was nice to meet you Mayor. I only wish it was under better circumstances."

Ann didn't know what to do next. "Ann, since it is going to be at least a couple of hours lets you, Samoka, and me go to the cafeteria for some coffee and talk about what you should do next."

"Okay, Dan, but tell the nurse where we will be in case, they need me."

While they were drinking their coffee Ann said, "What do I tell the kids?"

"Let Samoka go back to the house and have him explain what is going on. It is best you tell them the truth up front."

"They will want to come to the hospital."

"Samoka can tell them you will talk about what happen when you get home or in the morning."

"Samoka can you do that for me?"

"Yes Ann, I will go right now. When you are ready to come home call me at the house and I will come get you. Nija and I will stay at the house with the kids to make sure they are all right."

Ann reached over and kissed Samoka on the cheek and Samoka left for the ranch.

"Dan, you need to get home to your family. I called them and they are okay. Curly called my house and said he was coming to the hospital to stay with you and I would take his car and go home."

"You didn't have to do that."

"This was Curly's idea and not mine."

When Saomka got back to the ranch he gathered the kids in the living room and told them about Pitch being shot and that he had surgery and was in critical condition. Also, that Ann was staying at the hospital and she hoped to see him when he came out of recovery. It will be a long night for your Mom. The best thing you kids can do is wash up and got to bed and pray for Mr. Pitch."

Rory looked at the others, "Okay you heard him, lets go do what he said. That order came from Boss Samoka!"

They all laughed a little. Nija called her family and told them Saomka and her were staying at the McClure's house and she explained what happen. No sooner then she hung up the phone it rings again. This time it was Kinno and he was really upset. Pitch and Kinno were almost like brothers. In fact, Kinno was the one who taught Pitch how to speak Shoshone. Nija could tell he wanted to do something but there was nothing he could do. After Kinno's call Nija wouldn't answer the phone anymore because the calls were from the village people wanting to know about Pitch. She finally took the phone off the hook and didn't put it back until midnight. Samoka told Nija to go lay on Ann's bed because it was very late and he would lay on the sofa. Nija wasn't happy about that arrangement but she was really tired so she slowly went up the steps to Ann's room.

About two o'clock in the morning the nurse came to Ann sleeping in a chair next to Curly. "Mayor McClure she said softly," and then shook Ann's shoulder. "You can go see Mr. Wesley now he is in his room and resting. He is in ICU room 302. The nurse in the unit knows you are coming up."

Ann quickly woke up Curly and told him she was going to see Pitch and he could go home. Curly told her not to worry about him and that he would take a taxi home. Ann got on the elevator and her heart was beating triple time. The attending

211

nurse showed her Pitch's room and Ann quietly went in and when she looked at Pitch just started crying. Then she heard a weak voice, "It is okay Ann, I am still here with you."

She ran over to his bed and kissed all over his face. Pitch turned to talk but he was to weak. About twenty minutes later he spoke weakly to her again. "Why don't you get in bed with me," and he gave a little smile. The entire night beside his bed Ann prayed and prayed. When the sun started to come up the nurse came in the room. "Mayor McClure how about some breakfast, you will need your strength."

About nine o'clock Sheriff Douglas came back to the hospital and went to Pitch's room. "How is he doing Ann?"

"He had a hard night and they kept giving him medicine for the pain."

"Well, here is the plan for today. I have a deputy down stairs waiting to take you home. Go home shower, get some sleep and I'll stay with Pitch. You come back about two o'clock and relieve me. Besides, you need to talk to your kids. Please Ann, listen to me."

"Okay, Dan, I will go because you are right. I'll see you about two."

When Ann got home, she showered, took a long nap, and talked to the kids about Pitch's condition. They all wanted to go see him. "I will tell you what, I am going back to the hospital and if they let Pitch have visitors, I will call you. Then Tony can bring you to the hospital in the Cadillac. However, I think only one person is aloud in his room at a time. That means one of you of would go up and when that person comes down the next person can go up and so no. When each of you have seen

Pitch then you go back home until he gets out of the ICU. Does everybody understand?"

They shook their heads yes. Then Ann headed straight to the hospital to relieve Dan. The doctor gave Ann an update report and said Pitch would wake up for periods of about a half an hour and then would go back to sleep. He told her that Pitch is talking more and it looks like he will make a full recovery. Ann asked the doctor about the kids seeing him and he said it was okay but just one or two at a time and very short visits. The one thing Pitch does not need is excitement. Since Pitch was still sleeping, she ran down to the pay phone in the lounge and told Tony to bring the kids to the hospital. When she got back to Pitch's room, he was awake so she kissed him on the cheek and told him that she loved him very much. Pitch took her hand and held it very tight. After talking a little Pitch fell back to sleep. Ann went down to the lounge to see if the kids were here yet. As she got to the lounge, the kids just walked in the door. "Now, when you visit Pitch, he may be asleep and we can't wake him up because he needs his rest. Who wants to go first?"

Nellie raised her hand. "Tony you come with us so Nellie does not get lost on the way back."

The three of them got in the elevator and got off on the third floor. "Let me look in his room first. Okay, the both of you can come. He is sleeping so be quiet."

When Nellie and Tony saw Pitch, it caused them to worry more. Then Nellie started asking questions about the tubes and wires Pitch was hooked up to. Pitch's eyes opened and Nellie kissed him on the cheek and tears were running down her face. Then he saw Tony. "You are the man of the house now Tony."

Ann knew that was enough and sent Tony to go down and send the other two up. Rory and Tommy never got to talk to Pitch but they both knew he was hurt really bad. After the kids went home, Ann just sat by Pitch's bed and prayed.

About five o'clock Sharon Steward came walking in Pitch's room. She hugged Ann and Ann filled her in on Pitch's condition. Pitch heard them talking and opened his eyes. "Hi Sharon."

"Hello Pitch just came for a short visit to see how you are doing."

"I have a favor to asked of you and Bob."

"Anything for you honey."

"I need you to take Rory to the Coyote Club on Saturday. Ann can fill you in on the details."

"We would be honored to do that for you."

Pitch dozed off again. Ann told Sharon about Rory singing from eight to nine at the Coyote Club. She said she would have Tony take Rory to the band practices.

"No problem Ann in fact it sounds like fun. Tell Rory we will pick him up at seven so he has time to warm up with the bands."

"I really appreciate it because I didn't want Rory to miss the opportunity to sing with a band."

"Ann, I am sorry Gallon got away and the sheriff could not arrest him."

"Sharon, that son of a bitch is responsible for Pitch getting shot. If he was here right now, I would cut his balls off."

"Ann, I was thinking that Gallon's house must be worth at least $100,000 with that swimming pool and patio. I can not see him walking away from that kind of money. My question is, do you think somebody in his gang is going to try and sell it for him? If that person comes forward, I can bet you they know where he is so they can send the money to him."

"You have a good point. I was thinking of having the city confiscate it, sell it, and put the money in the city treasury. I don't know if I can do that but now, I think I will wait and see if what you said happens."

"Yea, you have nothing to lose. You can take the house any time you want it Mayor McClure."

They both had to laugh.

After Sharon left, the nurses had to change Pitch's bed sheets because of infections. While they were doing that Ann told the head nurse that she was going to the cafeteria to get something to eat. After Ann picked out what she wanted and sat down at a table Sister Martin came walking in the cafeteria. Ann waved to her, "Nice to see you Sister."

"I only found out about Pitch being shot when I read Sid Walter's article in the newspaper. It was really something to read all the things our mayor did."

"I will have to read it."

"I went up to Pitch's room but he was sleeping and the nurse told me where you were. How is he doing?"

"It seems like he is doing better each day and he is talking more. The doctor says he has a 60% chance of making it if the artery fix holds up. Oh, I have something to tell you. Rory is going to sing at the Coyote Club on Saturday night from eight until nine. He is going to sing four songs with the Bandit band."

"That is great because I strike out with finding a club with my Laramie contacts.

When Ann was finished eating, they went back up to Pitch's room and they prayed together for his speedy recovery. It was almost nine o'clock and Pitch opened his eyes. "What a beautiful sight to open my eyes to. Ann, my love, go home and get some rest. I'm not going anywhere I'll be right here in the morning."

Ann smiled and kissed Pitch three times. "Please, Ann, for me. Go home!"

"Okay, Boss Pitch I will see you in the morning." Ann kissed him and left the hospital.

When Ann got home, Tony and Rory were just getting back from Rory's practice with the band. Ann asked Rory what songs he was going to sing?"

"Mom, I don't know if you know any of these songs, they are pretty modern. However, if you really want to know they are; "I'm So Lonesome I Could Cry, Riders in the Sky, That Lucky old Sun, and You're Breakin' My Heart."

"I can't wait to hear you sing them."

"You're not going to be there. Sharon and Bob Steward are taking me."

"If Pitch is doing good, I am going to leave the hospital about quarter to eight and go so to the Coyote Club to hear you."

"That would be great Mom but only if Mr. Pitch doesn't need you."

It was time for bed and Ann couldn't wait to hit the shower and then her bed.

When Ann got to the hospital Pitch was sitting up some in his bed. Dr. Alexander said, "Pitch is doing just great mainly because he is in such good physical shape. The artery I repaired was pumping blood properly and his wound was healing nice. If he keeps improving over the next couple of days, I will have him moved out of critical condition to a regular private room."

"Thank you, Dr. Alexander, how long do you think he will be in the hospital?"

"If I had to guess right now, I would say about two more weeks because we really have to watch for infection in the wound. I have to run Ann I will keep you informed."

Ann kissed Pitch on the cheek and he woke up. "More, more, on the lips."

"I see you are back to your old self."

"Hon, I need to get home with the family. I miss them."

Just then the head nurse on duty came in Pitch's room with a very serious look on her face. Ann could tell by her skin that she was a full-blooded Indian woman. "Mayor McClure, Mr. Wesley you have two guests waiting to come in and see him if you will allow it."

Ann looked at her, "Who is it?"

"It is Chief Warki and his daughter Maomi."

Then Pitch said, "Tell them to come in."

Chief Warki greeted Pitch in Shoshone and Pitch said something back in Shoshone. While they were talking a little, Ann started talking to his daughter. "What is your name?"

"I am Maomi."

"You are the girl that helped Tony in school."

"Yes, Tony and I are friends."

"He said you helped him get to his classes and helped him make many friends."

"Tony is well liked in school now and he is very smart. Almost as smart as me."

That bought a smile to Ann's face. When the Chief and Pitch were done talking, he turned to Ann. "Chief McClure, I thank you for all you have done for the Shoshone. My son Kinno speaks very highly of you and says you are a great Chief. May the good spirits be with you in your journey."

Then the Chief and his daughter walked out of the room with his daughter behind him. "That was nice of the Chief to come visit you."

"Yes, it was Chief McClure"

Ann just smiled. "His daughter is very beautiful."

"Yes, and Tony really likes her big time."

"I guess he is getting at the girl age and will want to start dating."

"I think he is already there."

"I guess you will have to have that father to son talk with him about women."

"Pitch, you are crazy. The bullet didn't hit your brain did it?"

Pitch cracked a smile and dozed off, tired from all the conversations.

About seven-thirty Ann told Pitch she was leaving to go hear Rory sing. "Can I go with you?"

"I wish, but you will shortly."

Ann got to the Coyote Club ten minutes to eight and the place was packed to the walls. Stoney Mason spotted her when she came in the door and walked her to Bob and Sharon Steward's table. Stoney asked her if she wanted something to drink? "A coke will be fine, thanks Stoney."

Ann asked Sharon if Rory was nervous?'

"Hell, no Ann, he is just so calm and cool, like he has been doing this for years. If it was me, I would be shitting in my boots with all these people here."

Ann and Bob just laughed at Sharon and her comparison. Wes Holder came over to say a few words to Ann and then went back on stage. "Ladies and gentlemen, thank you for coming tonight. I am Wes Holder and this is the Bandit band. Our special singer is Rory McClure. Everybody applauded and yelled out Rory, Rory. The band played a warm up song. Then Rory stepped up to the microphone with his guitar, the band played a little introduction as Rory started to sing. "Hear that lonesome whippoorwill, He sounds to blue to fly, that means he's lost the will to live, I'm so lonesome I could cry." As Rory sang the entire song the place was very quiet until he ended the song. The crowd gave him a standing ovation and Ann heard one woman say, "He sounds like Hank Williams, what a beautiful voice."

Ann had tears running down her face. Sharon looked at her, "Cry all you want Honey, that son of yours is great."

Rory other three songs were just as good as the first. When Wes announced that Rory had to leave the place started booing. "Calm down, Rory is only thirteen years old and his Mom said he has to be in bed by ten. However, the good new is that he will be back next Saturday."

Ann told Sharon that she would take Rory home. "That's great Ann, Bob and I are going to hang out a little and dance some."

As Rory was walking out of the club everybody was patting him on the back. When they got to the jeep, "Well, Rory did you have a good time?"

"Yes, Mom, I loved it. I could have sung all night."

Now that Pitch was pretty stable Sheriff Douglas had to clean up the mess from the shooting. As he promised, he let the young man go free and told him he should go to California. As for the other guy who did all the shooting Dan had a list of charges against him a mile long. However, he was not happy that he had to deal with Tom Berry on the charges. Berry was his usual ass hole and questioned every charge against the guy. Dan figured there had to be more to this then the eye could see. Sheriff Douglas had a nephew in town, Charlie Douglas, who was trying to start a law practice after he passed the state bar examine. Charlie was twenty-eight years old and very bright when it comes to Wyoming state law. Dan went over to see him about the charges and why Berry was questioning them. Charlie looked them over carefully. "Uncle Dan, I don't know what his problem is the charges all have state law statutes that apply to them."

"I think this Berry guy has a personal agenda and I think the guy these charges are against has a connection with Berry. Anyway, how is your business going Charlie?"

"I'm afraid not very good. All the old established firms have the ranchers locked up and most of the businesses in town. If I don't find someway to make money I will have to close my office and look for a job somewhere else. I figure I got about four or five months left until I go bankrupt."

"If is anything comes up in the office, I will see if I can help you."

Since Pitch was doing good Ann started to spend more time on her mayor's job. Ann knew she had to make some changes on her staff but was taking her time so she made the right decisions. In the election results she got two new city council members and the other four was pretty reasonable guys to work with. Ann still wanted to find the mayor and bring him to justice but that was on her back burner now. When she was driving to Sharon's shop, she passed the Gallon house and it had a for sale sign out front. The realtor was the Kelly's and she was wondering who authorized Kelly to sell it. Instead of going to Sharon's she went to the Sheriff's Department. Dan was sitting in his office drinking coffee. Without any greeting whatsoever, "Dan who authorized Kelly to sell the Gallon house?"

"What are you talking about Ann?"

"There is a for sale sign in front of the house and the realtor is Kelly."

"It must have just gone up because it wasn't there yesterday. I don't have much to do so Curly and I will go talk to the Kelly's."

"Good idea, let me know what you find out."

Ann figured she did enough for the day as mayor and needed to get to the hospital.

When Ann walked in Pitch's new room he was sitting up in a chair. "Look at the big shot! Can I get you a glass of whiskey and a cigar?'

"No, but you can come over here and give me a really good kiss on the lips."

When Ann saw Dr. Alexander, he told her Pitch could go home in three days but he was to do nothing but sit around and get fat.

Sheriff Douglas and Curly went to the office Mr. & Mrs. Peter Kelly to find out information about who was selling the Gallon house. The Kelly's had lived in Sheridan a long time and for most part were as honest as a realtor company could be. The Sheriff asked them who told them to put the Gallon house up for sale? Mrs. Kelly wasted no time in answering, "Dan, three days ago in our mailbox we found an envelope with the property deed, one hundred dollars to clean up and five hundred dollars as an advance commission for selling the house. The note that came in the envelope said once a sold sign was put on the property, we would be contacted to close the deal."

"Do you still have the envelope and note?"

"Yes, let me go get it for you."

Mrs. Kelly gave the envelope and note to Dan. Curly, looked at the envelope and it had no post marks on it. "To me this indicates that somebody local put it in the Kelly's mailbox. Who ever did this printed the note so their hand writing could not be identified?"

"I agree with you Curly. Thank you for your help we will be in touch with you."

Riding back to the office Curly looked at Dan, "I got an idea."

"Okay, let's see if you are thinking what I am?"

"All we have to do is put a sold sign on the property and the person will contact the Kelly's to close the deal."

"That is what I was thinking but we can't do it to soon or the person will no it is a trap. I think we need to wait about two weeks and maybe get the Kelly's to show a few people the property in case this person is watching the property closely."

"Sounds like a plan Sheriff. We can have a couple deputies in plain clothes and their wives go look at the house like they are interested in buying it."

"I like that but don't make the visits to close together."

Sheriff Douglas told Ann the hard time Tom Berry was giving him about the charges against the guy who shot Pitch. Of course, she got really upset and didn't need any more pressure on her at this time. "Dan, I hate to say this but I can't stand Berry and I need to fire his ass but I can't afford to leave that position vacant. If I had a person to move right into that job, I would fire Berry in a second."

That got Dan thinking about his nephew. Dan knew Charlie could do the job but he was young with little experience and wasn't sure Ann would hire a relative of his. Dan decided to give it a shot because he didn't want Charlie and his family leaving Sheridan. "Ann, I have the person you are looking for to put in Berry's position."

"Go ahead Dan, I'm listening."

"I have a nephew here in Sheridan, Charlie Douglas, who is a smart attorney on state law. He is only twenty-eight years old and has little experience. I think he would be a great City Attorney General."

"I will tell you what Dan, you send him over to the hospital this afternoon and I will take a break from being with Pitch to interview him in the lounge. I am not promising you anything. Is that clearly understood?"

"Yes, Ann and I appreciate you giving him the opportunity. Thank you, Mayor."

When Dan left Ann, he was all excited and then he remembered he forgot to tell Ann about the Gallon house and the Kelly's. He figured he could tell her later because nothing was going to happen soon. Dan went right to Charlie's office and when he walked in Charlie was reading the want ads. "Hello Uncle Dan, what do I owe this honor to?"

"What are you doing reading the wants ads, looking for a job?"

"Just some part-time work to help with the bills."

"Charlie, how would like to be Sheridan's Attorney General working for Mayor McClure?"

"Okay, what is the joke?" I am serious. The job pays around $30,000 a year."

"Okay, I'll play your game. Yes, I would absolutely love the job and all my problems would be solved."

"Well, that is good because you have an interview with Mayor McClure this afternoon at the hospital."

"Come on Uncle Dan be serious."

"I am not kidding you. I will meet you there at two o'clock. She will be up with Pitch so I will go get her and then leave after I introduce you to her."

"This is for real?"

"Yes, this is your big chance and remember she loves teamwork. Just to tell you a little about her. She comes from New York city, her husband was killed in the war, his uncle left her the McClure ranch, she has three kids and one boy she took in off the street and she is engaged to Pitch Wesley. Ann is a take no shit type person and do not feed her any bull shit because she will see right through it. You have to convince her you can do the job with your little experience. Any questions?"

"No, Uncle Dan and thanks for getting me the interview."

"I will see you at the hospital at two."

Rory was the hit of the town. Sid Walter wrote several articles about him performing at the Coyote Club and many newspapers picked up the articles off the AP network line. Stoney Mason was in heaven because people were coming from other towns to hear Rory sing. Profits for the club were way up and the waitress's tips had probably doubled. Stoney wanted to talk to Pitch about seeing if Rory could sing till ten o'clcok instead of nine. Stoney figured Rory didn't have school the next day so it couldn't be a problem. He talked to Rory about it and he was okay but Stoney knew he had to deal with Ann and Pitch on this and with Pitch in the hospital the timing was not right. He told Rory to kind mention it to his Mom but not to push it. Rory looked at Stoney, "I think we would have a better shot if we asked them if I could sing Friday night from eight to ten because I can sleep in the next day. It will be harder to convince them about Saturday night since I have to go to church with the family for nine o'clock mass on Sunday."

"Dam, boy you are smart. Why don't you give that a try?"

With all the pressure Ann was under now was not the time for an interview with her. When Dan came up to the room and got her she was in a prissy mood because Pitch kept arguing with the nurses and wanted to get the hell out of the hospital. Dan introduced her to Charlie and then he left. "Charlie, I'm not in a good mood but let's see if you can change that for me. Tell me a little about yourself and your background."

Charlie told her he was married and had a three-year-old daughter. He graduated from the University of Wyoming with a law degree and was second in his class. He passed the Wyoming state bar examine about a year ago and loved Sheridan so he was trying to start his own law firm here. However, it is very difficult since the old firms have most of the business already. He told her that he didn't think his firm was going to make it and would probably go bankrupt and have to move. Ann decided to ask him a few questions, "What is your number one goal in life?"

"My top goal in life is to take care of my family. They are number one."

"What do you think the role of your boss is?"

"To oversee my work, to provide support and advice and to make sure we are working towards the same goals."

"What would be your responsibility to the city?"

"To always do my job to the best of my ability and make decisions that benefit the city and the tax payers."

"What do you think about teamwork?"

"I played baseball in college so I know the benefits of teamwork. In teamwork there is no I. Sometimes things don't benefit you but they are good for the overall team. I think teamwork is essential to success."

"Thank you, Charlie, your answers were good and very honest. I have a lot to think about and I will let you know my decision shortly."

"Thank you for your time Mayor McClure and I will pray for Mr. Wesley."

Ann got up and got in the elevator as Charlie walked out the door.

When Ann got back to Pitch's room the nurse told her to take him for a walk up and down the hallway. While they were walking Ann told him about her interview with Charlie Douglas. "If you want my advice, hire the young man and get Berry out of your office building completely."

"I am trying to be fair Pitch and Berry has not done anything wrong."

"You don't think he created a delay in arresting Gallon so he could get out of town?"

"To be honest, I am not sure. That reminds me I need to go see if the charges paperwork on the guy that shot you are ready. I'll take you back to your room and run over to the office to see it he has them done. I'll be back for dinner. Order me whatever you are having."

When Ann checked with Berry the paperwork was still on his desk. He told her he had a call into the city's municipal judge to ask him a question on one of the charges and was waiting his call back.

Since that didn't take long Ann decided to stop over the sheriff's office before going back to the hospital. As soon as she got in the door Dan asked her how Charlie's interview went. "I was very impressed Dan. The only thing that concerns me is his lack of experience working in the government environment."

"I know somebody else who had a lack of experience and she is doing one hell of a job."

"Your point is well taken. That brings me to another subject, our present City Attorney General is waiting to hear from our judge on something before he fills out the paperwork."

"That is total bull shit Ann. If I ever saw a clean-cut case of attempted murder this is it. I still think Berry is connected to Gallon somehow. That reminds me, yesterday I forgot to tell you about what the Kelly's had to say about the sale of Gallon's house."

The sheriff went through everything with Ann and told her about the trap Curly and he were planning. "Ann, I will bet you one hundred dollars that Berry is the one trying to sell the house."

"I'm not touching that bet. Let me know how you and Curly make out with your trap."

"Okay, hey, keep thinking about Charlie!"

Ann got to the hospital just in time for dinner. "What is this, tuna fish salad, tomatoes, carrots, and onion soup?"

"You said to get you what I was having!"

"You are really funny big boy."

"When am I going home? I really need to be helping Kinno out with the herd."

"You are going home not tomorrow morning but the next morning and as far as you helping Kinno that won't be until a month from now."

"Ann, why are you so hard on me?"

"Because I love you and want you around for a while cowboy."

Pitch asked her what was going on with the guy that shot him? "His story is that it was self-defense."

"Dan should beat the shit out of him until he tells the entire story and I know Berry is in this some way."

"I don't think that would be illegal and besides just give Dan some time and he will get the guy to talk his way."

Ann stayed at the hospital until seven-thirty and told Pitch she had to go check on the kids. When she walked in the house all kids jumped her with hugs and kisses all but Tony. When they were through, she went over and hugged Tony and kissed him on the forehead. Then each kid including Tony had something they wanted to talk to her about. Nellie wanted to know if Sara Song could spend Friday at the house? Ann told her to see if it was all right with Nija. Tommy wanted to know if she was coming to his lacrosse game on Saturday? She told him she would come to the next one because she had to bring Pitch home and get him settled in on Saturday. He said he understood with a disappointed look on his face. Next came Rory and he talked about singing Friday night at the Coyote Club. She said he would have to wait until Pitch got home so three of them could discuss it together. Ann looked at Tony, "What is on your mind young man?"

"I wanted to talk to you about something personal in private. Maybe we can talk later?"

"Okay, we can do that."

Ann gave them all the details on how Pitch was doing and that he was coming home on Saturday. At that point she decided to spring a surprise on them to see how they would react. "When Mr. Pitch comes home, I am putting him upstairs in my bed so I can keep an eye on him at night. I want to make sure he does what Dr. Alexander says."

Nellie thought she would handle that for all of them, "It's okay Mommy because Mr. Pitch will be our Daddy very soon."

The boys all shook their heads yes.

Ann was trying to put off Tony until Pitch got home. However, he was so moody that she called him over and said, "Let's talk something is really on your mind and I have time to listen."

"Are you sure I know you are really busy?"

"My ears are all yours for as long as you need."

"I would like to go out on a date with a girl but I don't know how to ask her?"

"Might this this girl be Maomi?"

"Yes, how did you know?"

"Honey, you talk about her all the time. I had a chance to meet her at the hospital and she told me she liked you."

"You think see likes me enough to go to the movies with me?"

"Do you know who her father is?"

"No, does it matter?"

"In her case yes because her father is Chief Warki the head of all the Shoshone and Kinno's father. The Shoshone have some very hard restrictions for their women."

"I am good friends with Kinno and he likes me."

"Kinno likes a lot of people but he still is a Shoshone and will follow their customs."

"Does this mean that I should not ask her to go to the movies with me?"

"My advice right now is that you should feel her out for a little while longer."

"What does that mean?"

"When you talk to, her ask her some questions like, do you like movies, now there is the movie theater here, have you ever been there, does your family let you go with other kids to the movies? See just simple questions and she might tell you more then you are asking. As smart as she is she will know you want to take her to the movies. Also, talk to Kinno and tell him you and Moami are good friends. Ask him if the Shoshone have any restrictions you should know about. After you get all this information from your questions you will know if she is allowed to go to the movie with you or not. Mr. Pitch is coming home soon and we can talk to him about how you should ask her. You may have to asked her father."

"Really, just to take her to the movies?"

"It depends on the Shoshone customs and Maomi is not just any girl so she is held to high standards. See what you can find out and then we can talk again to see what you have to do."

"Thank you, Mrs. McClure, I feel better now."

Bright and early Saturday morning Ann was at the hospital to bring Pitch home. It took forever to get all the release paperwork filled out, to get the doctor's instructions and prescriptions. Pitch was steaming because it took so long. Then he tried to walk out and the nurse told him that she had to take him down in a wheelchair. That just set him off and by now Ann had enough of his child behavior. "Pitch, sit your ass in that wheelchair and I don't want to hear another word come out of your mouth. Do you understand me. Am I clear?"

He looked at her and sat down in the wheelchair and out the front door of the hospital he went. On the ride home Pitch didn't say a word. "Aren't you happy to be going home?"

"Can I talk now Boss McClure?' They both broke out laughing.

Ann didn't tell him that she was putting him up in her bedroom. She figured she would surprise him.

When they pulled up at the front of the house there was a group of his wranglers, Kinno, Nija, Samoka, and the kids waiting to welcome him home. The kids all had to hug him even Tony. Samoka helped get him in the house and when Samoka turned to the steps instead of going down the hallway Pitch's eyes lit up. "What is this?"

"You are going to stay in my bedroom so I can keep an eye on you."

Pitch's face had a big grin on it and Ann just looked at him cross eyed.

CHAPTER 10

Pitch got all settled in Ann's bedroom and he was totally exhausted from all the morning activities. Ann told him to take a nap because she had some things to do and would come check on him later. Ann ran down the steps and told the kids to jump in the car quickly and she went up to the village lacrosse game. The second half of the game was just starting and they all waved and yelled at Tommy. He was all smiles and went on to score three goals in that half alone. His team the Tomahawks won 12-6 and Tommy scored five goals. After the game she told Tommy to get his equipment and get in the car because she needed to get home since Mr. Pitch was out of the hospital. "You can tell Mr. Pitch all about your game. I know he would love to hear all about it."

When they got home, Pitch was sitting in the kitchen eating and Tommy ran over and hugged him and told him the Tomahawks won. Ann looked at Nija with a pissed off look. "Ann, he just came down the steps and when I turned around, he was standing there."

"I understand Nija he is just hard headed. After talking with Tommy for a while about his game Pitch had to go back up stairs because he was starting to hurt. Ann took him up and he said, "Come lay down with me.""

"I have a lot of things I need to catch up on around here. You take your nap. I can see you are really tired and in pain."

Ann needed some fresh air and time to herself so she saddled up her horse and went for a ride. Her mind was on hard headed Pitch and trying to kept him under control until he fully recovered. She also was concerned about Tony and his dating problem. He did have to like the Chief's daughter out of all the girls in school. She wasn't sure but had a feeling that the Chief probably would not allow Maomi to date Tony. He probably wanted to keep the pure Indian blood line. Hell, they were only going to the movies and not getting married. Maybe Pitch could help with this problem. Ann also really wanted to hire Charlie Douglas mainly to keep him and his family here in Sheridan with Dan. She knew that Tom Berry was up to something but was not sure what it was. Ann hoped that Dan and Curly's trap worked so they could put Gallon behind bars. As she rode and looked out over the land it was hard for her to believe this all belonged to her. Then she thought about her upcoming wedding to Pitch and how God had put the two of them together. Ann knew her kids were getting older and Rory would have a singing career, Tommy would probably go to college and play lacrosse. Tony would get married and settle down somewhere. But hopefully she would still have her little Nellie. When Ann got back to the ranch, she was dirty and tired. Dinja told her he would take care of her horse. She went right upstairs to take a good shower. After showering she put on her three-quarters length silk robe and laid across the bed with her feet at Pitch's face. As she was dozing off Pitch started kissing her toes, then her feet, ankles, and calves. She through she was dreaming and then realized this was really happening. "Pitch, you are driving me crazy. I am horny enough and that even makes it harder on me." "Can I make love with you. I need you badly and all I think about is your sexy body."

"The doctor said no physical exercise."

"What does the doctor know?"

Ann got up off the bed and went and got dressed. "Let's go down stairs it is almost dinner time."

After dinner Rory asked Ann and Pitch if he could talk to them in private on the patio. They went out with him, "What's up Mr. Star?"

"I need to sing more and I love singing in front of a live audience at the Coyote."

Ann looked at him, "What do you have in mind?"

I would like to sing at the Coyote on Friday nights from eight to ten. That would give me a lot more experience and I could learn many new songs. I would till sing on Saturday from eight to nine so I can go to church with the family on Sunday. This would really help me advance my singing career."

"What do you think Ann?"

"What he says makes sense. I don't have a problem with it. What about the logistics of getting back and forth?"

"How about Tony driving and picking me up on Fridays?"

"No, that will not work. Tony has his own life and wants to go out with his friends on weekends. In fact, he has something he needs to talk to you about Pitch."

"I would think Stoney would be all right with this because it would help him pack the club on Friday nights just like on Saturday."

"Rory did not say a word that Stoney was in on the idea. "Here is the deal, if Stoney is willing to pick you up and bring you home on Friday night, I am okay with it. Ann and I will still go with you on Saturday. You okay with that Ann?"

"Yes, but the first time Rory is not home by ten-thirty on Friday, the deal is off."

"You okay with that condition Rory?"

"Yes sir, thank you both."

I will make a call to Stoney when we go in and see if he is okay about this plan. Remember now, if he says no you just keep singing on Saturday."

"Yes sir, whatever Stoney says goes."

After Pitch talked with Stoney everything was a go. Stoney told Pitch how great the club was doing. Pitch told him that he was going to try and talk Ann into letting him go with her on Saturday. "If I get there Stoney, I want you to assign a bouncer to be with me at all times because I am still recovering and can not be pushed around by people."

"You got it boss. I hope you can make it."

David Sarnoff the president of RCA Records finally got back in the states and called Sister Martin. She was so happy to hear from him and hoped that he would help Rory. "It seems funny calling you Sister Martin instead of Sylvia. How do you like being a nun?"

"This is the life for me David. I just love it."

"By the tape I know you can still play a mean guitar. Hey, that arrangement was beautiful. How in the world did you come up with that idea?"

"Rory and I worked on it together."

"How old is this young man"""

"He is thirteen but very mature."

"When can you get him to Nashville to see what we can do with him?"

"That could be a problem because he is still in school and I don't think his mother would let him go by himself."

"Doesn't she want to get rich?"

"David, she is already rich and is also the mayor of the town."

"He performances on weekends at the Coyote Night Club and the place is packed with wall to wall people."

"I'll tell you what Sylvia, I will send Chris Finley, one of my scouts, out to hear him sing and if he thinks the kid is great, he will talk to his parents about getting him to the recording studio in Nashville. How does that sound?"

"That is great David but tell this Chris to talk to me before he talks to Rory's mother."

"You got a deal. One more thing I would like to release that song on the tape with you and him at Christmas time. However, you both would have to come to the studio to record it."

"I'll think about it and let you know. Nice talking to you David. Thanks for your help."

"Anything for a mean guitar playing nun,"

Sheriff Douglas and Curly were hoping their trap worked after two weeks. Dan had the Kelly's put a sold sticker across the sale sign. The Kelly's got a call about the sale and they told the mysterious caller that it sold for $101,000 and the couple was ready to settle on the house. The caller told them to have the settlement on Thursday at eight o'clock in the evening because of his job. Mr. Kelly told him that he would check with the buyer but was sure it would be all right because they really wanted the house. Mrs. Kelly immediately called Sheriff Douglas and told him the situation. "Mrs. Kelly, Curly and I will at your office at seven o'clock and we will come in a plain car and park in your backyard. We think this person may be watching your office before he shows up."

Sheriff Douglas reported to Ann what was going down and would let her know the minute they have the person. While he was talking to her, he told her that he thought the prisoner was about ready to sing for him.

Pitch was getting stronger by the day and was bored out of his mind. One morning after Ann and the kids left, he told Nija he was going for a walk. Pitch walked slowly down to his truck and put it in four-wheel-drive and drove out to see how Kinno was doing. When Kinno saw a truck coming across the range he knew who it was. Kinno rode over to the truck laughing. "Hey, Pitch what are you a Ford Cowboy now?"

"Very funny! What is up with the herd?"

We are ready to drive the herd to the auction. We will start the drive two days from now."

"How long do you think it will take to get them to the train station?"

"With the size of this herd maybe three days or less. You know it depends a lot on the weather."

"I can't help with the drive but I will meet you at the train station for the auction."

"That sounds great. I would feel better with you there."

"I better go before Boss Ann comes back to the ranch and catches me driving. I'll see you back at the ranch."

That evening Ann told Pitch all about Tony wanting to date Maomi. She explained to him everything that she said to Tony and about the questions Tony was supposed to asked her. "Ann, I have to make a phone call. While I make the call get Tony and go out on the patio."

Ann and Tony only waited five minutes for Pitch to come out. "Tony, I hear you are having some women problems? Well, you better get used to it. Never mind, it was just a bad adult joke."

"Tell me where you are with Maomi?"

"I did like Mrs. McClure said and I asked her all kind of questions but the problem is she does not talk much so it was hard getting answers. I think she really likes me but then I think there is some type of Shoshone custom."

"Where did you get that idea?"

"Mrs. McClure said I might have to ask the Chief if I can date his daughter. It maybe that she can only date Indian boys because of pure blood lines according to Mrs. McClure."

"So, you got all this guidance from a Shoshone expert?"

"Pitch, I was only trying to help and I know the Shoshone believe in customs."

"That is right Ann and they also believe in spirits."

"Okay, Mr. Smart Ass what should he do?"

Pitch made like he was thinking really hard for a couple of minutes. "I got it! Tony walk up to Maomi and say, "I would like to take you to the movies on Saturday evening at six o'clock. If she says yes, you go to the movie, if says no then you know she does not like you like a boyfriend."

Ann quickly said, "That is it! What about being the Chief's daughter and Shoshone customs."

"I didn't say any of that junk you did. The Chief let's Maomi make her own decisions as to who she dates. Ann this is 1951, wake up. Where in the world did you come up with all the stuff?"

"Wait a minute you Shit Head, who did you make a call to minutes ago?"

"Just one of the cattle hands."

"Might this cattle hand be Kinno?'

Tony was standing there just laughing at the two of them making fun out of the other. "All I have to do is ask her out?"

"You got it partner. I hope you learned a lesson here today, never ask Ann anything about the Shoshone."

Then he started running for the house and Ann right behind him hitting him on his ass. "You Ass Hole, I owe you for that."

Dan and Curly set up in the back room of the Kelly's office so they could hear the conversations and had the door cracked so they could see the person. About five minutes after eight there was a knock on the door and when Peter Kelly opened it there stood Tom Berry. Peter welcomed him in and the three of them sat around a conference table where Mrs. Kelly had papers spread all over. To keep things polite, with a smile Mrs. Kelly said, "Mr.

Berry how did you come to own this property that belonged to the Gallon's? I only ask because the state tax register still has the Gallon's as owners." "I really don't own the property. I have Power of Attorney for the Gallon's. They have authorized me to sell the house as their broker. I will receive a 10% fee off the selling price and will send the rest to the Gallon's."

Dan and Curly had heard enough and came out of the back room. Curly had his gun drawn just in case of trouble. "Well, if it isn't my new buddy Tom Berry! Looks like you have gotten yourself in some big trouble."

"I have not broken any laws. I am just the broker for the property."

"Let me see now, aiding a fugitive on the law, obstruction of justice and I think I can up with a few more if I have too and I'm sure the city's new Attorney General will back me on the charges."

Both Dan and Curly had a big grin on their faces. "What I want to know Mr. Berry is how were you going to get the money to the Gallon's?"

"I was to mail it to them."

"That is a good start. What is the mailing address?"

"It is just a post box number."

"Where is the post box located?"

"I don't know."

"Sounds like another charge Curly."

"It sure does Sheriff. Berry when you send something to post box you have to have the town and state. How dumb do you think we are?"

"Thank you for reminding me Curly. Now, Tom you know I can go to our post office and find out where this post box is by the number. Why don't you just tell me and save us some work?"

"Okay, it is in Silver Springs, Colorado."

"So, that is where the Gallons are?"

"I am not sure, all I know is Silver Springs, Colorado."

"Tom, I don't like people who lie to me. You are just digging a deeper hole for yourself."

You could tell Berry was thinking very hard. "What kind of deal can I get?"

"Let me think about this for a couple minutes. If you tell us the Gallon's address and the FBI picks him up there here is what I will do. I will drop all charges against you and you will have two days to pack up and get out of Sheridan. That is the best offer you are going to get from me."

"Do I have to go to jail?"

"Absolutely, until the FBI confirms they have arrested Gallon."

Berry didn't know what to do and was just looking at the sheriff trying to figure out if he was buffing. His mind was really working. He knew he had already lost his job, he didn't own a house here, and he could move anywhere and start over without a criminal record. The sheriff was getting inpatient waiting for his response. "The deal is about to go out the door Berry. Going once, going twice."

"I'll take the deal. The Gallon's new address is 125 Michael Road in Silver Springs, Colorado."

"See that wasn't so hard. Curly put the handcuffs on him and take him to jail and then notify the FBI where Gallon is located. Mr. & Mrs. Kelly thank you for all your help."

"What is going to happen with the house?"

"The city is confiscating it, so go ahead and sell it for the city."

"What about the five hundred dollars he gave us already?'

"What five hundred dollars! We have to go, thank you again."

Since it was just nine o'clock Dan called Ann and shared the good news with her and she was very happy.

Rory's singing at the Coyote club on the weekends was working out really well. Ann would not let Pitch go to Rory's performance Saturday night and he was pissed. She promised him that he could next Saturday if he was a good boy. Tony and Maomi went on their first date to the movies on Saturday. Every time Ann got back from the office Pitch's clothes were dusty and dirty looking. Ann through something was going on and Pitch was hiding something from her. When she asked him about his clothes, he told her he had been going for long walks to build up his strength. "Sure, you have, something is fishy about your story."

"You can ask Nija!"

Nija shook her head yes. Ann, let it be for now but she knew he was up to trouble for sure. Later that night Ann pulled Nija a side and said, "Tomorrow when Pitch goes for a walk, I want you to call me immediately at my office."

The next day as soon as Pitch left the house Nija called Ann. "Nija how long is Mr. Pitch usually gone?"

"About two hours, sometimes a little longer."

"Thank you, I will be home before he gets there."

When Ann came back about just two hours later and she walked down to the stables to look to see if Thunder was still there. Since Pitch's horse was still in the stable, she went over the parking area and Pitch's truck was gone. She waited down at the stables figuring he would be back shortly. When he pulled into his parking space Ann popped her head out of the barn. "Where have you been big boy?"

Pitch was shocked when he heard her voice. "You caught me, I was out checking on the herd since Kinno will be driving them to the train station tomorrow."

"Look, I don't want to be your baby sitter and I know you have ants in your pants and are bored out of your mind. However, I want you completely recovered so we have a long life together."

"I am sorry for not telling you the truth but at least I took the truck and not my horse."

"I give up. I guess your head is just too hard."

"Here is something to think about besides me. When Kinno gets the herds to the train station you and I have to meet him there for the auction because Kinno knows nothing about selling cattle."

"When is that going to happen?"

"In three or four days. It depends on when the buyers get there."

"Okay, but try and get a firm date because I have all kinds of stuff going on. That reminds me, will you talk with Charlie Douglas with me about the Attorney General job?"

"Absolutely, when do you want to do it?"

"How about tomorrow morning, it will give you something to do."

Ann called Dan to tell him to have Charlie meet her at her office at ten o'clock because she didn't have Charlie's phone number. "Are you going to hire him Ann?"

"I am not sure but tomorrow I will make my decision one way or the other."

"Hey, guess what."

"What is it Dan?"

"When my prisoner saw Tom Berry being put in the cell next to him all of a sudden, he wanted to talk. He told us that Gallon had recruited the men from Arizona and he is the one that told them where to blast and Tom Berry was their money man. He said they already had $60,000 from the uranium. He also thinks that Gallon took off with all the money and didn't give a shit about them. He thought that Berry was getting the money they needed from the city by telling Gallon how to get it. Berry only met with them one time but he was a big part of the planning. Also, the FBI called and said they were on their way to pick up Gallon. It's been a good day, so far."

"I'll talk to you later Dan. Good work!"

When Pitch and Ann got to her office Charlie Douglas was waiting and he had on a suit and tie. "Charlie give us a minute and we will be right with you."

Charlie kept looking at Pitch like something was wrong with him. When Pitch got into her office, "Ann, why is that young man stirring at me?"

"I have no idea."

Ann picked up the papers she needed about the job and the three of them went in to her conference room. "Charlie, I like you and I think you have a lot of potential and could be an asset to the city."

Charlie kept looking at Pitch. "I'm sorry I forgot to introduce you to my finance'. Pitch Wesley."

Pitch started to say hello when Charlie went off. "I knew it. You are Sam Pitch Wesley and you pitched for the Dodgers. Our coach talked about you all the time when I was in college."

"Your coach!"

"I played baseball for the University of Wyoming where you went to school."

"Now, I know why you were looking at me so hard."

"Our coach had your picture hanging all over the place as an inspiration to the players.

"What position did you play?"

"I played centerfield and I hold the school record for the most home runs in a career."

"Okay boys, you can talk baseball later. Charlie your Uncle Dan says your specialty is Wyoming state law?"

"That is correct Mayor and you can talk to Judge Potter in Laramie about me. I did an internship in his court and he hated to see me move on."

I can see Pitch is impressed with you and wants me to hire you."

"You will be also when I work for you."

"A man with confidence. Here is the city's offer. You will become the youngest Attorney General in this city's history. You will report directly to me and work very closely with your uncle. Your office is right down the hallway and you have staff of four people including your secretary. The salary is $35,000 a year plus the city pays your health insurance. I think I covered everything. Do you have any question?"

"Yes, are you offering me the job right now?"

"Yes, I am Charlie, do you want it?"

"Absolutely Mayor, and I greatly appreciate you giving me this opportunity."

They all shook hands to seal the deal. "When do I start Mayor?"

"How about Monday?'

"That will be fine. It will give me time to clean up something."

Charlie almost ran out the door. "Ann, you did the right thing. I think he will be great. No doubt, you will be getting a call from Dan in about ten minutes."

Ann laughed.

Saturday night Pitch went with Ann and Rory to the Coyote club to hear Rory sing. Stoney had a table up front reserved for them. When they came in Stoney introduced Pitch to Jack who was one of the club's bouncers. Jack was about six-feet four inches tall and weighed about two hundred and fifty pounds and was nothing but muscle. Jack made his way through the crowd for them to get to their table while Rory went up on the stage. As soon as they sat down Sharon came running over to Ann. "Isn't this so exciting with your son singing? Bob and I have become Saturday night regulars since Rory started singing here. Pitch looks really good," Sharon was like a talking machine and just went on and on. Ann was so glad when she went back to sit with Bob. Rory was fabulous that night and the people kept yelling more, more. "Pitch looked at Ann, "Let him sing a couple more songs. We will leave at nine-thirty."

Ann agreed and Pitch put two fingers and mouthed to Wes that Rory could sing two more songs. When Wes told the crowd they all started cheering. On the way home Rory thanked them for letting him sing a couple more songs. "Have the both of you thought about the next step for me?"

"To be honest Rory we haven't given it much thought with my injury and your Mom becoming mayor. We promise to give it some serious thought."

Late Tuesday afternoon Kinno called Pitch and told him the herd made it safely and that the auction would start at noon tomorrow. "Ann, the auction starts tomorrow at noon so we have to leave the house at around five in the morning to get there on time."

"Are you kidding me? What happened to the advanced notice that you were going to give to me?"

"Ann, we don't control this, the buyers do and they don't give a shit whether or not you sell your cattle. They feel like they are doing us a favor coming to our small area,"

"I understand now. I will be ready to go in the morning. I can sleep while you drive, right?"

Charlie was getting adjusted to his new job and staff. Everybody in the office saw that he was full of energy and they would have to pick up their pace to keep up with him. Ann stopped by to see him, "Are you getting settled in Charlie? I need you to get those charges on the prisoner who shot Pitch over to Dan."

"He already has them and once he signs off on them, I will get them over to Judge Thomas."

"Good work Charlie, I think I am going to like working with you."

"Mayor, before you leave. What about the charges again Tom Berry? Do you want me to work up the paperwork?"

"You better hold off on those until we hear from the FBI and because Dan cut a deal with Berry if Gallon is arrested."

"Will do Mayor, have a nice day."

"Oh, Charlie before I forget, I will be going to the cattle auction the next couple days and I have left Fred Johnson in charge if you need anything. Hopefully, I will be back in on Friday."

"Got it, have a safe trip."

As Ann was walking back to her office, she thought maybe the entire office building will pick up Charlie's energy. Before Ann called it a day, she decided to go see Dan. Dan thanked her for giving Charlie this great opportunity. "Dan have you heard from the FBI yet?"

"Know, and that is starting to worry me. Curly put a call into them and he has not received a call back."

"That does not sound good!"

"You know Gallon is as slippery as an eel."

"If we don't arrest him are you filing charges against Berry?"

"Yes, he knows the deal. We have to arrest Gallon or the deal is off the table."

"Just keep me informed about what is going on. Oh yea, I am going to the cattle auction with Pitch and will be out of the office until Friday. If you need something Fred Johnson is in charge."

"Have a good trip and make lots of money."

Before sun rise Ann and Pitch were on their way to the train station for the auction. Ann slept almost two hours and when she woke up, she had a ton of questions for Pitch about the auction. "How many buyers come to the auction?"

"Probably only about six, compared to the large auctions where there are usually twenty or more."

"How many ranchers will have their cattle there to auction off?"

"Probably, seven or eight. Dick Bonne and our herd will be the two largest ones."

"How does the auction work?"

"There are many different ways but this one they kept really simple to get it over quickly so the buyers can move on to the next one."

"Where are the buyers from?"

"Mostly meat companies and large chain restaurants like McDonalds."

Pitch was impressed that Ann wanted to know all about the auction. However, he didn't want to tell her things were changing in the cattle industry and some companies were now raising their owns herds. Pitch personally thought that in ten to fifteen years there would be no more cattle ranches in Wyoming. When they finally arrived at the train station all the corrals there were filled so that meant the auction was almost ready to start. Kinno came over to them and told them the auctioneer would be starting in a half hour. "How does the prices look?"

"Really good, up from last years prices. The boys have coffee made you want some?"

The auction started right at noon and Ann could not understand a word the auctioneer was saying. She kept asking Pitch what he was saying and Pitch brushed her off and said, "Listen."

Most of the small herds went first and the prices were really good. By the time the auctioneer got to the McClure herd it was getting dark so he called a halt to the auction until eight o'clock tomorrow morning. Ann looked at Pitch, "So what do we do now?"

"There is a small town about fifteen minutes from here where we can get something to eat and a place to sleep over night."

"You didn't tell me we were staying overnight. I didn't pack an overnight bag and I have nothing to sleep in or clean clothes for tomorrow. What is the name of this small town?"

"It is called Cow Town!"

"Are you kidding me?"

"No, that is the name, I think only about thirty people live there and they all seem to be related."

"This small town has places for all of us to sleep?"

No. all the wranglers will just camp out here by the station. Only the owners, the buyers, and the auctioneer will need a place to stay. Kinno has reserved a room for us."

"Oh, so you knew we would have to stay overnight and didn't tell me?"

"Actually, I never gave it a thought but I am glad Kinno did or we would be sleeping under the stars with the cows instead of being in Cow Town."

"I bet this place is a real dive?"

"Well, it isn't a four-star hotel. Would prefer to sleep in the truck?"

"No, let's go check it out because I am hungry."

"I am on my way to Cow Town."

When Ann and Pitch checked into their room after a big dinner and some drinks the room actually was not that bad. "I am surprised by the quality of this room and we even have our own bathroom."

"You wouldn't be if you knew the price for one night!"

"How much is it?"

"Now don't scream or yell at me, $200 a night."

"Holy shit, you got to be kidding me!"

"No, the owner knows that all the people staying here are rich so he milks them for all the money he can get. The auctions only happen every quarter of the year so the town has to make their money during that time for the entire year." Well, that does make sense. I hate to know what you paid for dinner?"

Pitch took a shower and then Ann took hers. "What the hell am I supposed to put on now Pitch?'

"As far as I am concerned absolutely nothing. You can sleep naked."

"That will not work for me. I'll just put my panties and bra back on since you are wearing your boxer shorts."

The two them just laid in bed. "So, what do we do now Ann?"

"We go to sleep. It has been a long day."

She rolled over on her side facing away from Pitch. His arm immediately went around her wrist and his other hand was playing with her long hair. Pitch started kissing her on her neck several times. Ann started getting cool chills running through her body. "What are you doing Pitch?"

"Just feeling the lady, I love."

Ann turned to face him and they started kissing passionately. The next thing she knew was that her bra was unhooked. "This is trouble Pitch!"

"You know I love trouble."

Ann kissed all over his chest and the next thing she knew his boxer shorts were off. "Are you sure about this?"

Pitch was kissing all over her body and he worked off her panties. "Pitch I am worried about you re-injuring yourself."

"Just sit on my lap and don't lay on my chest and it will be fine."

They made love for a long time and when Ann rolled off of him, "On top is really hard work!"

Pitch broke out laughing and she hit him with a pillow.

As the auctioneer sold off the McClure herd Ann was still thinking about last night. When Pitch totaled up all the money from the different buyers, they had $265,000 to take home. On the ride back to the ranch Pitch was in some pain so Ann took over driving to let him just rest. "I told you last night was too much for you."

"Don't bother me I am picturing last night with somebody sitting on top of me."

"You are a real hard head Pitch. No more sex until you go for your check-up next week."

"I can't hear you."

"You might not hear me but I will show you."

The Tomahawks won the village lacrosse league championship and Tommy broke the season scoring record previously held by Dinja. Tommy made sure to bug Dinja about breaking his record. "You have better equipment to play with then back when I played. Our sticks were hand made not these custom factory fancy sticks like you have now."

"Don't cry Dinja, you did coach me so you get some credit. I'll probably break all your records next year."

"I don't think so, now that all the coaches know your ability, they will double team you and it will be hard to get open."

"We can work on that this winter."

"Only if you say please." They both laughed.

Sister Martin waited for Chris Finley from RCA to come to town. After school on Friday he came knocking on the convent door. Sister Mary answered the door. She invited Chris in and went to find Sister Martin. Chris introduced himself to Sister Martin and said that David Sarnoff spoke very highly of her. Sister told him all about Rory and how talented he is. "Rory sings at the Coyote Night Club downtown on Friday from eight to ten and on Saturday from eight to nine."

"Do you think you could go with me? I know it is asking a lot but I really would appreciate it."

"Let me talk to Sister Mary and see if I would be allowed to go."

"Mother Superior said it is okay because Rory has done so much for the church. I have to warn you the club will be really packed."

"That will be good. I will get to see him perform to a live audience."

"I will meet you at the door about quarter to eight."

"I can pick you up Sister."

"No, that will not be permitted. I'll just meet you there."

After Finley left Sister Martin called Ann at home and Ann and Pitch had just got back from the auction. Ann, I have Chris Finley a RCA records scout coming to hear Rory perform on Friday and Saturday. I was wondering if you could get Pitch to have Stoney Mason reserve a front table for us?"

"No problem, I will have Pitch call Stoney right now. Maybe Saturday night this Finley can sit with Pitch and I. Pitch can tell Stoney to watch for him at the door."

"I will be with Chris, Ann."

"I can't believe my ears. How did you pull that off?"

"Sister Superior thought the church owed Rory so it is good and I am trying to help him."

"Okay then, Pitch and I can sit with you and Finley on Saturday. I am anxious to see what he thinks about Rory."

On the way to her office Friday Ann stopped at John Riggins office and gave him the $265,000. "Ann, if Pitch does this every quarter you will be rolling in the money."

"Yea, but I have a lot of salaries and bills to pay."

"You are doing just fine Mayor."

Since she was in that part of town she decided to stop in and see the latest Dan has to report. "It is good to see you Ann. Did you make tons of money at the auction?"

"Just a little. What is the status with Gallon?"

"The FBI said when they got to the place where he lived it was empty. There were no signs of where he went."

"I guess that means we will have to prosecute Tom Berry?"

"Let's go tell him the deal is off and see if he has anything to say."

They walked in the part of the department where the cells were. "Hi Tom, say hi to Mayor McClure. She just instructed me to file charges against you."

"What happened to our deal sheriff?"

"Well Tom, it's like this, the FBI went to where you told them to pick up Gallon and guess what, no Gallon. Our deal was only good if they arrested Gallon so you are shit out of luck. To bad, you could have moved and started a new life."

Ann and Dan turned to walk back to his office. "Wait a minute, I might have something for you."

"This better be good Berry because I am tired of shitting with you."

"Gallon always rented a cabin up in Breckenridge for the snow season. He might be holding up there because it is the off season and nobody will be there. I went up there once with him and the place is called Snow Mountain Rentals and he had cabin number four."

"If I send the FBI up to Breckenridge and they do not find Gallon your ass is going to prison for a long time."

"I am positive that is where he is."

Dan and Ann went back to his office. "I will have Curly call the FBI but they will probably call the state troopers up in the Breckenridge area go check the place out before they go all the way up there."

"I can't blame them Dan, that's what I would do. I'll see you later, got to run."

Sister Martin was looking for Chris Finley at the Coyote Night Club front door. At the same time, Chris was looking through the crowd of people for a nun but Sister Martin was dressed in western clothes with her long black hair hanging down. When Sister Martin saw Chris, she yelled over to him and he just stood there looking at her. "Is that you Sister Martin?"

"Yes, Chris, I am just in regular clothes so I fit in and don't draw attention."

"I am sorry Sister but as beautiful as you are you are going to draw a lot of attention in any night club."

"Let me worry about that, you are here for Rory."

When they walked in the Coyote club, she could see that Stoney was looking all over for them. "Excuse me Stoney!"

"Yea, yea, what do you want I am very busy right now."

"I am Sister Martin. Are you looking for me?"

"Yes, I was looking for a nun."

"I am a nun"

"Where is your penguin outfit. You know the black and white all covered up look."

"I gave it the night off. Ann McClure said you would have a reserved table for us."

"I do, right up front. This must be the guy from RCA?"

"Stoney this is Chris Finley a scout for RCA Records. Stoney is the manger of the Coyote club."

"Looks like you have a big crowd here tonight Stoney?"

"Yea, ever since Rory started singing here on the weekends the place has been packed to the walls."

"Just wait here a minute Sister I'll be right back. Hey, Jack come over here."

"Yes boss, what do you need?"

"See that very beautiful Indian woman standing there with that guy?"

"I see her, she is dam pretty."

"Jack, that is Sister Martin from Saint Joseph's Catholic Church."

"You're shitting me. What is she doing taking a night off from the habit?"

"Knock the shit off, she is a very good friend on Pitch and Ann. You mean the owner of this place and our mayor. You are to stay with her the entire night and don't let any ass hole try to hit on her. Can you do that?"

"Sure Stoney, I got it."

"If you want to keep your bouncer job you better make sure nothing happens to her."

"I promise boss. It will protect her."

"All right come with me. Sister Martin, Chris this is Jack one of our security officers and he will be watching out for you both tonight. He will take you to your table up by the stage."

As they walked to their table Jack was moving people out of their way. "Sister Martin how come all this special treatment?"

"Let's see if you can follow this Chris. Rory's mother is Ann McClure who is the mayor of the town and owner of the McClure ranch. She is engaged to Pitch Wesley who is the owner the Coyote Night Club and is the manager of her ranch. Ann and Pitch are very good friends of mine and I taught Rory how to play his guitar and he is in my class at school."

"No wonder this guy is going to protect you."

While the band was warming up Rory kept looking at their table. Then he walked over, "Is that you Sister Martin?'

"The one and only Rory."

"You look so different."

"I know Rory. This is a friend of mine, Chris Finley who works as a scout for RCA Records."

"I have to run Wes is calling me."

The Bandit band played a warm up song and then Rory sang "I'm so Lonesome I Could Cry." When he finished the place went nuts. "What do you think Chris?"

"I need to hear a few more songs before I pass judgement."

At nine-thirty Sister Martin got up, didn't say a word and went to Stoney, "Would you please call me a taxi I have to leave now?"

"Are you going to the convent?"

"Yes, I have to be in before ten o'clock because the doors will be locked."

"Sister a taxi will take forever getting here. Let Sophie drive you to the convent."

"That would be great Stoney."

Sophie and Sister Martin jumped in the car and off they went. The convent was only about ten minutes away. Chris came walking back to where Stoney was standing. "Stoney, have you seen Sister Martin?"

"Yes, she left about ten minutes ago. Sophie took her to the convent."

"She didn't say a word to me. I would have driven her to the convent."

"There are a couple things you need to understand Chris. First, she didn't say anything to you because she wanted you to listen to Rory and she had to get back to the convent before ten o'clcok because Sister Superior locks and bolts the door. Also, she wouldn't let you drive her because she can not ride in a car with a man alone. That is why she let Sophie drive to the convent and not you. Remember all of that for tomorrow. Sister Martin may have been a professional guitar player once but now she is a true blue nun and lives by her vows."

'Stoney thank you so much for the explanation and for all your help tonight."

"Come on Chris let's got sit at the bar, drinks are on me."

They sat at the bar and talked for a while and Stoney asked Sophie to take Rory home. It was obvious to Stoney from their conversation that Chris thought Rory had a bright future in music. Chris really wanted to get Rory to Nashville so RCA could work with him but wasn't sure how to go about getting him there. "Chris, I like you so let me educate you a little. First of all, don't use money as an incentive for Rory to go to Nashville. Both Ann and Pitch are independently very rich and don't need the money. Then there is school, Rory has about three weeks left before school breaks for the summer. They want him to get an education. The last thing and it is a big one, Ann is the mayor of this town and has three other kids to worry about. Pitch is the Manager of her ranch and owns this night club. Are you getting the picture so far? They will not let Rory got to Nashville by himself and they don't have the time to go with him. So, when you talk to them tomorrow night keep all these things in the back of your head."

Rory was really happy around the house on Saturday and everybody kept trying to figure out why. Finally, Ann said, "Rory why are you happy today?"

"Last night at the Coyote Sister Martin bought a scout for RCA Records to hear me sing."

"So, why does that make you happy?"

"RCA is looking at me to make records for them and my career will be on its way."

"Aren't you jumping to conclusions pretty fast? What if he doesn't think you are good enough?" "Mom, Sister Martin thinks I am good enough to make records or she wouldn't have had this scout come here from Nashville."

"You know Sister Martin knows the president of RCA Records from her professional days. So, maybe he is just doing her a favor by sending a scout to hear you."

"Mom, you will meet Chris Finley tonight at the Coyote and you can see what he has on his mind."

Ann was worried about Rory being over confident and the big problem about him going to Nashville. She would have to get her genius Pitch to come up with the right solution.

Pitch, Ann, and Rory arrived at the Coyote club at seven-thirty. Waiting at the front door was Sister Martin and Chris Finley. After introductions Jack took them to their table. When the local people there saw Mayor McClure was in the audience they started chanting, "Mayor, Mayor, Mayor."

To acknowledge them, Ann stood up and they waved and said thank you. "You are very popular here Ann."

"This town has needed a new mayor for many years. I just think they are grateful for the change."

Wes Holder came over and did nothing but praise Rory. "So, Mr. Holder, what is Rory singing tonight?"

"Just call me Wes, Chris. He is singing a song he wrote."

"He writes music himself Sister?"

"He also plays the piano great. He has music in his veins."

Ann, Pitch and Sister Martin knew nothing about this song Rory had written so this was a surprise to them. The band played a couple songs then Wes came to the microphone to introduce Rory. Then Rory stepped up to the microphone, "Ladies and Gentlemen I am going to sing a song I wrote myself. I hope you enjoy it." The band played the intro to the song and Rory started singing, "Just pickin my guitar and singing my songs, letting each day go by with happiness inside, hoping that when I pass away my songs will bring happiness to people in many ways, so pick a little, sing a little in your life."

The entire place was on their feet applauding including Chris Finley. When the crowd settled down Chris turned to Ann, "That song could be a number one country western song in the nation. You have to let this young man cut some records for the public."

Between the tears running down her face Ann was smiling. Pitch hugged her. They both were so proud of Rory. After he finished up singing for the night and it was time to go home Chris said, "Is it okay if I come out to your ranch tomorrow afternoon to talk to you both about Rory's future?"

"Ann looked at Pitch, "That will be fine Chris. We go to church and then have lunch so about one o'clock would be great."

"Thank you, I will see you at one."

That night as Ann and Pitch laid in bed, "Pitch what are we going to do?"

"I have been thinking about this and maybe there is a solution. First of all, Rory has to finish school. Once he is out for the summer, he will be a available to go to Nashville."

"Okay, now comes the hard part."

"You are right Ann, he can't go by himself and it is crazy to think one of us could go with him. I think we have to ask

Chris how long Rory has to be in Nashville. Once we know that it might help us select the right person to go with him. I have a couple people in mind but I think we need to know the arrangements like, how does he get there, where does he stay, and things like that. We should make a list of our questions for Chris.

Both Ann and Pitch didn't get much sleep that night and were glad when church was over. Sister Martin came over and asked them what they thought about last night? Pitch said, "For one thing I think maybe I should start charging admission if that crowd keeps coming."

"I don't mean that. I am talking about Chris' reaction."

"You heard what he said by the song Rory wrote. He loves the kid!"

"Our problem is getting him to Nashville."

"I figured that would be the issue."

"We are meeting with him at one o'clock today at the ranch would you like to come?"

"I think it is best if the two of you handle it from here. But I will be praying hard that everything works out."

When Chris arrived at the ranch, he told Ann and Pitch that he talked to David Sarnoff this morning and he is ready to sign Rory. David said to tell you it would probably be best if Rory had an agent."

"That may be a problem because we want Rory to finish his education. He can do what you want him to during the three-month summer break. What about things like how does he get to Nashville, where does he stay and things like that?"

"RCA would send one of their airplanes to pick him up, he would have a suite at a five-star hotel. He would have a security man and a coordinator with him at all times. Of course, RCA is paying for all of this."

"What kind of money would he be making?"

"Ann, I couldn't tell you this but David wants to sign Rory to a five-year contract worth two million dollars."

"Holy shit!"

Pitch added, "I second that Ann! Chris, Rory has three weeks of school left and we need time to think things out carefully. Give us a week to get back to you with our plan."

"That will be fine Pitch. I look forward to hearing from you and working with Rory."

CHAPTER 11

Rory wanted to know everything Ann and Pitch talked about with Chris. When they told him the things Chris said he started jumping around like a crazy person. Both Ann and Pitch went to work on Monday but their minds were on the Rory situation. Ann took a break from her office and went to talk to John Riggins about everything. John said he could be Rory's financial advisor and handle the negotiation of his contract with RCA and set him up a bank account. Ann thought that was great. She always valued John's advice. "Ann, as for the other part, I think what you need is a traveling guardian who would be Rory's side-kick wherever he goes. I think you need someone who knows the music industry, a person about your age, Rory would listen to and value their opinion. If I were you, I would pay this person $50,000 a year plus expenses."

"That is a lot of money for just being a baby sitter!"

"Well, if Rory is going to make two or three million dollars it really isn't. If you hire an agent, they would cost you a lot more.

Plus, if the person is from here, that would be the best job in the world because they wouldn't want to lose this great paying job."

"John you are really good at what you do. I thank you so much that I could kiss you."

"I've never been kissed by a mayor."

Ann walked over and kissed him on the cheek.

When Ann caught up with Pitch that evening, she told him everything John Riggins said. "I thought about Samoka or Dinja but that wouldn't work because they are too important around here and we don't know how they would be treated in Nashville. You know as well as I do there are ass holes all over this nation."

"Yea, I think you are right Pitch. I thought about Sharon but she has to small kids and Bob couldn't handle the store and the kids. Sharon says he can't handle the store without her. You have many friends, anyone you can think of that we would trust?"

"I thought about Sophie but it wouldn't be fair to Wes. They just got married and bought a house. A man needs his woman around so he can have crazy sex whenever he wants it."

"That is all you have on your mind, sex, sex, sex."

"That's because I am a sex machine, baby!"

"Pitch, I hate to have to tell you this but you are not very good in bed!"

They looked at each other burst out laughing.

When Ann got to her office, she had a message from Sheriff Douglas that said he needed to see her. She told her secretary where she was going and said she would be back. When Ann got to Dan's office, he handed her a cup of coffee and told her to take a seat. "Ann here is the latest information. The saga of Mayor

Gallon continues. The FBI had the state troopers go check out the cabin in Breckenridge. When they got there Gallon's car and truck were parked on the side of the cabin. The state police captain figured Gallon was in the cabin and he called the FBI for instructions. The FBI told them to proceed with caution because Gallon was a dangerous fugitive and had gotten away several times. The captain called for three more troopers and they surrounded the cabin. The captain called out to the cabin with a bull-horn, "This is the Colorado State Police come out with your hands up."

After calling three times they started closing in on the cabin and Gallon started firing with an automatic rifle and his wife was also firing with a pistol. One state trooper got hit in his leg and went down. Then the captain threw in a smoke grenade through the cabin window. The Gallons tried to get out the side door to their car and when the troopers saw them, they opened fire and blow them both away. The FBI shot Gallon eight times and his wife three times. They both were preannounced dead at the scene. This ends the saga of the Gallons. What do you think about all of that Ann?"

"I guess justice was served but I would have loved to send him to prison for twenty years."

"I guess he figured he would be in prison a long time and decided he couldn't do the time so he tried to get away again."

"I am just glad it is over. What about Tom Berry now?"

"I guess I'll let him go as part of my deal with him. He did help us find Gallon but I think I will play with his head a little before I give him his freedom."

"Well, have fun Dan. I got to run. Good work sheriff."

Pitch was out with the wranglers in his truck moving part of the herd to a new pasture, he was thinking about the person they needed to travel with Rory. As Kinno moved the herd in his truck Pitch thought of a person who might work. However, he wasn't sure how Ann would feel about asking this person. Pitch was glad that his check-up with the doctor was tomorrow because he was tired of being a Ford Cowboy and really missed riding Thunder.

When Ann got back to her office Charlie informed her that Judge Thomas had set a trial date for Brad Hickory. "Charlie, you have to forgive me but who in the world is Brad Hickory?"

"He is the guy that shot Pitch and is locked up in our jail."

"Oh, I never paid attention to his name before. When does the trial begin?"

"Next Tuesday and Samuel Law Firm is representing him."

"I am surprised at that. How can he afford to pay that firm? They are very expensive."

"I think Hickory has a bank account some where outside of Sheridan and I don't believe Gallon got away with all the money from the uranium sales."

"What is his defense?"

"He is claiming self-defense and Samuel is okay with it."

After dinner Ann and Pitch went out on the patio so he could have his glass of whiskey and a cigar. "Ann, I have given Rory's situation a lot of thought and I think I have come up with the best person for the guardian job. However, I don't think you are going to like it."

"Okay, let me hear who your candidate is?"

"I think the best person for the job is Louise Lambert."

"Are you kidding me!"

"I know you told her off about her voting for the girl but at one time you thought the two of you could be good friends. In the end she did vote for Rory."

"Why do you think she would work the best?"

"There are a number of reasons and believe me I have thought this though carefully."

"Let me hear your logic for this."

"Louise has no tires so she is available for travel, she knows the music industry, her teaching makes peanuts, she is about your age, and Rory has respect for her. I could probably come up with a few more but I think that is enough."

"Everything you said is true and it would probably work. I think Rory would go along with her selection. So, now I have to eat crow and go kiss up to her?"

"You are a big girl you can handle it. Just remember you are doing this for Rory."

The next day Ann decided to bite the bullet and go talk to Louise Lambert. When Louise answered the door, she was shocked to see Ann standing there. "Can I come in Louise I have something to talk to you about?"

"Sure Ann, I never thought I would see you at my door again."

"Louise, I am sorry for the way I handle the voting thing and I know you were just trying to support one of your students. In the end you did vote for Rory and you supported him."

"I am glad you understand the situation I was in with the voting."

"I am here today to see if you will continue to support Rory. As you probably know RCA Records wants Rory to make records for their label. However, to do this he has to go to Nashville and perhaps some other places. Rory's music is important to Pitch and I but we don't have the time to devote to Rory's ambition right now. What we would like from you is that you be his traveling guardian. You know the music industry and Rory has a lot of respect for you. All you would have to do is travel with him and look out for his wellbeing. The job pays $50,000 a year plus expenses."

"Did you say $5,000 or $50,000?"

"I said $50,000 and when you are not traveling you could still do your teaching. Plus, most of your traveling will be in the summer months when Rory is out of school."

"Are you serious about the $50,000 salary? It takes me five or six years to make that much money."

"RCA is going to put Rory under contract but you won't have to be involved in that. John Riggins will negotiate his contract and will be his financial advisor. You would stay in five-star hotels and get to see a lot of places."

"This really sounds exciting. Are you offering me the job?"

"Yes, I am, RCA is waiting for a call from me to make all the arrangements for Rory to come to Nashville. You would be dealing with Chris Finley a really nice man. So, what is you answer?"

"Absolutely yes, I will take care of Rory like he was my own child. Thank you for giving me this great opportunity and I will not let you down."

"Once I call Chris, I will let you know all the details. Chris said RCA would send one of their airplanes to pick Rory and you up."

"I have never been on an airplane."

"Louise, I think we can have the friendship we once planned on."

They hugged each other.

School was out for the summer and Stoney Mason was amazed how fast Tony learned to keep the Coyote books. In fact, he got so good at it that Stoney had very little to do with the accounting part of the business. Tony was really enjoying doing the book keeping and several times he brought Maomi to the club to show her what it looked like on the inside. The two of them had been dating regularly and she even took him to meet her father, Chief Warki. They both got straight A's in all their classes and would argue who was smarter. Ann had Maomi over for dinner one night and they talked about their future. Maomi wanted to be a doctor so she could help her people. However, she wasn't sure she would get to college. "Maomi, surely you will get an academic scholarship from some college."

"I would like to believe that but most colleges stopped giving scholarships to American Indians. The reason being most of the Indians they gave scholarships to drop out of school after a year or so."

"That doesn't seem fair for the modern world of today. I think I am going to talk to the Rancher's Association about this because most of us have Indians as wranglers and we should give back to our communities. I will tell you one thing for sure if you keep your grades up, I will guarantee you will go to college one way or another."

"Thank you, Mrs. McClure, but I'm not alone."

"I got the picture Honey; your Mayor will address it."

Pitch just looked at her and thought, "What a great person I am marrying."

After Tony took Maomi back to the village and came back home, "Mrs. McClure I want to thank you for trying to help Maomi."

"Tony, two things, if I can't pull this off with the ranchers, I will pay for Maomi to go to college but don't you tell her that. Second, I am tired of you calling me Mrs. McClure, you can call me Mom or Ann whatever you chose."

Tony just looked at her, Okay Mom."

Ann had a big smile on her face.

Ann put a call into Chris Finley to let him know her plan. Chris was happy to hear from her and they got things ironed out. "Ann this is Rory's last week of school. Right?"

"Yes, it is."

"How about if I send the airplane to get him and Louise on Monday morning? This way Rory would have the weekend with his family."

"I like that very much."

Rory and Louise will be staying at the Nashville Hilton Downtown and he can call you every night from his room."

"That is great Chris. How long do you think he will be there?"

"I think two weeks to start. Tell him and Louise to bring enough clothes but the hotel does have a laundry service if they need it. Oh yea, make sure Rory brings his guitar. You may want to give him some spending money in case he wants to buy something in Nashville. I think that is it. Do you have any questions?"

"What time would the plane get here?"

"It is a three-hour flight so I guess about eleven o'clock."

"One more thing Chris. I know you will be planning to send him to different places over the summer."

"That is right, for media exposure."

"Well, Rory has to be in Sheridan the week of July 18th because he is in my wedding party."

"I will make sure of that. Congratulations are in order, are you marrying Pitch?"

"Yes, he is my man."

When Ann got off the phone with Chris, she immediately called Louise and told her the plans. "Louise, I will have John Riggins cut you an advance of $5.000 in case you need to buy something for the trip. Jeans girl, get into the country western look."

"Thanks Ann, I need some new clothes."

The trial of Brad Hickory started and the Samuel Law firm was not worried about facing Charlie Douglas. They thought of him as a light weight opposition with no experience in the court room. Ann knew Charlie had prepared for the trial and would not take anything for granted. The prosecution went first and Charlie presented all of his evidence and argued for attempted murder conviction. Then Samuel it was the defense's turn. Samuel made the big mistake of putting Brad Hickory on the stand to testify.

Then it was Charlie's turn to cross-examine the witness. "Mr. Hickory did you know you were on McClure property?"

"Yes, sir."

"Why were you on the McClure property?"

"To blast and drill for uranium."

"Did you know what you were doing was illegal?"

"I suppose so, but we were not hurting anybody."

"This isn't the first time that you have crossed paths with Mr. Wesley? In fact, Mr. Wesley chased you off the McClure property once before. Isn't that true?"

"Yes, the son of a bitch took our horses and equipment and threw us in a thorn bush."

Judge Thomas immediately jumped in the conversation, Mr. Hickory watch your language in my court room!"

"Yes, Judge."

"Mr. Hickory, did all of you have guns?"

"Yes sir."

"Why did all you have guns?"

"In case of a bear or some animal."

"So, you all needed guns for that reason?"

"Yes, sir"

"Did all of the other men fire their guns?"

"Yes, sir."

"So, let me get this straight, every one thought they were shooting at a bear?"

"No, we thought we were being robbed."

"Even after Sheriff Douglas told you to put down your weapons and hands up?"

"We didn't hear him."

"So, you thought a bear was talking?"

"No!"

"But you heard voices?"

"Yea."

"So, you just turned and started shooting?"

"I told you we thought we were being robbed."

"Isn't it a fact, Mr. Hickory that you thought it was Mr. Wesley again and you were not letting him put you though what he did before?"

"No!"

"Mr. Hickory, how many shoots did you fire?"

"Just two."

"Are you sure?"

"Absolutely, it was two."

"How come the investigation unveiled that you emptied your gun?"

"I guess I miss counted."

"Did Mr. Wesley have a gun and was he shooting at you?"

"Absolutely, that is why I fired back."

"Do you know that the investigation showed that Mr. Wesley never fired his gun."

"So, you have no reason to claim self-defense because Mr. Wesley never fired at you. Am I correct?"

"I just turned and shoot him."

"Were you trying to kill Mr. Wesley? When you shot and shot to kill. Are you surprised that Mr. Wesley is not dead?"

"Yes, I thought I got the son of a bitch in the heart."

"So, you really hated Mr. Wesley?"

"Yes, I do."

"Why didn't you shoot the other deputies?"

"I wanted to make sure I got Wesley."

"Your Honor the prosecution rest."

It only took the jury fifteen minutes to come back with a guilty verdict. Judge Thomas sentenced him to twenty years in the state prison. Mr. Samuel came over to Charlie, "Son, I under estimated you. That will not happen again. Good job."

Dan was so proud of Charlie he had tears coming down his face.

Ann and Pitch were headed to the hospital for his check-up. "Ann, since I have most of my stuff up in your room why don't I just stay there and give my room to Tony."

"I think that is an excellent idea he is older now and will need some privacy. I am sure Tommy is not going to like this one bit."

"I'll get Tony to help me move out and we can clean the room before he moves in."

"If the kids say anything, we will tell them the doctor still wants me to keep an eye on you."

"Okay, that is our story if they asked."

They didn't have to wait long for Dr. Alexander. He looked Pitch over really good and said, "I think you can start riding your horse again Pitch. Everything looks really good and I think you are close to normal. Only I wouldn't do any heavy lifting for about another six months. I will see you back here in six months."

"Thanks Doc, just in time for our wedding."

When they left the hospital Pitch immediately said, "Let's go home and have sex."

"I have a lot of work at the office so I'll give you a rain-check."

"How long before I can use this rain check?"

"You only have today or it is no good."

"Don't worry I will use it."

The weekend flew by and Rory told his audience at the Coyote Club that he would return to the club in several weeks. The RCA plane arrived at Sheridan County Airport at eleven o'clock and the entire family was there to see him off. The plane was an eight passenger so both Rory and Louise took window seats so they could watch the sights below. It took them only two and a half hours to reach the Nashville International Airport and there was a limousine waiting to pick them up. The driver took them to the Nashville Hilton Downtown hotel on 4th Avenue. Chris Finley was waiting for them to make sure they got checked in okay. Chris told them to get settled in their rooms and that David Sarnoff and he would have dinner with them at seven o'clcok tonight at Trattoria II Mulino restaurant right here in the hotel. He said the restaurant had great Italian cuisine. "I hope you both like Italian food?"

They both shook their heads yes. Chris told them if they wanted, they could check out the city because there is plenty to see. He suggested they ask the concierge for directions. Their rooms were on the fifteen floors over looking the city and they had adjoining rooms if they needed to talk.

They walked around the hotel to see where everything was and then took a walk a few blocks near the hotel. They didn't go far because they didn't want to get lost. Rory called Ann to let her know he got there safe and then he cleaned up for dinner. The two of them went down stairs and found the restaurant. Rory was looking for Chris because Louise had no idea what he looked like. When Chris came walking over to them, he had another man with him. Rory figured it must be David Sarnoff. He was a tall slim man with gray black hair and you could tell his clothes were very expensive. Chris introduced David and met Louise. Louise loved all the attention but did ask a few important questions. David named a few of their top county western artist, Hank Williams, Pee Wee King and Sons of the Pioneer. Chris informed them a chauffeur would pick them up at eight o'clock and for them to have breakfast here at the hotel and just charge it to their rooms. He said they would be going to RCA Record Label on Denorbreun Street. "The first thing they would do is a lot of testing of Rory's voice and sound acoustics and other things. After that they will have Rory sing a couple songs, he knows with the back up band. They would take a lot of pictures and try a song that they though were Rory's style. RCA would have a few people evaluate Rory's potential in the market place. This would take a couple days. Rory you with me?"

"So, far I follow you."

"Once all of this is completed David and I will determine what type of contract we want to offer Rory. I have been in contact with John Riggins who your Mom has authorized to negotiate your contract. Once the contract is agreed to in principal, we will start working on your first record. I hope that helps you both."

"Chris, does Rory have final approval on the songs you pick for him?"

"Good question Louise, absolutely. All of our artist have to like what they are singing because they have to market it for us."

"How long does it take to make a record?"

"Well Rory, it depends on many cuts we have to make. I guess to go though the twelve steps of recording probably three to four weeks."

"Once that is all completed what will we have to do from that point on?"

"Another good question Louise, we will set up a record promotion tour for Rory mainly to major cities like, Dallas, Houston, Birmingham, St. Louis. We know about Rory going back to school in September so we have to get a lot done between now and then."

David told Rory they were excited about having him join RCA Records. He asked Rory how Sister Martin was doing and told him all about how hard she worked to become a star in a world where most professional guitarist are men. When the evening was over at nine-thirty Chris told them to get some rest because tomorrow will be a long day. When they got to their rooms Louise suggested that they go to breakfast at seven o'clock and Rory agreed.

The house didn't feel right without Rory there. To keep busy so she wouldn't think about him Ann went over the plans for the wedding which was less than a month away. Everything was back to normal with Pitch, he was out on the range with the boys on Thunder. Ann was working hard as mayor to clean up Gallon's mess that went back years. Ann, Sharon, Nija, and Nellie went for their final fitting. Nija designed her own dress according to Shoshone customs but the dress maker made it for her. It was a soft light blue material with white beads coming down the front in a sun like pattern. When Sharon saw Nija's dress, "I want one like hers, it is so original and beautiful."

"To late Sharon, besides you are not an Indian."

Kinno decided to wear a tuxedo so Pitch took him and Tommy to get fitted. He also gave the tailor one of Rory's suits so he could make a tuxedo for Rory. Pitch didn't need one because he already had his own. Ann told Pitch she wanted Tony to have a tuxedo also since now she was his Mom. Pitch totally agreed and stopped at the Coyote club where Tony was working full time during the summer. Tony was a little shocked when Pitch told him he was getting a tuxedo because his adopted Mom said so. Ann, checked the hall, caterer, flowers, church, and told Pitch to make sure Wes and his Bandit band had the date on their calendar. Ann felt everything was taken care of and she decided to have Samoka orchestrate everything so it went right. She figured they would have about two hundred people at the wedding.

Rory and Louise arrived at RCA Records Label at eight-thirty and Rory was really excited. There were many studios and people were running all over the place. "Louise, look there is Hank Snow."

"I guess we will be seeing many famous artists here."

Chris Finley came out to them with another man. "Rory, Louise, this is Rex Flynn who will be the producer for your recordings."

After the introductions Chris said, "I have to run now but I will check on you through the day. You are in good hands with Rex, he is one of the best."

As Chris was leaving Rex said, "Chris is a great guy they just promoted him to general manager a couple weeks ago. Let me give you some highlights of what the process is in recording."

"That would be great Mr. Flynn."

"Rory, just call me Rex. Recording involves technical and creative aspects to make a recording successful. In order for me to produce your song I must consider the individual elements of, base track, rhythm, harmony, melody, and background fills. Each one of these elements must be addressed individually and then as a total package. The only thing you have to worry about is your singing. What we want for the record is the proper mixing of the elements. We have to make sure of the balancing channel levels, panning, equalization, compression, reverb, and automation. I know this is a lot but you will get to understand it as you make more records. To start Rory, let's go over here where the crew can start with the sound checks of your voice."

It was a long day for Rory and they finally stopped about quarter to five. While Rory was doing all the work Louise was walking around meeting people and basically trying to learn how the recording industry worked. Right after the crew stopped Chris came back over to them. "Rex, said you had a good day and his crew accomplished a lot today. Your chauffeur is waiting outside to take you to your hotel. You should go check out our city tonight. We have plenty of great restaurants. I will see you at eight tomorrow morning."

As Chris walked away, he yelled over his shoulder, "Rory don't forget to call your Mom."

The first thing Rory did when he got to his room was to call Ann. He told her all the things involved in making a record. They talked for about a half an hour and then Rory got ready to go to dinner. They walked about eight blocks from the hotel and saw a restaurant called Hillbilly Heaven and thought they would give it a try. After they ate, they looked in some of the shops. Then Rory said, "Louise I would like to go back to the hotel and go for a swim. I bought my bathing suit with me and it is really hot out.

When Rory went to the pool Louise decided to go down to the lounge bar and have a night cap while Rory was swimming. There were a lot of men in the bar and she heard one of them say they were here for a conference. One attractive looking guy came over to where Louise was sitting at the bar. "Hi, my name is Mike, can I buy you a drink?"

"Sure, why not Mike."

"Can I sit here with you?"

"Sure!" Louise thought it would be nice to have somebody to talk with. Mike told her he was from Atlanta, Georgia and that he was here for the entire week. The conversation was kind of one way with Mike doing most of the talking. Louise had no idea he was trying to hit on her because right now she really hated men. About three months prior Louise's husband just picked up and left her and headed to California. She was almost over the split-up and needed a little more time. After about an hour, Louise decided it was time to go check on Rory. "Mike, I have to go now. It was nice talking to you."

"Maybe we can go to dinner one night while you are here Louise?"

"I don't think so but perhaps we can have a drink another night."

Louise smiled as she got up and walked to the elevator with Mike's eyes on her the entire time. When she got on the elevator and was riding up to the 15th floor it dawned on her that Mike was trying to hit on her. She smiled to she self, you still got it girl, screwed that ass hole of a husband. When she opened the connecting door to Rory's room, he was sound asleep. She was still smiling about Mike and decided to turn in herself.

The next couple days were go, go, go for Rory and it was obvious that Rex really liked his voice. On Thursday Rory noticed Rex, Chris, and David Sarnoff huddle together talking about something. Rory was wondering what it was all about because he had done everything, they asked of him. Chris and Rex came over to Rory and they had a serious look on their faces. "Rory, do you have the music to the song you wrote and sang at the Coyote Club with you?"

"Yes Chris, it is in my guitar case."

"Could you give it to Rex he wants to see how it sounds with the studio band."

"Okay, I'll go get it for him."

Rory gave the song to Rex and he took it over to the band leader. They started writing things down and had the leaders of each section of the band look at it. "Louise said to Rory, "I think they are trying to determine the proper mixture for the band. You know who should play what and when to come in with their part."

"That makes sense, I only wrote it for a guitar."

The band must have played it a dozen times and finally the leader said, "Okay, let's get Rory up here to sing it with us."

While they tried it Chris went and got David to come out of his office to hear the song. When Rory sang it they could tell they needed to make some more adjustments. Louise over heard David says to Chris, "I like it, let's get it right and cut a tape for me to hear with the music evaluators.

While the recording was going on Chris called John Riggins to start negotiations for Rory's contract. John decided to handle this himself since it was so important to Ann one of his top customers. Chris initially offered two million dollars for a five-year contract. John countered with a three-million-dollar contract for three years. They went back and forth with offers and counter offers. Then Chris mentioned the song Rory wrote which John knew nothing about. After talking to Chris, he called Ann to find out what the story was. Ann informed him that Rory writes songs all the time. John cautioned her that RCA wanted the rights to his songs and that this should be part of his contract. Ann totally agreed. When John got back to Chris, he told him that their final offer was a four-million-dollar contract for four years with all song rights included. John stated, "Chris this is a great deal for RCA and if you don't like it, I will take it to Capital Records."

Chris said, "I have to talk with David and I will get back to you."

David was on the fence with the deal. "Let me go hear this song one more time."

The band and Rory had the song and music all ironed out and it sounded fabulous. "Chris we will get all of our money back just on this song and probably more. I want you to include in the deal that Rory will write one song a year."

"I think that will fly David."

When Chris got back to John, they both agreed on the song writing part and they had a deal. Chris said they would iron out all the contract details and overnight the contract to him for Ann to sign.

The studio never worked on Saturday but because they knew Rory had a limited time in Nashville, they came in to work. On Monday afternoon Rex brought the record evaluator team and David to hear the final cut. After they heard the recording, they all just applauded in approval. David told Rex to wrap it up and start producing the record. Listening over by the door was Hank Snow. "Rex, who wrote that song?"

"Rory McClure, the young man who just sang it."

"You think I can get him to write me a song like that?"

"Well Hank, he is now writing for RCA so you might get lucky."

Chris called Rory over and introduced him to Hank and Hank told him he thought the song was great. After Hank left Rory asked Rex if he could go home now?

"Rory, unfortunately not yet. The promotion people now take you over."

Rory called Ann that night and told her the recording was over but now they were going to work on promoting the record. When Ann told him about his contract, he didn't get excited. "Mom, I am in this because I love to sing and play music."

"That is fine son, but it helps your future if you have money. Remember in the Bronx when we had nothing but an apartment and food on the table. Now, you don't have to worry about going through something like that in your life."

"I know you are smart Mom; the money does help. So, when Pitch marries you, he will be rich like you."

"Rory my darling son, Pitch is already a millionaire and has more money then me. He made a lot of money playing for the Dodgers and he invested most of it. Pitch and I are getting married only because we love each other."

For the next three days all they did was take pictures of Rory. He had to change clothes so many times that he lost count. Rex told Rory his record was out now and that the radio stations would start playing it. The promotion team sat down with him and Louise to go over a traveling schedule for the up coming week. Rory reminded them that he had to be home the week of July 18th for his Mom's wedding. Rory and Louise first trip would be to three Texas cities, Dallas, Houston, and San Antonino. Rory would do radio interviews and be a guest singer at several western night clubs. Following that trip, they would go to Charlotte and Raleigh, North Carolina and then to Richmond, Virginia. Then he would be off for the wedding. After the wedding they would go to several California cities and then up to Seattle, Washington. At that point they would evaluate how sales were going and plan new visits from that information.

After two hard weeks Rory was happy to get home for a few days before Louise and him headed to Dallas. Everybody wanted to talk to him about his experience but all he wanted to do was rest. Stoney called to see if he would sing just "Pickin My Guitar on Saturday night at the Coyote club. He agreed to do it but he told Stoney only one song. Rory asked Tony to drive him over to see Sister Martin and come pick him back up in about an hour. When Sister Martin saw him, she hugged him tight. "I heard your song on the radio."

His conversation with Sister Martin was all about does it get any easier. "I hate to tell you Rory but it actually gets harder. They want you to be in several places at one time and you never have time for yourself. You should be fine because your Mom is making sure you go to school and that will give you time off from the rat race."

When Tony picked Rory up, he talked to Tony like Tony was his big brother. "Rory, you are thirteen going on fourteen and what I think you need is a girlfriend."

"Are you crazy?"

"I mean just to go out and have some fun, nothing serious. How about if I get Maomi to get you a date with one of her younger girlfriends and we all go to the movies and for an ice cream sundae after the movie?"

"I am really not sure."

"Oh, give it try, you have nothing to lose."

"I guess so but the girl better not be ugly."

Maomi was not happy with the arrangements Tony made with Rory. However, she did have a pretty younger friend in the village that was just starting high school like Rory. When Maomi asked Catina if she would go to the movie with Rory, she was all excited. She knew all about his singing and had heard him on the radio. Ann was not excited about Rory dating but figured he needed to have some fun with kids his own age since all he had been dealing with was adults. Rory liked Catina and they talked and talked. The movie was over at seven-thirty and Tony was ready to go to the ice cream shop. "Tony, I forget, I am supposed to sing at the Coyote club at eight o'clock."

"Why didn't tell me about this earlier?"

"I told you, I forgot about it. You all can come with me it will only take about fifteen minutes and then we can go for ice cream sundaes."

"Will Stoney let us in the place?"

"If he wants me to sing, he will."

"All right girls to the Coyote club we go."

The Coyote audience cheered Rory like he was a gladiator walking into the colosseum. His one song ended up being two but then he got out of there with Jack leading the way through the crowd. While they were eating their ice cream sundaes Catina wanted to know all he did in Nashville. She was so easy to talk to it was like they had been friends for years. When the evening was over Rory thanked Catina for a great time and she kissed him on his cheek. "When you get back in town perhaps, we can go out again."

"I would really like that."

CHAPTER 12

Rory and Louise were on the plane heading to Dallas where he had to run from one place to another to keep the local RCA coordinator happy. They spent two days in Dallas, a day and a half in Houston and one day in San Antonino. When they got back on the plane to fly back to Sheridan they were totally bushed. Rory could understand why Sister Martin called this the rat race.

Dinja picked them up at the airport because Ann was in a meeting with the City Council. The first thing Rory did when he got home was to call Tony at work and ask him if they could go on a date tomorrow night. "Haven't you talked to Mom yet?"

"No, did I do something wrong?"

"No stupid, she is having a barbeque in your honor tomorrow evening. So, we can not go out on a date."

"How about you bring the girls to the barbeque instead?"

"Mom, did all the invitations so you should ask her."

"But if it is in honor on me, I should be able to invite my friends."

"Rory what you say makes sense but if Mom gets pissed it is all on you, not me."

"She will be all right. I will tell her when she gets home."

When Ann got home, she hugged Rory and told him how much she missed him. I am having a big barbeque Saturday in your honor."

"That sounds great Mom can I invite a couple of my friends?"

"Sure Honey, invite whoever you want".

When Tony got home from work, "Mom told me I could invite my friends."

"Okay, I'll ask Maomi if they can come."

"I see you got a new room all to yourself?"

"Yes, and I am enjoying the privacy. I love Tommy but he wants to know everything I am doing. I'll let you know about the girls as soon as I can. If they are coming here, you and I need to have a little talk."

"You got it, just let me know when."

When Pitch came in the house, he grabbed Rory in a bear hug. "Boy, it looks like you have grown a couple inches. How did they treat you in Nashville?"

"Really good but all we did was work."

"How was the Texas trip?"

"Very tiring and boring. It was like I was on a merry-go-round and couldn't get off."

"That's the professional world, they keep you moving so they can make more money."

"Sister Martin called it the rat race."

"That is a great description for it. Are you doing anything now?"

"No, just relaxing."

"Take a ride with me to the tuxedo shop. I gave them one of your old suits to do your fitting but I think it may be to small so let's go get you measured right."

"Sure, let's go. I do want to look super for the wedding."

Maomi and Catina told Tony they would come to the barbeque on Saturday. "Tony, do you realize my brother will be there and maybe my father because he was invited."

"So, what are you telling me Maomi?"

"In their presence it is best that you and Rory do not touch us in front of our elders. They consider it disrespectful.

"Now that you mention it, I have never seen a Shoshone man hug, kiss or for that matter touch one of their women."

"Please make sure you tell Rory because by touching us in front of the elders would totally embarrass us both."

"I will make sure he understands. I promise I will tell him tonight."

"What time does the barbeque start so I can tell Catina?"

At three o'clock, I will pick you up about quarter to three. It will be very hot out so you should wear shorts."

"I don't think so Mr. Leg Man. We will be wearing peddle-pushers."

After dinner that evening, Tony said, Rory, would you like to see my new room?" Rory, just looked at him and Tony kept shaking his head yes. "Yea, let me see what it looks like now."

They walked down the hallway to Pitch's old room. "I told you we needed to talk."

"Okay, I'm here, so let's talk."

"Maomi and Catina are coming to the barbeque."

"Great, what time are you picking them up?"

"A little before three. But here's the thing, while they are here you cannot touch them."

"What does that mean?"

"You can't touch them, are you stupid? No holding hands, putting your arm around her, no physical contact at all. Maomi brother Kinno and his family will be there and Mom also invited Chief Warki so he might show up. The Shoshone consider it disrespectful if you touch one of their women in their presence. You could get the girls in trouble and we wouldn't be able to date them anymore. Am I clear Mr. Radio Star?"

"I got it Tony, no touching. How about kissing?"

"You are a total ass hole Rory."

They both laughed.

On Saturday morning Ann was running around like she was crazy. The catering people arrived and she was giving instructions left and right. Pitch told her to slow down or she would be exhausted by three o'clock. "Ann, the catering company has done this here before and they know what to do. Come in the house and have a cup of coffee with me."

"You are right. Coffee sounds good."

For the barbeque Ann had everything from steaks to hot dogs. About three o'clock people started arriving and Rory was at her side to greet them. Sheriff Douglas arrived with his wife. Charlie and his family came with the sheriff. Kinno and his family, many of the wranglers, Louise, Fred Johnson and even Judge Thomas and his wife. The turn out was great and people were still coming. Tony pulled up his four-door truck and two beautiful Indian girls got out. Ann just staired at them and Tony. "Mom you remember Maomi the Chief's daughter and this is Catina her friend. Ann welcomed them and they went to the patio and mixed with the other people. After everyone was here Ann made an announcement. "I am having this barbeque celebration in honor of Sheridan's new music star my son Rory."

Rory was standing next to Catina and he waved to everyone. "I hope you enjoy the food and have a great time," was Ann's final remarks. Ann kept looking at Rory and Catina standing together. "Ann, you look like you just saw a ghost." "Pitch, I think that must be the girl Rory is going out with."

"From the looks of things, I would say you are right! Come on, they are only going to the movies. What are you afraid of losing one of your babies?"

"Pitch, you need to have that father son talk with Rory."

"Really, Ann, can't I wait until I'm really his step-father?"

"No, the sooner the better!"

"Why don't you do it."

"Because I wasn't very good at it when I talked to Tony."

"Oh yea, I forget about that mess. Okay, Ann I will talk to him the first chance I get."

The barbeque was going great but Chief Warki didn't come so Tony and Rory were grateful for that. Ann decided to talk to Catina. "Mom this my friend Catina."

"Yes, Rory we already met earlier. What grade are you in Catina?"

"I will be freshman just like Rory."

"Do you live in the village?"

"No, Mayor McClure we on Chester Street right off of Main Street. But I spend a lot of time at the village and I saw you at couple lacrosse games. Your son Tommy is really good."

"Is your father a wrangler?"

No, he works at the bank and handles all the Indian business for them."

"I would love to meet your parents."

"My mother died two years of cancer but my Dad and I are doing fine."

"I am sorry to hear that about your mother."

Ann moved on talking to the other guest. But she kept thinking about Rory and Catina. When the barbeque was over Tony, Rory, Maomi and Catina jumped in Tony's truck and Rory yelled, "See you later Mom, thanks!"

Ann was not smiling. "Pitch you need to have that talk with Rory soon. Where do you think they are going? Probably to make out somewhere."

"Ann, they are going to the ice cream shop where all their friends hang out. You need to chill out. Let me assure you those indian girls won't even let those boys get to first base."

"Well, that is good to know."

Besides Rory is focused on his music career right now and nothing will get in his way. Come on let's go take a shower together and freshen up."

"How about we each take a shower and go to sleep."

"I thought I would try!"

Sunday afternoon it was time for Rory and Louise to take off for Charlotte, North Carolina. From Charlotte they would go to Raleigh and then on to Richmond, Virginia. The radio announcer in Charlotte informed Rory that his song was now number thirty-two on the music ranking chart. They stayed in Charlotte just one day and then their chauffeur drove them to Raleigh which was only several hours away. The ride passed beautiful scenery and it gave Rory and Louise time just to relax and talk. Rory asked Louise how she was doing without her husband? Rory, I actually think it was a blessing that he left. We just argued all the time and he couldn't keep a job long. When I look back now, I actually don't know what I saw in him."

Rory just smiled but Louise laughed out loud. "Rory, do you think I am pretty?"

"Absolutely, especially now with your new clothes which show your fit body. I bet the men will be after you very soon."

"I have to tell you this. When we were in Nashville, I went down to the hotel lounge bar for a night cap while you were swimming. This guy, Mike, came over and bought me a drink and talked with me for an hour. Then he asked if I would go to dinner with him."

"God, the guy was hitting on you Louise."

"Yes, isn't that wonderful."

"You know who I think really likes you?'

"Who, tell me!"

"Chris Finley!"

"Isn't he married?"

"Mom said he was single and lived by himself in Nashville."

In the morning they went to a Raleigh county music radio station and the announcer was a smart-ass skinny guy who kept calling Rory Roy. He started asking stupid questions and Louise was getting pissed off by the minute. "Hey Roy baby, what are you going to be when you grow up?"

They only been there about a half hour and Louise finally said, "That's it Rory we are out of here right now. Let's go!"

They both got up and walked out of the radio studio and were heading to the door. The RCA local coordinator came running behind them and when he caught them, he begged them not go. Then Louise went off on him, "You are supposed to control ass holes like that skinny ass announcer. That is why you are with us in the first place. When I tell David Sarnoff about this bull shit interview you will be lucky to keep your job. Now, get out of our way."

Rory had never seen Louise so fired up like that. He was really surprised. Since they had some time on their hands Louise suggested they go downtown Raleigh and visit some of the city's county bars. "What do you think Rory? I could really use a good drink?"

"Let's do it boss lady."

They stopped in four places and everybody they talked to loved Rory's song. One bartender told them this weekly ranking just came out today and Pickin My Guitar was number twenty-three on the chart. Louise looked at Rory with her drink in her hand, "That is really good you jumped nine positions in one week. I bet RCA will be calling you to Nashville soon to start work on another song."

From Raleigh thy flew to Richmond, Virginia and the radio station rolled out the red carpet for Rory. Louise just loved the announcer and his positive attitude about everything. This was the place that asked Rory who wrote the song. When they left the radio station people were waiting outside for Rory to get autographs. He must have signed fifty pictures of himself thanks to the radio station giving them out to the people waiting. At that point Rory knew he was on the right road because the fans loved his music. They were happy when they got on the plane to go back to Sheridan but on the way the plane had some mechanical problem and they had to land at the Pittsburgh Airport so the pilot could check out the problem. They came back and told Louise and Rory the problem was the fuel pump and it would be three hours or more to replace it. Louise immediately called Chris from the airport and told him about the plane and that it would take hours to fix it. "Louise there is a great county western radio station in Pittsburgh. You and Rory take a taxi to this address and I will call them to let then know you are coming."

"Okay, but we better not miss our plane!"

"That plane is not going anywhere without the two of you on board."

"Just spend an hour and then get a taxi back to the airport."

"I got it Chris, goodbye. Rory I am going to call your Mom so she knows we will be late getting in. It rang four times and no answer. I guess Nija is shopping."

Rory and Louise got a taxi and it took a half hour to get to the radio station but at least they were waiting for them. While on the air, they asked Rory all different kind of questions including was he going to move to Nashville? "No, I am still in school and my Mom wants me to graduate from high school."

"Don't you care about all the money you could make touring?"

"I only care about what the public thinks about my songs and singing. I hope the people can appreciate good county western music which our country was built on."

"You heard it here from the man himself so run out right now and buy his record Pickin My Guitar."

Louise and Rory thanked the announcer and took a taxi back to the airport. The captain told them the plane was all fixed and they headed for Sheridan once again.

Dinja waited at the airport for an hour just in case the plane was late. He decided he better call Ann because it was getting late and maybe Rory called the house. After talking to Dinja Ann started to panic and she told Samoka to take a truck and tell Pitch I need him. In about an hour Pitch came running in the house. "Ann, what is the big problem?"

Ann told him about the plane not arriving and if there was trouble flying. Pitch immediately grabbed the phone and called Chris Finley. Chris explained what happen and said they would be arriving between eleven and twelve tonight and told them not to worry everything was fine. Pitch was pissed, "Chris the next time shit happens involving Rory you call us immediately to let us know."

"I am sorry Pitch. You are right I should have called you but things like that happen all the time."

"When it involves Rory, you call us or I'll kick your ass up and down Broadway Street'

"I believe you. I promise I will keep you and Ann informed."

Rory got back to the ranch around midnight and Ann and Pitch were waiting up for him. Rory made it sound like the plane problem was no big deal and went into the kitchen and made a sandwich for himself. While eating the sandwich he walked to the steps and said, "Good night I am going to bed."

Ann and Pitch were right behind him up the steps. As they laid in bed Pitch started a conversation, "Ann when we get married Saturday are you keeping your McClure last name?"

"I have not given it any thought."

"You know your kids are McClure's and the ranch is named McClure."

"What do you think I should do?"

"Oh no, don't put that on me. That is your decision alone."

"Everyone knows me as Mayor McClure in the town and all my property and finances are under McClure. I would have to change a lot of things. This is really a hard question. Would you mind if I kept my McClure name?"

"Ann you do what you want and not what I would like. No matter what you decide, I will love you just the same."

"I have to think about this some more."

"You better decided soon we are getting married in four days."

"I know and I think I know my answer but I want to be sure."

On Friday evening the wedding party had a rehearsal at the church and they all went to the Carter Restaurant for dinner at

Ann and Pitch's expense. Ann was very talkative and excited while Pitch was kind of quiet and he looked nervous. Ann pulled Rory aside, "If you want to bring your friend Catina to the wedding you can. Tony already asked me if Maomi could come so they would have buddies to hang out with at the reception."

Rory wasted no time getting to a phone to call Catina. He didn't want it to look like a last-minute invitation so he told Catina that his Mom invited her long ago but he forgot to tell her because he was focused on going out of town. She said she understood how busy he was with all the traveling and would love to come to the wedding. "I'll call Maomi and catch a ride with her family."

After the call Rory was all smiles so Ann figured Catina was coming to the wedding. As Pitch laid in bed that night waiting for Ann, the name thing was in the back of his mind but he decided not to bring it up. When Ann came into the room, he just looked at her, "Just think this is our last night as a single couple. This time tomorrow we will be man and wife."

"It is about time you made an honest woman out of me."

"Come here, you wild thing."

The wedding day was finally here and Pitch went to the Coyote Club so he wouldn't see Ann in her gown before the wedding. He took Rory and Tommy with him and said that they could change into their tuxedos at the club when it was time to get dressed. Tony stayed at the house because he was Ann's chauffer. Sharon came over to the ranch early to see if she could help Ann but Nija already had that under control. When all the women and Nellie were dressed the photographer took a ton of pictures. Ann really liked the one of her coming down the steps so he took about ten different shots of that alone. Tony held the doors open for the party to get in the Cadillac and Nellie got to sit up front with Tony. Down the dusty road they went with Nija on one side of Ann and Sharon on the other side.

Pitch, the boys and Kinno were waiting at Saint Joseph's for the bride to arrive. Pitch could not believe all the people coming into the church. When Tony pulled up to the front of the church, the church usher told the men to go up to the front of the church and wait on the right side which they already knew from rehearsal. When the men were in position Father Daniel came out and stood in front of the altar. The ladies lined up to go into the church with Nellie in front. Then Sharon, Nija and Ann. At the last-minute Ann grabbed Tony's arm. He looked at her trying to figure out what she was doing. "Tony, since I don't have a father to give me away, I thought my oldest son should walk me down the aisle."

Tony felt so proud and took Ann by the arm. The organist started playing the Wedding March and Nellie started walking down the red carpet. The church was so filled, it was standing room only. People who were not invited must have come just to see the wedding ceremony. All the people in the church stood up as Ann came walking down the aisle. When Ann and Tony got to where Father Daniel was Pitch stepped forward and Tony handed Ann's hand to Pitch and stepped to the side. Father Daniel welcomed everyone to this great occasion and made a funny comment that he wished the church was filled like this on Sunday. Father Daniel started reading a couple verses from the Bible about marriage. Then has said a prayer asking God to bless Ann and Pitch. Finally, it was time for the vows.

Father Daniel went through all the vows and Tommy gave them the rings to put on each other's finger. Then came the big moment, "By the power vested in me by God and the state of Wyoming I pronounce you Mr. & Mrs. Samuel Wesley."

Pitch almost broke down crying. He kissed Ann and said, "Thank you."

"I wouldn't have it any other way."

As they exited the church and rice was flying everywhere, they both saw Chris Finley standing in the crowd. When they got in the car Tony told them that he was going to drive them around for ten minutes and then take them back to the church for pictures.

According to Pitch the photographer must have taken ten thousand pictures. Finally, he was done at the church but would take more pictures at the reception. Tony drove them to the reception hall which was only ten minutes away. When they walked in the hall Wes Holder announced, "Ladies and Gentlemen please welcome Mr. & Mrs. Pitch Wesley."

Pitch smiled at Wes and waved because he didn't use Samuel because he actually hated the name. The newly weds walked over to the beautiful wedding party table. Once they sat down Pitch said, "I need a beer, Ann you want a drink?"

"Yes, but just a coke now."

Kinno's wife sat at the wedding table but Samoka would not so Nija was all alone. Ann looked at him, "Samoka please sit with your wife for me on my wedding day."

Saomka could not say no so he went and sat with Nija at the wedding table.

Chris Finley didn't know what to do with himself because all the people he knew were in the wedding party. Then somebody tapped him on the back, "Chris, would you like to sit with me?"

"Louise, I would love it. Actually, you rescued me because I don't know a sole here but the people in the wedding party."

"Don't I count?"

"You count more than the wedding party."

They found a couple seats at a table and Chris went to the open-bar to get them a drink. "I am surprised to see you here Chris with your busy schedule."

"I really needed to take a little break and I liked this town when I was here before so I thought I could come to the wedding."

"That is really nice of you. I thought you came to see me!"

"That was another big reason for the trip."

Louise could not believe what she just heard. A later Chris told her that Pitch was upset with him because he didn't call them when the plane had mechanical problems. "Chris, I called Ann four times from the airport and nobody answered the phone."

"I bet Pitch didn't know that?"

"Well, I will casually make sure he knows about it because it isn't all your fault."

The Bandit band stared playing and Chris asked Louise to dance. She was a little shocked because her ex-husband would not put a foot on the dance floor. Chris was a good dancer and Louise was having fun for the first time in a long while. They sat down to take a break from dancing. Chris politely asked, "Louise, what is your status? I heard that you were married?"

"As of two weeks ago I am a divorced woman."

Chris just smiled and said, "I am single, never been married.

That was when it was time for another dance.

The food was served at the reception but before they started eating Kinno gave his toast to the couple. "I want everybody here to lift their glasses to two great people who really care about every individual here and would do anything for you. They are great bosses and like a brother and sister to me. Drink up!"

The food was great and so were the people serving the food. It was time now for Ann to throw her bouquet of flowers. All the single women got behind Ann and she turned around with her back towards them and counted 1, 2, 3, and threw the bouquet over her shoulder. Louise almost caught it but Maomi got it. When they all got back to the table Pitch was laughing because Tony's girlfriend caught the flowers. "It's not funny Pitch, Tony is going to college and so is Maomi."

"I thought if you caught the bouquet it meant you would be the next to get married."

"Not is this case."

Then Wes announced the couples first dance as Mr.& Mrs. Wesley. After Pitch and Ann danced a little while Wes told the guests they could cut-in now. Ann danced with almost every man in the hall and some women to like Sharon. Pitch didn't last as long as Ann and he went to the bar for a beer. Before a half hour later it was time for Pitch to take Ann's garter off her leg and throw it to the single men. Pitch was really funny. He rubbed up and down Ann's leg and tried to look under her gown until Ann finally hit him in the head and everyone laughed. Finally, he got the garter off and threw it over his shoulder and Dinja caught it. This was a little funny because Dinja was engaged to be married.

Louise went over and sat by Ann while Pitch was walking around talking to the guest. Their conversation was just the normal chit-chat until Louise said, "I was so glad when they got the plane fixed so we could make it home for the wedding. I called you and called you from the airport to tell you about the problem. I guessed Nija and Samoka were grocery shopping."

A light went off in Ann's brain, "Thank you for trying Louise."

When Pitch came back to the table Ann said, "I think you owe Chris an apology. Louise told me she called the house four times with no answer to let us know about the plane problem."

Pitch got up walked over to Chris. "I owe you an apology for the other day. I understand that Louise tried to call us but nobody was home."

"No, Pitch, you were right I should have called, it is part of my responsibility to take care of my singers."

They shook hands and closed the door on that subject.

When Chris got back to his table where Louise was, he smiled, "Thank you for telling them you tried to call."

They danced a couple more dances and then Chris looked at her, "Would you have dinner with me this evening?"

"I think I would like that."

It was time to cut the cake. Ann had warned Pitch not to do anything stupid. Pitch and Ann cut the cake hand in hand and then they fed it to each other. About a hour later it was time for their departure from the reception hall. When they got outside the kids had decorated the Cadillac and even had tin cans dragging behind the car. They were going to the Sheridan Hotel where they had already checked in and had all their luggage there for their trip to Las Vegas. Ann was the one who picked Las Vegas for their honeymoon because it was growing in popularity and a lot of stars were performing their now. Pitch really didn't give a shit since he traveled all over with the Dodgers. If he had his way their honeymoon would be at the McClure Ranch.

Since it was blazing hot out Ann couldn't wait to get out of her gown. She underdressed and immediately took a cold shower and Pitch was right behind her. Then they laid on the bed, kissed little and actually fell sound asleep. By the time they woke it was dinner time so they got dressed and went down to the hotel restaurant. When they walked in the restaurant, they saw Chris and Louise at a table with drinks in their hands. Chris got up and went over to them and asked if they would like to join Louise and him. Pitch and Ann decided to join them and Louise was tickled when they came over to the table. Louise told them what a wonderful wedding they had and how much she enjoyed herself. During the conversation Pitch asked where Rory and she were heading next?"

"We are going to three cities in California and then up to Seattle, Washington."

"That seems like a lot of ground to cover in less than a week, was Pitch's comment. Chris then jumped in, "They are going to San Diego and then to San Jose, which are not far apart. From there to Sacramento and then up to Seattle. After that they get a break until we evaluate how we are doing in the market. I think Rory's record will be in the top five by then. We are now looking for a new song for him to record."

"Have you talked to Rory about a new song?"

"No Ann, we have to see what our writers come up with for him."

"Do you know that Rory has a suitcase filled with songs he wrote?"

"Are you kidding me?'

"No, you should ask him about them. The ones I have heard are really good, of course that is my opinion."

After dinner Pitch and Ann said they had to go because the had an early flight in the morning and had to pack for the trip. Louise and Chris continued talking at the table and told Pitch and Ann to have a great honeymoon as the newly wed couple walked away. On the elevator, "Pitch do you think something is going on between the two of them?"

"I think so, he is single and Louise is divorced now. They both probably need some good sex."

"You have sex on the brain."

"That is because you are so good. You probably should have given Louise some tips."

"You are awful!"

"You won't be saying that in about an hour."

Ann just laughed.

Chris asked Louise where she lived? "Not to far from here, it is a small house but I like it. Would you like to see it?"

"Sure, we can drive over in your car and I can walk back to the hotel and get some fresh air."

When they walked in Louise's house Chris saw her teaching area with the piano. "Do you play the piano?"

"Yes, would you like to hear a song or two? I'll get us a drink first and then I'll play for you.

When Louise started playing Chris was amazed. "Where did you learn to play like that Louise?"

"I went to Peabody Conservatory."

While Louise was sitting at the piano playing another song. Chris walked up behind her and kissed her on the neck. Louise stopped playing and turned to him and they started kissing like crazy. The next thing Chris knew was that Louise was taking him to her bedroom. At that point clothes started flying off and they laid naked in her bed holding each other. They had wild, crazy, and passionate sex for hours. Finally, Chris said, "I better get going now."

"Why don't you just stay the night and I'll fix you breakfast in the morning?"

Ann and Pitch boarded their plane at seven-thirty in the morning. They would have to fly to Denver and they change planes to get to Las Vegas. After a night of love making, they both were tired and slept most of the way. When they arrived at The Desert Inn people were running around all over the place. It reminded Ann of Time Square in New York City. There were all kind of stars performing in town but the one Ann wanted to see were Frank Sinatra. All the people running the place seemed like Italians who were from New York. Ann had the entire trip planned out and Pitch just was going along for the ride. If Pitch had his way, they would still be home on the ranch.

Chris went to the airport with Louise and Rory but he was leaving on a commercial flight to Nashville and they were going to the west coast on a company plane. While they were waiting to board the plane and talking Chris remembered what Ann said about all the songs Rory had written. "Rory, your Mom said you have a suitcase filled with songs you wrote?"

"That is correct Chris. I am writing new ones all the time."

"How many do you have?"

"Oh, probably twenty to thirty. I stopped counting them. Some still need work but most of them are finished."

"Just by chance, do you have any with you?"

"Yea, I have three really nice songs that are finished and two I am working on."

"Do you think I could take the finished ones back to Nashville with me?"

"I guess that would be all right but they are in my guitar case which has already been loaded on the plane with our luggage."

Chris went immediately to the captain of the company plane and instructed him to get Rory's guitar case and bring it to him.

The captain returned fifteen minutes later and was carrying the guitar case. When Rory opened it there were all kinds of music sheets behind his guitar. "Let me look through the sheets and find the right ones Chris."

It took Rory about ten minutes to find what he was looking for. "Here they are Chris. The names of the songs are; Spirit of Love, Lonely Wrangler, and My Dream Girl. All the music is for a guitar so you have to do the arrangements for the other instruments. I personally think the one called Lonely Wrangler would be a good song for Hank Snow."

"I'll see what Rex can do with them. I hope you guys have a safe trip. I think the captain is ready for departure."

Then Chris kissed Louise very sincerely. Rory just looked at them and thought, "What have I missed. I didn't see this coming!"

When they got settled on the plane Rory turned to Louise, "Okay, tell me what in the world is going on?"

Louise didn't know where to start or what to tell Rory. "Let me see how to start this. At your Mom's wedding Chris and I sat together at the reception and we danced and had a lot of fun together. He asked me out to dinner that night and in fact we had dinner with your parents at the hotel. We talked about our lives and how we both were lonely. Then he decided to kiss me and I kissed him back. We kissed a few more times and he drove me to my house and kissed me goodnight and said he would see me in the morning. I am not sure where this is going but I really like Chris and I think he likes me. By him just kissing me in public meant a lot to me. I hope there is more to it then just this weekend. That's it my friend." "Chris is a great guy Louise. You should try to hold on to him."

"It might be hard with him in Nashville and me in Sheridan."

"If he makes you an offer you can't refuse there is nothing holding you back from moving to Nashville."

"I know you are right. I guess I'll just have to wait and see."

A little later in the flight Rory told Louise he had a girlfriend named Catina. "Is that the girls you were with at the wedding reception?"

"Yes, that is Catina. She had a friend Maomi with her who Tony is dating."

"She is a very beautiful girl. Is she a Shoshone?"

"Yes, but her father works at the bank in Sheridan and she lives downtown not in the village."

"How many times have you gone out with her?"

"Three times counting the wedding."

"What does your Mom think?"

"She thinks I am to young to be dating but she doesn't stop me."

"Rory you have plenty of time and you will meet plenty of girls."

Louise and Rory's west coast swing started in San Diego where it seemed like the majority of the people there were Mexican or half Mexican. Rory couldn't believe how much they loved county western music. When he was being interviewed on the radio some times the announcer would speak to the listeners in Spanish. Rory was really fascinated by the language that he decided he would take Spanish in high school. That thought made him realize that school was only a month away.

Next, they went to San Jose and the radio studio had a huge picture of Rory in their window. The announcer told Louise that he gets about twenty calls a day from listeners requesting him to play Rory's song. By the time they got to Sacramento, the capitol of California the new weekly rankings were out and Pickin My Guitar was number two on the chart right behind Hank Snow. They got to see the Pacific Ocean and all the surfers. Louise asked Rory if he wanted to try surfing. "Do you want me to kill myself? I am a cowboy not a fish."

Las Vegas was not quit what Ann thought it would be. They tried gambling at the casino. Pitch taught Ann to play black-jack because it was the easiest game to learn. They sat side by side at the black-jack table and Pitch kept winning and Ann kept losing. After losing a hundred dollars in twenty minutes she decided to play the slot-machines which only cost a nickel. This was their nightly activity accept for the night they saw Frank Sinatra. During the day they would hang out at the pool and both of them got burnt really bad by the second day. After four days of the same thing over and over Ann said to Pitch, "Can we go home and go for a horse ride out in the open range?"

"I thought you would never ask."

They packed up and were heading back to good old Sheridan.

For Louise and Rory this trip seemed harder then the other ones and they both were exhausted by the time they got back to Sheridan. By the time Rory got to the ranch it was nine o'clock Friday night. Nija fixed him something to eat and told him that Ann and Pitch were on their way home but had a delay in Denver because of heavy storms. "Rory, you also got a call from Chris Finley of RCA who said he will be here to talk to you this weekend."

The first thing Rory thought was more cities to visit before school.

Ann and Pitch didn't make it back to Sheridan until eleven o'clock Saturday morning. They did get a good night's rest at a hotel in Denver but were glad to get back home. The kids were glad to see them and so was poor Nija. Ann told them all that after church on Sunday they were going for a family horse ride and they all cheered. Right after lunch Ann got a phone call from Chris Finley saying he needed to come out and talk to Rory as soon as possible. Ann wanted to know what it was about? "I want to talk to him about making his next record and the songs he wrote."

"He and Tony just left for the village. I will call you back when he gets home. I'll call you at the hotel."

"I'm not staying at the hotel, I am at Louise's house."

"Okay, I will call you there."

When Ann got off the phone she turned to Pitch, "I think Louise and Chris are getting it on."

Pitch relied, "Good for them."

When Ann called Chris back to tell him Rory was home, she invited him and Louise to have dinner with them. After he checked with Louise he said, "That would be great. We can talk business after dinner."

"Sorry Chris, but that won't work. Rory and Tony are going out for the evening so why don't you get here about five o'clock so we all can talk."

"That works for us. I'll see you then."

Rory was happy to be home and he must have talked to Catina on the phone for about an hour. They made plans to go to the movie but Catina wanted him to meet her father before the movie. This shocked Rory a little and he wasn't sure how to handle it. Since he was a little nervous, he decided to talk to his step-dad. Pitch's advice to him was to just be himself and always be polite no matter what the circumstance was. "Pitch, did you have to do this stuff when you were a star baseball player?"

"Sure, I dated a few girls but never had to meet their parents. My advice to you is stay focused on your music career and don't get serious or worry about the other bull shit. That will all come when the timing is right."

Rory looked at him, "Thanks Dad," and he smiled.

Chris and Louise got to the house at five and they decided to handle the business before dinner so Rory could get out of there. "Rory, here is the deal, we would like you to come to Nashville next week and cut your next record. We want you to record your song Spirit of Love. Rex has done all the arrangements so we can probably get it out int three or four days. We also would like your permission to let Hank Snow record your song Lonely Wrangler."

"That is okay with me."

"One more question. Do you have any more songs that are good?"

"Yea, I have a suitcase upstairs filled with songs I wrote."

"Could you pick out maybe the best three or four and bring them to Nashville with you when you come Sunday evening."

"I can do that for you."

"Your plane will pick you up Sunday at six o'clock."

After Rory left Ann couldn't wait to get Louise alone so she could find out what is going on with Chris. She suggested to Pitch, with one of her looks, that he shows Chris the horses. After they left, "Okay, Louise what is going on?"

"I think I am in love with Chris but I am not sure he is. We have only been together for a couple of weekends and he has come to Sheridan a couple times to see me."

"Have you had sex?"

Louise smiled, "Yes and it was great for both of us. I honestly don't know where this is going but I am enjoying it for now."

"I think the big test will be when you go to Nashville next week and if he ask you to stay at his house."

"I thought about that but what about Rory?"

"He has been to Nashville already and knows the hotel. Besides, he will be working long hours. I think if you and Chris take him to dinner it would be all right. He can sleep in the hotel without you being next door as long as he locks the door."

"So, you are saying I can stay with Chris if he ask me?"

"Sure, I don't want to stand in the way of love. By the way here is your quarterly pay check."

Oh, my God, that is more than I made in a year. Shopping here I come."

Rory was all nervous going to Catina's father's house. He knew her last name was Mosley which didn't sound like an Indian name. Her dad were really nice when they greeted Rory and asked him to sit in their living room to talk. All Rory wanted was to get the hell out of there. Catina's father started the conversation, "Catina's tells us you are a big county western star?"

"I wouldn't say that, I only have one record out but I'll be making another one next week."

How does that work? Do they pay you by the number of records sold?"

"No, I have a contract with RCA. Mr. Riggins negotiated it for me. You know him, he deals with your bank all the time."

"Yes, I know John very well. If you don't mind me asking, how much is your contract worth?"

"I don't mind. It is for four million dollars."

Rory thought Mr. Mosley was going to choke. "I don't really care about the money only my music."

Then Catina's mother came into the conversation. "How come you like indian girls and not white girls."

"Rory wasn't ready for that question but he remembered what Pitch told him. Mr. Mosley, I just look at the inside of a person not the color of their skin. Catina is a beautiful person who he enjoy spending time with."

After all the questioning was over Rory couldn't wait to get out the door. When they got outside where Tony and Maomi were waiting Tony looked at Rory and his face was all red. "How did you make out Brother?"

"As Pitch always says I could use a beer."

They all laughed and headed to the movie.

CHAPTER 13

Louise and Rory were on their way to Nashville and Chris was going to meet them at the airport instead of their usual chauffeur. Rory knew something was up but he decided to wait until Louise told him. About half way through their flight Louise decided to come clean to Rory. "Rory, Chris is picking us up because he asked me if I would stay at his house instead of the hotel. I asked your Mom about it and she was okay with me not staying at the hotel with you."

"That is fine Louise, we work almost all day and it looks like you and Chris are getting serious."

"Thank you, Rory, I hope you are right about Chris!"

When they got off the plane Chris greeted Louise with a kiss and Rory immediately said, "Where is my kiss?"

They all laughed. When they got to the hotel Chris made sure Rory checked-in okay and got to his room. He told Rory if he was hungry to order room service. "I can do that?"

"Sure, it just goes on the hotel bill to RCA. Make sure when you sign for the food you leave the deliverer a tip."

"I'll be fine, you guys take off. I know Louise really wants to see your house."

When Louise and Chris arrived at his house Louise could not believe her eyes. "This isn't a house it is a mansion."

"Just a little place I call home."

As he gave her the grand tour of the house Louise was overwhelmed. His back yard had a huge patio and a beautiful swimming pool. "You live in this place all by yourself?"

"Oh no, my dog Rusty lives here with me. I know you are tired from the trip so why don't I call for pizza and we just relax?"

"That sounds great to me."

Chris took her up stairs and showed her the bedrooms. Of course, his bedroom was a giant size room. "Louise you can have your own bedroom or stay in mine with me?"

"How about a compromise? I will keep all my things in this bedroom and bathroom but will sleep in your bed. That way we won't be in each other's way in the morning."

"That is a great idea."

When they were eating their pizza, Chris hit Louise with a big question. "Do you think you could live in Nashville?"

Louise was dead silent for a minute. "I guess so if the conditions were right."

They finished off the pizza and took a shower and then went to bed, but not to sleep.

The chauffeur dropped Rory at the studio and Chris and Louise were waiting for him inside. "Did you two have a good night?"

"Yes, Rory it was great," was Chris's reply."

Then Rex Flynn came over to them. "Rory those three songs are really great and we did a lot of work on the arrangement on Spirit of Love which we picked for your next recording. Are you ready to go to work?"

As Rex and Rory went over to the band area Chris took Louise with him to show her how the music business worked. About five-thirty Rex called it a day. All Rory could think about was the swimming pool at the hotel and room service. Louise asked him to go to dinner with Chris and her but he turned her down saying he was tired and just wanted to get to the hotel. After he took his swim he was refreshed and decided to go for a walk. As he walked, he started getting hungry and he saw the Bluebird Café with all kind of singer's pictures in their window and somebody was singing inside. He walked in the door and a lady was standing there collecting money. "Excuse me, but can I get something to eat in here?"

"Sure honey, just as long as you don't order alcohol. That will be two dollars."

Since it was only a little after seven the place was not overly crowded. The waitress came to Rory's table over by the wall, "Can I take you order sir?"

"I'll have a hamburger, French fries, and a coke."

The waitress just kept looking at him and she went over to the other waitresses and pointed to Rory. He wasn't sure what the problem was and then he thought maybe it is because I am young and here by myself. When the waitress bought him his food she said, "Do you mind if I asked you a question?"

"No, you seem nice, ask away."

"Are you Rory McClure the singer of Pickin My Guitar? The picture on the wall over there looks just like you."

"Yea, I am Rory, what is your name?"

"Sally, can I have your autograph?"

"Sure, what do you want me to sign?"

"My blouse!"

Rory looked for a place to sign in the front but decided it would be safer to autograph the back of her blouse. The next thing he knew all the waitress came over to get their blouses autographed. Then the manager stopped the singer right in the middle of his song and took the microphone from him. "Ladies and Gentlemen, we have a recording artist here in the Bluebird Café tonight. Would you please welcome Rory McClure the singer of Pickin My Guitar the number one record in the nation."

All the people applauded and came over to Rory for autographs. He decided he better get back to the hotel before more people came in the café. He thanked Sally and as she walked him to the door, she kissed him on the cheek.

Rory was really working hard to finish the record so he could get back home. On the other hand, Louise didn't want to go home. Finally, on Friday Rex told Chris to go get David and the evaluation people to see if they had it right. Rex told Rory to take a break until the boss gets here. About a half hour later David and the evaluators made it to the studio. David came over and shook hands with Rory and asked him how he was doing. "I am pretty tired and can't wait to get home." "You know your song is number one on the rating chart now?"

"Yes sir, I hope they like this new one and buy the record."

"Well, let me see what you have."

David took his seat. Rex announced, "Recording Spirit of Love evaluation track."

Rory got up to the microphone and the band played the introduction. Then Rory started singing, "When love is around you, you can feel your spirit grow, but a broken love has no spirit to cling to, that is why you call the spirit of love."

After Rory was done. David stood up, "That is a wrap, print it, and get it out the door immediately." He waved to Rory, "Great job son, keep up the good work."

Then he turned and was out the door with the evaluation team just sitting there looking stupid. Rory immediately asked Chris if he could go home now? "Rory, just let the marketing people get some new promotion pictures and I'll have you on the plane by six o'clock. I will call your Mom and tell them to pick you up at about nine o'clock. Is that okay?"

"That is fine Chris."

Chris was trying to talk Louise into staying the weekend in Nashville and he would pay her way home on Monday. Louise didn't know what to do so she decided to talk to Rory and see what he thought. "Louise, I know my Mom really well and I know how she thinks. She gave you a break by letting you stay with Chris but if you don't fly back with me you will be risking your job. She hired you to be my traveling partner and is paying you lots of money for an easy job. My advice is you don't want to cross her if you still want to keep your job. Don't get me wrong

I like Chris but it isn't like he made a commitment to you or you are engaged. Right now, all you have is a love affair."

"Everything you say is true Rory but I am in love with the guy."

"Has he told you that he was in love with you?"

"No, but maybe he will."

"I will guarantee you if I get off the plane in Sheridan without you my Mom will fire you. You have to make your choice and your choices are stay here for the weekend or keep your job and fly back to Sheridan."

"I have to really think about this Rory."

"Well, you have about two hours before we have to leave for the plane."

Louise went to look for Chris but he was tided up in meetings. She didn't want to lose her job or Chris. Finally, he came out of his meeting to talk to her. "Are you staying here?"

"My thoughts are why don't you come on the plane to Sheridan with me?"

"I am really busy and have a ton of things to do so it is impossible for me to leave now."

"So, you will have to work over the weekend?"

"Just a few hours on Saturday. We can still be together and go to dinner."

"So, I am just supposed to sit at your house and wait for you?"

"I promise I will not be long at the studio."

Louise turned around and walked away. When the chauffeur came to pick them up Louise was waiting with Rory. "I hope

I didn't influence your decision Louise?" "No, Rory you had nothing to do with it. Chris was okay with me losing my job but he didn't want me to interfere with his job. No, Rory I made the right choice to go home with you."

Ann and Pitch picked up Rory at the airport and dropped Louise at her house. On the way home Rory told Ann what happened between Louise and Chris. "She made the right choice otherwise she would have been unemployed."

Rory had only two weeks before school started and Pitch really didn't want to travel anymore this summer. On Saturday Chris called Ann and told her that Rory needed to make one more week trip before school started. Ann argued with him, telling him Rory was tired and needed time to rest. "He can rest when he goes back to school. We are paying him a lot of money."

Ann didn't like Chris' tone during the conversation and was getting pissed off by the minute. "I am sorry Ann, I am just so upset, I think I lost the woman I love. Oh, the trip, Rory will like this trip he is going to New York city, Baltimore, and Atlanta. He can visit his old neighborhood and friends. These are big market cities and it is the kick-off of his new song."

"Okay Chris, he will go because I think he will like to go back to New York. I am sorry about Louise and you. But you asked her to lose her job to spend a day and a half with you."

"What do you mean lose her job?"

"If Rory would have gotten off that plane by himself, I would have fired Louise on the spot. She is his traveling partner. So, she decided to keep her $50,000 a year job."

"I didn't know all of that."

"Yea, you men are stupid and only think of yourselves. Earlier you said the woman you love. Have you told her you love her?"

"What should I do?"

"If you really love her buy her a big ass engagement ring and propose to her. If she says yes, move her to Nashville and marry her."

"What about Rory? He will need a new traveling partner."

"I have a couple people in mind and I am positive I can find somebody in this little town who would want a $50,000 job."

Chris laughed. "I don't know what to do first?"

"Call her and tell her you love her. That is enough from me. What time is the plane getting here Sunday?"

"At four o'clock Ann. I can't thank you enough."

Chris wasted no time and called Louise that evening. "First, I want to apology to you for not taking into consideration your job and only mine. Next, I want to tell you I love you and that you make my life better."

"Chris, I love you and want to be with you. It is not easy finding someone you enjoy being with all the time."

"Louise I am proposing to you right now. I am not letting you get away. Louise will you marry me?"

"Absolutely, Yes Chris!"

"Consider yourself engaged and when the plane picks you up on Sunday the captain will have your engagement ring to give to you from me."

"That will be wonderful. Where are we going to this time?"

"To New York City, Baltimore, and Atlanta and make sure Rory gets to visit his old neighborhood. I love you and wish I was with you."

Ann were having problems with the City Council because she wanted to improve the road from Sheridan to Interstate 25. In Ann's opinion this would draw more people to Sheridan and help the city's economy grow over the long term. She had studies conducted that showed with the new road the economy would grow 23% after the completion of the road. The city population itself was split. Some wanted it for there children's future and others wanted it to remain the quiet small town it presently is. The six City Council members were split on their decision, three for and three against. Chester Newton the chair of the council was totally against it and would not listen to the benefits for the city. All Newton saw the seventeen million dollars to pay for it. Ann knew if he voted for the improvement the other council members would follow. She decided to have a private meeting with him to see if she could change his position.

Louise and Rory were boarding the plane for New York when the captain came up to Louise and handed her a small box. "This is from Chris Finley he is sorry he is not here to give this to you himself. When Louise opened the box, it was a beautiful large diamond in the middle of the ring and a smaller diamond at the top, bottom, and both sides. Louise stated crying and Rory hugged her. "I think Chris really loves you."

"He does Rory, he told me last night and we are going to get married."

"I told you things would work out, it's the Spirit of Love."

Louise laughed because that is the title of his new song. The captain prepared for take off and they were on their way to the Big Apple."

Landing at the New York airport bought back memories for Rory. He wondered if the fish market was still there where he sang for the first time in public. Their first stop was WKTS radio station the main country western station in New York. The announcer was the same guy when Rory lived in New York, Hal Harris. Everybody just called him Double H. They talked on the air about Rory's time in New York and how he liked Wyoming. Hal Harris let several of the listeners directly asked Rory some questions. One person asked Rory who wrote the Spirit of Love?"

When Rory answered he did, Hal asked him if he had a girlfriend? Rory told him he was dating a Shoshone Indian girl Catina. Hal thought that was a beautiful name and asked Rory if she was beautiful?

Rory laughed, "You can't believe how beautiful."

The total time at WKTS was great and Rory spent two hours there.

After Louise and Rory had lunch it was time to got to the Bronx. Rory had the chauffeur drive them to his old neighborhood and told the chauffeur to drop them off on Preston Street and come back to this corner in two hours. You could tell Rory was really excited as he pointed out things to Louise left and right. He decided to first show Louise the fish market. Mr. Anthony still had his stand in the market so Rory asked the men working there if he was around. Unfortunately, they told Rory Mr. Anthony just left for the fishing pier to buy some fresh fish. Then he took Louise to Saint Patrick's Catholic Church and School and told her this was where the McClure kids went to school. Next on the agenda was the garment district where Ann worked. When he opened the door to one of the sweat shops Louise was shocked. It had many women in a row sitting behind a sewing machine and they were going 90mph. She was just standing in the shop and had a hard time breathing. "Those poor women," was her comment. Rory told her Ann worked in this shop ten hours a day five days a week for peanuts. Next, he wanted to show her where they lived and as they walked down Preston Street Rory saw his old best friend, Sonny Tanbello. Rory called to him, "Sonny, Sonny," and he walked over to Sonny. "Why if it isn't Rory the Cannery. How you doing my friend?"

"Really great Sonny. How about yourself?"

"Not that good, I just got out of juvenile hall. Hey, can you loan me five bucks?"

"Sure, but all I have is twenty-dollar bills."

"I'll just take one of those. Thanks Cannery I'll see you around."

Sonny went walking down the street a lot happier with Rory's twenty-dollars. The last stop on Rory's tour was where they lived on Preston Street.

When they walked up to the apartment building it needed lots of work. "This is where we lived Louise. See that third-floor window that was our apartment."

"How did all of you sleep in that small area?"

"It has two bedrooms. Mom and Nellie in one and Tommy and me in the other. We had to make it do because that was all Mom could afford." Rory looked at a man coming out of the building. He looked again and called "Mr. Zario."

The man looked at Rory, "Is that really you Rory McClure?"

"Yes, sir."

"I thought you moved out west somewhere?"

"Yes sir, I am just visiting here."

"Well, you are lucky because this place is turning into a shit hole. Look how nice the buildings next to it are. The owner won't fix one dam thing and he keeps raising the rent which the people here can't afford. You know your Mom almost killed herself working so hard to keep this shitty apartment for you kids. But there isn't a dam thing we can do about it."

Rory's brain was working really hard and he felt he had to do something to help these people. "Mr. Zario, I have an idea if you will help me."

"If it will help, let me hear it Rory."

"I will buy this apartment building and give you $50,000 to fix it up. Then you could set the rent payment for what you think is fair and manage the building for me. What do you think of that plan?"

"Sure, sure, sure that sounds good."

"Rory, he thinks you are feeding him a lot of bull."

"I think you are right, Louise."

Rory got a piece of paper and pencil from Louise and wrote down John Riggins name. "Mr. Zario, this name on the paper is a man who will get things started. His name is John Riggins and one of his people will contact you."

"Sure, sure, I got you."

"He still doesn't believe you Rory."

"That is okay Mr. Riggins will get somebody to contact Mr. Zario and then he will know it is the truth."

"This is really nice of you. What will your Mom think because this will cost some big dollars?"

"She will be all for it."

After going back to his old neighborhood Rory thanked God for all the good things that changed his life.

After they ate dinner Rory called Ann and told her about Mr. Zario and their old apartment building. He told her what he wanted to do and she was so proud of him wanting to help others. Ann said, "I will talk to John Riggins and asked him to get his people working on your project."

They talked all about his tours and about the diamond ring Chris give to Louise as an engagement ring. "Mom, we were so blessed by the dear Lord and I could not let the people living in our old building suffer any more."

"I understand Rory, I feel the same way."

Ann's meeting with Chester Newton of the city council went nowhere. For some reason he wouldn't even listen to the facts and he even got a little smart mouthed with her. She could not figure out why Newton was so set against the road improvement. What she needed was some type of action plan to make sure when the people voted they would approve the road construction. After given it some serious thought she came up with two actions. She would get Charlie Douglas to investigate Chester Newton's background and see if he could fine the reason for Newton's attitude. She also would talk to Sharon Steward about getting the Sheridan Women's Association to promote the road improvement project. Ann decided to first handle the Rory project and called

John Riggins. Ann informed John what Rory wanted to do and he said he would assign one of his men to it immediately.

After visiting the other radio station in the morning Louise and Rory headed to Baltimore. Their plane landed at Baltimore/Washington Airport and their chauffeur along with the RCA local coordinator was waiting for them. The radio station they were going to the next day was actually not in Baltimore but in Waldorf, Maryland. Since Waldorf was just twenty miles south of Washington D.C. their coordinator made reservations for them in the nation's capital just in case they wanted to go sightseeing. Louise and Rory thought that was a great idea. After checking into the Hilton Downtown Hotel their coordinator told them that he would put them up at eight o'clock in the morning and after the radio interview he would take them to the airport for their next leg in Atlanta.

Louise and Rory quickly changed into their casual clothes and hit the streets of Washington D.C. Since they both had never been to D.C. before and they knew their time was limited they decided to hire a local cab to drive them around to all the sights. The local cab driver told them he would show them all the sights since it was not a busy evening and would only charge them $250. Louise could not believe the high price and thought the taxi driver was trying to take advantage of them because they were from out of town. Louise politely said no thanks and they got out of the cab. Since they really didn't know where to go, they tried another taxi driver and his price was $200 so they figured the prices in D.C. must be really high so they told the driver okay.

He drove down Pennsylvania Avenue and stopped in front of the White House and Louise pulled a small camera out of her pocketbook and took some pictures. Then the driver showed them the Lincoln Memorial, the Supreme Court building, all the museums, the Ford Theater, and all the department agencies of the Federal Government. Rory had Louise take a picture of him standing in front of the FBI Building. Their taxi driver was really good and he would give them a little history as he showed them each location. When the tour was over, they thought he was so good they give him $250. Since now they were hungry, they decided to just eat in the hotel restaurant and call it a night.

Ann called Sharon and asked her to meet at her office. Ann asked Sharon what she thought about Ann's road improvement plan. "I think it is great and should have been done years ago. We need the road to grow the city because eventually there will be very few cattle ranches around here to support the job population."

That statement raised a big question mark in Ann's mind and made a note to talk to Pitch about that. Sharon was sure most of the ladies in the association was for the improvement. "Ann, they are thinking about the future of their children. None of us want our children to grow up and move out of Sheridan. We want them to stay here so we can be with our grandchildren but the city's economy needs to change to support that."

Ann felt the same way Sharon did. She didn't want Tony, Tommy, and Nellie moving away but Ann knew Rory would. "Ann, here's what we will do. You give a speech to the women's association and get them all fired up like we did for your mayor campaign."

"God, girl where did you get all those brains. Let's do it!"

John Riggins assigned one of his best men, Troy Sullivan, to the Rory project mainly because he was originally from New York. Troy wasted no time and found the owner of the building from the city records. He made an offer of $120,000 for the property to the owner. Troy was playing hard ball with the owner and told him the offer was a one time offer and only good for three days. The owner knew the building was in terrible condition and it wouldn't be long before the city cracked down on him. On the third day the owner called Troy and accepted the offer. Troy then called a building contractor friend of his family, Jack O'Neal and together they went to see Mr. Zario.

When Mr. Zario opened his door, Troy introduced himself and told him he was working for John Riggins handling the Rory McClure project. Mr. Zario looked at him with an are you nuts look. "You remember what Rory McClure told you?"

"Yes, but I thought he was just making it up."

"No, sir, it is for real. Rory has already bought the building I have the deed right here."

Mr. Zario was amazed and also confused. "This is Jack O'Neal a local building contractor here in the city. He is going to fix up everything wrong with the building and I want you to work with him so he fixes everything. Once all the repairs are finished, I will be back to see you and show you how to manage the building. Are you okay with all of this?"

Mr. Zario walked over and hugged Troy. "Sir, you don't need to thank me. You need to thank Rory McClure."

Louise and Rory's trip to Baltimore/Washington D.C. was more fun then they expected. The radio Station people were great and promised to promote Rory's new song. Now they were on their way to Atlanta, Georgia before going home. Rory asked Louise about her wedding plans. "I'm not sure Rory, since I have been married one but Chris hasn't, I don't know if he wants a big wedding or to go to the Justice of Peace."

"If it was me, I would just go to the Justice of Peace since you both are in your mid-thirties and then I would go on a great honeymoon like to Puerto Rico for a week."

"That is a great plan. I hope Chris sees it that way." Why go through all that trouble and expense since all that matters are, we are together?"

"I am sure Chris will be asking you so just tell him that plan. I think he would want to get married as soon as possible so he can get you to move to Nashville."

"I guess we will have to wait and see what is on his mind."

Ann's speech to the women's association was fabulous and the women were pumped up ready to take on the world. They organized a campaign team just like before and were putting posters up all over town encouraging people to vote for the road improvement. Ann decided that since the campaign was going so well it was time to talk to Charlie. Ann's secretary scheduled a meeting with Charlie for the late afternoon so most of the people in the building were going home. Charlie showed up in Ann's office at four-thirty. "Charlie, I want your department to investigate Chester Newton's background very carefully. I want you to pick only people you really trust because there can not be links to Chester."

"I got it Ann. Do you think he is up to something or better yet why the investigation?"

"He is really against my road improvement plan and will not look at the studies or listen to reason. He is just totally against it and is influencing people. I don't know if this is personal or just him being a hard head. Just see what you can find."

"I am on it, Ann. Just give me about a week and I'll report my findings to you."

Louise and Rory couldn't wait to get out of Atlanta because they had other things on their mind. Rory was looking forward to seeing Catina and was hoping she was in most of his classes when he registered for high school next week. Of course, Louise was thinking of Chris, getting married, and moving to Nashville. The amazing part of their Atlanta trip was that Rory could not believe how many people there had cowboy hats on. Even the radio station announcer had a cowboy hat. The one big question the announcer asked Rory was if he was coming out with an album? Rory never gave that a thought until now. Knowing all the work it took to make a record, he figured an album would take months and he was going back to school. Louise told him to stop worrying about it and that Chris knew his circumstance and would figure how to work around it. They finished up in Atlanta and were back on the plane heading to Sheridan which Louise wished was Nashville.

Jack O'Neal and his crew were working very hard to get the apartment building fixed up as fast as they could. When Ann told Rory, what was going on he was happy and called John Riggins to thank him. John told him that Troy would go back to New York when the job was completed to educate Mr. Zario on how to manage the building and its tenants. John said that Jack O'Neal was going to put a cement intendment on the on the front of the building that says McClure Building. Rory really like that saying, "Then the McClure's will always be part of New York City.

When Rory called Catina, "Rory did you see the article in the New York Post newspaper?"

"No, how did you get that newspaper?'

"My father gets it to follow the stock market."

"So, what article are you talking about?"

"There was an article on your visit to New York. The article talked all about you and your success. Then the article said you were dating me and I was very beautiful."

"Oh, that interview with Hal Harris."

"It's okay Rory. My Dad loved the article and is showing it to everyone but now he wants me to marry you."

They both laughed and made fun of her father. Then Rory asked her to go to dinner with him. "That sounds great. What about Maomi and Tony are they going with us?"

"No, it will be my Mom and Step-Dad."

"Are you for real or just kidding me?"

"I'm just kidding you, we are going with Tony and Maomi. I thought I would let you see how it feels when you are asked to meet your parents."

"Okay, you owe me!"

Chris caught the early flight to Sheridan and Louise was surprised when he showed up at her door ten o'clock in the morning. After she realized it was Chris standing there she jumped in his arms and very quickly dragged him to her bedroom. Later they sat on her front porch looking at the sky. "Louise, what do you want to do about getting married?"

"I wasn't sure what you wanted to do and I figured I would just do what you wanted."

"That's not an answer and I am lost about this kind of stuff. Help me!"

"Okay, you want my opinion here it comes. Let's go to the Justice of Peace get married and go on a great honeymoon in

Puerto Rico and come back and move me to Nashville. That is, it. Remember, you asked!"

"I absolutely love you. That is our plan. I am so glad you didn't want a big wedding like Ann and Pitch had."

"Since Rory's traveling is done. What if we pack up everything I need, we load up my car, lock up the house, and drive to Nashville so we can get married on Monday."

"Let's start packing."

Charlie had his two most trusted people investigating Chester Newton. They were looking at everything from his finances, taxes, education and family tree. So, far their investigation had not turned up a single thing. Charlie told his team that he felt Newton was somehow connected to ex-mayor Gallon. When they started digging, they found tracks to Gallon. Newton was Annie Gallon's brother. Before she got married, she was Annie Newton. Charlie guessed this was a big secret in their families so Chester Newton could control the city council while Mayor Gallon conducted all his illegal business. Charlie also thought since Ann was the person that uncovered all of Gallon's illegal actions and caused them to run, she was responsible for Annie Gallon getting shot to death. It was obvious to Charlie that Chester Newton was on a revenge trip and wanted Ann to pay for his sister's death. Charlie wanted to make sure all his bases were covered before he told Ann.

One evening on the patio Ann asked Pitch about what Sharon said about the cattle ranches going away. Pitch explained to her that more and more of the meat companies and hamburger chains are raising their own herds of cattle. That means it will drive the prices of our cattle down and evemtually it won't be profitable like it is now to raise cattle. To be honest it is just a matter of time.

"How soon do you think this will happen?"

"My best guess would be twelve to fifteen years but it could be sooner."

"What will happen to the ranches?"

"Many of them will just close down but a lot of the big ranches will become what they call Dude Ranches. This is where people come to stay on the ranch and do all the things cowboys do. It is like taking a week's vacation and learning the total cowboy experience of riding, roping and the other stuff. Rich city people will pay big bucks just to give this a try."

"Won't all the wranglers lose their jobs>?"

"Probably about 80% of them but the owners will still need some ranch hands."

"Are you sure this is really going to happen?"

"We talk about it all the time at the ranch owner's association meetings which I go to for you. They projected that the smaller ranches will close down in about seven years or so. If the train stops coming to Cow Town it will kill off the big ranches because we would have to drive the cattle to far to get them to market. Richard Boone already is building a hotel/lounge on his property and will start trying Dude Ranching in about two years. He will still raise his cattle until it becomes unprofitable."

"Should we start doing what Richard is doing?"

"I don't think so because we have an ace up our shelves."

"What does all that mean, ace up our shelves? I only know black-jack?"

"It is just a saying Ann. I think we can raise cattle for another twelve years which would put Nellie in college. Then we tap into your ace, uranium. Your property has tons and tons of uranium. When the cattle business dries up, we mine uranium. We would continue to utilize the Shoshone people. Instead of being wranglers they would be uranium miners."

"You have really thought this out!"

"I wish that I could take all to the credit but good old Uncle McClure knew what he was doing when he bought this property. Why do you think all the free-loaders keep coming back to your property? Out of all the ranches around here including Richard Boone's ranch they don't have big deposits of uranium only your ranch."

"All of that makes sense. So, I don't have to worry about the future?"

"Darling, you are Mrs. Wesley now and everything is under control."

CHAPTER 14

Ann's campaign for the road improvement was going strong and Chester Newton was totally pissed off. He started giving speeches himself telling the people where they could better use the city's money instead of the road. Charlie had checked his information over several times so he decided it was time to meet with the mayor. He called Ann at her office and asked her if she could have a beer with him after work at the Bonfire Tavern. She thought this was a funny request but was sure Charlie had something important to tell her. "Charlie, I will meet you there at five o'clock."

"That will be great Ann."

Charlie wasn't really sure what Ann was going to do with the information but in reality, Chester Newton had not done anything illegal. He tried to figure ways to help her but he could not think of anything legal.

Jack O'Neal finished the McClure Building and it looked great. The city inspectors praised him for his work and the tenants were all happy. Troy Sullivan made the trip back to New York to work with Mr. Zario. The first thing Troy did was take a lot of pictures to take back to Rory. Mr. Zario was so pleasured to see Troy and just kept telling him all the things Jack's crew did. Mr. Zario insisted that Troy call him Hank from now on and not Mr. Zario. Tory went over all the tenants monthly rent changes with Hank. He then asked Hank to describe to him each tenant's financial situation in the building. The families that had children Troy cut their rent by 25% and the others by 15%. Hank then looked at each individual rent payment very carefully and sked Troy if the rent was good or did it need to be lowered some more. Troy told Hank that each tenant would get a letter from him telling them what their new rent would be, that it was due the first of the moth, and payment was to be made to Mr. Zario. Troy gave him a sample of the letter so he knew what it actually said.

Next, he told Hank that he opened a bank account at the Union Trust Bank. The account was in Rory McClure's name and that is where he would deposit the tenants rent payments each month. Troy informed Hank that he would be monitoring the account from Wyoming. Then he gave Hank a bank card which authorized Mr. Zario to make withdraws if he needed money to fix the property. He told Hank he that established a maintenance contract with Herbie's Building Maintenance Company that would do all the small repairs in the apartments. He added that if there was a major repair that he needed to draw out money for, he needed to call Troy and let him know. "Do you have all of this so far Hank?"

"Yes, Troy, you have made it pretty simple."

"Okay, you are now the building superintendent and you will receive a $1,000 check from me each month for your service."

"Are you kidding me?"

"No, this your pay for being the superintendent of the building. If you run into any problems call me immediately. Here is my business card. I will check in with you about once a quarter. Are we good to go?"

"Absolutely, Troy. Tell Rory we love him and will pray for him."

"Take care Hank. I got to go catch my plane."

Tony took Rory to register for his classes and the students there were all over Rory with thousands of questions about making records. Finally, Tony yelled, "That is enough he will be in school all year so you have plenty of time to talk to him."

"Thank you, Tony, it is nice to have an older brother who is a senior."

Rory only got to pick two classes the others were all standard for freshman. The two electives he picked were music and Spanish. The only chance he had of being in Catina's classes was if the school put them together because no way Catina was taking music and Spanish for her electives. Rory would have to wait until they mailed him his schedule in a couple days. When Tony registered the counselor there asked him if he was going to apply for any academic scholarships because he was one of the school's top students. "Sorry, but I am not going to college. When I graduate that is it for me."

The counselor quickly replied, "Does your mother the Mayor know about this?"

"I think this is my decision."

Rory was standing there listening to their conversation and he knew Ann wanted Tony to go to college. When they walked back to Tony's truck Rory looked at Tony, "Are you going to tell Mom you don't want to go to college?"

"With your big mouth I guess I am going to have to tell her before you do!"

Ann caught up with Charlie at the Bonfire Tavern. He was sitting at a table far in the corner up against the wall. "Do you want a beer Ann?"

"Sure, it is really hot out and a cold beer sounds good."

Charlie signal to the waitress for two beers while Ann took a seat. "Okay, Charlie let me have what you got me over here for."

"I will get right to the point; Annie Gallon is Chester Newton's sister."

"You are shitting me?"

"No, I think Chester controlled the city council so Gallon could do what he wanted."

"But why now with the Gallon's dead?"

"I think this is personal because he blames you for his sister's death and probably hates your guts."

"That makes sense and nobody in this town knew they were related?"

"I think they kept it a secret so Gallon could spend the city's money on things like a commercial truck and swimming pool. I believe Newton must have received a kick-back from Gallon somehow. However, we did not find any evidences of it. The bottom-line Ann, is Newton has not done anything illegal for us to file charges."

"I understand Charlie but when people find out he is related to the Gallon's his name will be mud in this city."

"Just be careful, no false accusations."

After Ann drank her beer, she told Charlie she had to run because dinner was on the table.

After Louise and Chris loaded up the car, they took off that evening. Since the drive to Nashville from Sheridan would take about twenty-three hours about two o'clock in the morning they stopped at a motel. They only slept about five hours and were back on the road. The 1,500-mile ride went by fast as they talked about everything including their family background. They stopped to eat one more time and finally arrived in Nashville at ten o'clock Sunday night. They both were so happy when they saw Charlie's house and could get out of the car for good. They both were not hungry so they decided to take a shower to feel better. "Louise, I have to make one phone call while you are showering."

"That is fine Chris."

"Hello David, this is Chris I am sorry for calling so late but Louise and I just got into Nashville. I just wanted to tell you I will not be in work tomorrow because I am getting married."

"Are you shitting Chris?"

"No, Louise and I decided to get married and we are going to the court house tomorrow."

"Well, congratulations, I will talk with you later."

Louise heard who he was calling, "Now, I know I am really important to you if you are taking off work."

Chris just smiled at her and grabbed her up off of her feet and carried her to the bed.

After a great night they went to the court house early in the morning. When they got there the bad news hit them. They had to buy a marriage license first and wait three days before they could get married. Louise told Chris it was not a big deal and if he wanted to drop her off at the house and go to work it was fine with her. "Are you really sure?"

"Yes, because you will have to take off Thursday. Now, that I have my car here I can go shopping and check out Nashville's stores."

Ann had a meeting with the campaign team and told them about Chester Newton being Annie Gallon's brother. Ann told them they had to be careful not to say anything illegal. The team came up with all kinds of suggestions. They settled on putting up posters all around town that said, "Don't let Annie Gallon's Brother Chester Newton influence you vote." They also decided to do a second posters, "Vote for Road Improvement, "Don't listen to Gallon relative Newton."

Ann laughed, "There posters will get the hair on his back up."

Sharon said they would get the posters made quickly and assigned team members to areas to put them up.

When Ann came home that evening Tony asked her if he could talk to her later. After dinner they went out to the patio and Tony thought that Pitch should come also. "I just wanted to tell you that I am not interested in going to college."

Ann could not believe what she just heard and was not sure what to say. Pitch was waiting for her to say something and when she didn't, he spoke out, "Tony, what do you plan to do for a living?"

"I thought I would just keep working at the Coyote club."

"The job you have for the summer is not a real job. I created it for you so you could learn finance and accounting. When you go back to school that job goes away and you just work on Saturday like now. Tell me what you are going to do to make a living again?"

"I can find a job."

"Doing what, working on the trash truck. Do you think Ann took you into her family so you could work on a trash truck? What about your girlfriend. She is going to college to become a doctor. Do you think a doctor is going to marry a trash collector?"

Then Ann took over, "It would be different if you were having a hard time in school but you are one of the top students in the school."

Tony was just looking at the two of them and he started to question himself as to what he was doing. Pitch went back at it, "You have a great mind for working with numbers and accounting. If you go to college you could be the next John Riggins in the town."

"Going to college cost a lot of money and you both have done so much for me already."

"Tony do not base your decision on the money issue. Ann and I together have more money then we know what to do with it. Why do you think your Mom told Maomi she was going to college even if she did not get a scholarship? You don't know, right? That's because Ann is going to pay her way."

"Is that the truth Mom?"

"Yes, Tony it is the truth but don't tell Maomi, yet.

"I don't want to let you both down. I want a future with Maomi but I am not sure what to do?"

Ann had to say the last words, "We love you Tony and want you to be successful in life and have the family you want."

"I will think about it some more. You both told me things I didn't know."

The new posters were all over town and people were laughing at Chester Newton. It was so bad that his wife wouldn't even go grocery shopping in the public. To top things off Sid Walters wrote a big article in the Sheridan Prairie newspaper all about Newton's connection to Gallon. He was so mad that he went around town tearing down the posters of the poles and buildings. Sheriff Douglas told him to stop doing it or he would lock him up, so he did. The five other council men kept trying to call him but he would not return their calls. Chester Newton tried to speak at the men's club and they all booed him. Sheriff Dan and Curly were keeping a close eye on him because they figured he was going to break sooner or later and would do something stupid. Newton's children did not want to go to school because the other kids were making fun of their dad. That was the last straw and Newton decided he had to talk with Ann because she was the one behind all of his misery. Newton didn't call for an appointment, he just dashed into Ann's office. "You little bitch, you are destroying my life with those postures.

"What posters Chester?"

"Don't play dumb with me or I'll knock that smile off your face."

When Ann's secretary heard him say that she ran down the hall to get Charlie Douglas. Just as they got to Ann's door Newton raised his arm back and hit Ann in the face and she fell to the floor. Charlie quickly tackled Newton and yelled to the secretary, "Call the ambulance and Sheriff Douglas to come get this ass hole."

After Charlie tied up Newtons hands and feet, he went over to look at Ann. Her mouth, nose, and lip were bleeding really bad. Charlie tried to stop the bleeding and tried talking to her. Just then the medics arrived and took her to the hospital in the ambulance. When the Sheriff and Curly got there Charlie gave them six charges, they could hold Newton. They picked him off the floor and put handcuffs on him and out the door they went.

Charlie looked at Ann's secretary, "Somebody needs to call Pitch?"

"Don't look at me, you do it."

Charlie called the house and Nija answered the phone. "Nija, is Pitch around?"

"He is out on the range working."

"Can you send Samoka out to get him?"

"Why!"

"Ann has been hurt really bad and is in the emergency room at the hospital."

All Charlie heard was the phone drop,

When Pitch saw Samoka coming in the truck he went over to him so he didn't spook the cattle. "What brings you out here Samoka?"

"Mrs. Ann has been hurt and is in the emergency room at the hospital. "Give me that truck and you ride my horse back."

Pitch went straight to the emergency room with his chaps still on. When he saw Ann laying in an emergency room bed, he got tears in his eyes. Walked over and took her hand softly to let her know he was there. Ann's face was all bandaged up and she looked like she was in serious pain. Then Pitch yelled at the nurse, "Where the hell is the dam doctor."

The nurse ran out of the room and came back with the doctor. "I am her husband what is her condition. She looks like she is in lots of pain."

"Mayor McClure has a broken nose, a burst eye vessel, one tooth knocked out and I put six stitches in her lip so no kissing for a while. Her face will probably be black and blue for about three or four weeks. I think she will recover fully over time."

"Can she go home?"

"No, I think we better keep her over night and if everything is okay, she can go home in the morning after I check her."

"Thank you doctor."

Just then Sheriff Douglas came walking in to see how Ann was. "Is she going to be okay."

"The doctor said she would fully recover but it will take a little time."

Pitch pulled Dan over to the side. "Now, tell me what the hell happened to get her injured like this? Did she fall down the steps at work or what? The one side of her face looks like it took all the damage. Tell me what you know."

Dan did not want this job because Pitch would probably go nuts. However, he didn't want to send him to Charlie because Charlie had done enough. "Okay partner, you need to be calm after you hear the total story."

"I promise Dan. Right now, I only care about Ann."

Dan was telling him the entire story and when he got to the part where Chester Newton hit Ann in the face with his full power you could also see Pitch's blood pressure rise. "So, if Charlie didn't come in and tackle Newton, he could have killed Ann?"

"I'm not sure what he would have done next. I only wish Charlie could have gotten there a little sooner."

"Newton is in your jail?"

"Yes, Charlie has filed six charges against him with the two big ones being attempted murder and assault and battery. He could get twenty years in prison just alone for those two."

"Thank you, Dan.,"

"I'll leave you alone with Ann. You better let the family know what is going on because Nija keeps calling may office."

Just as Dan was leaving Ann came to. "Is that you Pitch?"

"Yes, Ann I am here you just take it easy."

"Newton really did a job on me. I feel like a train ran over my face."

"Yea, he hit you pretty hard and he is a big man. He is in jail now looking at about twenty years in prison."

"Can I go home?"

"The doctor just wants to keep you over night. I can take you home in the morning if you have a good night without problems."

"I guess I can live with that compared to what you went through. I am really in a lot of pain."

"Just try and rest. I am here with you."

Ann fell back to sleep as the pain medicine kicked-in. Pitch thought this would be a good time to call the house so he went down to the lounge and found a pay phone.

When he called the house Nija answered the phone and would not get off. She wanted to know everything about Ann's condition. Finally, Pitch had to tell her to get off the phone and get him Rory. He explained to Rory everything that happened and that Ann would be coming home tomorrow. Pitch told him it was no need for the kids to come to the hospital and that he was staying all night with Ann. "Is she in the critical condition room section?"

"No, she is just in a regular room on the second floor. I got to go back up stairs Rory we will see you all in the morning, hopefully."

When Rory hung up with Pitch, he got Tony, Tommy, and Nellie together and told them what happened and that Ann would be coming home tomorrow. They all were worried to death about their Mom. Finally, Tony said, "That's bull shit everybody gets in the truck we are going to see Mom at the hospital."

They loaded up the truck and were at the hospital in twenty minutes. Pitch was shocked when the four kids came walking in the room, yet he was proud of them. They waited a little while and Ann woke up. She assured them she was all right just a little beat up. She told Nellie it was hard to talk with her lip and that Nellie would have to take care of her when she goes home. At nine o'clock the nurse in charge told them they all had to go but Pitch. On the way home Rory said, "I feel like going to the jail and beating up that Newton guy."

"I think we all do Rory but putting him in prison for a long time will be much better."

Pitch felt like he just wanted to get in bed with Ann and just hold her. The room only had a bed, night stand, and two chairs. Pitch moved the chairs out of the way and found a blanket, pillow, and a sheet in the closet. He laid the blanket on the floor sided Ann's bed, put the pillow at the top on the blanket and the sheet would be his cover up. He took off his boots and jeans and put them on the chair next to his hat. Pitch checked Ann one more time, turned off the light and laid down in his make shift bed on the floor. Every time Ann groaned during the night he would get up and check on her. In the morning when the new morning nurse came to check on Ann, she saw the boots and jeans laying on the chair and wondered what was going on. Then a head popped up along side of Ann's bed and the nurse started screaming. Pitch jumped to his feet in his boxer shorts," It's okay, I'm her husband, settle down."

Then he quickly put on his jeans as the nurse left the room. As he finished dressing, he could hear all the nurses at the nurse station laughing. Ann heard them laughing as she woke up. "What is so funny Pitch? I could use a good laugh."

When he told her, she did get a laugh? The doctor came in at nine o'clock he said everything looked good and that Ann could go home. He gave Pitch medicine prescriptions and said he wanted to see Ann in a week. Ann was glad to get her clothes back on even though her shirt had blood stains. Last night Pitch had washed it the best he could and it did look better than it was. Once they were in the truck Pitch kept asking every five minutes how she was doing and was he going to fast? "Pitch, stop the questions, put the truck in gear and get me home. I smell like blood."

When they got to the house Nija came out to help Ann get in the house. "I'm okay, I can walk, my face is what is hurt not my legs."

Ann went right upstairs to shower and then she laid on her bed for a nap.

Louise and Chris finally got married at the court house. It was just the two of them and the Justice of Peace. Afterwards they went to lunch as Mr. & Mrs. Chris Finley. While Louise was shopping downtown, she came across a travel agency and went in to check about their honeymoon. The agent planned the entire trip for them and all Louise had to do was to call the agent with the dates. Louise even paid for the trip at the time. When she told Chris about it he got all excited but would have to check with David to see when he could take off a week. After lunch they drove over to the studio to let everybody know they got married. When he talked to David, he told him he wanted a week off for his honeymoon. David just looked at him. "Do you know Rory's Spirit of Love song is number eight on the charts already. He has two songs in the top ten. I know the public has really taken to his music. We got a gold mine with this kid. Chris, I am having a little celebration for you and Louise at my house on Saturday evening. As far as the honeymoon, you can go next week because things seem to be under control. One thing you have to take care of tomorrow before you leave is, we got a call from the Ed Sullivan Show producer. You need to call him and see what they want."

"I'll get right on that tomorrow. Thanks boss, you have been great to me."

"Chris you are a hard worker and I hope you and Louise are happy."

Tony decided to talk to Maomi about going to college. She still wasn't sure she would get to go to college but she encouraged Tony to go. "Maomi, we can go to the same college and be together."

"That sounds great Tony but there is not a chance of an Indian getting an academic scholarship."

"Maomi, you are going to college to become a doctor for you people."

"How!"

"Okay, but you can't tell this to anybody. It is a secret for now. You will receive the first McClure/Boone college scholarship that only goes to Shoshone Indians."

"What in the world are you talking about Tony? Are you going crazy on me?"

"Since the McClure and Boone ranches have so many Shoshone Indians working for them, they decided to create a scholarship fund just for the Shoshone. It is called the McClure/Boone Shoshone College Scholarship Fund and Mom said they have selected you as the first winner of the scholarship."

"Are you serious Tony?"

"Yes, but you can't tell anybody until they announce it in the newspaper."

"You don't know what a relief that is to me. Now, you have to go with me. I will major in medicine and you in financial management. We both will have great careers and raise a family."

"I love you Maomi, very, very much!"

"I feel the same way Tony."

When the word got to Nashville that Ann was beaten up Louise called to talk with her. Ann told her she was doing really good and felt good all but her nose and lip. When Louise told Ann, she was married Ann got excited for her and wanted to know all the details. She was surprised that Louise was settling in Chris's house so fast and that she had moved a lot of her things already. Louise informed Ann they would have to find another traveling partner for Rory and thanked her for the great opportunity and for being her friend again. No sooner than Ann hung up with Louise the door bell rang. Nija answered the door and it was Sharon. "Oh, my God Ann, look at you. You look like you have been in a bar fight."

After Ann told her everything that happened Sharon replied, "Well, at least you will get your road improvement project approved by the city. What are you going to do about the Newton's spot on the City Council?"

"Well, I have been giving that some thought being laid up with time on my hands. I think it is time to have a woman on the City Council and that woman is you. It will not require much of your time. The council only meets a couple times a month. What do you think?"

"I like it, I'll do it."

"First, I have to get Chester Newton to resign his position because he hasn't been convicted of anything yet. Once he does that, I can put you in as the interim city council member replacement until the election. Of course, there is no doubt you will be elected with our campaign team behind you." They both smiled.

Later Ann took off some of the bandage off her face. "It isn't that bad once the nose goes down and the black and blue disappears. I think I'll go to the office tomorrow after Pitch goes out on the range."

Rory finally got his got his class schedule in the mail and he quickly called Catina to compare classes. Out of the five standard classes they had two of them together. They had English and Math and the English class was right before lunch so they could have lunch together. "Rory, did you see that both of your records are in the top ten this week?"

"No, I really don't follow the rankings. I know my songs are good so people will buy them."

"When are you going to start making an album?"

"Everybody is asking me that question and I don't know the answer. I will be back in school so it will be hard to find the time to do an album. I guess when Chris gets back from his honeymoon, we will talk about it. Right now, I have a question for you? Do you think I can kiss you?"

"I have been waiting forever. What took you so long?"

"That sounds like I have to make up for lost time tonight."

The next morning Pitch had already gone so Ann jumped in her jeep and took off for her office with Nija yelling the entire time, "Where are you going?"

Everybody in the office was glad to see Ann up and around. Of course, injured or not injured, everybody knew who was still the boss. She told her secretary to tell Charlie that she wanted to see him. About fifteen minutes later Charlie came to her office. "Mayor, you look better then the last time I saw you. How are you feeling?"

"I'm okay. By the way, thanks for all you did to help me out because I don't know what could have happened next."

"When I tackled Newton, I think he was bending over to help you. I think his sane mind came back to him and he realized what he had done. Those postures really did him in, his wife couldn't go out in public, his kids didn't want to go the school and the entire town was making fun of him. I think he just broke down and did something he regretted."

"Yes, that would make anybody break down. I'm the one who got beat up but I feel sorry for Newton's family."

"So, what can I do for you."

"I seriously want you to give me some advice and tell me whether I am crazy or not."

"Go ahead, I'll try my best."

"I was thinking about offering Newton what I think you call a plea-bargain agreement."

"What is the plea-bargain agreement?"

"I will drop all charges and he can go back to his family and their tire business. In return for that I want Newton to resign from our City Council and promise to never run for any government position the rest of his life."

"That's a great deal for him because this is an open and closed case with him probably getting twenty years in prison and who knows what will happen to his family and business. Are you sure you want to do this? You know Pitch wants to kick his ass up and down Main Street."

"How about it if we put in the agreement that Pitch gets to hit him like he hit me?"

"Then you would have to arrest Pitch for assault."

"Charlie come on, what would you do?"

"If you can control Pitch so he doesn't do something stupid, I would offer the deal to Newton. I think he knows he is headed to prison for a long time and is worried about his family. Before I go Ann, can you do me a favor?"

"Sure!"

"Have your ladies take those posters down. You won the battle and the war."

"That is a good idea Charles. I will get Sharon to have the team take them down."

"Let me know when you want me to work up your plea-bargain agreement?"

"Hopefully, I will let you know in a couple days after I talk with Pitch."

Chris went into work on Friday and the staff was really excited because they had three songs in the top ten rankings. Two of Rory's and Lonely Wrangler by Hank Snow. As soon as Rex Flynn saw Chris, he asked him if he had a minute. "Sure, Rex, what can I do for you?"

"Do you think you could get Rory to share all his other songs in his suitcase with us because two of the three he gave us are in the top ten?"

"I know what you are saying but I think we would have to talk to John Riggins Rory's advisor first. His advisor states that he has to write one song for RCA a year and we have already gotten two. If we want to go for the suitcase, I think Riggers will want to amend his contract."

"It was just a thought boss; the kid can write some good music."

"It is a good thought Rex."

Chris went to his office and finally called the Ed Sullivan Show producer. What they wanted was for Rory to come on the show in mid-October. Chris told them he would have to check with Rory's parents and then get back to them. They informed Chris they only had a two-week window for his decision or they would have to fill the spot reserved for him.

Ann made it home before Pitch got back from the range and she told Nija not to say a word. As she was sitting in the kitchen talking to Nija, Tony popped in the house. "Oh, there you are. I've been looking for you all day."

"What can I do for you Mr. Tony?"

"I just wanted to tell you I have decided to go to college, that's all."

Ann couldn't believe all that worrying she did and that one little pretty girl, Maomi, could make him change his mind in five minutes. When Pitch walked through the door Ann's heart skipped a beat because she knew she had to ask him about the plea-bargain deal. The entire family had a nice dinner and Ann said to Pitch, "Let's go out on the patio for some fresh air. You can even have your whiskey and cigar."

"It won't bother you?"

"No, I'm fine. If I wasn't on these drugs, I would have some whiskey with you."

"So, what's on that pretty little mind of yours?"

"I have been thinking about the Newton thing."

"I could break that son of a bitch's neck."

"Calm down cowboy everything is okay. I even have been thinking all day about having sex with you tonight. Ann was figuring the sex thing always worked for her to get what she wanted. "This must be big for you to play the whiskey, cigar, and sex decoys."

"You know I have been thinking about the Newton thing and I know my postures really pushed him over the top. I know his family is really suffering because of this and they didn't do a thing. I feel somewhat responsible for him hitting me and I think after he hit me, he regretted doing it and was going to help me when Charlie came flying at him."

"Ann, I hear all of this but the man hit you and he probably weighs a 150 pounds more than you. He could have killed you."

"I understand Pitch but I am really hurting for his family. Charlies investigated him and the only thing he could find was that he was Annie Gallon's brother. Nothing illegal or dirty like Gallon."

"Where are you going with this Ann?"

"I am thinking about giving him a plea-bargain deal."

"Does this deal keep him in jail or prison?"

"No, Pitch, it does not. It returns him to his normal life all but being a member of the City Council."

"Ann, this is not right! For God sakes, look at yourself. It is going to take a month or more for you to fully recover. I can't buy into this, I am sorry. The man needs to go to prison, end of subject!"

"Will you at least think about it a little more and think of his wife and two kids?"

"Ann, you can tell I am upset with the deal bull shit but since I love you so much, I promise you I will think about it. However, the subject is closed for now."

Ann wasn't sure Pitch would change his mind and for good reason. Maybe she needed to go talk to Chester Newton at the jail and see what his attitude is. Perhaps giving Pitch some loving tonight would soften him up.

Chris called Ann to talk about Rory going on the Ed Sullivan Show. However, Rory answered the phone. "Rory is your Mom there?"

"No, but I did want to talk with you because everybody wants to know when I am making an album? I have a suitcase filled with songs ready to record."

That reminded Chris that he needed to talk to John Riggins about the song writing. "Rory, in your suitcase how many songs do you think are really, really good?"

"Let me see really, really good. I think about ten or eleven."

"Holy shit! I am sorry about the language Rory but you got your friend here all excited with those numbers. With you going to school now it is going to be hard because albums take time."

I know Chris but I have a plan I have been working on."

"That's great because I don't. Let me hear what you think?"

"I can pick out eight songs from the suitcase and we have two songs already out so that would be ten songs for the album."

"Go ahead, I am following you so far."

"I would send the eight new songs to Rex and he could work on the sound, orchestration, and all his stuff. Then he sends me the music cut and I practice at home. Then every other Friday you send the plane for me to come to Nashville and we work all day Saturday and part of Sunday before I go home. When I am off for Thanksgiving week I can come for the week and we can cut the album."

"I think that is a great solution that could work. Let me think about it while I am on my honeymoon and talk to you when I get back. You might want to run your plan by your Mom."

"She just came in the door."

"I need to talk with her just a couple minutes on something very important."

"Okay, Mom, Chris needs to talk to you."

"Ann, I am trying to finish up things before I leave for my honeymoon."

"What do you need Chris?'

"The producer of the Ed Sullivan Show wants Rory to be on the show in the middle of October."

"What do you want me to tell him? This would be great exposure for Rory."

"Tell them yes!"

"That is great I will get all the details when I get back."

"Have a great honeymoon."

As soon as Chris got off the phone with Ann, he called John Riggins. "John, we need to talk about the songs Rory writes."

"I thought I would be hearing from you Chris. What is your offer for songs beyond the four his has written for RCA already?"

"I was thinking $25,000 a song."

"I was thinking double that. Rory has given you four songs he has written and three of them are in the top ten and I am sure the other one will be there also."

"John let me talk to David and get back to you and once we agree on the price, we can do a separate contract."

"Sounds good to me Chris, just give me a call."

On Saturday. Pitch was branding cattle and all the kids were doing their own things so Ann decided to take a ride to the Sheriff's office to talk with Chester Newton. She knew Dan would be off and Curly would be in charge but that was okay. Curly welcomed the Mayor and asked what she was doing here on a Saturday.

"Curly, I want to talk to Chester Newton in private."

"I guess it is okay since you're the mayor. You don't have a gun or any weapons?"

"No, Curly, I just came to talk to him about a plea-bargain deal."

"Let me put him in the conference room and handcuff him before you go into the room to see him."

Curly had Chester seated and handcuffed and then called her in the room. "That will be all Curly."

"I'll be right outside this door if you need me Mayor."

"Thank you."

Chester looked really calm and it looked like he was losing weight. "How are you Chester? See what you did to my pretty face?'

"Ann, I am so sorry, I just lost control of myself. I regret everything I did and deeply apology for my behavior. I am not a violent man, I just cracked from all the pressure and took it out on you. I have been praying for you to get well, I am truly sorry Ann."

"How is your family and business during?"

"The business is still doing okay but my family is a nervous mess. They are afraid to go out in the public and the kids don't want to go to school."

"Why were you against my road improvement project? Was it because of you sister's death?"

"Yes, I held you responsible but after sitting here thinking clearly about it the one responsible for my sister's death is Gallon. Are you going to make a full recovery Ann?"

"Yes, Chester, the doctor said I would be fine in about a month. Chester I am a forgiving person and a family person. So, I am considering a pled-bargain agreement with you. You know if you go to trial you would probably get twenty years in prison?"

"Yes, Ann, I figured that would be the sentence. I would appreciate any deal that could get me back to my family sooner."

"Here is what I have in mind. You resign as City Council member and agree to never run for a government office again, I will drop all the charges and you can go back to your normal life"

"Oh my God Ann, that would be absolutely wonderful. I would also volunteer one more thing. That I pay all your doctor and hospital bills."

"I like that Chester. You need to keep this to yourself until Charlie Douglas offers it to you. It will take a little time because Pitch is really against this. He wants to kill you."

"I can understand how he feels."

"So, I have to work on him before I offer you the deal. I think he will come around because he is a family man. However, if this deal works out and you see him coming your way you best turn around and go the other way, as fast as you can."

CHAPTER 15

A t dinner that night Ann told the family that Rory is going to be on the Ed Sullivan Show. They all started yelling, "Can we go, can we go?"

Pitch spoke out first, "I think the whole family should go."

"Okay, I will talk to Chris when he gets back for all the details."

Rory couldn't wait to tell Catina that he was going to be on television. "Now, that you will be a television star all the girls will be after you and you will forget me."

"I don't think so, besides they just love my music, not me."

"I wouldn't count of that young girls go crazy over recording stars."

"All I know is you are my girl and I enjoy kissing you."

Rory sat down with Ann one evening and told her about his plan for making an album. "I think you might have something

Rory. You can still go to school and do the album. I think we need to look for a new traveling partner for you. I will talk to Pitch and see if he has anybody in mind."

"Just make sure it is somebody I will like to be around."

"I think we may need a man this time because I believe

people will start recognizing you and will be all over you."

"You have a good point Mom because when Tony and I went to register for our classes he had to rescue me form all the students. Plus, I don't think you have to pay that much money for the little that is required of the job. I think maybe $30,000 is plenty for anybody from Sheridan."

Even after a wonderful night together Pitch still seemed upset about the potential Newton deal. When he took Ann to the doctor for her check-up everything was fine and the doctor took her stitches out and released her. On the ride from the hospital Ann said, "Let's go have lunch Pitch?"

"Okay, where do you want to go?"

"How about the Bonfire Tavern they have a great lunch menu and I could use a cold beer."

"Now, you are talking."

The tavern was half emptied so Ann figured they could talk some more about Newton. Pitch, quickly read her mind, "We are here because you want to talk about Newton?"

"Yes, and some other things."

The first thing she addressed was Rory's plan to do an album. Pitch thought it was a good plan but he would be away from his family for Thanksgiving."

"What if we all go with him and check out Nashville and the RCA studio."

"I like that idea but I don't think Tony will want to go."

"That is okay we will have Nija keep an eye on him. He is going to be eighteen in January so he knows how to take care of himself."

Next on Ann's agenda was finding Rory a new traveling partner. She told Pitch that Rory wanted a male partner this time and her concerns about his safety."

They talked about a couple people and then Pitch said, "I got it."

"What does that mean, I got it?"

"The person who should be Rory's traveling partner."

"Okay, let me hear your candidate."

"Jack Waltowski."

"Who is Jack Waltowski?"

"You remember the bouncer who looked out for us at the Coyote club. He is as big as an ox and could stop a train. He is single and pretty smart. He went to a junior college for a year. Plus, you could probably pay him less money than Louise. What do you think?"

"That sounds really good, do you think he will take the job?"

"I think so because he makes peanuts at the Coyote club. How much are you thinking of paying him?"

Both Rory and I felt $30,000 a year for the limited requirements of the job."

"I think he would jump at it in a heartbeat."

"Won't that hurt Stoney's security at the club?"

"Big guys are a dime a dozen, it will be easy to find a bouncer."

After covering all the little things, it was time for Ann to address the Newton deal. "I went to the jail and talked to Newton and he admitted he lost control of himself and regretted hitting me. He said he understands how you feel Pitch. Chester said his family was suffering because of him and they didn't deserve it. He is afraid his wife is going to have a nervous breakdown. If I let him go to prison, I will be destroying a family and I can't do that Pitch. Please help me."

"Since I believe everything you said is the truth and this is tearing your insides out, I will go along with you giving him the deal. I am only doing this because I love you so much and you really want to do this."

"I love you for being who you are Pitch and you know I wouldn't go against you. If you don't want me to do this I will not."

"I know Ann and I know how important family is to you and that means more to me then kicking his ass. I am okay with you offering him the deal. I think you and Chester Newton owe me big time."

"Oh, I also added to the deal that he has to pay all my doctor and hospital bills."

"That's good!"

When Ann got home, she called Charlie Douglas and told him to work up the papers on the plea-bargain for Chester Newton and to include that he would pay all her doctor and hospital bills. "Ann, is Pitch okay with this or is he going to go nuts when he finds out?"

"He is okay with it Charlie or let me say he can live with it. When you present this to Chester, I want to also get his resignation from the City Council. He can type it and sign it in Dan's office before you give him his freedom. Is everything clear?"

"Yes, I will present it to him tomorrow afternoon and his resignation letter will be on your desk in the morning. This is a good thing you are doing Ann."

The following afternoon Chester Newton walked out of the police department into the arms of his wife and children. Sid Walters of the Sheridan Prairie Newspaper was there taking pictures and interviewing Chester and his wife. The next day he had a big full-page article with pictures in the paper. The headline read, The Mayor with a Heart. The article talked about looking beyond her injuries and her concern for the family. At the end of the article Sid wrote that Sheridan should thank God for Mayor McClure Wesley. On the same day in a different section of the newspaper there was an article on the establishment of the McClure/Boone Shoshone College Scholarship Foundation. It stated that Ann McClure Wesley and Richard Boone were the sole fund providers but that other ranches and businesses could join the foundation. Then the article went on to say the first scholarship winner was Maomi Warki who is a senior and honor roll student at Sheridan High School.

When Ann got home Nija told her the phone wouldn't stop ringing. "Ann, everybody wants to tell you what a great person you are. But we already know that."

Just as they sat down for dinner the doorbell ring and when Nija opened the door she quickly backed away from it in a bow position. When Ann saw her, she ran to the door. It was Chief Warki and what looked like the entire village. Maomi was standing with her mother and her brother Kinno. The next thing Ann knew was that her entire family was standing behind her looking out. Then Chief Warki said, "We are here in number to thank you for what you have done for the Shoshone people. You are a true sister of the Shoshone and our spirits will always walk with you. My daughter Maomi will make you proud of her and she will become a doctor for our people." Chief Warki walked over to Ann and hugged her. Then all the Shoshone people started chanting some song. After it was all over and the family went back to finish dinner Ann said to Pitch, "What was that they were chanting in Shoshone?"

He smiled at her, "They was asking the spirits to watch over you."

The next day Pitch went into town to the Coyote club. He first told Stoney what he was going to talk to Jack about and Stoney had no problem with it. Stoney let Pitch use his office and told Jack, "The boss wants to see you in my office."

Of course, Jack immediately thought he was in trouble. "Have a seat Jack, I have something I need to discuss with you."

"Yes, sir, what can I do for you?"

"No, Jack, it is what I am going to do for you. How much money do you make a year?'

"Besides being a bouncer here, I deliver mail for the post office. From both jobs I make about $11,000 annually."

"Are you single?"

"Yes, sir, I live in an apartment over on 3rd Street. What is all of this about?"

"I have an opportunity for you to make $30,000 a year plus expenses. You know Rory McClure?"

"Yes, sir, he is a great guy and we get along good."

"The job is for you to be his traveling partner. When he goes on a trip you travel with him and look out for him. You make sure he is where he is supposed to be. Basically, you take care of him like he was your young brother. What do you think?"

"When do I start? I am ready to go."

"You will be working with Chris Finley of RCA Records and he will provide all the details of the trips to you. You will stay in first class hotels, eat in great restaurants, you will have a chauffeur to get you both around and you will fly on one of RCA's private planes. Your first trip will probably be to Nashville in several weeks."

"What do I do while Rory is in school?'

"Have fun and enjoy your life."

"This is great Mr. Pitch, and you are going to pay me $30,000 for doing this?'

"That is right Jack. But you better take really good care of that kid or you will answer to me."

"You can count on it. God bless you!"

After his week-long honeymoon Chris came back to work on Monday exhausted. All the guys were kidding him that Louise wore him out. Chris gave John Riggins a call to iron out the song writing deal. "John, I talked this over with David and this is what we are willing to offer. $35,000 per song and if the song makes it into the top ten ratings, we will give Rory a $10,000 bonus."

The other end of the phone was silent for several seconds, "Chris, you got a deal. Work the contract up and I'll get Ann to sign it."

"That is great John. Is it okay to move forward now because we have a lot of work to do on Rory's album?"

"Absolutely, Chris, we have an agreement the rest is just paperwork."

"Thank you for your help John. I got to run."

Next, Chris called Rory at the house and he had already gone to school but luckily Ann was still at the house. Chris told Ann about the song writing contract and said that John would have it for her to sign. "Ann, did Rory get to talk to you about his plan for making an album?"

"Yes, he did and we are good with it. In fact, when he goes to Nashville the Thanksgiving Day week, we all are going with him, except for Tony. Can all of us fit in the plane you send?"

"There is plenty of room. I think it has fifteen seats. My secretary can make hotel reservations for you at the Hilton where you will get the RCA discount."

"That would be great Chris."

"Louise will love to hear you are coming. Perhaps we all can have Thanksgiving Day dinner together?"

"We would love that Chris."

"I have got to run I'm trying to catch up from my week off. Oh, one more thing tell Rory to get in touch with Rex so they can start work on his album."

"I will tell him. Have you heard from the Ed Sullivan Show because we all want to make the trip to New York with Rory?"

"Let me check all my messages and get back to you on that."

"Have a good day Chris and say hi to Louise for me."

When Rory got home, Ann told him to call Rex about the album and that RCA was going ahead with his plan. "Rory, we all decided when you go to Nashville for the whole week, we are going with you so we can have Thanksgiving together."

"That is great Mom. Did you find me a new traveling partner?"

"Yes, Pitch did and he is all ready to go."

"Well, who is it Mom?'

"Oh, Jack Waltowski the bouncer at the Coyote club."

"That is great. I really like Jack and we will have a good time together. I have just one more question for you Mom."

"Okay, what is it Cannery Boy?"

"I know this is a big one but here goes. When we all got to the Ed Sullivan Show can Catina come with us?"

"That is a big one. I will have to talk to Pitch about it and if he is okay with it we would have to talk to Catina's parents."

"Please Mom for me."

"I will try Rory, that is all I can promise."

The next morning Ann had Sharon Steward come to her office. She had the other five members of the City Council there in her office. Ann asked them if they all knew Sharon and all but one did. Then Judge Thomas came walking through the door. "Judge Thomas I appreciate you coming here this morning and I know your calendar is full so let's get on with it."

The judge swore in Sharon as the interim City Council member making her the first woman to serve on the council. The other council members congratulated her and said they looked forward to working with her. Of course, Sid Walters was there so he could write about it for the newspaper. After everybody left the office but Sharon, she hugged Ann. "We have come a long way as girls."

They both smiled at each other.

Chris got all the details for the Ed Sullivan Show and called Ann. "Rory will be on the show Sunday October 15th. He has to be there Saturday at 1pm for the show rehearsal. They want him to sing both of his songs. One at the beginning of the show and the other near the end. You and your family will have to fly in on Friday night. I will keep in touch as we get closer but I would make your reservations for the family as soon as you can they will five tickets for you at the pick-up window."

"I think we may need six. Rory wants to bring a friend."

"I'll tell them to make it six tickets."

With everything for the Ed Sullivan Show settled Ann and Pitch went to see Mr. Mosley about Catina going to New York with them. Ann was not looking forward to this but she promised Rory. "Pitch, you do all the talking."

He just looked at her. The Mosley greeted them and they all went to their living room to talk. "We would like to take Catina with us to New York city to see Rory on the Ed Sullivan Show." Pitch wasted no time and got right to the subject. Mr. Mosley said, "How long will this be for?"

"We will leave Friday October 13th after school and return Monday morning at about eleven o'clcok. Catina will only have to miss one day of school."

Then Ann finally jumped in the conversation, "Catina will stay with Nellie and me while the boys stay with Pitch. The trip won't cost you a penny because RCA is picking up all the bills.

Catina started begging her father "Please dad let me go it will be a great experience for me and I will get to see New York City."

"Okay, Catina can go and I appreciate you taking her."

Pitch and Ann thanked Mr. Mosley and almost ran out the door. "We did it Pitch, Rory will be so happy."

The following Tuesday it was the day of the special vote on the new road improvement plan. The women's association was encouraging everybody to vote for the project. To Ann's surprise Chester Newton was also out encouraging people to vote for the project. When the final vote was in 90% of Sheridan's population voted for the road improvement plan. Ann was excited that her plan was approval and she told Charlie to have his procurement staff get the bid out to the construction companies.

Rory was having a ball traveling every other weekend to Nashville with Jack. Rex had really worked hard on the music arrangements for the new songs and he thought the album would be ready for release the first week of December. Louise flew back to Sheridan one Sunday with Jack and Rory to clean out her house and have the Kelly's put it up for sale.

Before they knew it the weekend on the Ed Sullivan show was here and everybody boarded the plane, including Catina. The flight only took four hours and a chauffeur was waiting to pick them up at the airport. When then they got to the Hilton Hotel Rory received the red-carpet treatment and right there and then knew he was somebody important. Since it was late, they decided to have dinner at the hotel restaurant instead of going out. When they all finished dinner, they were ready to call it a night. Catina and Nellie went with Ann to their suite and the boys with Pitch to their suite.

Saturday after breakfast they decided to go walking around the city and show Tony and Catina some of the sights. The one they liked the best was Time Square and they had a hard time believing all these people lived here. It seemed like they were crammed in and there was no fresh air to breath. Rory had to go to his rehearsal at one o'clock so they decided to have a late lunch while he was at the studio. Rory caught up with them at the restaurant and said that he got to meet Mr. Sullivan and the rehearsal went great. Since they had the entire afternoon and evening Ann wanted to visit her old neighborhood and show Pitch the other part of her life. When they walked down Preston Street to their old apartment building Ann could not believe her eyes. The apartment building looked beautiful and on the front in cement it said the McClure Building. Ann started crying and Pitch hugged her dearly. Rory pointed to the third-floor window and told Catina thats where they lived. Just as they were leaving Mr. Zario came out the front door. "Hey, Mr. Zario, how are you doing?"

Mr. Zario looked and looked again, "Is that you Rory McClure?"

"Yes sir!"

Mr. Zario actually ran over to Rory and hugged him so tight Rory had a hard time breathing. "Rory, you don't know what a difference you have made in the lives of the people who live here."

"That is great. I was glad I could help out my old neighborhood."

"Why are you here in the city?"

"I will be on the Ed Sullivan Show tomorrow night."

"I will tell everybody in the building to watch it so they know who made their lives much happier."

"That would be great. We have to go now but it was great seeing you."

They walked down to the fish market where Rory first song in public. Ann even showed Pitch the garment district where she worked. However, the shop was closed so she could not show him how the sweat shop really looked. They had walked so much they were glad to see their chauffeur pull up so they could get off their feet. While riding back Catina said, "Mrs. Ann you had a hard life here and the spirits bought you to Wyoming. They knew you would come out west and help others."

"That is very nice of you to say that Catina."

When they got to the hotel, they were all bushed and Pitch says, "Where are we going to dinner in the Big Apple?"

"I don't know about all of you but the restaurant I like is called Room Service."

They all took a vote and Room Service won out. When they got to their rooms the girls were not sure how to order. Rory said, "Just pick out what you want and I will take care of the ordering for you."

You could tell Rory had done this a few times because he had it down. Ann reminded everyone they were going to the ten o'clcok mass at Saint Patrick's and told them to be ready when the chauffeur shows up to take us there.

After church and talking to some old friends they went to have lunch at Tribeca's Kitchen which was one of the oldest restaurants in the city. The chauffeur took them down Church Street and dropped them off and said he would be back in two hours. They all had a big lunch because they missed breakfast and was not sure when they would eat again. Once their bellies were filled, they all were ready for a little nap so the driver took them back to the hotel to rest up. Since Rory had to be at the theater at five o'clock so he kissed everybody goodbye and the chauffeur drove him over to the theater.

After a nice nap they all got dressed up for the theater and Pitch picked up their tickets at the window. They had special tickets so they were allowed to enter at six-thirty. Their seats were up front in the second row. The stage crew was working hard to get everything ready. They checked the stage lighting; sound system and the band were tuning up their instruments. At seven o'clcok they let the general audience come in and the place filled up quickly. The sound manager did one more check," Testing, testing." The audience manager told the people to watch the red light on the side and when it turned green to start applauding. When the light turned green Ed Sullivan stepped out on to the stage to open the show.

"Ladies and gentleman we have a great show for you tonight. So, sit back and enjoy it. Our first performer tonight is a young man from Sheridan, Wyoming. He will be singing the number one song in the nation, Pickin My Guitar. Please help me welcome Rory McClure!"

The End

BOOK SUMMARY

Ann McClure is a widow raising three kids in the Bronx. She fights daily to make ends meet and worries about the future of her children. One of her sons is a very talented singer and only the people who come to the fish market know how good he is. Ann's deceased husband's uncle dies and leaves Ann a ranch in Sheridan, Wyoming and a substantial amount of money with the condition that she must live on the ranch. As she becomes the owner of the ranch, she meets the ranch manager, Pitch Wesley who helps her understand the ranch and the way of life out west. The ranch employs many Shoshone Indians as wranglers and other jobs and her family befriends them. She helps her son Rory broaden his musical skills by having him take piano lessons and buying him a guitar. Ann finds out quickly that besides the cattle ranch her property is rich with uranium and everybody wants to steal it from her land. As she becomes a member of the Sheridan Women's Association her popularity increases and they convince her to run for mayor against the present dishonest mayor who is stealing from the city. Her children learn how to ride and take care of their horses and become good friends with the Shoshone people. As Rory wins a talent contest his singing ability is starting to be noticed. He fines a great mentor in Sister Martin and she is determined to help him. As the problem of uranium poachers grow, the sheriff and Pitch confront them and Pitch is critically wormed and must fight for his life. When Ann is elected mayor, she uncovers many misuses of city funds by the ex-mayor for his personal good. Ann is determined to bring the ex-mayor to justice but he escapes and the FBI pursues him. Rory starts performing at the Coyote club and sings the National Anthem at a University of Wyoming football game. With help from Sister Martin he gets a contract with RCA records and releases his first record. Ann continues to face many challenges and her determination causes her to be beaten up badly by a city council member. Rory uses some of his money to help out his old neighbors in the Bronx and comes up with a plan to make an album in Nashville. As Rory's abilities are noticed in the business industry, he is recruited by a television show.

ABOUT AUTHOR

B orn on April 16, 1944 in Shamokin, Pennsylvania a small coal mining town. Grow up in the inner-city of Baltimore, Maryland and lived there for approximately twenty year. Received an athletic scholarship from the University of Baltimore and attended graduate school at the University of Pittsburgh and The Wharton School of Business at the University of Pennsylvania. Majority of education was in marketing and finance. Was honorably discharged from the U.S. Army as a Platoon Sergeant during the Vietnam War. Business career included working as a General Manager for AT&T, President of Litton Network Systems and Chief Operations Officer for Virginia Transformer Corporation. Presently, retired living in Murrells Inlet, South Carolina for the past twenty years. Has been married for 55 years and have a deceased daughter and one granddaughter. Loves playing golf, working in the yard and active in his church.

CPSIA information can be obtained
at www.ICGtesting.com
Printed in the USA
BVHW070849290421
606134BV00004B/636